MARGARET

FROM NEWTON TO NERJA

JOYCE C. GRAND

Margaret - from Newton to Nerja
Copyright © 2013 by Joyce C. Grand. All rights reserved.
First Print Edition: November 2013
ISBN-10: 0-615-86151-2
ISBN-13: 978-0-615-86151-7

Cover and Formatting: Streetlight Graphics

DEDICATION

For Rachel, Carly, Joey, Josh, Stella, Gus and Sam who have permission to read this novel when they reach the age of eighteen.

Newton

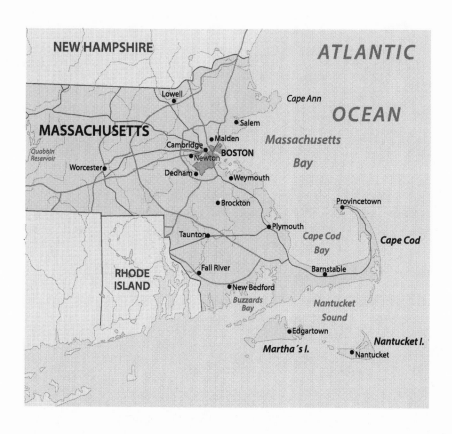

Nerja
(Pronounced "Near-ha")

PROLOGUE

MARGARET COWERED AS SHE CROUCHED in a corner of the cave. Seeking protection and cover, she felt herself backing as far as possible into the recesses of the rock.

She had come to the caves of Nerja, as she did routinely, whenever she wished for quiet and a place to gather her thoughts. Now, a refuge was being threatened.

On Saturday, she had been sipping coffee at an outdoor café when she became aware of someone watching her. At the time, she rejected a surging sense of fear and continued to enjoy the early spring warmth as she lifted her face to the sun. Nonetheless, the hair on the nape of her neck began to prickle. Someone was observing her. Margaret turned her head just slightly. A man, or what she presumed to be a man from the look of his fingers, ducked his head beneath the open newspaper. When she dared turn again, the figure was gone.

She dismissed a feeling of alarm and continued her usual routines of teaching, taking long walks, and swimming in the pool behind the home she'd rented. The white house was nestled into the bottom of the hills among all the white houses. A paradise! She had loved it from the first. It had afforded Margaret a sense of unparalleled freedom and abandon, security and privacy.

This life-style allowed her to throw off constraints. She was now in the habit of swimming topless in her private, heated pool. The lovely terrace and spacious pool were hidden from the street and prying eyes. Or so she thought! This week as she lay on her back doing a slow, rhythmic stroke, she again sensed someone watching her. Grabbing for her towel, she climbed out of the pool and looked far up into the hills.

Without a doubt, there was a person looming at the top of the crest. Even from this distance, Margaret could tell that it was a masculine figure staring down at her through a set of binoculars. As soon as Margaret's actions were noticed, the figure fled. He was gone too rapidly for her to examine him carefully. She could not distinguish his features, nor decide on his height or complexion.

This sighting left her feeling very apprehensive and exposed. This man had seen her. . . and fully well at that. Was it just a random tourist who, while eyeing the scenery, glanced upon a semi-clad female form? These hills did seduce those who had a penchant for traveling off the beaten path. She would just have to shake this feeling of being stalked.

Margaret resolved to continue as if nothing had happened. After all, nothing had really happened. Perhaps, she was just overreacting.

On Sunday, Margaret went to Mass as was her wont. Just as she loved the caves, Margaret looked forward to sitting in the pristine, white church that was the center of Nerja, and now the center of her world.

This Sunday, the church was crowded with more worshipers than usual. Perhaps, because it was shortly after Easter, more people were caught up in a religious mode. Margaret eased into a center pew where a vacant seat remained.

As Father Eduardo rose to give the homily, someone standing in the rear gave a short cough. Margaret turned toward the sound. A man quickly turned his back and exited rapidly.

Had Margaret been imagining all of this? Was she becoming paranoid? She had been so surprised by the presence of this man that it took her a few seconds to focus and comprehend. With several masses recited on Sunday, why was he present now? Was this the same individual who'd had his binoculars trained on her earlier in the week?

This was the longest and closest view she'd had of this person. There was no denying that it was a he. In addition, she could see that he was fairly tall and moderate in build. He had moved so quickly, Margaret noted nothing more. Now, her fear was tangible. The incident left her with a tingling spine and dry mouth. She was barely able to make it back to her house. As she entered, she searched each room, looked past the windows up into the hills, and made certain all outer doors were locked. She remained indoors throughout Sunday afternoon and evening. She regretted terribly being too frightened to swim or lounge by the pool. She found that she jumped at any noise, at the ringing of the telephone. There was no one in whom she could confide. She would just have to be wary.

There were no further sightings of the man and, by Wednesday, Margaret began to relax. She decided to enjoy some hours at the caves that had originally drawn her to Nerja and where she'd found such contentment during the many months while living in Spain.

She wandered along, captivated as always by the magnitude and beauty of this underground wonder. Suddenly, she became aware of a figure lurking in the shadows along the edges of the caves' walls. She quickly tried to melt into a niche in the rocks and prayed she would pass unseen.

Now, Margaret listened intently. All the tourists had left and she heard no voices. She could hear her rapid breaths and the thumping of her heartbeat. She felt as if her chest would burst.

CHAPTER 1

MARGARET SAT IN THE TRAFFIC inching its way toward Boston. She was driving in a direction opposite the commuter traffic and had assumed she'd have no problem getting into town this late in the day. But as the Chrysler idled, she wondered if she had acted rashly. It was unlike her to do anything in haste. Now, she was having a niggling sensation that surprising Andrew at his office might not be prudent even if it were their eighteenth wedding anniversary.

He'd made no mention of the date when he'd left that morning and simply said he might be working late. She'd been in the midst of getting her haircut when she decided she'd race home, change her clothes and appear at his office with an invite to dinner.

Andrew was not an impulsive person, nor a romantic, and Margaret usually took her cues from him. However, her best friend, Missy, had convinced her that Margaret and Andrew could do with a little spontaneity and romance, and an evening at "The Bay Tower" near the south side of Faneuil Hall might be just the spark. It had the most glorious views of Boston and the harbor in addition to the good food and excellent service. The restaurant had been a favorite of theirs in the early years, but they hadn't been there in a long time.

She glanced at herself in the rear-view mirror. Her newly-cut carrot top stared back at her. Missy, whom she'd known from elementary school, had convinced her to buy the dress she was wearing. She said the dress accented Margaret's figure and showed off her long legs. The deep green color set off her red hair. Hence, Margaret was equipped with more confidence than was her custom of late.

The traffic finally broke and Margaret was able to ease her car into the parking garage beneath the office building by 6:30 p.m. She wrote "Margaret Cleary" in the little box for visitor and Cleary, Caan and Davis for the office. The elderly security guard noted her name and that of the office and said in a heavy Irish brogue, "Ah, we don't see you here very often Mrs. Cleary. Ye be goin' right on up now."

As Margaret stepped from the elevator, she marveled at the beautiful marble floors, wood paneling and expanse of the office. It was certainly impressive and must be to clients and adversaries alike.

Several years ago, Andrew had urged his dad to merge their prestigious and recognized law firm with the emerging team of young, capable legal minds that were Caan and Davis. The senior Cleary retained an office in the old brownstone which remained in the family while additional office space was rented to outside corporations. It became a win/win situation. The old brownstone continued to appreciate; Mr. Cleary collected high rents; and the building in which Margaret had entered was a modern, sleek high rise in the center of relatively new office buildings.

Margaret's long legs traversed a spacious, richly-carpeted reception area. She saw no one, nor heard any sounds emanating from the offices. Since the staff had a reputation for working late, the quiet surprised her.

She was debating whether or not to sit in the reception area and wait for someone to appear, or to simply knock on Andrew's office door. She opted for the latter and proceeded toward the offices in the rear. She strode, hesitantly, her feet sinking into the plush carpeting as she padded through the corridors. Her eyes took in the magnificence of the expertly-carved black walnut conference table surrounded by its two dozen leather swivel chairs where the partners and associates gathered or met with their clients. The carpeting changed to marble flooring as she approached a work station to her left. Here, she noted that the large central area that housed the copier, shredder, fax machine, paper cutter, some files and the small kitchen seemed unusually still.

As she continued to the rear of the complex and approached Andrew's office, she heard what sounded like a male voice moaning and groaning. Andrew? Suddenly, a woman screamed. Were people hurt, being murdered, what? Margaret stopped in her tracks not knowing if she should follow the sounds, call for help, or flee the scene. She stood transfixed.

Then, she heard thudding noises, gasping and a woman's purring sound. My God, someone was having sex. It was her turn to gasp! What had she come upon? The sounds were definitely coming from her husband's office, although she couldn't recall Andrew responding to an orgasm in this manner.

Margaret still could not get her body to move. She was having great difficulty processing all of this. She should have heeded her premonition while she was driving into the city and turned back. What was she doing here? What was she going to do now? How would she confront Andrew?

Her head felt dizzy, her knees weak. She could barely breathe. She wanted to beat a hasty retreat, but barely managed to get herself back to the reception area where she, dazedly, sank into a couch. Her inclination was to get out of there as quickly as possible, but her legs wouldn't carry her. She must compose herself and make her way to her car. If she could just stop her legs from wobbling, maybe she could walk several blocks and clear her head before driving home.

She wasn't seated but a couple of minutes when Andrew appeared flushed, slightly disheveled, and looking very upset. She hadn't expected to face Andrew just then and was not prepared to deal with the situation. Andrew, for his part, must have heard her gasp and heard her retreating footsteps. His shocked reaction, when he saw her, clearly indicated that he had anticipated seeing a client or a member of the cleaning crew, not his wife.

It was Andrew's turn to act stunned and speechless, a response most uncharacteristic of Andrew. However, he managed to gather himself rather quickly, probably from years of appearing before juries and reacting to witnesses' surprises. He exploded! "How dare you barge in on me like this? This is MY domain; what right have you to appear without alerting my office staff?" Getting redder in the face, he continued to harangue, "What ever got into your head? Where do you come off to show up unannounced?"

Margaret sat in numbed shock. Nothing came out of her throat but a muffled, muted sound. She could not form words. She could not cry. Her body was visibly trembling. It was as if he had struck her; indeed, he had struck her straight to her heart, to her core. Her whole being felt shattered. And this, on their eighteenth wedding anniversary!

CHAPTER 2

MARGARET SIDLED DOWN THE AISLE trying to compress her tall, gangly body. She was sure that the overnight bag, laptop, large overstuffed shoulder purse and tennis racquet were bound to smack a fellow passenger in the head as she wended her way to her seat. She fervently wished the Andrew of yore or one of her sons was here to relieve her of this task. She longed for another pair of hands. There must be a better way, she thought, as she maneuvered to find an empty overhead bin that would accommodate all her paraphernalia. The airline needed a conveyor belt that would carry passengers along the floor and another above to hoist their belongings. Maybe, she could invent one. The thought made her smile.

People on the plane reacted. Otherwise gloomy faces returned her grin. Their response reminded her that smiles are infectious and welcoming. She needed to remember this. Perhaps, when she was feeling lonely or isolated in a foreign country with an unfamiliar language and customs, a warm smile could ease the pain and invite a warm response.

Margaret settled into the window seat at the very rear of the airplane feeling grateful that she could nestle in and, perhaps, avoid conversation. She needed this time to collect herself. Nothing had prepared her for what she'd found at Andrew's office. Now, she was taking flight.

What was she doing planning to spend several months or more away from home? Living in a foreign country? Speaking a language with which she had barely a nodding acquaintance? Being apart from everyone she ever knew, even her children? Had she lost her mind? She felt as if she were being thrust forward without direction or brakes. A state of upheaval she had been in ever since she'd witnessed Andrew's unfaithfulness just six months ago.

She hadn't always been this way. There was a time, even early on as a child, when Margaret knew who she was, knew where she wanted to go, and had a sense of how she was going to get there. All that seemed to disappear when Andrew came into her life. At the time, however, she'd viewed him as the catalyst for reaching her dreams.

They had been students at the university, and she was instantly attracted to Andrew. With his perfect features, clear skin, penetrating blue eyes, and trim physique, he was ogled by all the young women in her dorm. More than that, he was tall . . . taller than Margaret. At five foot nine, Margaret was very self-conscious about her height. Andrew was older, taller, better educated, and a strong leader-qualities that Margaret deemed attractive in a mate.

Andrew seemed to embody all these characteristics and then some. Not only was he a handsome law student and strong-willed, but he also came from a well-to-do, prominent family that had long-established roots in Boston. To his credit, Andrew never spoke of his family ties, but his good breeding and air of confidence were self-evident.

Just then, the pilot broke into her musings to welcome them aboard, explain the air route, weather patterns, estimated time of arrival, and probable temperature they would find when they landed in Madrid. Margaret used this time to glance at the man who'd seated himself beside her. He was a rather attractive-looking gentleman probably in his early fifties. She noted his dark business suit, white shirt and bright red and white foulard tie. He was actively engaged in a rapid-fire conversation with the man on the aisle whom Margaret could not see unless she twisted herself forward. Instead, she settled back, heard the pilot wish them a good flight, and added a silent prayer and amen to his wish.

Her mind wandered back to Andrew. Over the years, Margaret had wondered what Andrew had seen in her. She was awkward and shy particularly with the male gender. She'd had little contact with men while growing up. Her dad had died when she was thirteen. Her entire schooling was at the local parochial schools which separated the sexes with a chain link fence. Margaret often thought, 'more fences, more interest'.

Her mother painted a different picture of the fences. She shared with Margaret that when she was in Catholic high school, while the fence sparked their interest, the nuns and their mothers were feeding them a different line. Each Saturday, during her mother's senior year in high school, a bus would carry the girls up to the nearby convent for indoctrination. At the time, Margaret's mom and her friends had seriously thought of entering the convent. Margaret's mom said, "The place felt serene, the sisters cheerful, warm and enthusiastic. There seemed to be a complete commitment to God and acceptance of the life they'd chosen. Nevertheless, we were not ready to retreat from the real world. We were too intrigued with boys. Besides, the thought of never being able to tweeze eyebrows, wear makeup or shave legs was totally unacceptable." Margaret had laughed.

However, her mom did reinforce that "good girls" didn't 'go all the way'. Several of Margaret's friends, however, did. They liked it, and, they lived to tell about it.

Margaret had spent the summer between her junior and senior years of high school at the Cape as a guest of Missy and her family. She and Missy had been best of friends since kindergarten. They were known to their friends as M&M because they had an easy, unforced camaraderie that didn't exclude anyone, yet neither relied on anyone else. Always and always, Margaret thought, they'd had each other.

They seemed the antithesis of each other. Margaret was tall and redheaded. Missy was perky, petite, and fair-skinned with jet black hair. While Margaret was the more serious student, she admired Missy's spunk and athletic prowess. She wished that she, too, could be a cheerleader, march in St. Patrick Day Parades and have lots of guys hanging around.

Nevertheless, she never felt left out of the fun. M&M were not only good friends to each other, but they also had a large circle of bright, fun-loving, high-energy girlfriends. Together, they engaged in all sorts of pranks from strewing toilet tissue across lawns and houses of good friends, to spray painting boys' nicknames out on the streets in front of the guys' houses, to dancing in the streets accompanied by loud music emanating from a car radio or tape deck, to sipping on a beer before their birth date allowed.

They experimented with smoking cigarettes. These were introduced in the girls' restroom behind the church sanctuary. Even when one of the girls became ill and fainted at her first drag, she recovered swiftly and they were not forced to call upon the clergy or parents to come to the rescue. The experience sobered them for a time. However, looking back on all the mischief, Margaret realized how benign it all had been, how few headaches they had caused their elders.

Again, the cockpit interrupted her thoughts to announce the plane's imminent departure. A flight attendant described the use of seat belts, life preservers and oxygen masks. She drew attention to the exits. Margaret wondered if anyone were listening. She did, barely, but knew that in case of an emergency she would panic and not recall any of the instructions although she'd heard the same litany dozens and dozens of times before.

She glanced in the direction of the man adjacent to her. This time he was absorbed in his reading material and jotting copious notes. Margaret always liked people-watching and invented little scenarios of what their lives might be like. Unobtrusively, she studied the man. He had strong features, craggy eyebrows, and a well-proportioned face. He was handsome in a rugged sort of way. Despite his necktie and jacket, he was suntanned and looked the outdoors type.

Thinking of outdoors brought Margaret back to that summer at Cape Cod where she and Missy worked as waitresses at a well-known Hyannis restaurant. It was an establishment that attracted the locals as well as the tourists. One of the good-looking young locals had been hired by the Hyannis police during the summer's influx of residents. Margaret and Missy would see him when they worked the evening shift and were sprawled on a beach blanket soaking up the sun during the day. She remembered that his name was Jack, and he often stopped on his beat to watch them play a game of *Scrabble.* Very soon, Jack was coming around to the restaurant when Missy finished work in the evening.

Occasionally, Margaret would join them with a date she'd found or with a fix-up Jack had engineered. When it became obvious that Missy and Jack preferred to be off by themselves, Margaret would go to a movie by herself or join other friends. More often than not, however, Margaret found herself having to cover for Missy.

She was uncomfortable lying for her friend, and worse, she was beside herself when Missy, inadvertently, let slip that Jack was married. Although Margaret did not wish to think about it and was pretty much in denial, it was hard to imagine that Missy and Jack were not sexually engaged. They were crawling all over each other at every turn.

Margaret began to think that the sexual act must be quite compelling to keep her friend coming back for more. Certainly, it was not without complications, and especially given that Jack was married.

She, for one, was not ready for the complications. Margaret had dated some in high school, but was never in any long-term relationship. She was not sufficiently drawn to any one person. She knew that she would have to feel emotionally committed to a relationship before allowing such physical intimacy.

Thus, when Andrew first approached her for a date, she was thrilled but reluctant. She was inexperienced, not at all sure she was ready for the experiences he might expect. He appeared so smooth and worldly that Margaret was in awe of him and ill at ease. She wondered now if she'd ever felt truly composed in Andrew's presence.

For the first time, instead of asking herself what Andrew had seen in her, Margaret had begun asking herself why she'd been drawn to Andrew. She surmised that Andrew and his family probably epitomized what Margaret and her family lacked.

Where Andrew was sure of himself, Margaret's dad had hesitated; where her father appeared weak, Andrew was strong; while her family lacked for power, money, and a solid reputation, Andrew's family represented it.

Margaret's father, though he managed to hold a job, had been a quiet alcoholic. The women in the household tiptoed around him, hid his drinking from prying eyes, and felt that they were the cause of his affliction. He was not actively engaged in Margaret's upbringing, but his behavior fostered her need to be circumspect and to make something of herself. His early death from cirrhosis of the liver, which left her and her mom and her younger sister to fend for themselves, only heightened those ambitions.

Andrew, coming from a privileged background, was polished, well-mannered, well-traveled, well-spoken, knowledgeable on many subjects. His natural athletic ability was enhanced by the many lessons in the hands of professionals. The country club staff offered instruction in swimming, horseback riding, tennis and golf. From an early age, Andrew was in the capable hands of ski instructors. He moved with grace.

His good manners, however, could turn to a cold abruptness and derision if challenged or annoyed. His take-charge attitude, while giving her security and strength, also made Margaret feel small and inept.

Again, the loudspeaker boomed overhead, this time to announce the plane's cocktail service. As her tomato juice with a twist of lime was passed to her, the man seated next to her assisted the flight attendant. Margaret could not help noticing that her seat-mate's hands, though strong, moved gracefully. His fingernails were clean, well shaped and professionally buffed. For a brief instant, Margaret pictured those hands lightly caressing her breasts and running eagerly down her torso. She was quickly brought back to reality when he said, "Madame" and proffered the tomato juice and bag of nuts. She thanked him and, as she did so, he seemed to notice her for the first time. He engaged her with his eyes, looked directly at her and smiled. Then he turned away to get his glass of wine and to resume a conversation with the man in the aisle seat.

Margaret thought to herself, What did he notice when he looked at me? Did he see my wrinkles? Did he notice the worry lines, the lack of sleep? Did he observe my red hair, my hazel eyes, my little turned up nose, and freckles? Did this gentleman from Spain detect the Irish in me? Are people attracted to opposites of themselves? Is it alluring to be in the company of someone from another culture?

Was this the fascination that drew Andrew and me, she wondered? Andrew had said that he first noticed her while she was running along the campus during a rainstorm. She and some of her buddies were trying to find a building in which to take refuge from the downpour and were obviously unsuccessful. As they found the doors locked, they'd run to the next while laughing and giggling all the way. Their hair was hanging down their faces, their clothes soaked to the skin giving a clear outline of their bodies, and the water was pouring off them. Margaret, being so much taller than her friends, stood out. In addition, she'd been leading the pack.

The next day, he'd seen her playing volleyball. She learned later that he'd watched her and liked her abundant energy, enthusiasm, ability to focus and great legs. He thought she was mighty cute. Margaret had a clean, fresh-scrubbed look about her that Andrew found appealing. He waited for her and approached her as she came off the field. When he introduced himself, she was flabbergasted and could hardly reply. She had known who he was, but was astonished that he'd be interested in her. When he struck up a conversation, she could barely open her mouth to give her name.

Over the next few months, as they sat with their books in the library, caught a movie, grabbed a beer at one of the campus hangouts, danced together at the campus Inn, or just hung around, she was impressed with how much he knew, how composed and self-assured he was, and how all heads turned when they entered a room. She felt certain everyone was admiring Andrew. Now, when she looked at photographs from those days, she had to admit they'd both been very striking.

Although she didn't remember laughing with him as she always did with her girlfriends, his stability, strong sense of direction and take-charge attitude felt good to her at the time. It was almost as if she were a child and needed a strong parent figure, and Andrew played the role. She felt safe with him.

It was only when he invited her to fraternity functions and, finally, to meet his parents that she felt out of her element. The fraternity house reeked of money. The brick building contained mahogany paneling, a mahogany bar, two winding staircases. Unlike most fraternity houses, where the mismatched upholstery is coming apart and reeking of beer, here the large living room held lovely settees and chairs that were newly upholstered and bespoke a decorator's touch. Where most fraternity houses held old rickety furniture, here an ebony concert grand piano stood in a corner of the living room and the men's bedrooms were all outfitted with built-ins.

Even the fraternity brothers were different. They were clean cut, carefully groomed, and wore more jewelry at one time than Margaret owned collectively.

Margaret's reverie was, once again, interrupted. Dinner was to be served. Did she want chicken, fish, or beef? Did she care for a glass of white or red wine? Margaret made her selections knowing that whatever main dish she requested would be presented in a sea of sauce with vegetables swimming in butter, a skimpy salad, and a soft roll. Truly unappetizing! But, she was hungry. She wondered if a glass of wine would react well with the Dramamine she'd taken before boarding. She decided to go with it knowing she wanted to get some sleep before arriving in Spain. Moreover, Murphy's Law required that as soon as airplane food was served, turbulent skies would follow; she might as well be lulled.

She straightened her seat to its upright position and pulled down the tray to await dinner. As she did so, the gentleman sitting beside her also adjusted his and, again, made eye contact.

In barely accented English he asked, "Where are you headed?"

Margaret replied, "To Spain."

"Oh, are you traveling for business or pleasure?"

"I guess, hopefully, for pleasure," she answered while averting her eyes.

"Ah, I see," he replied, but with a hesitation in his voice that implied he didn't really see.

"Have you been to Spain before?"

"Yes, for a short visit, just two weeks." Now with more enthusiasm to her voice, Margaret continued, "I loved spending time in Madrid, exploring Toledo, seeing the gorgeous Alhambra in Granada, and, oh yes, I was fascinated with the sophistication and history of Seville." Margaret's voice had a dreamy quality.

The gentleman beamed with obvious pride in his homeland. "Well, I hope you will have an opportunity to stay longer this time."

"Perhaps, six months. I'm not sure."

"May I ask where you will be staying?"

"I've rented a small house, a bungalow, above Nerja."

"Really! It's such a beautiful town. I own a small condo not too far from there. Have you been to Nerja before?"

"Yes, but only for a few days. It was so charming. And, I remember the people being very warm and welcoming. I hope they'll welcome a stranger in their midst. . ."

Margaret's voice drifted off.

Sensing her reluctance, he abruptly changed the subject. "Where do you live in the States?"

When Margaret mentioned Boston, he seemed to light up.

"My name is Tomas Nunez," he added quickly as if he'd forgotten to introduce himself earlier. When he extended his hand toward Margaret, she grasped his in a firm handshake and said with a genuine smile, "Margaret Cleary."

As they ate, Margaret tried to answer each question with a reply that would be construed as polite. However, she frankly did not know why she'd chosen to flee to Spain as opposed to elsewhere nor, for that matter, how long she would remain. The circumstances were too painful and she wasn't about to share them with a stranger. As a result, she asked few questions of him.

Still, he had a warm way about him and she found herself comfortably sharing stories of growing up in Boston. She learned that Tomas had attended graduate school at Harvard which, she presumed, accounted for his fluency in English. His business also required him to return, periodically, to the States.

They shared a love of Boston. They both salivated at the mention of Italian food on the North End and agreed they'd much rather be eating there tonight, were impressed with the area around Faneuil Hall and thought the concept was a lot of fun, and loved going off to Rockport for 'lobster-in-the-rough'.

As Margaret had predicted, the pilot came on the intercom to warn that there was turbulence ahead. He would attempt to fly at a lower altitude to avoid some of the upheaval, but everyone was to remain seated with seat belts fastened and to prepare for some jostling. Suddenly, it seemed as if all hell broke loose. The plane gave a deep dive; pieces of food, clothing, purses flew; and Margaret felt as if her stomach were about to heave. Without thinking, she grabbed for the hand next to her. Tomas responded by placing an arm about her shoulders and holding on to her hand while she dug her head into his shoulder and closed her eyes. They remained in this position while the plane lurched and tossed. She prayed in English, he in Spanish, his companion in French. From the familiar cadence, Margaret discerned, they were each reciting the rosary.

Margaret thought for sure this was to be the end. Passengers were screaming all around them and were fastened to their seats. There were no sounds coming from the cockpit. Its silence was deafening.

Just as suddenly, the plane righted itself and continued on course. The pilot's voice could be heard from the loudspeaker with an apology for the inconvenience.

Inconvenience? Right, Margaret thought.

Flight attendants, wobbly and somewhat green in color, made their way down the aisle checking on the state of the passengers. One doctor emerged to examine one or two people who had been hit by some of the flying debris. Miraculously, no one appeared badly hurt, but everyone on that plane was badly shaken. Few spoke; several quietly sobbed.

Margaret lifted her head slowly, embarrassed to have been buried in the shoulder of a stranger. She had trouble meeting his eyes, but knew she must thank him for being so solicitous. Tomas seemed to sense her embarrassment and he began to talk about the experience and just how frightening it was. His words seemed to validate her feelings and her behavior, and she felt herself relax. It was so rare to find someone who would intuit what another person was feeling, own up to his own feelings, and, in addition, be brave enough to verbalize them. This man was truly sensitive and kind.

Kindness. Now there was an interesting attribute and one she hadn't experienced in a long time. She certainly could use some kindness in her life.

When she'd first met Andrew's family, they were polite and cordial to her as their breeding dictated; she was, after all, a guest of their son. However, they were none too pleased with Andrew's choice and their disappointment made itself known to her in infinite little ways.

His mother would look up from the Sunday *Boston Globe*'s society section to announce in a particularly pseudo-snobby voice, "Oh, I see that Charlotte Mayer is engaged to wed Henry Snotgrass. I remember her elegant coming out party. She is a beauty. Her ability to run a household and to entertain will certainly be a fine enhancement to Henry's business interests."

Andrew's father was entranced with the whole world of genetics and had amassed every bit of current material he could find. He would wax eloquently on the subject throughout an entire dinner. Often, he'd stress the importance of good breeding. To this day, Margaret wondered if the man confused humans with cattle. She knew that Andrew's father did not consider her to be the perfect breeding stock for his grandsons.

Margaret and Andrew felt the disappointment from each set of parents. Margaret's mom was none too happy to see her daughter involved with someone outside the Roman Catholic Church. With Margaret teaching and not dependent on her mom for financial assistance, money was no longer an issue. At issue, was the Church. There was an abundance of suitable Roman Catholic men on the scene whenever Andrew wasn't.

Thus, she or Andrew had broken off their romance any number of times throughout the last years of college and during Andrew's years in law school. Andrew was the one who usually revived the relationship. Like many, he was drawn to Margaret's spontaneity, her eagerness to fully participate in life's adventures, and her upbeat nature.

Having attended few professional theatrical performances while growing up, Margaret would happily accompany Andrew to any and all live stage performances of Andrew's choosing. Many of the women in Andrew's social circle were more discerning.

At restaurants, Margaret readily allowed Andrew to choose from the menu offerings. It would be her first experience tasting frogs legs, oysters on the half shell, stone crabs, Alaskan King Crabs, snails in garlic and butter sauce, rabbit, venison, pheasant under glass. She tasted all with an adventurous spirit and exuded delight at the new flavors.

His country-club set had dipped their taste buds into these delicacies many times before. They greeted his selections with ennui. Those young women now contented themselves with salads and vegetable platters while they watched their waistlines and searched for husbands.

When Andrew suggested that he and Margaret travel together to Europe during a break from his law-school studies. Margaret jumped at the chance. By then, Margaret had been teaching first grade for two years, and she insisted that she pay for her share of the trip. To accommodate Margaret's budget, they backpacked, stayed at hostels, spent nights on trains, hitchhiked, and consumed bread and wine while sitting on the ancient stone walls surrounding beaches, rivers and lakes. Although Andrew had visited Europe on several holidays with his family, he had never experienced it in this fashion. He met many more of the "natives," enjoyed the pubs and trattorias, and saw far more sunrises and sunsets.

Seeing it through Margaret's eyes made everything new. Her reaction to the unknown, her nonchalance in meeting strangers, her facility with other languages, and her acceptance of accommodations that were substandard amazed Andrew. He found her greatly refreshing compared to the women who had always surrounded him. Unlike those women, Margaret had never been pampered. Margaret could get soaked in the rain or covered with mud, could stroll among the sheep or swat flies in a tent. Her spirits rarely faltered. He found himself absorbing her aliveness.

Despite their parents' disapproval, within six months of their return from Europe, they eloped.

Margaret knew the Clearys would never fully accept her and she would always be walking on eggs in trying to evade their cutting barbs. Her insecurities and diffidence led her to be very dependent on Andrew's family.

Right from the start, she sought the advice of his mother and sister as to what she would wear, who should cut her untamed locks, what perfume would be most acceptable, what conversational topics would be proper among their friends. Although this did not endear Margaret to them, it allowed them to be less apprehensive about Margaret committing a major faux-pax and embarrassing the family name.

This acquiescence in all facets related to her life and her life with Andrew assuaged the initial reluctance her in-laws had toward the marriage. Her mother-in-law, for all intents and purposes, selected the town, neighborhood, and the house in which they were to live. Andrew's mother hired the housekeeper who virtually ran Margaret's home.

Although Margaret did not fit the breeding expectations of Andrew's dad, he did think her an attractive sort and in acceptable health. Most important, she did manage to give him two fine looking and healthy specimens for grandsons who consistently delighted their granddad.

Margaret and Andrew remained at the exclusive country club where Andrew's grandfather had been a founding member and had served on its first board of directors. The family had been members ever since. Andrew was not about to break with tradition.

At first, Margaret was grateful for all the assistance from Andrew's family. She would have had difficulty knowing what to look for in a house, how to go about furnishing it, how to entertain. Certainly, these were not crucial elements that were a part of her upbringing, so she was totally unprepared. On her own, Margaret would have hesitated long and hard before spending the kind of money necessary to achieve the perfect wardrobe, the perfect party, the perfect home and the running of the place.

Initially, Margaret was enthralled with her new lifestyle and grateful to Andrew and his family for providing it. She became caught up in all the hoopla of parties, theater, concerts, luncheons, and events for causes. Her natural ability to lead had her at the forefront of many dances, dinners and musicales on behalf of one charity or another. These small successes emboldened her, and, over time, she became a little more assertive. Nevertheless, she still remained within the bounds prescribed by Andrew and his family and their expectations of her. And, as long as she stayed within those guidelines, Andrew's family tolerated her presence.

Margaret was jolted by the pilot's voice announcing their approach to Barajas Airport in Madrid. Sometime during the night, she had fallen asleep, her head resting on Tomas' shoulder. Although she started to apologize for her behavior, he'd hear none of it.

Very soon, they were touching down in Spain. Tomas expressed his pleasure at meeting her, wished her a good trip and told her to telephone if she required assistance while in Spain. With that, Tomas handed her a business card and set off to make his meeting. She stuffed the card into a pocket of her jeans as she thanked him again for his kindness.

Once again, she struggled with all of her hand-held belongings as she made her way down the aisle. She still had to claim her two grips from baggage. Then, she would be off for, what she hoped would be, a new beginning . . . in Nerja.

CHAPTER 3

MARGARET FLOATED ON TOP OF the water and felt the muscles in her whole body go limp. Slowly, she stretched her arms and legs into a leisurely, rhythmic crawl, swimming lengthwise across the beautifully tiled, heated pool. Her strokes were graceful and precise. Every part of her body was aching. The warm water and motion had a soothing effect. It was just what her body was craving after being cramped into an airplane seat for several hours and then onto a train and automobile. Now, she could reflect on the long, arduous trip she'd just completed that brought her to this place.

After landing in Madrid, Margaret had opted not to drive to the Costa del Sol. Instead, she took a high-speed train between Madrid and Malaga. She had debated about spending the money, but then realizing that it would be a brutally long day, she had purchased the train ticket and a first-class seat. It was a wise decision. The car was clean, modern and cheerful. In addition, she was offered a menu choice of a very appetizing dinner and intermittent snacks.

With memories of the horrific terrorist bombing attacks on Madrid's trains during one day in 2004, Margaret had to overcome her understandable fears of entering the Madrid rail station and getting on board. Fortunately, her concerns were unfounded, and she relaxed sufficiently to thoroughly appreciate the train and the scenic views it afforded.

The passing panorama was lovely, just as she recollected. Once again, she thrilled to the gorgeous scenery that Spain provided . . . the fields, vineyards, acres and acres of olive trees arrayed as if on checkerboards, towns with walled Paradors atop, and the open countryside with rugged stone mountains rising and falling in the distance. She stretched out in the spacious seat . . . dozed and woke, dozed and woke, the kaleidoscope passing swiftly across the train's window. Her senses heightened, her anticipation slowly outweighing the trepidations of this entire expedition.

When Margaret arrived at Malaga, the car and driver she'd arranged before leaving the States were nowhere to be seen. After several faulty and frustrating conversations in broken Spanish and English, a driver emerged to carry her to her destination.

As they'd slowly driven along the shoreline and on to the Interstate, her eyes scanned the scenery. It was suddenly all so unfamiliar. Shock, bewilderment and disillusion were her immediate responses. She was appalled by the numbers of new condominiums and resorts lining the path looking out onto the water. The high-rise buildings stood as modern, ugly fortresses guarding the coastline while blocking the sun and view to those living above. They reminded Margaret that progress and growth were not always beautiful and welcoming.

When she finally drove into Nerja, she was heartsick to see that there, too, hotels had cropped up where she remembered open spaces. Even in the beautiful hills of memory where she'd rented this house, cranes, like her sons' erector set, dotted the landscape. Small sub-divisions and lavish homes were springing up and down the hills. Her disappointment was palpable.

The home she had rented was known to her from only a brief description and a half-a-dozen pictures she'd found through the Internet.

The blurb read:

> *Terraced house with 2 bedrooms in a quiet area only 2 km. from Nerja. It has 2 bedrooms, bathroom en-suite, bathroom, lounge-dining with fireplace, kitchen, 2 Terraces, 2 roof terraces with lovely views of the sea and the mountains. Swimming pool on premises. Furnished. Garage beneath.*

The white stucco house topped by a clay tile roof rose about one third of the way to the top of the hills and nestled, quite modestly, among the larger houses. From her research, Margaret knew that the house could sell for the euro equivalent of approximately five hundred thousand dollars. She was fortunate that the owners were renting at the last minute and were willing to make accommodations on the rent.

When the realtor escorted her inside, Margaret had not known quite what to expect. When the door opened, Margaret was pleasantly surprised. It looked as lovely as the photos she'd uploaded on her laptop. However, she barely could suppress the giggle which suddenly erupted. "This layout reminds me of similar ones I've visited in retirement communities in Massachusetts and Florida. I'm not even forty-three yet; is someone trying to tell me something here?"

Senora Rios returned a limp smile of bewilderment, oblivious to Margaret's humor. A language gap here?

Margaret composed herself and, with a more subdued mien, addressed the house.

The living and dining areas were one large room. The kitchen could be seen through a waist-to-ceiling pass way. Hence, the area appeared more spacious.

The furnishings enhanced the effect. Fabrics on the sofa and two chairs in the living room were in hues of yellows and white. Two white wicker chairs, a coffee table, and a round, sturdy white wrought-iron dining table with six matching chairs completed the room. Soft recessed lighting shown on white-stained hardwood floors and creamy-white painted walls. The opposite wall was comprised of windows divided by a center, wood-burning fireplace. All added to the feeling of space and light.

A white eyelet-lace comforter was tucked neatly over a king-sized bed in the master bedroom. Large windows made the bedrooms feel commodious, as well. All in all, it put Margaret in a wonderfully uplifting mood.

The kitchen cabinets were a light oak with corresponding granite counters. Margaret spotted a small microwave, toaster, and coffee-maker on the far counter.

Senora Rios opened cabinets so that Margaret could see there was an adequate number of dishes, utensils, pots, pans, Pyrex dishes, and table mats.

The major appliances were clean and up to date. Margaret was pleased to see there was a dishwasher and stacked washer/dryer in the kitchen, as well.

The two bathrooms were compact and nondescript, but adequate. Toilets, sinks, tub and showers appeared to be in working order as Margaret tested each. There were sufficient bath towels and bed linens that were attractive and new. They would accommodate her and her sons when the boys visited.

Then, the realtor slid open the patio doors and they walked out onto the terrace. Margaret felt her breath being sucked in by the views for, from every angle, each scene was more breathtaking than the next. The water gleaming in the pool surrounded by small palm trees, bushes of bougainvillaea and jasmine. An arrangement of rocks in which small cacti were placed stood at the corner of the large swimming pool. Margaret knew that these boded a feast for her senses when Spring arrived.

Awaiting her gaze was Nerja and the beautiful blue waters extending as far as the eye could see. Above her were the hills of Frigiliana. Margaret was awed by the sheer beauty of it all. She watched . . . mute.

Senora Rios smiled to see Margaret's pleasure. Then, since Margaret appeared satisfied with her inspection of the house, Senora Rios handed her the keys and wished her, "Buena Suerte!"

"Thanks for everything. The e-mails, virtual photos and phone calls really helped. Still I couldn't visualize this place until seeing it."

The realtor assured Margaret that she could be counted on in a pinch. With that, she left Margaret to her own devices.

With the realtor escorted out the door, Margaret's disposition changed dramatically. She suddenly felt depressed and very alone.

She slumped onto one end of the "L" shaped sofa. Her emotions were on a roller coaster. One minute anticipating with joy a new life, a new beginning. Another minute and she was cascading down a steep slope into the depths of despair longing for her home, her children, and a past life that was no longer hers. Perhaps, that life had been a fantasy, a state of denial. Her head was aching and her stomach sour.

Margaret was shocked to hear herself speaking aloud, "Well, Margaret, if you're to drown in your sorrow, you may as well drown in that pool." As if someone were propelling her, Margaret walked into the bedroom, tore open one of the suitcases scattering clothes hither and yon, and pulled out a two-piece bathing suit.

Thus, to her amazement, Margaret was in her pool before unpacking, before alerting her sons and Missy that she'd arrived safely, before stocking her fridge.

Now, she let her body go limp once more as she held her breath and did a prone float in her private swimming pool. She laid in this position for some time allowing little bubbles to escape as she expelled air. Her body curved almost into a ball, and she felt herself relax.

Then she rolled onto her back and stared up at the bluest, clearest sky she'd seen since she couldn't remember when. She closed her eyes, and when she opened them again, she skipped past the cranes and viewed the white houses that dotted the hills above Nerja. From this supine position, her eyes looked north, scanning the white towns . . . one of the splendors that had drawn her to return to this region. She remembered their stark, pristine beauty. As she lay on her back, she heard a sigh escape her lips as she drank in the sight. From this vantage, she could see the rolling hills, all the houses above her, and up into the village of Frigiliana. She was right to come here. Already, she was feeling its healing powers.

She emerged from the pool and wrapped herself in a towel. Upon entering the house, she looked with a discerning eye. The furnishings were sparse, but cheerful and adequate. Still, it lacked for any personal possessions, trinkets, objets d'art. As a result, there was little warmth in the house.

Before leaving her Massachusetts home, Margaret had tossed some of her framed photographs into a suitcase. Now, she tucked these into some of the barren spots in her new bedroom and living room and smiled poignantly at her two sons, her sister and brother-in-law with her niece and nephew, and her friend Missy with her family. At the sight of her loved ones, she felt a sense of comfort mixed with a rush of longing. The photos helped to define the space as her home, and she promised herself she would search for some objects in Spain that would add a personal touch. The expectation of having an opportunity to select some pieces of her own choosing began to excite her. Perhaps, she could find some flea markets and out-of-the-way shops at the beginning of next week.

Tomorrow was Sunday. She knew she would head for the little white church which stood in the center of the town not far from the water's edge near the historic Balcon de Europa.

CHAPTER 4

A S SHE AROSE THE NEXT morning, she pulled her hair back with a yellow and white polka-dot ribbon and donned a deep-yellow knit dress with its matching jacket. Margaret had taken several nice clothes whose material would pack well.

She put on comfortable walking shoes for the long hike to church. It was early enough so that the sun was just breaking forth in the sky. It appeared as a flaming red ball. Margaret took a deep breath. The sight reminded her of other mornings heading off to church in Newton.when she'd been a part of a complete family. It was so hard to swallow; that chapter of her life had ended. An unbearable sadness enveloped her. Perhaps the rhythms of the Mass would bring her comfort.

Margaret slipped into the back pew and glanced around the church. The Church of El Salvador dated from the 17th century. She remembered the simplicity and whiteness of it all. The last time she'd visited here, the church walls had been decorated with children's art work. They were mostly immense pictures of butterflies and flowers. The depictions flowed with the ambiance of the building, and, at the time, Margaret had considered it a very beautiful and moving testament to God's gifts. She was somewhat disappointed that they were no longer on display.

Instead, she focused on all the gold surrounding the figure of Christ and the communion altar; the massive wooden doors to the sides; the elaborate stained-glassed windows; and the diamond-shaped pattern of black and white marble beneath her feet.

A new roof outside, and a simple yet handsome wood-beamed ceiling within, added greatly to its beauty. She looked with admiration at the four contemporary-styled chandeliers which were each held by a gold pole dropped from the new ceiling. Their geometric shape with clear glass and tapered lights added to the fresh look.

Margaret had arrived early. The church bells overhead pealed loudly every fifteen minutes to remind worshipers that the Mass was about to commence. The women were still laying out the candles, chalice for the sacramental wine and the wafers to be used in the Eucharist. Young boys and girls distributed photocopied, stapled hymnals. Margaret watched the comings and goings with great interest.

The church pews were quickly filling. Several individuals stood to the rear.

Only two women were wearing hats. Dress was fairly casual.

At last, a relatively young priest appeared with a deacon by his side. They were about to begin.

Since Margaret's command of the Spanish language was very limited, she did not expect to comprehend any of the readings, sermon or songs. Surprisingly, the priest did translate into English much of what was said and done. Just being a part of the setting, hearing the priest's mellifluous voice and the tones of the choir culminated in a calming effect. She pushed all thoughts out of her head and tried to capture the moment.

After the service, the priest greeted each parishioner at the door. As Margaret approached, she shook his hand, murmured a quiet, "Gracias, padre," and almost did an abbreviated curtsy. The priest had been aware of her presence in the rear of his church. Even with her hair pulled back, her red locks stood out. In seeing her, the priest switched to English and asked Margaret if she were just passing through Nerja or if she were staying awhile. Margaret explained that she had a six-month lease that could be renewed and she hoped to be attending his church.

As there were still parishioners waiting to greet Father Eduardo, he asked if she would like to continue the conversation. Margaret indicated that she would be pleased to do so, and he motioned to her to enter through an adjacent door around the back of the church.

When Margaret sat down in the modest but pleasant-looking study, she noticed that a computer and telephone took up much of the desk. A window fan indicated that there would be no air conditioning in the building during the hot summer months. The small study was lined with mostly books, photos, and memorabilia. She twisted her body around to take it all in while trying not to look too inquisitive.

The priest entered within a short time and greeted Margaret warmly. Shaking her by the hand, and in a light-hearted voice, "Hi, name's Father Eduardo, but, feel free to call me Edward or Eddie." Noticing Margaret's questioning eyebrow, he added, "Picked up the nicknames while I was at Siena College in upstate New York." He, then, proceeded to casually slide into the desk chair which did not appear big enough to fit his frame and protruding legs.

From that introduction, Margaret gleaned that Father Eduardo was both a Franciscan and seemingly unpretentious. "Your English made me think you were a native. Oh, I'm Margaret Leary . . . from Newton, Massachusetts . . . not too far from Loudonville, NewYork. My folks used to take my sister and me into Albany, New York when we were little. My dad had a second cousin or something we'd visit. I've not been back there too frequently."

"Well, not much to see and do there unless you're caught up in the college scene. I was!"

Margaret wondered if he were going to pursue that thought, but he seemed to think better of it. "So what brings you to Nerja?"

"I'd been here ten years ago and loved the area. I thought it would be kind of neat to live 'in the culture' so to speak." And under her breath, "and to sort out some things." She didn't elaborate, and the priest didn't pry. He seemed to understand that she didn't wish to delve further.

Margaret was of the opinion that people reached a certain point in their lives where they just knew, almost immediately, whether or not they and another individual would click. She did this easily at cocktail parties or at large gatherings.

This priest, who appeared to be about the same age as Margaret, seemed to have a good sense of humor and a capacity to reach out to others. His questions of her, though probing, did not demand an answer. She took an immediate liking to him and felt they'd be simpatico.

When the priest realized that Margaret was planning to walk home, he offered to drop her at her house. The next few Masses of the day would be overseen by another priest, and Father Eduardo welcomed the break.

Margaret hesitated.

"Is there something I said to offend you? Did I make you uncomfortable?"

"Oh, heavens no. " Margaret quickly tried to reassure him. "You see," she said laughingly, "I just arrived yesterday and have absolutely nothing in the house to eat. My breakfast consisted of a stale roll and sweet bread that I saved from the airplane."

"Oh dear, you must be famished. Anyway, that's no problem. There's a local supermarket at the far side of Nerja right on the way to Frigiliana. Let's go load up your pantry and fridge."

Father Eduardo led the way with long strides and a light gait. He seemed bent on this happy mission.

As they rode the short distance in the priest's old, black and badly dented four-door sedan, Margaret asked, " Would you have any idea where I might rent a car for the length of my stay? I'll need some 'wheels' to do daily errands as well as take some day trips."

"There is a showroom along the street . . . at the upper end of town. It's in a small storefront and has a few cars on display. Not much for you to actually see. I'm thinking. You know, it might be more economical for you to purchase an inexpensive model or a used car and sell it whenever you decide to return to the States. I have a parishioner who might be of assistance, and he owes me a favor or two. Are you free tomorrow? We can drive out along the highway where there are several dealerships." Without waiting for a reply, Father Eduardo offered to take her to see the car dealer the next morning. Margaret was extremely grateful and eagerly accepted his offer.

Margaret sensed that the priest's kindness extended beyond finding her food and a means of transportation. His curiosity, regarding her, had not been sated. Margaret had shared little about herself save the fact that she desired some time to sort out her personal problems. He must have sensed that she had needs far beyond food and transportation.

CHAPTER 5

SINCE MARGARET HAD BECOME AWARE of Andrew's infidelity, she had unburdened herself only to her good friend Missy. Margaret was not one to bare her soul and hang her dirty linen in public.

She rarely shared her disappointments or displeasure regarding her husband even with her younger sister. Margaret believed it counterproductive for Eileen to think ill of Andrew. Eileen had a very happy marriage to Tony which produced two adorable youngsters. Margaret felt her sister had been blessed and thanked God for it. Andrew liked Eileen and Tony well enough, but he considered them blue collar and chose to socialize with them infrequently. However, to his credit, he never cast aspersions nor protested when Margaret sent her niece and nephew outfits from Saks or Nieman's or good hand-me-downs to her nephew. Andrew understood Margaret's generosity toward her sister and brother-in-law and never discouraged it. Thus, Eileen and Tony thought well of Andrew, and Margaret wished to keep it that way.

After the episode at Andrew's office, Margaret had driven home in a state of shock and ultimate despair. She did not know where to turn or what to do. As she drove into her driveway that night, she was consumed with grief. This was the home that had always felt safe and given her whole being a lift as she'd enter the circular drive. Now, on her eighteenth wedding anniversary, her whole world had been torn asunder.

Was she to toss Andrew's belongings out the front door? Would she change all the locks? Should she call a lawyer, and, if so, which one? Did she need pictures to catch him in flagrante delicto? What was to become of them? What was to become of her? It was all too overwhelming, and she'd had a huge headache and felt nauseated.

Andrew had not called or tried to see her that night. Missy came the next morning as soon as Margaret telephoned. The women sat with a pot of coffee while Margaret sobbed. Poor Margaret looked awful and felt worse. She kept repeating, "What did I do wrong?" Margaret was berating herself, whipping herself. How had she let this happen? Maybe she should have dressed more attractively, paid more attention to her hair and nails, really excelled at golf, been more exciting in the bedroom. What had she done to throw Andrew into the arms of another woman?

Missy tried reassuring Margaret that this wasn't her doing. She was glad that she had rushed here this morning; Margaret was beyond being rational and was caught in a painful web of self-denigration.

Missy dreaded resurrecting an even greater wound. Yet, she had to remind Margaret that Andrew was, indeed, capable of going behind Margaret's back, inflicting extreme hurt, and totally negating Margaret's feelings, needs and wishes. Hadn't he, unilaterally, made the decision to send the boys off to boarding school at the age of fifteen and sixteen, respectively?

Margaret stopped short with a jerk. Her spasmodic sobs caught in her throat. She couldn't breathe. She, once more, felt a severe pain to her chest and doubled over. Yes, Margaret thought, that had been an even harder blow. Now, she was crying uncontrollably. She had to admit she'd been in agony for months . . . ever since Andrew had come home and announced that he'd enrolled the boys at boarding school. He'd wanted to surprise her and them with this news.

It would never have occurred to Andrew to have consulted with Margaret or, for that matter, with their sons Brandon and Richard. Both Andrew and his father had graduated from the old prestigious prep school and it was expected that all Cleary males would get a fine academic education there and love it in the process.

By living in the town of Newton, the boys were offered the excellence of one of the best school systems in the nation. Margaret had been extremely pleased with the Newton public schools and expected her sons would be in attendance there from kindergarten through high school graduation.

She had pleaded with Andrew to allow the boys to remain at home. Wasn't their present school giving the boys a first-rate education? Didn't they have a great bunch of friends? Was she not a good mom?

Andrew reluctantly agreed that all was going exceptionally well, but her pleas fell on deaf ears. Andrew was buying none of it. Classes at the prep school were small and often met as seminars with only six to eight boys seated around a table discussing a wide variety of subjects with their instructors. The student body represented some of the most prestigious families in the nation making future business contacts more readily accessible. It would be good for the boys to be in a more rough and tumble environment and out from under their mother's skirts. He wanted the boys in a boarding school. Period!

Margaret's imploring, weeping, arguing, and reasoning with Andrew didn't make a dent. He just became all the more adamant. He wanted his sons to share his learning experiences and to graduate with a diploma from the old, established and very reputable institution that granted one to him and to their grandfather. Besides, the school was only one and a half to two hours away, so what was all the fuss?

While Brandon and Richard were not so far away that they could not come home frequently, or she could not visit them, their not being home on a daily basis was pure torture to Margaret.

She knew that the best time to reach a child was just as his head was laid on the pillow at night. In the darkness, as she stroked their hair and whispered, "Good night," they would often blurt out whatever problems might be disturbing them. This was the moment that they were the most vulnerable and open to baring their souls. It eased them into sleep, allowed her a glimpse into their inner selves and offered her the opportunity to occasionally assist them with a possible remedy. It seemed awfully young to pry them from their nest.

She missed them terribly. Her sons missed her, too. However, they were adjusting surprisingly well. Despite occasional bouts with homesickness missing their folks and friends, they were caught up in the daily activities the school offered. They liked their classes, their roommates, most of their classmates and faculty, and appreciated the excellent athletic facilities the boarding school offered.

After being there a few months, the boys surprised Margaret by going out for extra-curricular activities in addition to the intramural sports teams. Just prior to Thanksgiving, Richard had invited his parents to see him perform with the Drama Club. Even with his relatively minor part in the production, it was obvious to Margaret that her son was thoroughly immersed in the character he presented on stage and displayed no noticeable stage fright. Of course, she had a difficult time separating the character on stage from the person she knew as her son. However, her child really seemed to believe he was the character he was portraying. His mannerisms, gait, voice, and carriage were indicative of a person she'd never met.

Brandon had signed on to write for the student newspaper. Margaret was pleased to see him honing his skills while researching, interviewing, and looking for scoops.

Their teachers were most supportive and were happy to have these well-adjusted, bright, inquisitive youngsters under their tutelage. In addition, the boys were good athletes and personable; they made friends easily. The twenty-five acre campus, with its long history, had much to offer.

Margaret knew the boys were doing well despite not being in her daily care. Yet, the ache in her heart persisted. When she came into her home, her teenagers were missing.

She had tried to busy herself with activities in the town, at the club, and in Boston proper. Recently, she was toying with the idea of returning to school. Boston has a huge number of colleges and universities from which she could get a master's degree. Boston College was situated right there in Newton, and she was quite sure she would gain acceptance to enroll in a graduate program.

She'd also scanned the Sunday paper's employment section to see if something might be of interest. Nothing grabbed her.

Andrew, on the other hand, continued with his daily routines. Unlike Margaret, Andrew would take his sons to the golf course or play a set of tennis with them, but he did not experience that day to day contact which Margaret had and now pined for. Andrew was proud of his sons and certainly loved them. Yet, his attachment to them was nowhere near that of Margaret's.

Missy knew, only too well, that Margaret had always gone the extra mile for Andrew, their children and his family. They lived where Andrew wished, sent their boys to the schools of Andrew's choice, belonged to the family's country club, socialized with Andrew's friends and business acquaintances. On top of all that, Margaret accepted the bedroom as one of her wifely duties along with entertaining, keeping their lives in order, and juggling with a young family's demands.

Missy watched her friend always acquiesce to Andrew's wants even when they were totally contrary to Margaret's strong beliefs. Margaret would quietly question or even protest, but she was summarily beaten down.

Andrew's involvement with other women was only the last straw. Missy was irate; she could have choked Andrew. She recalled the deepest hurts that Andrew had inflicted over the years when she felt like killing Andrew. Margaret, on the other hand, would try to present him in the best light.

It had disconcerted Missy so to see her best friend's spunk and will eroded. She insisted that Margaret not back down this time. If Andrew wished to act as if nothing had happened, Margaret was not to welcome him with open arms. Missy made Margaret swear to her that she would not be manipulated again.

This was not an easy promise to exact. Andrew's mom had already phoned that morning. Although there were no specific references to the night before, his mother intimated that boys will be boys. She suggested that they all go for dinner on Sunday at the club to celebrate Margaret and Andrew's anniversary. She asked what Margaret and Andrew might like for a present. Filled with anger and hurt, and feeling exhausted, Margaret could barely speak. She mumbled to her mother-in-law that she'd contact her later.

While Margaret and Missy were seated at the kitchen table, flowers arrived with a note attached. "I am sorry that you were so upset last night. I hope you will let me explain. Love, Andrew" The Clearys were certainly not going to make this any easier for Margaret.

Margaret knew Andrew and his family were deathly afraid that this little event might go public. What would the neighbors think? How might this information impact on Andrew's practice, the family name? For sure, Margaret would grow up and realize adultery is practiced in proper circles; it's just that sophisticated people don't talk about it. The Clearys did not need to verbalize their concerns, justifications and smug philosophies, Margaret knew them well enough to know what they were thinking and contemplating.

Missy was right, of course. Margaret could no longer kowtow to the Clearys' demands. Their lifestyle and judgements ran counter to Margaret's very soul. She'd been involved in an internal tug of war for years. This was the breaking straw.

Nonetheless, Margaret had her sons to consider. She couldn't ruin Andrew's livelihood; her sons needed to be supported. Nor could she ruin the Cleary name; her sons would be carrying that name throughout their lives. For the sake of Brandon and Richard, she did not wish the family to become the object of scuttlebutt. Thus, few people could know of the mounting tensions behind the Clearys' door.

With Missy to bolster her, Margaret telephoned Andrew's office. She asked that he pick up his belongings and move out. She would need time to think. Since the boys were in school and unlikely to be home for a couple of months, she asked that he not bring the boys into this conflict. She would contact Andrew when she'd decided how to proceed. She needed some breathing time.

Surprisingly, Andrew did not act in an argumentative and combative fashion. Perhaps he'd had the night to do some thinking on his own and had begun to realize that being caught might possibly upset his tidy little applecart. He would not push Margaret further. It was clear she knew she had the upper hand although her strained voice showed certain defeat.

Andrew drove up that evening with a pick-up truck and a driver. He said little to Margaret, nor she to him. He and the driver loaded up Andrew's wardrobe, toilet articles, books and belongings from his study, and a few of his favorite CD's and DVD's. It was so civil. It was so Andrew.

For the next six months, Margaret continued to live in the house and Andrew continued to pay the mortgage. On his own, he offered Margaret a very comfortable allowance which Margaret readily accepted. Margaret and Missy termed it "hush money." While Andrew was now begging for a reunion, she was asking that they be legally separated.

Andrew requested that Margaret meet him for lunch or dinner. Margaret agreed to see him at lunch. She waltzed in displaying far more confidence than she was feeling and wearing the identical dress she'd had on the night she'd caught him at his office. The sight of her in this garb caused him to simultaneously wince and draw in his breath. He'd forgotten the impact that Margaret could have on a man. Margaret, with her striking red hair, tall, well-proportioned figure and sculptured features, turned every head in this businessmen's establishment. Eyes followed as she circled the restaurant to reach the table at which Andrew was seated. He realized that he was proud to be seen with her.

Margaret had wisely calculated that looking her best and walking with her head held high would give her the upper hand in any discussion or dissuasive points that Andrew might raise. She tried to exude self confidence throughout the lunch. When she informed him that she'd rented a house in Spain for several months and would appreciate it if he would allow the boys to fly there for their Spring Break, she suspected that this latest news would cause him to be apoplectic and it did. She dismissed all of his warnings, arguments, and cajoling with the explanation that she felt they both needed additional time and space to make important life-decisions.

Now, she recalled almost word by word their final conversation. Margaret had summoned all of her courage to say, "Through an acquaintance, I've managed to rent the house in Newton to a young professor and his wife." To herself, Margaret thought, the small income should offset the cost of my Nerja stay, and, hopefully, keep you, Andrew, off the premises.

Andrew was aghast. "I cannot imagine you taking such a bold step. And renting our house!"

Trying to keep her voice under control, Margaret had intoned, "You're no longer living there, Andrew. I have to make decisions for myself now."

Andrew, for his part, was amazed at, and taken aback by, the strength of her convictions. It was evident that she was not going to readily back down. For the first time in their marriage, Andrew capitulated.

This was a major victory for Margaret. It added greatly to her self-esteem which had been badly bruised having to come to grips with the knowledge of Andrew's cheating on her. She was still apprehensive about going it alone in Spain. However, once she'd shared her plan with Andrew, she was committed.

Thus, here she was . . . in Nerja.

CHAPTER 6

FATHER EDUARDO ARRIVED BRIGHT AND early Monday morning. They had not discussed a time to meet. Since Margaret's landline had not been installed and she'd omitted giving him her cell number, he'd not given her a heads up. Hence, she was not quite ready to be on her way. She had just emerged from the shower and had barely managed to grab her bathrobe and firmly tie the accompanying belt before opening the front door. A towel was still wrapped around her head.

The priest, his face reddened, appeared obviously embarrassed by the sight of her. It was not every day that he viewed women in a dressing mode. Margaret quickly excused herself while she hastily dried her hair and jumped into the wardrobe she'd previously laid out on her bed.

Emerging from her bedroom, she invited the priest to join her for breakfast rolls and coffee. He readily agreed and settled himself at the table on the terrace. Their conversation ranged from the beautiful view overlooking her pool, the open, airy feeling of the house, this gorgeous sunny day, and her purchase of a car.

The priest had sensed Margaret's reluctance to answer questions related to herself. He realized he would have to win her trust if he were to help her work through her pain. Therefore, he kept the conversation focused elsewhere.

As they drove, he asked, "What are your specific requirements for a car? You know automatic cars are far more expensive and not as readily available as in the States. Can you drive a car with manual transmission?"

"Oh my! I haven't driven a stick shift in years, but maybe with a little brushing up on the mechanics I could handle one again."

"The stick here operates a little differently from cars in the States. You have to press down on the gear shift as you shift into Reverse, and it's located on the upper left hand side."

Margaret looked as if she were processing this information and moving her right hand to activate the reverse gear.

"As to my other requirements, I will insist on air conditioning," she piped in. "You know, I've been amazed at the huge number of motorcycles I see up and down Nerja and Frigiliana. This morning one woke me with a roar. All morning, I've been hearing the cyclists tool around these hills and heading into Nerja or onto the highway. Is everyday a Harley Convention? Maybe, I'll get me one!"

The priest laughed. "You wouldn't have air conditioning."

"No, and I wouldn't have room enough for my two sons."

The priest looked at her with great curiosity. She explained about her sons' impending visit in a few months, but then chose not to comment further. Father Eduardo did not push that line of questioning.

Instead, he asked, "How did you choose to come to Nerja? Not many Americans seem to land here even if they visit the southern coast of Spain."

Margaret replied, "Ten years ago, we spent a week in Nerja at the Parador on the beach below. I fell in love with the views, the paths along the ocean, the quaint white towns and with your church. Even more so, I was drawn to the caves. To me, the caves represent a city under the ground, a mammoth, magnificent, awe-inspiring work of God's hand."

"You sound like a travel brochure, but I heartily agree. I'd gladly take you to the caves later in the day if we can accomplish the car purchase in a reasonable amount of time. I love visiting the caves."

What the priest didn't say aloud was, God forgive me, I really don't enjoy spending the day shopping for a car. The promise of a visit to the caves might hasten the process.

The priest introduced Margaret to the owner of the car lot, a parishioner, whom Father felt could be trusted. Francisco Burgos willingly showed Margaret his new and used automobiles.

Compared to the U.S., prices were outrageous. The euro was at a much higher rate than the dollar. Furthermore, the value-added-tax placed an even heavier burden on the purchase.

Margaret thought briefly of buying a bicycle, but the incline of the hills and the lengthy distances from place to place discouraged that idea. She excused herself to the car dealer and sought out Father Eduardo for feedback. "Any recommendations?"

Father Eduardo jerked his thumb back toward his own clunker and laughingly said, "Do you think I'm in a position to give advice? Go ahead, pick what suits you."

Margaret zeroed in on a year old black, four-door sedan. It seemed reliable and roomy. She drove the car around the parking lot and was satisfied at the way it handled. She dug through her purse and produced her credit card.

As she did so, out of the corner of her eye, she spotted the sun bouncing off a car parked three rows away and off to her left. "Whoa!" Shoving the credit card into her pants pocket, she walked forcefully to a white two-door convertible. Did she dare? She suddenly felt rather giddy. "Why not?" Margaret thought. Wasn't it her turn for some fun?

"Sorry, but would you be kind enough to allow me to see this Ford Escort convertible," she shouted. The astonished priest translated, and he and Senor Burgos quickly came to her side.

Almost in unison, "you wish to see THIS car?"

Now feeling slightly uncomfortable, Margaret replied in a quieter tone, "Yes."

Then, emphatically, "Yes, I really do."

As she peeked inside, she saw that it did have a full-sized seat in the back that would serve passengers. She stretched her long legs behind the wheel; checked out the gear shift, brakes, lights, windshield wipers, air-conditioning, and radio; looked under the hood; checked the mileage; looked for possible accident-related damage; checked the size of the trunk; sat in the rear seat: kicked the tires; and realized that she didn't know much more about the mechanics of the car than she'd known before. Did men? She would just have to trust the lot owner and women's intuition.

This time, all three went out for a test drive. The priest stretched out in back saying, "I could get used to this." Margaret sat in the passenger seat. The dealer drove right onto the highway. Margaret liked the car's pick up, quiet motor and sporty feel.

Since she didn't feel comfortable practicing standard shift out on the open road, she drove around the side streets and back into the parking area of the dealership.

She surprised the priest at the way she bargained. At one point, she, regretfully, turned to leave without a sale. The owner looked at the priest who had rolled his eyes heavenward. The stymied dealer continued to negotiate until Margaret was satisfied that they'd hit rock bottom. She closed the deal with a smile and a handshake. With everyone satisfied, the priest emitted an audible sigh of relief. They thanked Francisco and continued on their way.

Margaret was most grateful to Father Eduardo and insisted that she treat him to lunch. She followed the priest toward a restaurant, her car bumping, jerking, and stalling. They drove slowly and, somehow, Margaret managed to arrive at their destination. She hoped she would not strip the gears of this thing before she mastered the art of driving five on the floor.

Over lunch, Father Eduardo expressed his great admiration for her car-buying skills displayed this morning. He praised her thoroughness in appraising the vehicle and her skill at negotiation. In fact, he went so far as to ask if she'd kindly accompany him when he made his next car purchase. It would have to be soon as his old heap was just about ready for burial. She had noticed how it seemed to be wheezing and on its last breath.

Margaret, for her part, was overwhelmed by the priest's praise and exhausted from the stress of selecting this major purchase. She confided in him, "Since my marriage, I've never chosen my own automobile. My husband always purchased the car through a client's dealership. It was always an expensive model and suited me just fine, except, when it pulled into the driveway . . . it was a fait accompli."

Father Eduardo was having a difficult time filling in the blanks, but he realized that Margaret did seem to have a means of support. He wondered, however, how she would occupy her time and he voiced his thoughts.

Margaret replied, "Oh, I think I'll enjoy having the time to read, swim, comb the villages, hike some of the mountains and amble along the seashore, return to Gibraltar and Marbella, and I hope to spend lots of time at the caves."

"That's right," said the priest, "I did promise to escort you there and I've been looking forward to it. We can stop there en route."

As soon as they'd finished lunch, Margaret tailed the priest's car. This time, she stalled out only twice. "Well," she giggled softly to herself, "maybe I'll get the hang of this yet!"

Margaret purchased a long-term pass that would enable her to visit the caves on a frequent basis without breaking her budget. As they proceeded down below, Margaret could feel the tightness in her chest. The descent was a mixture of exhilaration and trepidation. Margaret remembered the Cuevas de Nerja as unlike any other caves she'd ever visited. Their expanse is enormous. From one end, one can see far into the distance.

Margaret read from her Fodor's guide book to refresh her memory. "These huge Paleolithic caves are thought to be between twelve thousand and twenty thousand years [composed of] floodlit spires and turrets created by centuries of dripping water. One suspended pinnacle, two hundred feet long, claims the title of world's largest stalactite. .. these awesome subterranean chambers provide an impressive setting for concert and ballet performances."

After reading aloud to the priest, Margaret intoned, "No matter how eloquently they write about these caves, no one can grasp its beauty and magnificence except by being here." The priest solemnly nodded. He and Margaret walked silently and slowly, eyes searching out the hidden recesses, straining to see the heights, drinking in the sight.

They continued in this fashion for close to forty minutes speechless and lost in thought. As they stood off in a corner, Father whispered that he came here often to meditate, to gather ideas for sermons, and to feel God's presence. He said that he often felt the caves of Nerja held him captive. Margaret concurred. Margaret knew she, too, would return here many times in the months ahead.

CHAPTER 7

THAT NIGHT, AS SHE LAY in bed, Margaret felt a degree of self-satisfaction she'd not had in a long time. She had purchased a car of her choosing, mastered the stick shift . . . well, sort of . . . and revisited the caves. The latter provided inner peace and a lift to her spirits. She was feeling far more confident in striking out on her own.

The next morning, the telephone installers actually came to do their job. Margaret had expected that their arrival would take weeks. She had pressed the realtor to make the arrangements prior to her arrival, and, low and behold, that pre-planning had actually sprung results. Margaret was surprised and euphoric. She would no longer have to rely solely on her iPhone to telephone her sons before their bedtime.

Now, she would use her new landline to call Father Eduardo to, again, thank him for being so generous with his time and his help. She reiterated how much she appreciated his efforts on her behalf. In addition, she'd had a wonderful time in his company and wanted him to know that. He was equal in his enthusiasm. The priest confessed that he had dreaded the prospect of shopping for a car, but was surprised how much he'd enjoyed the day.

Actually, he'd been thinking about Margaret's situation. Although she had an agenda in mind for occupying her days, Father Eduardo realized that she would be spending much of her waking hours alone. He believed that she needed opportunities for her own thoughts, but too much time spent detached from the company of others might not be time well spent. Father sincerely believed in Divine Providence and he now thought that his and Margaret's confluence might be ordained.

He remembered Margaret mentioning that she'd taught first graders for three and a half years before starting a family. He'd asked her if she'd ever taught students whose first language was not English.

Margaret had responded, "Not among my first graders, but I did help some foreign-born through our church. There was a man from Egypt who'd settled in our parish and another family from Greece. I used many of the same teaching techniques and skills as I'd used with my first graders. Teaching is such a creative process. There are so many ways to present material, and it's challenging and fun to dream up ideas and see results take hold."

She spoke with such enthusiasm that Father Eduardo knew that teaching was in her blood and something she loved to do. It had given him food for thought.

Now, on the phone he said, "I spent the morning on the telephone with several of our Board Members. They were willing to authorize two hundred fifty euros a month to allow a qualified individual to teach English to interested parishioners. It will mean a commitment of two evenings a week and, of course, preparation time."

Not giving Margaret a chance to get a word in edgewise, the priest continued, "This is a plan I've been trying to implement for some time. More and more, English is the international language. Some of our church attendees are on the lowest rungs of the pay scale. Some are in the tourist industry where we are seeing tourists from the United States, Canada and much of Europe. Still, others are in business and professional positions where fluency in English is almost a requirement. I truly believe that if they had a better command of the English language, they would greatly increase their chances for economic advancement. Six months of speaking English twice a week with you should be of great benefit to their employment opportunities. You don't have to answer on one foot, but I would like you to seriously consider this project. Will you please think about it?"

In a markedly uncharacteristic reaction, without hesitating a moment, Margaret responded, "I'd love to do that." In a flash, Margaret saw herself having a purpose, a role, a reason to get out of bed in the morning, and a place to go. Furthermore, it was an invitation to partake in the community of Nerja. Margaret could not resist.

Father Eduardo could not believe his luck. His intuition had borne him out. Margaret was an individual who liked to make a difference in this world and she would bear a sense of responsibility toward her students. More importantly, Margaret was, clearly, someone who was looking for a chance to get back into life.

Afraid she might still back out, he did not give her an opportunity to think. Instead, he went straight about his plan. "I'm going to send notices to the congregants and post notices at the church and in store fronts advertising the classes. In addition, what do you say, we'll charge a fee of five euros for pre-registration. This would commit people and, also, give us a head count prior to the first class. Furthermore, it should allow you a small stipend to buy supplies. Shall we schedule the first class then in two weeks? Will that give you sufficient lead time?"

"I guess so," Margaret replied now somewhat in a daze.

Father thanked her profusely, and before she had a chance to yell "STOP," he hung up.

Margaret had been standing throughout this conversation. Now, she could feel her legs buckling and looked for a chair in which to collapse. Was this really happening? Into what had she gotten herself? She could say only a few words in Spanish. How was she to communicate with her pupils? How many students would show?

Margaret had always prided herself on her ability to focus on an issue and think things through at length. She would argue the pros and cons of a decision letting it go round and round in her head for hours and even for days when necessary. Since that night in Andrew's office, however, she found that she was, impulsively, jumping into events. Insisting that Andrew leave their home and, then, six months later, flying off to Nerja were two major acts that she would never have dreamt of doing years before. Now, she'd jumped into another without so much as a second glance.

She lifted herself from the chair and changed into a bathing suit. Maybe a long swim would clear her head. As she glided along the water, ideas came leaping across her skull. When she was student teaching, she remembered a French teacher giving lessons to third graders at a private school in the suburbs. The woman had labeled pictures from magazines and used them and objects around the classroom to introduce new words. Margaret's task was to keep in mind that her students needed a grounding in English that would prepare them for employment opportunities. She would have to find magazines and picture books with an eye toward that goal. She had a plan.

Margaret sprang from the water, hastily toweled off, hurriedly dressed and jumped into her new car. Now, she strolled among the shops in and around Nerja. She searched out magazines in the Safeway and in pharmacies and prowled a second-hand book store where she found some picture books she thought adequate. Before she finished, she'd spent close to one hundred dollars. She smiled to herself and wondered if she were going to spend more on this job than she would earn. Teachers always managed to shake a chunk of their salaries for classroom supplies; some things never changed.

Returning home, she sat at a table overlooking the swimming pool while busily searching, selecting, cutting, pasting, and labeling throughout the better part of the late afternoon and early evening. She rose only once to swim in the heated pool, dry off, and jump back into clothes. She worked relentlessly at her task. When she looked at the clock, it was past seven in the evening. She couldn't believe how quickly the time had flown.

The following morning, refreshed after a sound-night's sleep, she headed straight for the church. As she entered the building, she ran into Father Eduardo. This was her lucky day; she had so many questions ricocheting across her brain.

The priest was delighted with Margaret's quick response. Although he was busy, he paused to answer questions and act as a guide. "You and your students can enter from a door at the rear of the church."

Margaret followed the priest to the entrance and, almost immediately, found herself in the classroom. Under the priest's bemused eye, Margaret walked off each foot-long floor tile and pronounced the room eighteen by twenty feet. An ample chalk board was at one end with two large oblong tables and chairs perpendicular to it. "It'll be tight, but I guess we can squeeze in the twenty students you hope will sign on," trying to make her voice sound on a positive note.

Bookcases lined one wall, and Margaret noted an old tape recorder sitting on the lowest shelf. "Oh, great. If it operates, that will come in really handy."

"I believe it should. While you're here, I'd like to introduce you to my administrative assistant, Helen. You two ladies might enjoy each other."

Margaret was quickly introduced to an attractive woman slightly older than herself who greeted Margaret with a pleasant smile and calm demeanor. Just as the women were about to speak, Helen was interrupted by the ring of the telephone and nodded in Margaret's direction, saying simply, "Welcome aboard" as she proceeded to respond to the caller. Margaret detected a British accent, but there was to be no opportunity to have a conversation with Helen as she was, clearly, attempting to answer several questions from a parishioner.

Since the priest had appeared intent on some project when Margaret arrived, she quickly thanked him and was ready to leave.

"By the way, if ever you need me, you can just cross the sitting area which separates your classroom from my office."

"Hopefully, I'll not have too many problems or questions, but thanks." Shaking her head from side to side, "I can't believe I've committed to this project and we'll be starting so soon."

In fact, the next couple of weeks flew. She managed to visit the caves at least twice a week, to purchase her grocery supplies, and to bring some clothes to the laundry in walking distance of the Parador. She had a recollection of looking into that same window ten years before and seeing the proprietor standing over a baby in a play pen. Then, she spotted a ten-year-old seated at a table copiously taking notes from a textbook. The sight gave her a warm feeling.

As she drove back to her house, Margaret felt a rush of memories. She and Andrew had spent five days in Nerja traversing many of these same streets; visiting the beaches, the caves; enjoying the perfunctory glass of Spanish sherry served before each delicious dinner at the local restaurants; traveling the coast of Spain through the towns and villages; poking their heads into the shops and the local church; cavorting in the Jacuzzi in their suite at the Parador.

They had visited Spain ten years ago: and, at the time, Margaret felt the romanticism and sensualness of the region. Perhaps she had returned to Nerja to recapture one of the happier moments in their marriage. Perhaps, too, it's easier to return to a spot where you already know the lay of the land. Margaret could picture herself living here and conducting her daily routines.

CHAPTER 8

NOWHERE, HOWEVER, IN HER PICTURE of life in Nerja was there a suggestion of standing in front of a roomful of adults to instruct them in the English language. Yet, here was Margaret doing just that.

She looked out upon a sea of strangers comprised of a broad range of ages and states of attire. From the list of registrants, Father Eduardo had informed Margaret that she would have a class of twenty individuals from all walks of life with varying degrees of facility with the English language. Quite a challenge!

After introducing herself and asking their names, she offered simple sentences that covered any and all social or business situations. "How do you do. My name is _____. I'm so glad to meet you."

She directed their attention to items in the room . . . a chair, table, desk, window, door, pen, pencil, paper, man, woman, and so on. Margaret then introduced her labeled pictures of other common items that might be found in an office as well as at home . . . the bathroom, kitchen, computer, keys . . . Over the weeks, they reviewed the days of the week, months, time, seasons, holidays. It became obvious that some in the class had familiarity with all of the items. Her job was to give them a sense of ease with the language, assist them with proper pronunciation and grammatical phrasing. Her ultimate goal would be to get them to think in English where sentences would flow easily from their lips.

She found the time flew by. Her pupils were eager to learn and their eyes shone with interest. They were attentive and responsive. They displayed all the necessary ingredients that ignite the adrenalin in a dedicated teacher. Margaret was off and running.

As the ability of the class increased, she introduced role playing. They pretended to apply for a job, dine in a restaurant, shop in a boutique, go to a supermarket, and use public transportation.

Margaret marveled at the group's stamina. Most of her students were coming to class after a day of work. They met for two hours and persevered despite an occasional stomach's rumbling. Spaniards eat dinner after ten in the evening and this class ended around nine. These people were tired and hungry, yet their spirits never flagged.

Only one individual seemed to require more assistance, and Margaret occasionally stayed after class to supply additional guidance. Luis was a day laborer dressed in work boots that were caked with dried cement. He wore a cap over hair that was covered, depending on the day, in dust or paint. His pants appeared as if they'd been shrunk. He was an intense young man who was committed to learning English and he exerted all his effort in that direction.

His knowledge of the English language was, by far, the most rudimentary of the group. He had been exposed to a smattering of English in the elementary grades and little beyond. Luis greatly appreciated Margaret's patience and respect. Had she mocked him in any way, the class might have followed. It was clear from Margaret's approach that behavior like that would never be tolerated. Everyone seemed to follow her lead and her students were careful to encourage and support each other.

Margaret found Luis to be an extremely sweet, gentle soul and tried to draw him out as best she could. One night, he remained after class and, hesitantly, proffered a portfolio from which he extracted a handful of drawings, sketches, and charcoals. These he presented to Margaret to peruse. Enclosed were landscapes of ships along the water's edge, women's torsos, some still life, and portraits of, what she suspected, were members of his family. Margaret was intrigued. His work had captured her imagination and she found herself wanting to know far more about this young man.

Margaret said, "Luis, these are beautiful. Did you do all of this yourself?"

When he replied in the affirmative, Margaret's interest was really piqued. Although his portfolio contained work that was not polished, it showed great promise. She asked if he would allow her to treat him to a bite of dinner where they could talk about this wonderful collection of art work. He nodded happily; and they walked down one of the narrow, windy streets immediately behind the church to Café Carabeo.

During dinner, Margaret asked Luis a million questions. From his very broken English, Margaret gleaned that he would love to take some art courses, wished he had more time to sketch and paint, and hoped someday to be considered a true artist. He had taken the class with the dream of being able to communicate with potential buyers who spoke English. He had sold a few of his paintings and sketches at out-door art shows at the church. In addition, while painting down by the coast, some tourists had offered to purchase his art. Margaret suspected that they'd picked up these lovely pieces for a song. Perhaps, she could help Luis to know the value of his work and to negotiate, in English, a fair market price for his labors.

Moreover, she wondered how she might further his talent. Aloud, she said, "Luis, how much would art lessons cost?" At his reply, she asked if she might offer him a loan.

He thought a moment, blushed, and said, "I can no take money from you. I save from my job and my grandfather he will help to give me money." Again, he blushed and then seemed to blurt out, "Miss Margaret, you are much pretty. I would be happy you sit for me and I put you on my paper."

Margaret almost choked on the food she was swallowing. Did he really mean what she thought he'd said? He was looking at her with a mix of apprehension and anticipation. She couldn't respond. She was flattered and disquieted at the same time. She did not wish to hurt his feelings, so she did not say no immediately. Instead, when she regained her composure, Margaret promised Luis she would think about his suggestion.

True to his word, she'd been speaking with Father Eduardo a couple of times each week to review the progress of the class and to gather data regarding her students. To exchange information, she'd met with the priest for an occasional lunch, or in the sitting room that separated her classroom from his office. He enlightened her about some of his parishioners, but, obviously, would not impart what might be considered confidential.

Now, she called the Father and asked if he might have some time to speak with her. They arranged to meet the following afternoon.

Margaret thought about Luis' suggestion and it caught her up short. While she knew that she was not unattractive, she was not in the habit of dwelling on her looks or having others stare at her endlessly.

While getting into her bathing suit for a morning swim, she stood before her mirror and eyed herself with a discriminating, long, hard look. Her face and skin color had taken on some of the bright burnished glow that comes with daily exposure to the sun. More freckles were about as well.

Swimming and walking the hills and streets of Nerja had firmed the muscles of her body. Her breasts were still tilted upward as she approached middle age. Her friends complained of all their body parts heading south. As Margaret surveyed her image, she saw reflected a healthy, attractive, confident looking woman.

Suddenly, the thought of posing as an artist's model left her with a dangerous, suggestive, sensual feeling. It dually excited her and scared her.

She knew she would not dismiss Luis' proposal out of hand. It was one to be considered seriously.

At lunch the next day, she spoke with Father Eduardo about several of her students. She did not think it advisable to discuss Luis' proposal per se, but she did want to reassure herself that he was as upstanding and honest as he appeared.Therefore, she mentioned Luis only after inquiring of some of the others.

The priest confirmed her thinking. "Luis comes from a very poor, but decent, family. They work hard, pull together, are church goers, and want something better for their children. I'm pleased, Margaret, that you are willing to go the extra mile for Luis.

I'm familiar with Luis' dream and think the boy has a lot of potential. I'd like to see it fostered."

Margaret wondered what the priest would think of her posing for this developing talent, but she thought better of pursuing that line. With the priest's information, Margaret would now have to make that decision for herself.

CHAPTER 9

INSTINCTIVELY, MARGARET HAD KNOWN THAT if she were to pose for Luis, she would want to keep these modeling sessions in a public venue. She had not come to a firm decision, however when Luis hung back at the end of the next class. Almost on impulse, she suggested a day's outing where they could find some picturesque scenery to use as background. Without really dwelling on it, Margaret's natural shyness led her to hope that Luis would concentrate on the scenery.

She gave some thought to her attire for the day. What colors and configuration of clothing would best suit her as an artist's model? She pulled several garments from the closet, but soon settled on a woolen, champagne-colored turtleneck sweater worn over a pair of black wool slacks. She completed the outfit with a large colorful black woolen-silk paisley shawl whose design picked up the champagne color in the sweater. She flung the shawl casually about her shoulders and tied a loose knot. The stylish soft black boots with a raised, narrow heel gave her an even taller and leaner appearance and complemented the outfit. Next, Margaret grabbed her Gortex jacket. Although the temperature would be in the fifties, staying outside for a length of time could get chilly. The thinsulate jacket was always in her knapsack along with a pair of black leather gloves. She included a pair of running shoes to tramp up the mountain.

She and Luis had agreed to meet at the foot of the hills beneath Margaret's home. From there, they drove in Margaret's car toward Gibraltar. Driving along the Costa del Sol is always a beautiful, relaxing, and invigorating experience. The day offered a clear, blue, picture-perfect sky. A great day to view the Rock of Gibraltar, take the tram up the mountain, and look down upon the waters separating it from Morocco.

She recalled the town at the mountain's base with its quaint homes and school children scurrying past the shutters and balconies. The beautiful weather would draw the small, tailless apes outside to frolic among the tourists. Margaret could hide among them and in the many niches of the rugged mountain. Margaret was looking forward to returning to this natural play land. In this setting, posing for Luis seemed inviting.

En route, they passed through the small towns of Malaga and Marbella where wealthy Europeans, and now some Americans, have their second homes in the many elegant condominiums and small villas that fight for limited space overlooking the water. Their capacious, mahogany-outfitted yachts moored at the marinas.

While driving, Margaret tried to engage Luis in conversation. She rhapsodized for almost half an hour about the captivating scenery and the monkeys to be found on Gibraltar. There was little or no response from Luis. When Margaret and Luis arrived at the gates of Gibraltar to enter the British garrison, they were required to show their passports. Margaret produced hers, but Luis had no identification whatsoever. He hadn't known it was required. In a flash, Margaret realized that what she thought was a difficulty in communication was, in reality, the fact that Luis had never made the short trip to Gibraltar and couldn't relate at all to Margaret's memories. Oops, thought Margaret, now what do I do?

They returned to her car and headed back to Marbella. Luis could sketch at the water's edge. They parked the car and walked to the Puerto Banus. The first time Margaret had visited this idyllic spot, it reminded her of St. Tropez in the South of France. She loved the luxurious feel of the place, its natural beauty and the total relaxation derived from the surround of calming waters. Although it did not have the sense of antiquity associated with St. Tropez, it had the first class boutiques, cafés, restaurants, and the huge, privately-owned, mahogany outfitted yachts docked in the marina.

Margaret had loved watching the people who were so elegantly groomed. Even their play clothes screamed money. It was fascinating to see the pages of Elle and Vogue come to life. She noted some stunning young women on the arms of silver-haired gentlemen.

The area surrounding the water was bustling with strolling pedestrians. Sitting there by the water's edge, Margaret knew it would be impossible to meld into the background.

Luis pulled out his sketch pad and charcoal and seated Margaret on the raised sea wall in front of one of the large, impressive yachts. People paused as they walked past and craned their necks to see his work. Others observed Margaret while they ate their lunches at the cafés which lined the walk that separated the diners from the water. Since it was a warm afternoon for early February, a few hearty souls were lunching outdoors. Margaret, feeling most embarrassed, patiently sat for Luis for the better part of the afternoon.

It was painstaking to maintain one position. Posing, Margaret concluded, is not an easy task. She gained new respect for fashion and artists' models. Occasionally, Luis would indicate that Margaret was slumping and needed to change her body's position. He would move her head slightly and give it a tilt, turn her shoulders in one direction while her torso was heading in another, place her hands in her lap, or cross her legs.

After watching a most beautiful sunset of fiery red that turned to streaks of purple hues across a pink sky, Luis indicated that he could no longer see his drawings. Margaret welcomed the halt with great relief. The sunset had drawn a very large cocktail and dinner crowd to the adjacent restaurants, and she did not enjoy being on display. In addition, her body ached.

She decided to treat the two of them to dinner. By earning the small salary from her evening classes, Margaret was allowed a measure of independence and indulgence. A lovely, though expensive, dinner was called for.

Luis was helping her with the Spanish while she was interpreting some of the esoteric menu choices. They were deciphering the menu when a figure appeared at her side. Thinking it was the waiter, Margaret, in her best Spanish, begged for more time. "No, no, senora. Didn't I see you on the airplane to Madrid? Aren't you from Boston?"

Margaret looked up and stared into the handsome face of her seat mate, Tomas. Unlike the business suit he was wearing on the plane, Tomas was now casually attired in a bright blue and yellow checkered shirt open at the collar.

The shirt peeked from beneath a sweater in the same blue. He wore dark slacks and loafers. For a fleeting moment, Margaret thought he'd stepped out of an ad for Ralph Lauren or Calvin Klein. In addition, his posture seemed more relaxed than when she'd seen him on the plane. He appeared taller, younger and very good looking.

"I have been out of the country for several weeks and in Madrid, but I did wish to know how you are getting on," he said. Then, he looked quizzically toward Luis.

Suddenly, Margaret realized that it looked as if she'd taken up with a young gigolo. In a rush, Margaret blurted out the news of her teaching English at the church and introduced Luis as one of her students. She raced on to say that Luis was a fledgling artist with talent. Tomas replied that he'd seen them together while Luis was sketching. Margaret felt herself redden uncontrollably. It was one thing to be on display for total strangers. Here was someone she'd already known. It made her terribly uncomfortable. However, Tomas seemed not to notice her discomfort. The restaurant was dimly lit and dark enough that she hoped he would not see her deepening flush.

In truth, watching her sit for Luis had heightened Tomas' interest in the American. He was aware that she held herself with new confidence which made her more alluring. In addition, she seemed less restrained. As Margaret had noticed earlier, her walking and swimming had, indeed, firmed her figure and added a healthy glow. Tomas had thought her attractive enough when they'd flown together. Today, while watching her, he found himself drawn to her.

He asked if he might phone her and produced a pen and paper to record her telephone number. They said their goodbyes, and Margaret wondered if she'd ever hear from him. Her thoughts were disjointed. He did approach her table, so he must have been interested. However, he could be asking for her number just as a courtesy. Margaret tried to see with whom Tomas was dining, but she could not do so without turning around and stretching this way and that. Her actions would have been terribly obvious. She forced herself to return to the menu choices and to converse with Luis. She was determined to put Tomas out of her mind, at least for the time being.

That night, however, as she lay in bed, she thought of several scenarios that included Tomas. She finally felt a warm rush between her thighs, convulsed, and fell into a peaceful sleep.

CHAPTER 10

MARGARET HAD BARELY FINISHED BRUSHING her teeth, when the phone rang the next morning. Margaret hesitated. She wanted so much for it to be Tomas, yet feared the unknown. Her life had somehow settled into a contented flow of teaching her students; attending Mass; walking in varied directions to discover new facets of Nerja and its environs; exploring the caves; taking a swim; and talking to her sons on the telephone or exchanging messages through the Internet several times a week.

She occasionally suffered with bouts of loneliness, but remembered that a smile on her face caused, otherwise, gloomy visages to return her grin. She was managing well. Did she need a disruption to the routines in her life?

She answered on the fourth ring. "Margaret? Tomas Nunez here. I have been called back to Madrid today," and here he paused. Margaret was caught between relief that she would not see him again and disappointment at the thought. But, he continued, "Would you be free on Wednesday evening? I plan to return that afternoon."

Margaret was free almost every evening when she was not teaching. She usually used the time to bone up on her Spanish. She'd study from a grammar and vocabulary text or watch the Spanish television stations. Since she taught on Tuesdays and Thursdays, the likelihood of her being busy Wednesday night was very slim indeed. What came out could only be described as a catch in her voice as she kind of grunted a "uh."

"Oh good," replied Tomas, "may I pick you up say around seven? I know it's early for dinner in Spain, but I'd like to have sufficient time to resume our acquaintance. I'll need to get you back fairly early as I fly to New York the following morning. Where are you living? I'll pick you up there."

Before Margaret could think of a good enough reason NOT to meet him, she'd given him her address. He assured her he'd be on time and was looking forward to continuing their airplane conversation.

Margaret stared at the receiver. She was of two minds. No, maybe three. Perhaps, she might have suggested that she meet him at their destination. That would have made her seem like a modern, independent woman. Wasn't that who she was now?

However, if she faced the truth, her real concern was that she'd given him her address. Her home might be her castle, but this castle did not include a moat, guards and servants. He was virtually a stranger, and she was totally on her own here. She knew nothing about this man other than what he'd told her on the plane. Margaret remembered Ted Bundy. Wasn't he good looking, well-spoken, and seemingly a fine young man? Hadn't he been responsible for murdering young women who had grown to trust him? Who could tell a person's character by his looks and demeanor? Even if she were to leave the door wide open as he came up the drive, who would hear her holler for help? Margaret could hear her mother's voice in her head remonstrating. She's turning in her grave, Margaret surmised.

At times like this, Margaret especially missed her friend, Missy. Missy would stop her from working herself into a state of panic. If Missy were here she'd know what to do. She'd had far more dating experience and would know how to appear more casual about all of this. At the very least, she'd welcome Missy as a sounding board. She had told Missy, on the phone, of meeting the Spanish businessman on the airplane. Now, she'd like to update her friend. She'd try to contact Missy tonight.

Margaret moved her body to the kitchen and sat down to a hot cup of coffee. In the few months that Margaret was living in Spain, she missed not only Missy, but all female companionship as well.

She knew she should get more involved with a community of ex-pats from America who gathered on Mondays. They were always polite and welcoming the once or twice Margaret had popped in and introduced herself. But the group consisted mainly of retired couples, and Margaret's circumstances did not conform. It would take more psychic energy than she cared to allow to start explaining her particular situation.

A lady, older than Margaret, had approached her one day among the fruits and vegetables at the Safeway in Nerja and inquired if Margaret were from the States. Margaret was ecstatic to be meeting someone with whom she might be able to strike up a conversation. However, her enthusiasm in meeting a fellow American waned quickly. The stranger immediately grated on Margaret. This woman spoke without coming up for air and tossed her head and body around as if she were still a teenager. Most individuals have nervous habits that reveal their stress. Margaret always tugged at a lock of hair, her mom would wipe her hands on her apron, Andrew raised and lowered his eyebrows, their sons would often look at the floor to manifest discomfort. This lady constantly yanked at her blouse and at the well-matched strand of black South Sea pearls around her neck. She jumped about so that Margaret thought her body had been invaded by Mexican jumping beans. It was comical to behold. Then, she waxed surprise that Margaret shopped routinely in a Safeway with so many of the natives. She, on the other hand, spent her winter in the well-to-do resort of Marbella and was running in for only a few items since her maid usually did the shopping.

As starved as she was for female companionship and as much as she longed for conversations in English, Margaret was eager to remove herself from this person's clutches. She'd, happily, left several of these snooty types back home in Newton . . . and elsewhere. Margaret wondered how she might extricate herself from this expensively groomed and perfectly coiffed woman who went into a monologue about her husband the developer, her extensive jewelry collection, her personal trainer, her fine taste in acquiring Oriental rugs and art work, her love of clothes, and on and on. In the span of ten minutes, it was all about herself and her affluence. Never a word to inquire about Margaret.

Women like this were off-putting. Margaret used to be intimidated by them. As she matured, she realized these women were to be pitied. They rested on their husbands' laurels and were at the mercy of those husbands for their generosity. Furthermore, these souls appeared so insecure and self-absorbed as they tugged at their clothes and worried about their aging appearance with little of real substance to their lives. She imagined them appearing at St. Peter's Gate: "And, what have you done to gain entry?" "Oh, I always looked beautiful and had a magnificent home."

Margaret believed that there must be a balance in life between looking your best, having a comfortable home, enjoying travel and entertainment without it becoming all-consuming. She fervently prayed that she would always be able to maintain that balance and keep things in proper perspective.

By the time Margaret finally convinced this woman that she was running late and had to complete her errands, Margaret was truly in despair. She had spent time in Nerja seeking out a book group, study group, church group, anything that would have given her access to English-speaking women with similar interests. She wished for someone nearby in whom she could confide, someone to mosey through the shops with her, someone to sit beside her at church, someone to hit tennis balls or chat over a lunch or coffee. All of her efforts had proved fruitless. The women she met spoke a fluent and rapid Spanish and their command of English was often limited.

Margaret's Spanish was still a struggle as she slowly formed her thoughts and pronounced them in a halting voice. If she mulled over her question or idea, it came out quite fluently. However, when people responded to her, she was caught off guard and stumbled around for words. She might find the vocabulary and, then, confuse the grammar or visa versa. Most of those she'd encountered did not have the patience to try to converse at length. It became a tiring exercise on both their parts. Therefore, conversations were brief. An evening with Tomas seemed very inviting.

As with the priest, here was someone who spoke English well, and she was looking forward to Wednesday.

Without a female friend on the scene, however, Margaret would have to rely upon herself to decide what to wear, what was expected of her throughout the evening, how much she ought to reveal about herself. She wished she had an instruction book in her possession outlining what one does on a date. It had been so many years since she'd had this experience. For the second time today, she heard her mother's voice in her head. "Child, you are making mountains out of molehills."

Yes, Margaret thought, I definitely am. Margaret began giving herself a pep talk. She'd certainly been in the company of others since coming here, and some of that company represented the male gender. "I managed just fine, thank you," she said aloud to no one in particular.

However, time spent with Luis could hardly be considered dating. He was a child really, and probably looked upon her as a mother figure.

She'd had occasional lunches and spent time at the caves with Father Eduardo. He was always very gallant opening doors, pulling out her chair, helping her on with her coat, walking on the curb side of the pavement. She was now comfortable enough in his presence to ask if these amenities were part of a priest's curriculum. He laughingly said, "No, good manners were expected by my mother, and in our house HER word was canon law."

One day, Father Eduardo had phoned to tell her he'd come upon two tickets to hear an evening concert in the Nerja caves and asked if she would care to join him. Margaret was thrilled and flattered that he would ask her to be his guest. He knew of her love for the caves and of music. Yet, she was surprised that he wasn't acquainted with others who shared these same pastimes and hadn't offered the promise of such a wonderful experience to someone else. Margaret did not waste too much time wondering, however, as she was so excited with the prospect of listening to the beautiful voices and music in the caves she loved. With the caves having a permanent setting for these events, Margaret anticipated the music to resound throughout. She jumped at the chance.

Father Eduardo arrived at her door promptly at seven forty-five. Margaret was wearing her green dress which showed all her curves and threw highlights of color against her red hair. The latter had been recently shaped into a very chic European style. The priest seemed startled at the sight of her. Margaret hesitated wondering if she should have been more restrained in her appearance. She tossed a light-weight coat over her outfit which seemed to relax both of them.

Dinner reservations were at a small, very fine restaurant, *Udo Heimer*, en route to the caves. The menu was written in Spanish, English and German.

"Do you mind if I select a bottle of wine for us? There is one that I really like from Ribera del Duero." When he saw Margaret's puzzled look, he added, "It's situated just north of Madrid and considered a leading wine region."

For starters, they shared a Carpaccio of Beef Fillet with Vinaigrette of Pine Nuts, pickled Oyster-Mushrooms and Parmesan Flakes. The priest ordered the Roast Rack of Lamb with garlic, chick-pea timbal and Compote of Apples while Margaret chose a Breast of Duck in Juniper Sauce and Orange Reduction with crispy wild rice. Eddie offered her a taste from his plate before he commenced, and was quick to accept Margaret's invitation of a sampling of her duck and wild rice. They deemed the dinner absolutely delicious. Margaret did wonder to herself how Eddie knew so much about fine wine and expensive food. He'd insisted on paying the bill. How could he even afford it on a priest's salary? She thought no more about it. By the time they reached the caves, Margaret was already experiencing a warm, mellow sense of relaxation.

They proceeded down the steep steps into the caves and across the span into a corner. Margaret said, " I can't believe that a theater so large can fit into one small corner of this place. It's absolutely awesome."

"Yes," the priest replied, "I, too, marvel at it. I once counted five hundred and twenty-two seats located on this tier and another hundred in the tier below. Those below are reserved for the functionaries of the caves. And tonight on that stage," he continued, "we are to hear a glorious rendering of the *Phantom of the Opera*."

The evening surpassed any of Margaret's expectations. She had seen Andrew Lloyd Weber's hit on Broadway several years before. She and Andrew had planned a weekend in New York at the Waldorf when a client of Andrew's had managed to snare two tickets for them for a Saturday night performance. Margaret adored the music, the voices, and the unique and dramatic staging. As a lover of caves, even then, the concept of an underground abode fascinated her. Now, here she was experiencing it in the flesh.

Being down in the caves made the performance even more believable. She visibly shivered when the heroine is swept off by the masked suitor. The priest, sensing her fear, placed his arm around her back and shoulder and Margaret crept into his safe embrace. She viewed the remainder of the performance thus, particularly, in anticipation of the descent of the large, heavy crystal chandelier.

Margaret sat with rapt attention throughout the performance. She was still sitting motionless at its conclusion. The sensation was one of being pulled into the great beyond. Reality was the caves and the underground life it represented. She clung to the music and the moment. Father Eduardo seemed to recognize her need. He, too, remained still.

After a few minutes, the crowd was on its feet exploding into violent applause while emitting great whoops of "bravo," breaking the spell that had wound about her.

Father withdrew his arm and gently whispered, "Margaret." The experience left her nerve endings tingling.

Both of them were overcome with the emotions of the music within the aura of the caves. They barely spoke during the car ride home, but were silently drawn together by this shared experience.

Feeling the need to physically connect, they had embraced at her door. Margaret gently kissed him on the cheek as she thanked him again for such a special time.

It had been a perfectly marvelous and memorable evening. The lovely gourmet dinner, the gorgeous voices, the beautiful music in such an exquisite setting, and, Father Eduardo such a kind, generous, and sensitive gentleman. Not to mention his striking good looks. Ah, but there were strict rules within her (and she assumed within the priest) that eliminated romantic courtship. Smiling to herself she thought, if I were back in high school, we girls would be referring to him as "Father, What a Waste!"

CHAPTER 11

FATHER EDUARDO SAT BACK IN his chair and closed his eyes while heaving an audible sigh. What was he thinking? What was he doing?

Hundreds of worshipers packed his church each Sunday. Most were foreigners, many from the States and Great Britain. There were so many that often he'd give the Mass and homily in English. He'd greet them after the service, but rarely connect. Most of these individuals were "short term." They'd stay a week or two or, perhaps, a month or two for the winter. He was genuinely welcoming, but their conversations were fleeting and equal to the briefness of their stay.

He did know most of the retirees who now had homes or apartments in Nerja and attended church on a regular basis. He'd see them at services, socials and other events. They became a part of the rhythm of the church.

How had he become so well-acquainted with Margaret? Why had he singled her out the first day he'd seen her and ask that she wait for him at his office? With so many English-speaking permanent residents, why had he asked Margaret to teach English classes to his Spanish-speaking parishioners?

Why did he look for her among the congregants at Sunday Mass? True, her flaming-red hair was hard to miss, but with so many in the audience and so much activity to divert him, why was he aware of her presence or lack thereof? Where were his thoughts of God during the services?

He realized, too, that he was conjuring ways to spend more and more time in her company. First, suggesting he help her look for a car; something he dreaded doing for himself let alone for someone else. Yet, with Margaret it turned out to be a delightful day. Then the lunches to presumably discuss her work with the students. Then the trips to the caves. Finally, the evening of dinner and his great enjoyment at the performance of *The Phantom of the Opera*. He'd seen the much more professional cast on Broadway, yet it had not held the same magic. Why? What was happening to him, to his life?

He could not deny that Margaret was terribly attractive and held a special fascination for him. During dinner, she had opened up much more than in past conversations with the priest. She managed to give an abbreviated look into her past. He was now aware of the causes for her separation from Andrew, of their respective families, and how each of those families differed.

As they arrived at the entrance to the caves this evening, he was pleased to learn that she was expecting to bring her sons to church with her for the Easter celebration. He knew that her boys were important in her life, and she would be eagerly awaiting their arrival in April from the States. The mystery of her past, her loving anecdotes of her sons, the intensity of her gaze when he spoke to her, her quick wit and child-like giggles, the warmth and compassion in her eyes when she spoke of her students, the delight she took in spending time at the caves, her initial hesitance then exuberance for seeing and doing something new, her carriage when she walked or seated herself. It was like a perfume that enveloped him, and he couldn't seem to break through.

How fetching she had looked this evening. When she'd leaned into him, or he helped her on with her wrap, or he'd had his hand behind her chair there was something very sensuous, feelings he'd not experienced in many years. Very unnerving.

Embracing her at her door, albeit in the manner of a relative, could it have mushroomed into something greater? He had brushed aside the flickering remembrances of dreams in the night that occasionally surfaced in the early morning awakening. Memories of them lay deeply buried in his subconscious, too disquieting, too embarrassing to allow to rise and ponder. Yet, they burned there waiting to be dwelt upon. He thought he'd shelved that part of himself long before he'd taken his final vows. Was he still so human? Was he still just simply 'a man'?

As many of his fellow priests, was it time for him to return to the lay community, to forsake his vows, to give up all that he'd worked for and aspired to? These thoughts were reverberating through his head, and if Eduardo were to confess, they'd been rolling through his head for some time, in fact, ever since meeting Margaret.

When he'd left Spain for an American college, he was merely a boy, a teenager ripe for anything. His father had insisted that he attend a Catholic college if he were to leave Spain. Eduardo supposed that his parents felt he'd be more protected, better supervised. At the time, he'd, reluctantly, acquiesced. However, he found that Siena College allowed the boys plenty of space. Eduardo became

Eddie in the full sense of change. He drank from the well of freedom with a headiness he'd never known.

Although Loudonville, New York is a speck on the map, there were dozens and dozens of colleges and universities within easy reach. Eddie had a full complement of young women, lots of beer, an occasional joint, and plenty of time to party, ski and dance while managing to fulfill his class requirements. He did take in the museums and theater that New York City and Boston offered, as well, but the urge to party was paramount.

He spent his first two and a half years at Siena in this manner. Yet, he was subtly influenced by the calm and clear thinking of the Friars who taught many of his required theology classes and those whom he'd meet on the golf course. Slowly, he was drawn more and more into their inner sanctuaries. By the last semester of his Junior year, he was seriously considering entering the priesthood.

CHAPTER 12

B Y THE TIME WEDNESDAY ARRIVED, Margaret was in a total state of ambivalence. She had psyched herself to believe that she could carry off her date with Tomas with no problems. She had mentally walked through her vision of the evening and found herself equal to the occasion. What she couldn't master were the palpitations, the butterflies in her stomach, and the choice of wardrobes. She was hyper-energized and tore everything from her closet. Clothes came out one at a time, or in combinations, and most lay discarded on top of her bed. When she'd finally narrowed it down to two or three outfits, she'd exhausted herself. She realized that she had no idea where they were going, had no way of reaching Tomas, and, therefore, had no clear idea of what type of wardrobe would begin to suit the occasion.

Should she, again, reach for the dark green dress. It had made the priest take notice. How did she want Tomas to react? Was this to be a business-like get together, a start of a nice friendship, or a hot romance? What did she want from this relationship if anything? Why was he interested in seeing Margaret? Was Margaret to be patient and allow this to play itself out, or was she to step in and take the reins? For the moment, she decided to take a wait and see attitude. Once she resolved this in her head, she felt more on top of the situation. Do all people need to feel some control over their own lives?

Since Margaret could only make suppositions, she figured she'd best get back to something more pragmatic and immediately solvable. She resumed checking out her wardrobe. Once again, she reached for the green dress . . . then stopped. She decided upon a more subdued camel-colored cashmere knit, turtleneck dress. It, too, was clingy, but with a softer, quieter texture and feel. In lieu of a scarf as an accent piece, she chose a simple lavalier hanging from a long gold chain. It accented her bosom without seeming blatantly bold. Margaret drew on high heeled, dark-brown pumps that elongated her, already, long legs, and pulled out a small brown clutch to complete the outfit. She perused her image in the mirror from all angles and pronounced it a done deal. Of course, throughout the rest of the morning, she was second guessing.

In order to limit her decision-making, she decided to don her sweats and running shoes and head out the door for a long brisk walk. It was a good idea, and she was able to clear her head and drink in the calming views of Nerja. She walked down to the water's edge and along the vacant beach at a fast clip. The serenity of her surroundings left her composed.

When she returned to the house a few hours later, she was feeling pleasantly fatigued. She awoke from a nap refreshed and felt ready to face whatever presented itself. The knots in her stomach, however, returned.

By the time she heard his knock, Margaret was in quite a state. She took several deep breaths while heading toward the door. As she opened it and Tomas stood in the doorway, he surveyed her with one quick sweeping glance. His face registered a look of approval and sincere delight in seeing her. Her spirits were buoyed to be in the company of someone whose emotions were easily read by the expression on his face. It took away some of the mystery, but it alleviated having to go through the process of attempting to read someone's mind without any road maps.

Tomas apologized for being several minutes late and suggested they leave immediately for the restaurant. He must have sensed her reluctance when she spoke with him on the phone earlier in the week and had not waited for an invitation to enter the house. Margaret was grateful to him. As he helped her with her coat, his hands lingered a moment on her shoulders. Margaret welcomed the intimate gesture.

She was surprised to see that he was tooling around in an old Alfa Romeo. It was certainly not a rental. He must garage this car in Marbella at his condominium home.

Since it was a cool evening, the convertible top was up on the little two-seater. They drove in relative silence to the restaurant. Margaret was able to steal a few glances in Tomas' direction. He was still wearing business attire and looked quite handsome.

Conversation began hesitantly. It was relegated to the lovely weather they'd been having and how much Tomas missed being able to be out on his boat or, at the very least, have a couple of hours to spare for a tennis game. This last bit of information caught Margaret's attention. Although she had carted her tennis racquet to Nerja, she'd found no one with whom to hit. Had Tomas recalled her struggling with the racquet as she alighted from the plane? Was he looking for a conversation starter? Was he wanting to hit with her, or was he merely desirous of being outdoors in this glorious weather? She didn't wish to appear too forward by suggesting that they spend time together on a tennis court. She did not know his level of proficiency nor his interest in spending time with her. For that matter, how did she know that she'd want to ever see him again? She reminded herself, better to just let things evolve.

Their drained sherry glasses signaled the waiter to take the dinner orders. Tomas highly recommended the assortment of canapes: salmon, anchovy and caviar for them to share as a starter. "I'm delighted that your taste buds are adventurous. Do you often try new dishes?"

"I do like to try, yes. Can't always say I enjoy everything," Margaret added with a giggle, "but I find I like most."

For the main course, Tomas ordered a smoked trout while Margaret had a grilled swordfish. As they sat awaiting their dinner, Tomas complimented Margaret, "You've found a lovely home in Nerja. Are you enjoying the place?"

He wanted to know what she was doing with her days, if she were homesick, and all the details about her English classes at the church. He questioned Margaret at length.

She found herself chattering away about the priest who'd been especially helpful, her teaching methods, her students, her purchase of mementoes to personalize her quarters, how much she was missing her sons and friends. He kept peppering her with questions as she spoke. He seemed truly focused on all she was doing and feeling. Margaret was welcoming this special attention.

She looked toward Tomas expecting a continuation of his barrage of questions. Instead, he began to loosen his tie and the top button on his white dress shirt as he stared directly into her eyes. If he were trying to arouse her, he was making a good case. Margaret found the gesture to be quite seductive; her limbs felt weak. Tomas seemed totally unaware of the effect he was having on her, but she wondered, nonetheless.

Dinner was set before them, and they ate with great gusto. "Would you care for a taste of the trout? That swordfish looks good, too."

Margaret found the sharing of food an intimate expression and was pleased that Tomas was relaxed in her company. She gladly accepted his offer.

As their plates emptied, Tomas apologized again for being a few minutes late arriving at her house. "I've spent the entire day in meetings in Madrid and barely made it down to the Costa del Sol for our evening together.

The CEOs who deal in olives and olive oil production in Spain have reached a consensus. They wish to arrange a large gathering of their compatriots from the olive-producing countries of Spain, Italy, Greece, Turkey, Portugal, Israel, and, hopefully, some of the Arab states including Morocco, Tunisia, Algeria and Syria. Although most of the olive-growing countries are centered around the Mediterranean Sea, I'm hoping there might be representation from the United States, as well."

Margaret listened, fascinated. Except for having viewed acres and acres of ancient olive trees each time she'd headed to the Costa del Sol, she knew little about the olive industry.

Tomas had been asked to oversee the details of this upcoming conference.

"I'm embarrassed to speak of this. For centuries, my family has been held in high regard as leading producers of olives and olive oil. They are one of the families in the forefront of this important industry in Spain.

"However, to organize an international conference feels . . . daunting. There's a wonderful staff at the

IOOC . . ." When he saw Margaret's eyebrows raised in confusion, he elaborated, "Sorry, the International Olive Oil Council based in Madrid. They have an excellent staff and they usually plan, implement, oversee and do most of the work. This year, for reasons I won't go into, I must take some responsibility. I must confess to you, I don't know where to begin."

Margaret did not know how to respond. They sat in silence for a few moments. Margaret's curiosity caused her to speak up. Upon questioning, Margaret learned that the event was to be held in Madrid in less than three months.

Slowly, and with great deliberation, Margaret asked, "Have you someone to select the menu and sample the foods and beverages being served; to check the table arrangements, the lighting, the microphones and sound system, the location of the restrooms? Who will check the guests into the conference? Who will arrange for the guests lodging and for activities for any accompanying spouses or companions?"

"Goodness. It seems even more than I imagined. I'm not sure any of my staff or I are aware of all the work involved. Besides, we are already up to our eyeballs."

"Maybe, you ought to consider using a conference planner?"

Tomas just stared at Margaret. He was overwhelmed by all the specifics. He was also surprised at how much Margaret seemed to know about the preparations necessary for a successful event and noted the professional tone in her voice as she ticked off just what might be required. He looked at her with new respect. As a rule, his assistant saw to many of these details. However, this project was on a much grander scale and would require far more hours to work through all the minutiae. How had Margaret come by all this knowledge?

Margaret demurred. The knowledge she had of event planning seemed so ingrained that she never thought of it as an acquired skill. Thinking back, Margaret realized that over the years she had arranged her sister's wedding; entertained large gatherings of friends and Andrew's business associates; conducted large fund raisers for the boys' elementary and middle schools; had chaired major events at their Country Club for the Boston Bar Association and for some worthy non-profits. As she recounted, she was amazed at how many successful activities she had actually organized. Surprisingly, perhaps, she did have some expertise to offer him.

Although neither of them had room for it, they dallied over the cheese assortment that was dessert and slowly finished the bottle of wine. Neither seemed to want the evening to end.

Margaret knew she certainly didn't, but Tomas suddenly looked at his watch, "Oh, my goodness, I still have to pack; I take off early tomorrow morning for New York."

Most reluctantly, Margaret allowed her feet to carry her out of the restaurant and into the evening air.

When they arrived at Margaret's door, she was not certain what to do. Should she wish him a goodnight at the door, kiss him on the cheek as she'd done with Father Eduardo, or was she expected to invite him in?

Tomas solved that dilemma, too. He put both her hands in his and drew her to him. She looked into his face, and, as the European gesture, he lightly brushed his lips on each of her cheeks. "May I see you during the weekend? I'll be returning from New York on Friday night. Would you be free for dinner on Saturday?"

Margaret was elated. She jumped at the opportunity to see him again.

"Do you like to dance," he asked? When she readily replied in the affirmative, he said, "Well, put on your dancing shoes. I know where there's a great little combo for dancing and they have delicious tapas and wines. I'll pick you up around nine in the evening, when Spain comes to life."

She leaned up against the closed door, her body trembling. When had she last felt this way? As a teenager? She'd better look at herself in the mirror to remind herself that she was a grown woman with two teenaged sons . . . and a marriage which, though kaput, wasn't officially ended.

Oh, how she wanted to talk to Missy. She picked up the phone and began punching in the numbers. Stop! What was she doing? She'd be calling Boston in the wee hours of the morning. Even Missy would not appreciate that. Margaret would have to contain herself until tomorrow. She kept replaying the evening in her head. It took quite some time before she could settle down and finally get a few hours sleep.

When she did reach her friend, Missy was ready to fly out the door. Margaret quickly poured out the events of the last week and her reactions to it. Missy said little while Margaret chirped her way through the details. In the old days, Missy would have been bouncing along with Margaret's enthusiasm. Today, she said, "Oh, that's great that you're having so much fun." Yet, there was an undertone in her voice that Margaret sensed was being cautious and wary. Margaret's joy was deflated a bit by the time the conversation ended.

What was going through Missy's head? Since Margaret did some of her best thinking underwater, she grabbed her suit and headed for the heated pool outside the house and proceeded to swim laps.

She knew it was customary for wives to feel rejected and thrown to the wind when husbands sought the company of other females. Margaret was obviously buoyed by a male's attention whether from the priest or Luis or Tomas. Was that a juvenile reaction; something built into the way women were raised? Was that really necessary? Shouldn't a woman find herself attractive and personable on her own merits, and not require male approval? Shouldn't people, in general, know their own strengths without having to seek assurances from others? Margaret had felt quite confident through her school years. When had she begun to question her self-worth?

Of course, she had generally behaved as her parents saw fit adhering to their guidelines and to those of the Church. There were few grays. Most of life was measured in blacks and whites.

Moreover, all her life she'd heard her parents say, "What will the neighbors think?" Margaret now reflected, Did the neighbors really care? Was it really necessary to be concerned about the neighbors if you knew you were doing the right thing and felt yourself to be a capable person and not hurting anyone?

Was her time spent with Tomas a harmless act? She doubted the Church would approve. What did she really know about this guy? What was his agenda? She might be lonely for companionship in Spain, but he'd lived here most of his life. Why was he interested in her? Perhaps, she ought not let things just evolve.

CHAPTER 13

WITH HER GREAT RESOLVE TO step more cautiously with regard to Tomas, Margaret spent her Thursday and Friday preparing and teaching her English Second Language class, shopping at the grocery, running to the cleaner, walking on the beach, and taking another swim to keep her head clear and her hormones in check.

Luis had approached her again to pose. His first drawings of her had met with enough success to gain a small scholarship enabling him to take an art class. She was pleased for him and knew that Father Eduardo would be, too. Although reluctant to continue acting as his model, the initial poses had been harmless and she could not find sufficient reason to turn him down.

They agreed to meet at the beach early Saturday afternoon. However, when they'd arrived, the weather was too chilly to allow Margaret to remove her jacket. Instead, they wound up at Margaret's house and she stood or sat in front of the windows and door leading to the pool. At Luis' request, she sat patiently while he, again, drew her at different angles. They broke only once for a soft drink.

About four in the afternoon, Margaret explained that she really had to ask that he leave as she had to ready herself for her evening plans. Luis seemed surprised and disappointed at this interruption, but begrudgingly acquiesced. That was the first time Margaret sensed him asserting himself, which was good. She, nonetheless, was upset that he appeared somewhat annoyed and unable to respect her needs.

As soon as Luis left, she put him out of her mind. She drew a hot tub with soapy lavender bubble bath and laid her head back in the delicious warmth. She lounged there for as long as possible feeling the warm water and bubbles soak into her body. The pleasant aroma filled her nostrils. She felt relaxed and sensual; all her nerve endings were awake.

When the water in the tub finally cooled, she washed her hair under the shower and decided to let it dry naturally. It would appear a little wild. Did she wish to appear a little wild for tonight, or did she simply not have the strength to bother? She sensed that her vow to not let things get out of hand was, definitely, slipping out of her hands.

She collapsed on her bed and dozed for a good half hour. When she awoke, her hair was, without a doubt, . . . wild. She knew there was no use trying to tame it unless she washed it once again. She hadn't the desire or time. And, in truth, a part of her was allowing a daring side to emerge. She knew she was definitely out of control.

Was this to be HER little fling? A little voice went off in her head saying, "Margaret, what will the neighbors think?" Margaret laughed aloud and heard herself say, "By God, I don't even know my neighbors!" At which point she bolted upright and fairly bounced out of bed.

Margaret selected her clothes for the evening in no time. She quickly identified the sexiest belongings in her wardrobe. Out came the black lacy underwear to be followed by a short black, gauzy-silk cocktail dress. The sleeveless bodice had a low- scooped neckline in front and back, and ended in a fitted-empire cut which fell just beneath her bust. The garment then continued as a straight skirt where it gave a gradual flair with a double flounce at the irregular hemline. It was her perfect dance dress and very in style.

Black high-heeled sandals and a little black silk purse completed her outfit. She topped this off with a pair of large gold dangling earrings and a, very in vogue, thick gold bracelet at her wrist. Everything was strewn atop her bed.

She sat in the living room with her silk robe fastened by a self-sash about her waist. Before dressing, Margaret took pains to give herself a careful pedicure and manicure and to allow time for the red polish to adequately dry. While drying her nails, she tried reading a magazine. However, her excitement was building for her evening with Tomas, and she found it difficult to concentrate.

Margaret had determined that some moisturizer, eye shadow, liner, and mascara really brought out her eyes. Her somewhat ruddy natural complexion from spending time outdoors was enhanced with a little Clinique bronze gel and Borghese blush. She experimented with the makeup until she was satisfied that it appeared natural and evenly applied.

She doused herself lightly at the pressure points with Chloe. She liked its sharp, light aroma. Heavy and sweet perfumes did not suit her.

Satisfied with her appearance, she sat down to await Tomas. Again, her stomach was tight and she could feel her heart beating.

The waiting seemed interminable. In truth, his knock on her door was promptly at nine. With no hesitancy, she flung open the door. Her appearance must have stunned

Tomas. He stared, mouth open. In a barely audible tone he blurted out, "You look . . . lovely."

It was uttered so softly and spontaneously that Margaret was both embarrassed and pleased. They stood momentarily transfixed until Margaret ran her hands over her bare arms.

Tomas snapped to attention, "You are going to need a coat or wrap. It's chilly this evening."

Margaret motioned him in while she went toward her bedroom to fetch her black wool shawl. Tomas' attention was drawn to the framed photographs set about the living room. When Margaret returned with the shawl and purse in her hands, she saw Tomas smiling at a picture of Brandon and Richard. "These are handsome young lads. Do you claim them?"

Margaret returned his smile somewhat wistfully. As if to cut to the chase, she pointed to each of her sons by name and quickly explained that they attended boarding school in Connecticut. "I miss them terribly, but, then, I was missing them in Newton, too. Their father insisted they attend the prep school from which he and their grandfather had graduated. The boys do like it there, but I've felt a hole in my heart ever since."

"I know that feeling", Tomas responded. "While I was in New York for business, I managed to squeeze in dinners with my son. He's a graduate student at Columbia. It's always a delight to spend time with him. Antonio always seems to look forward to seeing me." Then Tomas laughed, "I hope he looks forward to being with me and not merely coveting the expensive restaurant fare." "Anyway," he added, still grinning, "I make it a point to have business in that city every couple of months. Killing two birds with one stone as you Americans put it."

Margaret welcomed his sharing information about his personal life. It made her feel closer to him and, she continued to see him as a warm and caring individual. As they headed toward Tomas' car, she found herself inching toward him. He really appealed to her and she wanted to get close to him in every respect.

As they drove off in his Alfa Romeo, he mentioned that they were heading to Torremolinos which is located almost half-way between Malaga and Marbella. Looking directly at the road as he drove, Tomas continued, "Torremolinos is noted for having some of the best discos anywhere; many geared to the gay community." Tomas noted Margaret's eyebrows rise in a questioning, but non-judgmental, look. "The one I have in mind, if it suits you, is an old-established night club which caters to couples like us where we can dance and munch on tapas."

"Sounds terrific. I'd love it."

Driving the Costa del Sol is a magnificent stretch of highway in the daylight. However, since dusk had long settled into a night sky, Margaret laid her head on the back rest and hunkered down hoping to hear more about Tomas. Instead, he spoke up first and asked if photographs he had noted in her living room were of her daughter and another son.

Margaret explained that they were her sister's children, and then took the opportunity to segue to his family. "Have you any other youngsters beside Antonio?"

"I have a daughter who is a second year student at the University in Madrid. I see her often as I keep an apartment there and an office, as well."

When the conversation might have drifted to their children's other parent, each of them appeared to hedge. Margaret, for one, wished Tomas to know her better before delving into that aspect of her life's history. Nor did she want to know too much about Tomas' spouse just yet. Since Tomas didn't spend too many days in one place, she assumed he wasn't able to spend a great deal of time with any one person. Was he a widower, divorced, separated, having affairs as so many European men were wont to do? In time, perhaps, all would be known. Meantime, Margaret opted for patience. Tonight was to enjoy!

They were quickly seated in a quiet corner not too far from the dance floor. The band members were quietly readying their instruments. Tomas took the opportunity to order a variety of tapas. He included some beef, chicken, shrimp, mushroom canapes, and eggplant dishes.

It would be a smorgasbord of delicacies. Margaret actually preferred that to a full entree. She often got bored eating a lot of one thing.

She knew that Tapas dishes never came out at the same time nor in any particular order. She and Tomas could just nibble away all evening. They'd be served leisurely and with small portions that the two of them could share. Although it didn't seem possible, if they were still hungry, they could order more.

The music began at ten o'clock. The bulk of the patrons would not arrive until later. Folks in Spain are late-nighters.

Their pitcher of sangria arrived as the five-piece band began playing. Margaret half expected that Tomas would suggest they dance. However, she had just inquired about the olive industry, and Tomas became passionate in his description of his family's land.

"The soft gray-green barks and leaves with their gnarled trunks are breathtaking. They're scattered throughout the acres of the property."

Margaret had seen, what appeared to be, hundreds of olive orchards as she traveled between Madrid and the Costa del Sol and did, indeed, believe them to be startling in their unique loveliness.

"Olive trees survive for centuries and are considered sacred," Tomas continued. "In the Middle East, there are olive trees that date back to the early days of Christianity. Even there, where hostilities result in savage battles, few enemies will engage in the bombing or destruction of the expansive olive orchards or of the olive trees that are scattered throughout that region. It is almost an unspoken rule."

When Margaret asked if he spent most of his time at the orchards, his enthusiasm suddenly evaporated. Looking extremely deflated and with a sad voice, he replied, "No, unfortunately, that is no longer possible."

As if to stave off any further discussion, Tomas reached for Margaret's hand and held it firmly in his grasp while he led her to the nearly-empty dance floor. He drew her to him as they glided in rhythm to slow fox trots sung in Spanish. Margaret wondered at his reaction to her question, but sensed that his sudden disconsolate tone needed the warmth of another human being to stem this despair.

Consequently, cuddled into him, with his hand pressed firmly against her back, he gently led her through the steps. She followed his lead with ease, and, after a few minutes, an observer might have thought they'd danced together always.

Tomas' proficiency on the dance floor hit a nerve. Andrew had been such a klutz. She stifled a giggle as she recalled her teenage years when the girls used to surreptitiously rate their dance partners. They'd equate a boy's agility as a dancer with his potential as a lover.

Probably not the best gauge, but what had they known at fifteen. Now, with a sly grin, she thought she probably wouldn't mind testing that old hypothesis. Tomas caught her smiling to herself, and his face lit up.

They continued in this fashion until the tempo picked up with Latin beats. With hips swaying, Margaret shook to the pulsating rhythms of the rumba and meringue. When Tomas led her into a salsa, she, laughingly, stumbled around a bit until she started getting the hang of it. Tomas joined in the laughter . . . his melancholy eased.

Margaret thought, laughter unites people. It allows individuals to enter the same wave length and share the intimacy of a personal experience. They were now looking directly in each other's eyes, lingering in the moment.

When they returned to their table, Tomas' customary good spirits had returned. Both he and Margaret plunged into the waiting platters of tapas. The choices were good, and they ate ravenously commenting only on the delicious variety of flavors.

As they came up for air, Tomas looked directly at Margaret and, as he'd done on their first date, locked her with his teasing eyes. Margaret could not glance away. His action felt beguiling and at the same time disquieting. Was he pleased at her presence, or just toying with her affections, or being lascivious? She could not read him, but felt captivated nonetheless. A tingling sensation consumed her body. Uncomfortable as it made her feel, Margaret was reluctant to let it go. She matched his smile and his stare. Neither of them blinked for what seemed an eternity. In reality, it must have been only a matter of minutes when Margaret finally averted her gaze.

In the ensuing silence, she, once again, heard the band's offering. The music had swung into the songs she'd bounced to in her youth, Margaret began to hum or sing with some of the familiar American tunes. Tomas asked her to dance, and she readily popped up from her seat and fairly boogied out to the dance floor. It was a relief to have an opportunity to release some of the sexual tensions she'd just experienced.

They swung to *Run Around Sue*, *Mr. Lee*, and *Let's Go to the Hop*; and later, moved to a disco beat. Each following the other's dance steps while, again, sharing the laughter. Margaret recalled all of these melodies from her parents' collection of music from their own teen years. She moved with reckless abandon, portions of her body flying in varying directions. Tomas seemed to be reveling in her sense of freedom. When the music ceased, they were both panting. Tomas drew her to him holding her in a long embrace. The band broke into a rendition of the Doo Wop melodies of Motown. The long-familiar repertoire of the Platters, the Temptations, and the Marcels were aptly performed by the vocalists. Margaret and Tomas moved as one to the lush harmonies of *Smoke Gets in your Eyes*, *Earth Angel*, and *Blue Moon*.

When they returned to their table, more tapas had been placed before them. Neither reached for a bite. Their comfort with each other on the dance floor now manifested itself as an embarrassment. They hardly knew one another, yet were caught up in a euphoria of enjoying each other's company. The ease with which they could converse, dance, and sense each other's need was profoundly affecting them. Neither quite knew how to respond. Each of them sat looking out on the scene; this time avoiding eye contact.

Finally, Margaret broke the silence by asking Tomas how he was so adept at American-style dancing. From their conversation on the airplane, Margaret had surmised that he had been an exchange student for only a year in the U.S.

Tomas replied, "I spent several years living in the States. I did my undergrad at Berkeley. Then, I spent more than a year in New York working for a business conglomerate before heading to Harvard; I realized I needed an MBA."

This was all said in a very unassuming, matter-of-fact manner. Margaret realized that Tomas was quite an outstanding student, but unaffected by all he'd accomplished.

In a teasing voice, he said, "I can assure you that while I was hard at work, I still managed to squeeze in some time for fun and a social life."

"Well, I guess that explains your ability to jitterbug, lindy, fox trot, disco. Do you rap?"

He laughed.

"It also accounts for your fluency with English. You not only have the grammar and vocabulary down pat, but also our American slang and its idioms."

Between the pitchers of sangria, the headiness of her reactions to Tomas, and the pulse of the music, Margaret felt complete abandonment of any inhibitions she might have otherwise held. When the band began to play, Margaret did not wait for an invitation. She took Tomas by the hand and fairly dragged him onto the dance floor. She began to do the fish. a dance step that could only be described as seductive to the 'max'. She crooned in Tomas' ears a very poor rendition of the Capris' *"There's a Moon Out Tonight . . . let's go strolling dear."*

Her arms about his neck and leaning into him with three gyrations on the right leg followed by three gyrations on the left. He matched her steps while gazing at her in wonderment and with pleasure. His expression looked bemused, yet delighted.

He surprised himself by murmuring in a most approving tone, "You are unlike any woman I know."

Margaret stopped her singing and grinned up at him, then dug her head into his shoulder.

The band broke into *Why Must I Be a Teenager In Love?* which cued Margaret into a free-style dance step as she sang aloud, "Why CAN'T I be a teenager in love?" Tomas roared with laughter and led her back to their table. He quickly gathered up her belongings, paid the bill, and eased Margaret out toward his car.

Although Margaret was not tipsy, she moved with total abandonment. The sips of sangria mingled with the rhythms of the dance had eased the conversational flow between them and promised a lightness to the evening. Moreover, Tomas' reactions to Margaret's antics permitted a liberty which she rarely experienced with others. He seemed not only to approve of her comic sense, but to find it attractively compelling. Margaret could not remember the last time she was so filled with happiness and a sense of well-being.

She recalled dancing at their club in Newton when Andrew and her in-laws rushed to her side and cautioned her to . . . "act like a lady. Your movements on the dance floor resemble a 'loose woman'. Margaret, you are embarrassing us in front of our friends."

Everything in their lives, Margaret had thought at the time, was measured by appearances. Finally, here was someone who took pleasure in her joy, welcomed her gaiety, and manifested a bit of the free spirit himself.

She heard herself saying, in a soft voice, "Tomas, I have enjoyed this evening so much. Thank you; it's been wonderful."

He beamed broadly and leaned across the seat of the car to clasp her to him. She lifted her face to his and their lips pressed together. As he pulled her toward him, they both stopped and burst into laughter. Their torsos were being shoved into the gear shift of the Alfa Romeo. A romantic car without a very romantic floor plan, thought Margaret chuckling to herself. I guess I can no longer be a teenager in love. At least, this car is not geared to front or backseat necking.

Almost immediately Margaret had a sinking sensation in her gut. She knew she didn't want this evening to end and she began to feel desolate at the thought of not being able to spend more time with Tomas.

As if reading her thoughts, Tomas asked, "I apologize for asking so last minute, but, are you free to play some tennis tomorrow morning? I took the liberty of reserving court time at ten-thirty with the hope that you could join me."

Margaret was flattered that Tomas had made plans to include her in an additional day of his weekend. She was eager, too, to get out and hit some tennis balls. Yet, she hesitated. Although she longed to spend Sunday with Tomas, she felt obligated to attend morning Mass. She wondered if Father Eduardo would notice if she were not present. Although a piece of her acknowledged that it would be highly unlikely, she resolved to try and do both.

CHAPTER 14

LIGHT WAS POURING INTO THE room when Margaret opened her eyes. She groaned, put her hand over her eyes and allowed her body to come alive. Her hands lightly caressed her arms, torso and down her legs. She was savoring the memories from the night before and grinning like a Cheshire cat.

They had stood in her entry way softly lit by a lamp from the far corner of the living room. Without speaking, their mouths had searched hungrily for one another. This time they kissed deeply, again and again.

Tomas' hands moved slowly exploring each and every part of her. Slowly, he removed her shawl and allowed it to drop to the floor. Margaret responded in kind. She caressed his face, his neck, across his shoulders and down his arms. He pressed her buttocks and drew her tightly against him.

Suddenly, Margaret had gasped, "Tomas, I'm not prepared for this." He stopped in his tracks. "Not prepared?", he questioned. "Ah", as if he finally understood. Sheepishly, he replied, "I guess I'm not either. I hadn't thought this far ahead."

He kissed her again this time very gently. Clearing his throat, he said almost in a whisper, "If we're to make our tennis time, we'll need to leave here before ten tomorrow morning. May I come by at nine thirty?"

Margaret thought she'd try to make the seven o'clock Mass which would allow her time to get home before Tomas arrived. She'd set her alarm for six in the morning; she'd get five hours sleep.

Now, she looked at her clock. "Oh, my God." Margaret careened out of bed and raced toward the shower. Tomas would be here in less than half an hour.

She tugged at a tennis skirt and top as she tried to free it from the hanger. She was still dripping wet while she rummaged through her belongings for sneakers, shoes, two sets of undies, and an outfit for the remainder of the day. She was dashing around to put on her deodorant, makeup and clothes and was barely finished when she heard the knock at the door.

In a state of total disarray, she opened the door for Tomas then flew back into her bedroom to gather all of her belongings. As they walked out her door and into his car, she was mentally enumerating all the things she'd packed or forgotten. She prayed that the clubhouse would have hair dryers and other amenities in the ladies' locker room.

"Oversleep?" Tomas said as looked at her with a grin. She collapsed into the seat. "Uh, huh." He continued to give her a teasing smile. "Guess you didn't get breakfast either? I bought us some baked goods from the bakery near you." Margaret brightened. Not only had he found her favorite place for pastries, but he'd also anticipated her needs . . . and topped it off with that teasing grin that left her weak.

They munched on his purchases both from hunger and with relief. Neither was fully adjusted to the newness of their situation. They were each displaying those awkward signs of shyness that accompany a couple's unaccustomed sense of familiarity. At this moment, it was easier to eat together than to converse.

The car turned left somewhere between Puerto Banus and Marbella. A super- deluxe, modern hotel surrounded by a complex of low-slung, white stucco buildings was just above the horizon. Tomas' pass flashed across the seeing-eye control and the gate lifted. A guard standing inside a small entry saluted as they drove through the gate.

She was still trying to locate the country club when Tomas pulled alongside the tennis courts. With one quick leap, he checked his watch, opened his door, grabbed their tennis paraphernalia from the car trunk, and went round to open Margaret's door. She took hold of her racquet and followed him to one of the courts.

Tennis, as in many other sports, requires a total focus on the ball. Margaret knew if she thought about last night, or possibly of the night to come, she would lose her concentration. Furthermore, she would have difficulty playing with anyone with whom she'd never hit before, and her feelings toward Tomas only compounded the challenge. In order to play her own game, she would have to relax, play the ball, and not rivet her attention on her opponent across the net.

She was feeling very pressured. She wished to reach Tomas' level of play so that they would be compatible on the courts. It would be far more fun for each of them if they could sustain a rally. In addition, she hoped she could give him a good enough game so that he would look forward to playing another day.

Feeling more than a little out of practice, Margaret bemoaned, " I've not held a tennis racquet since arriving in Spain. It's been a couple of months you know."

"Sorry. I saw you lugging your racquet off the plane. I should have had you out here sooner."

"Oh, that's okay. I didn't mean it was your fault."

Tomas returned her smile, "How would you like to warm up?"

"Well, if you don't mind I usually start at the mid-line. It allows me to have better control."

"Never did that before, but I'll give it a try."

They sent the balls back and forth in this tightly-concentrated area practicing forehands, backhands and some overheads. Margaret noted that Tomas was able to place the ball, a sign of a seasoned player.

Margaret concerned herself with getting to the ball, standing sideways to it, and keeping her arm and wrist firmly level while she swung out in front of her to connect. She had to remind herself to keep her eye on the ball at all times, turn her body, and shift her weight. She'd been playing this game for so many years, most of the time her reactions were automatic. Nonetheless, it never hurt to review.

"Guess I'm as ready as I'll ever be. Shall we move to the baseline and continue to hit?"

Margaret tried to get into a rhythm, keep her feet moving and her eyes glued to the ball. Once, while retrieving balls, she took note of Tomas' muscular legs and forearms and flat stomach. She found herself wondering how her abbreviated tennis skirt was impacting on him. Did he like her hair pulled back under a cap?

Back on the court, an easy shot sailed past. Tomas looked at her quizzically. She pulled her attention back to the little yellow ball.

Margaret managed to revive her game and hit with greater force and accuracy as the remainder of the hour ticked on. As she poured her strength into her swing, Tomas increased his velocity and power. Unlike other opponents she'd played in the past, Tomas was looking for a competitive game, but was not out to kill her. He, as she, was looking to play the best game possible and still have fun.

He had Margaret on the run. Fortunately, her swimming, power walking and jogging were paying dividends on the court. She was able to get to most of his returns and send them back with a resounding hit. She successfully executed swift cross courts, some lobs, and even passed him down the line. He was obviously enjoying the challenge she was presenting.

Breathless, she finally came to a halt. "I'm sorry," she said. "I really am out of shape."

He looked at her with pride, "Not at all. Not to sound sexist, but there are few women I've seen play better. And, your play is far more competitive than many a man."

Margaret felt herself beaming like a silly puppy and felt sillier knowing how she must look. Nonetheless, she couldn't stop. She was so happy to have had such an elevating experience. Rarely had she ever heard words of praise in all her years of marriage. Tomas' words floated quietly and gladly in her brain.

They ambled along together toward a set of water fountains while they maneuvered their tennis racquets back into their respective cases. Looking up, Margaret noticed a thermometer displayed along the far wall. Although it registered fifty-nine degrees, each of them was perspiring profusely. Margaret looked desperately for the clubhouse; its showers would be most inviting.

Margaret decided to take a stab, "Where might I find a very needed shower? Is there a clubhouse?"

Tomas, with a confused and somewhat self-conscious look, said, "I can drive you back to your place to take a shower and get dressed, or we can shower here. My condo is to our right at the end of the complex."

"All these low buildings that surround the hotel are apartments," questioned Margaret almost to herself. "The tennis courts, swimming pools and other facilities belong to the hotel and condominium residents?" Tomas shook his head to signify agreement.

Margaret had not anticipated this turn of events and was unsure how to respond.

She hesitated. He, noting her awkward silence again stated, "It's no trouble, Margaret, I'd be happy to drive you to your house."

Well, Margaret mused, he'd been a gentleman throughout so she shouldn't anticipate problems in his apartment. Besides, the thought of spending time alone with him was not exactly uninviting. With that in mind, she blurted out, "I need a shower NOW. Can't wait."

Tomas laughed heartily, and they hurried themselves and their belongings into his car. They drove the few seconds to the parking area attached to the two-story condo and quickly climbed out of his car. Almost simultaneously, a luxury Cadillac parked to their left. Tomas greeted his neighbors, and Margaret drew in her breath. She would have given anything to hide her red head and go unrecognized.

Immediately, the woman from the Safeway piped up, "My goodness! What are YOU doing here?" Without waiting for a response, she turned to Tomas. "I didn't know you knew HER." Poor Tomas looked into the face of an equally stunned Margaret as if to yell for help.

Margaret summoned all the presence she could muster, reached to her full height to tower above this female, and in one breath quietly explained that she and Tomas had met on her flight from the States and Tomas was kind enough to ask her to play tennis. As she was speaking, Tomas was heading upstairs toward his apartment door with Margaret following in tow. He opened the door, acknowledged his neighbors with a pleasant, "Have a good day," and he and Margaret disappeared behind the door. They faced each other in total disbelief and discomfiture.

Margaret was feeling caught in the act. It all had seemed perfectly innocent. This woman made her feel illicit. Moreover, her tone not only sounded disapproving, but also condescending. It was as if Margaret, who shopped at the Safeway, had no business behind these cloistered walls. These beautifully manicured lawns and gardens surrounding the elegant buildings, tennis courts, and swimming pools with paths descending to the beach were not to be tread upon by the likes of Margaret . . . only by the elite.

Tomas was muttering to himself in Spanish. It was too soft for Margaret to hear and too fast for her to understand. However, she could judge by the expression on his face that Tomas was confused and angry. "How did this woman even know you, Margaret?"

Margaret explained her previous encounter with his neighbor while they were at the Safeway. She described the woman's lengthy discourse all about herself.

Tomas nodded his head. "She is very wrapped up in herself. I avoid her at all costs. Not to toot my own horn, as you say in America, but I feel as if she is throwing herself at me whenever her husband is not present. She is totally unappealing, and I find her behavior makes me terribly uncomfortable."

All amorous thoughts were now quickly laid to waste. Margaret hopped into the shower, soaped up her entire frame from head to toe, rinsed off just as rapidly, and toweled off in a matter of minutes. Tomas, in answer to her query through the door, informed her that the hair dryer could be found in the cabinet beneath the sink. As Margaret reached in and brought it forth, she noticed an unopened box of condoms.

She wondered if they'd been purchased sometime overnight or this morning, or if they'd lain on that shelf, unused, for a long time. However, the thought of Tomas' neighbors listening to a shifting bed squelched any romantic inklings.

Margaret did not need to question if Tomas was being impacted in the same fashion. His manner had changed dramatically, and he, too, rushed through his shower and dressed. Barely conversing, they scurried out the door, and Margaret thought that Tomas probably slammed the door quite loudly to signal their hasty departure.

Since neither of them had eaten a hearty breakfast, Tomas suggested that they stop for an early lunch. Although the complex where he lived had two restaurants with excellent reputations, the possibility of bumping into his neighbors for a second time caused them to seek elsewhere.

They headed toward the Marbella Club where the maître d' seated them near the patio which overlooked a lush subtropical forest. Magnificently colored songbirds could be seen flitting about. For the first time since meeting the neighbors, Margaret and Tomas visibly relaxed.

Margaret took note of how handsome Tomas looked. He was wearing a shirt open at the collar and a pair of chinos. A sweater was slung across his shoulders and looped in front. He was wearing loafers with no socks. She wondered how he could do that since the temperatures were only in the low sixties.

Margaret had put on a teal colored, wrap-around dress that tied above her left hip. She was wearing black thigh highs under a pair of black low-heeled sandals. A black sweater covered her arms. They were both dressed casually but appropriately for the setting.

Tomas explained, "I have a membership to the health club here, and occasionally schedule dinner meetings for when I've finished my workout. I can vouch for the excellence of the food. May I make some suggestions?"

"Please do," Margaret nodded enthusiastically.

"Well, for starters, I'd highly recommend the gazpacho. I know for a fact that the ingredients are blended with a pestle and mortar rather than through a Cuisinart. I feel sure that the consistency will be to your liking."

"I didn't even know there was such a process. The few times I've made it or seen it made everyone used a Cuisinart. I'm trying to picture how it can be blended differently. Sure, I'd love to try it."

The cold soup arrived almost immediately, and the waiter placed extra chopped garlic, peppers and tomatoes in small bowls beside their soup. They were free to please their own taste buds.

"This is delicious and refreshing. Much better than I've ever tasted."

A bottle of a fine white wine, 'Vina Sol', produced in Spain accompanied their meal. They slowly sipped while awaiting the entrees. Margaret took in the whole tableau. Tomas, the elegantly groomed and polite people seated about, and the beautiful panorama beyond the patio. She sat back in her chair feeling thoroughly content.

Tomas had suggested they order the fresh fish of the day. "It's always a pleaser on the Costa del Sol; it tastes as if it has been caught this morning. And, it may well have."

Served over a bed of greens and surrounded by fresh fruits, it was beautiful to behold as well as to taste. They ate leisurely, relishing each bite.

Tomas broke the silence, "I'm heading to Madrid this week. Among other things, I have to make plans for that gathering of the olive companies' representatives. Do you recall that I told you about the International Olive Oil Council?"

Margaret nodded, "Yes, but you didn't fill me in on any details. Just that they exist."

"Oh, OK. The IOOC was formed in 1956 to safeguard olive trees and the olive oil industry. There's also a lot of research being done on the premises of the building."

"I guess it's primarily Spain, Italy, California, and a couple of countries in the Middle East?"

"Oh, no; it's much more encompassing. Let me see, members include: Morocco, Israel, Jordan, Lebanon,

Tunisia, all of the European Community and the United Kingdom, er . . . , Slovenia, Montenegro, Croatia, Cyprus, Egypt, Algeria . . . I'm sure I'm leaving out others."

"Wow! Isn't the United States a member?"

"Actually, no. It's an observer. There are even more countries who are observers than there are members. For example, Russia, Argentina, Australia and New Zealand, Japan, Iran, several in Latin America, Norway, . . . am I boring you, yet?"

"No," she laughed. "I'm fascinated. I had no idea that all of this existed. But, why would YOU be having to be put together their conference?"

"Well, we do have a smoothly-run operation with very capable olive producers in the role of directors, and an extremely proficient staff to back them. Usually, they run the show."

"The French-speaking gentleman who was seated beside me on the plane is our new Executive Director. As such, he was making his first visit to the U.S. as the IOOC representative. As I speak some French along with English, and had business in the States, he asked that I accompany him as a friend, colleague and translator. Normally, he and the Deputy Director would have been in charge of the conference. However, the Deputy has not been appointed, and won't be until the conference."

Shaking his head as if in disbelief, Tomas continued, "Since I sit on their Board, I volunteered my help and that of my staff. Frankly, I'm still uncomfortable having that responsibility on my shoulders. In addition, my administrative assistant, who normally can be counted upon, is tied up with prior business that must also get done. Margaret, this is quite a favor I need to ask of you . . ."

Margaret looked up from her food with great surprise written on her face.

Tomas continued, "Would you be able to meet me in Madrid to interview some hotels? Maria, the assistant I just mentioned, could provide a list and arrange appointments. I just have this hunch that you would have an understanding of our needs and could represent my corporation as a polished professional."

Margaret was overwhelmed. She had never thought of herself in that role. Her stomach tightened. She suddenly felt very insecure and unprepared to meet his request.

Tomas must have sensed her reluctance, because he said, "You needn't tell me just yet, I will not be heading to Madrid until Tuesday evening." Then he smiled at her in a very doting fashion, "Believe me, I would never put you in this position if my years of business experience did not tell me you ARE qualified."

She relaxed some and replied, "I'll promise to think about it."

When Tomas excused himself to use the men's room, Margaret did indeed think hard and fast. She was flattered that he had such confidence in her, and she certainly would like to spend extra time with Tomas. Realistically, however, she might get to Madrid and discover that he was tied up in business meetings or running home to a wife. Worse, she might not be up to the job and fall flat on her face. She didn't want to be seen as incompetent. What if she signed up a hotel and the results were disastrous?

When Tomas returned to their table, it was time to leave. He showed her through the club's facilities and, since it was a beautiful day, they decided to walk around the beautiful grounds. They continued down to the beach and walked around the piers.

Margaret fairly chirped, "What if I were to leave for Madrid on Friday morning? Would there be sufficient time for me to visit the various hotels?"

Tomas answered quickly, "No way. Why must you wait until Friday? Why can't you get away sooner ?"

"I have my English classes to conduct on Tuesdays and Thursdays; I can't leave before."

As much as Tomas would have liked the process to start earlier, he valued Margaret's work ethic. He had been questioning his own motives as to why he was involving Margaret in this assignment. Her careful deliberation and professional demeanor reassured him that he had managed to maintain some objectivity and made a correct judgement call.

"OK," he said, "I suggest you come to my office directly from the train station on Friday, get the hotel list from Maria, and make appointments for Monday and early Tuesday. You can stay the weekend, and I will escort you through Madrid.

"My firm will pay for your rail ticket and lodgings and food. I'll make arrangements for you at a hotel. It will be one of the ones you will want to look at for the conference anyway. On Tuesday, both of us can leave mid-day and fly back here. I promise to get you to the church on time . . ." They both chuckled aloud as he sang the concluding phrase to the tune from *My Fair Lady*.

The joined laughter caused them to lean into each other. Margaret lifted her face toward Tomas and he bent down and kissed her long and hard. Although they were unobserved, they were in a fairly public setting.

Without a word, they headed toward Tomas' car hand in hand. They continued to hold hands or stroke one another as they drove toward Nerja. Although their conversation consisted of light, meaningless banter, each of them had other thoughts in mind. Their bodies resembled the toy black and white Scotty dogs that are magnetically attracted. At every turn, funny remark, or matter of discussion, Margaret placed a hand on Tomas' arm or stroked his shoulder as if to stress a point. They couldn't contain their hands or their need to join bodies. They were mentally readying themselves for a new chapter in their relationship. Neither seemed embarrassed by the possibilities, merely eagerly anticipating.

Margaret's skin was feeling highly sensitive to his touch and key muscles in her body were twitching. She noticed the beginnings of a lump forming beneath Tomas' slacks. The hair on Margaret's arms were standing erect as if she'd been hit with a gust of ice cold air-conditioning after perspiring on a hot summer's day. Each pore tingled. Upon entering Margaret's house, the two practically lunged for one another.

Margaret had already removed her cardigan while they were driving. She didn't know if the outside temperatures were heating up or if her body temperature was. All Tomas had to do now was release the self belt of her wrap-around dress. It was no more protection than a bathrobe.

With their mutually penetrating kisses and strong caresses, Margaret's arousal was at full tilt. Her body ached for his. Should she unhinge the wrap on her dress or wait for Tomas to tug at the hanging material? Margaret decided to take matters into her own hands. As Tomas pressed against her, she slid her hand down to her waist band and released the tie. When they came up for air, she leaned back slightly allowing the dress to partially open. Tomas inserted his arms beneath the dress and across her back at the waist. Her bra and panties were now revealed. He leaned down to lightly kiss the tops of her breasts and run his hands along her back, shoulders and breasts. He inserted his hands beneath her panties pressing on her buttocks. Her body thrust toward his. They moved as one to the bedroom. Tomas was releasing his belt as Margaret tore open the buttons on his shirt.

When they lay on her bed, he clumsily released her bra. Slowly, they removed their remaining garments. Tomas guided Margaret's body to ease down on his. He closed his eyes and brailled her skin. He seemed to be savoring every inch of her. Instinctively, her back arched. Margaret was feeling her body attractive and all her nerve endings awakened. She slowly moved her torso up and down receptive to his touch. When she was feeling that her blood vessels were fully engorged, he turned her over and dug deeply and in rhythm to her urging. Margaret had never experienced such a complete consumption of her mind and body. She felt the sensations moving up and up and up until she experienced a shuddering explosion. It left her whole body on fire. They both lay sated, holding each other, neither speaking.

CHAPTER 15

MARGARET WAS BARELY OUT OF bed and stumbling around when the telephone rang. She wasn't sure she was up to answering it. Her voice had a frog in it as she strained to croak out a cheery, "Good Morning, Buenos Dias." By the time she was responding, her answering machine had kicked in. She could hear Father Eduardo asking in an agitated voice, "Margaret, are you all right? I didn't see you in church yesterday. I've been calling your house and leaving messages on your machine. Is something the matter? Where have you been? I was tempted to drop by to be certain you're OK."

Margaret stifled embarrassed laughter and took a deep breath. Like a train racing out of the station, she quickly blathered, "I'm fine, Father. Someone asked me to play tennis yesterday morning. I'd planned to attend early Mass first, but overslept."

Her excuse seemed rather lame even to her own ears. Margaret was hit by embarrassment and shame. She prayed that the priest would not pry. She was caught between a rock and a hard place. It was not her nature to lie, but she did not want to spill all to the ears of the clergy. Besides, she hadn't yet processed last night.

"I didn't know you played tennis, Margaret. I would be delighted to hit with you."

Oh great, thought Margaret, now what do I say?

Before she could respond, Father questioned, "With whom did you play and where were you all day and evening that I couldn't reach you? No, you needn't answer. You're a big girl. I've just been terribly worried; I'm glad you're OK."

Margaret was touched by the priest's concern for her, but she really didn't wish to give him the details. When he suggested they meet for lunch, she knew she had to find a means of postponing.

"Believe it or not I'm expected in Madrid at the end of this week to work on a business project. May we connect the following week? I'll fill you in on the specifics and run through the details then. I'll call you as soon as I return and we can arrange a time and place."

Now satisfied and sounding much relieved, the priest said, "That will be fine, Margaret. Take care. Ciao."

Margaret was left with a knot in her stomach and shivering. She proceeded to the kitchen where she stared at the two wine glasses, the two dinner plates, the two coffee cups and multiple flatware lying in the sink. She sank into the nearest chair and closed her eyes. She wanted to recapture the beauty of last night.

After making love, she and Tomas had lain together, not speaking, for what seemed an eternity. Margaret surmised that they each had probably dozed off. The clock showed 7:20 when Margaret had looked at it. At first, she mistakenly thought it was morning and Tomas must have spent the night. It took her a few minutes to orient herself.

Tomas was still wrapped around her and felt her move. She stepped into the bathroom, showered and put on her underwear and bathrobe . . . her dress still remained on the floor by the entry door.

Before Tomas could get out of bed, Margaret stood in the kitchen scrambling some eggs with cheese, and preparing coffee and toast as she hadn't much else in the fridge. She could hear the shower going while she was cooking, and she felt herself moving on automatic pilot.

When the supper had been set on the table, Tomas appeared fully attired. He leaned toward Margaret and kissed her tenderly on her forehead. "Please don't be upset; you are so special to me."

From the moment Margaret arose from the bed, she'd been racing around trying not to think. Now, his remarks softened her, and she smiled up at him with a new-found ease.

Tomas looked about her room. He located the Bose radio/CD player. From a nearby shelf, he pulled out an easy listening album and proceeded to play it at a low decibel. He put a match to the logs and kindling that were stacked in the fireplace. It was a signal to Margaret that the situation needed some soft lighting. She had purchased a pretty votive candle while out walking one day. This, she lit and placed in the center of her table. In the dim light, they proceeded to eat their supper in relative silence before the hearth. They spoke in a hush if barely at all; so much had transpired.

After supper, Tomas assisted Margaret in removing the dishes. As they neared the kitchen sink, Tomas stopped, "I'm still hungry", he laughed wistfully and drew her to him. Between the recent shower, the room's ambience, the memory of their tryst still fresh, and Tomas' handsome presence, Margaret, too, felt hungry. She encircled his neck with her arms and kissed him hard. Now, as she reminisced, she was shocked at her boldness. She didn't recall ever initiating sex with Andrew nor ever responding quickly to his overtures.

She and Tomas had left the dishes to soak in the water overnight as they moved to the thick rug which Margaret had purchased to partially cover the polished wood floor of Margaret's living room. They swayed to some slow dance tune emanating from the radio. Holding her to him, Tomas slowly removed her robe and lowered her to the rug. He kneeled above her and, once again, they were moving in unison.

Thinking of it now, Margaret smiled and hugged herself. She could still feel Tomas' arms around her, his legs entwined with hers. The memory felt so good.

She remained in this position until a piece of paper caught her eye. It was lying on the end table next to the couch. She rose and walked over to read a hastily written note.

Margaret dear,

Hated to drag myself away. Need to be at a conference first thing this A.M. Will call you.

The note remained unsigned.

Margaret smiled and fairly floated back to the kitchen. Giving no thought to her task at hand, she began to attack last night's remains washing, drying and putting away. Her state of mind would not allow for anything more substantive.

If she permitted herself to think, she was wrenched by ambivalence. How could this be happening to her, Margaret Cleary? Who, knowing her, would believe she could find herself in this situation . . . an adulteress really? It was barely eight months that she was separated from her husband, whom she'd married in the Church. His actions had caused her such pain. Yet, here was another man bringing so much joy into her life. She would have loved to confess all and try to make some sense of things. Father Eduardo seemed like such a reasonable, caring, and intelligent individual. Perhaps she really could confide in this priest. Pondering that decision, Margaret caught herself. She'd be walking a thin line here. He would be a wonderful sounding board since he was a person she highly admired. It would be a great relief to get it off her chest, but she would be risking the priest's respect for her and, ultimately, their friendship. Better that she find a neighboring church and slip into a confessional anonymously. Was that legal?

With proper penitence, could she be absolved? Could she receive Communion? Would it mean giving up Tomas? Was that too great a loss? Which was the greater loss?

She disciplined herself to power walk or jog each morning along the beach. One afternoon, she squeezed in some time to find solace at the caves. Fewer tourists than usual were on hand, and Margaret welcomed the silence. She entered one of the niches in a part of the caves that was off limits. The solitude satisfied her need for introspection and calm.

Millions of questions rang through her head as she struggled to reconcile herself with this sudden relationship and her feelings toward Tomas. Was she falling in love with this man? Was he in love with her? Was she just lonely and reaching for the nearest pillar?

Margaret could not remember when she had last agonized so. Insisting Andrew leave their home was an instinctive response to her hurt and anger. Even today, she did not know where she had found the strength. Come to think of it, where had she found the fortitude to be seated here in Nerja? She sensed that she had not only traveled a long way in miles, but in breaking out of a mold as well.

This was another Margaret Cleary from a year ago. Did she like the new person? Was she comfortable in this new skin? Margaret wondered from where all these questions were popping? She realized that she'd never thought through so many layers before. Does this come from age, from experience, from pain, from reading, from talking to others? Where and when had she suddenly emerged as a person who, once again, weighed her thoughts and predicaments and attempted to make her own decisions?

While the burden of making her own choices hung heavily, the experience provided a release. She was feeling much empowered.

She spent the remainder of the week fluctuating between feeling marvelous and burdened by the "A" on her chest. Alone, she agonized over her conduct. While she kept seeing Tomas in her mind's eye and glowing with the vision, she was still weighed down by the anxieties attributable to their relationship. Could she open up to him? She really knew so little about him. Was he married? If so, what was his marriage like? What were his true feelings for her? He certainly appeared to enjoy her and feel affection. Was this all too premature? Yes, but not really; they were already intimate. For Margaret, that had opened a Pandora's box.

On the other hand, she fairly danced down the aisles of the Safeway. Thoughts of Tomas raced through her brain . . . things he'd said and done. Her legs were pirouetting behind her cart while her face was beaming. Teaching her classes, she moved with a boundless energy that even superseded her usual stance and pace. People responded to her accordingly. As a mirror, many reflected her smiling face and joy. She couldn't wait until Friday and Madrid.

She tried to pack and to prepare for the work that was ahead of her. Her brain, however, would not hold still. Her thoughts were a diversion to her tasks.

CHAPTER 16

S EATED, AT LAST, ON THE high-speed train that was to take her to Madrid, Margaret drew a yellow legal pad from her over-sized purse. She forced herself to concentrate on the project at hand. While suffering from insomnia these last few nights, Margaret had risen and made pages and pages of handwritten notes, listing what she assumed would be the necessary details regarding the upcoming meeting of the olive-oil magnates. Most of these details she had ticked off quickly in her Sunday luncheon conversation with Tomas. Now, in columns, she categorized all of the pieces she felt were required for a successful event. At the far left of the paper, she noted each of the hotels she would be interviewing. Margaret left room to write her comments as each meeting progressed.

Satisfied that she had covered all her bases, Margaret put down her pad and closed her eyes. She had time now to let her thoughts roam freely.

Earlier in the week, while teaching, she noted that Luis would not make eye contact or linger after class. She attempted to approach him and ask how his art work was progressing and inquired how he was enjoying the program being provided by the scholarship fund. Luis merely shrugged and excused himself saying he had to get home. His response was brusque. Margaret hypothesized that Luis was still indignant toward her for not continuing to pose for him or to spend time with him. She would have liked to be more available to him, but time did not allow. Her order of priorities now were Tomas, the upcoming meetings in Madrid, and her teaching.

As was the case in recent days, her mind slid toward Tomas. In the very brief time she'd spent in his condo on the Costa del Sol last Sunday, it did not suggest his primary residence.

The floor plan was magnificent and three times the size of where Margaret was presently living. One entered a commodious entry. The dining room and living room were one large area with a cathedral ceiling. In addition, the kitchen was state of the art. A gourmet chef would be elated to prepare meals there. More than ample granite counters, top-of-the-line Miehle appliances including a garbage disposal, and sufficient cabinet and pantry space to satisfy the needs of a large family. However, from all indications, Tomas was not in the habit of preparing elaborate meals for himself, and the appliances appeared little used.

Although he had a makeshift office in the smaller of the two bedrooms and some photos of his children scattered about, there was little to connote the man himself. The variable hues within the spectrum of blues and browns defined the space; it was very masculine. Yet, Margaret did not feel as if Tomas had outfitted the place himself. Margaret concluded that he might have hired someone to pull it together or the apartment conveyed as is. The lack of a woman's touch was noticeable. There was little attention to detail and less in the way of 'collectibles'. Furthermore, there was no history here. Tomas, himself, seemed to be a detail-oriented person and the little she knew of him suggested a family history embodying a rich and complex tapestry.

Perhaps, his main residence was in Madrid. He had previously mentioned a place in Madrid as he did so much business there. She recalled him saying that he kept a place in New York, as well. Was there another dwelling in addition to the Costa del Sol, Madrid and New York? Which was his primary home? She felt reasonably sure that someday she'd know.

In the meantime, it stood to reason that Margaret would stay alone at a hotel while Tomas went to his own home and, presumably, to his wife. Then again, maybe there was no wife. She'd seen no pictures of her in the apartment, and he'd never mentioned his spouse. How could he be available to spend so much time with Margaret as he'd done these last few weeks? Yet, if he were widowed, wouldn't it have more than likely arisen in conversation by this time? Was he separated as she? Was he divorced? Was divorce acceptable in Spain; it is a Catholic country. How could she broach the subject without seeming to pry or to be judgmental? Perhaps, some of the answers would come this weekend.

As she pondered, she must have fallen into an exhausted sleep. Awakened suddenly when the train pulled into a station, Margaret sat in a half trance. Thoughts were barreling through her head like the engine of this train. In an almost semi-conscious state, they veered toward her future. She sat with her head tilted back on the reclining seat and fantasized a life with Tomas. Questions came roaring past her. What would it be like to be with Tomas on a routine basis? Where would they live? Again, did he have encumbrances. . . like a wife? She still knew too little about him to conjure up a very clear picture of how life would present itself.

Margaret half-smiled as she played this game. It was so many years since she and her good friend, Missy, would sometimes share their day dreams. Often, Margaret reflected, they had not even met the boy. . . usually a blind date. Yet, they could contrive all different scenarios of possibilities. They'd each 'married' a half dozen to a dozen different guys during the course of their teen years. Some of these young men were one-time dates.

She wondered if guys did the same thing. She figured all the boys concerned themselves with, at that time, were the cost of the evening and whether or not they would 'score'. They probably never went beyond in their fantasizing. Was this the case today? She'd have to question her sons when they visited during Spring Break.

As she drew back into the real world, she found herself eavesdropping. In the days of her youth, as she traveled the Boston "T", she was a pro at hearing the dribs and drabs of conversations and creating a 'life' for the individuals sitting near her. Now, except for a few instances, most of the Spanish was too rapid for her to latch on to anymore than drifts of sentences or ideas. Smiling to herself, Margaret concluded that a foreigner to American shores would probably much prefer to speak English with someone from Georgia than with a Bostonian or New Yorker.

Margaret felt a queasiness rise in her stomach. She'd suddenly reflected upon the words of one of the teaching sisters at her high school. "Always look your best, ladies, for that is what people see first. Next, they hear how you speak before they listen to your thoughts. If you have an educated speech, your words will carry greater weight."

Educated speech? In Spanish? Was there such a thing as pidgin Spanish? If so, that's what Margaret spoke. Margaret wondered how she would manage to conduct herself with the personnel at the hotels. Her Spanish was still terribly stilted. If people were to measure her words from her Spanish delivery, she wouldn't go too far in Madrid. Her only hope was that her audience spoke English.

Nonetheless, she found herself mentally running through her lists, questions, and pleasantries in the best Spanish she could muster. Occasionally, she resorted to her dog-eared Spanish-English Dictionary.

As they pulled into the station in Madrid and alighted from the train, Margaret was greatly comforted to see that it was her own name prominently displayed on a piece of cardboard held high above the head of a young woman. She was greeted in English and squired into a waiting taxicab. Anna introduced herself as a University intern in Tomas' office. Her Dad, a diplomat, was a good friend of Tomas. According to where her Dad was posted, that's where the family had lived. As a result, her Dad counted on Tomas when he or one of his family members returned to Spain.

Now, Anna bubbled enthusiastically as to how she would assist Margaret on their rounds of the hotels. Anna also divulged the fact that Tomas appeared so much more relaxed and buoyed since Margaret was to handle the mechanics of this event. This news lifted Margaret's spirits. She was pleased that she had removed some of the onus from Tomas' shoulders. Hopefully, too, some of his buoyancy was due to Margaret's presence. This conjecture she chose not to share with Anna.

She sat back in the taxi feeling relieved and happy that Tomas had not left her in the lurch. He seemed to be anticipating Margaret's needs every step of the way.

He'd even timed her entrance. When Anna and Margaret stood in front of Tomas' personal assistant, Maria greeted Margaret and informed her that her boss had just stepped into his office. He was awaiting Margaret there. . . first door to the left.

Margaret could feel her legs turn to Jello. She wondered how they would carry her the few steps down the hallway. Her stomach was churning as well. Her brain commanded her legs to move. Drawing a deep breath, she put one foot in front of the other.

The door swung open as she was upon it. Tomas quickly drew her toward him as he closed the door behind them. Margaret could barely get her breath as his powerful kiss sucked the air out of her. His arms were wound tightly around her waist. He held her to him with such fierceness that Margaret wondered if he'd ever let go. She wanted to cry with joy, but contained any sound for fear of being heard through the door. When he finally released her, his hands gently caressed the features of her face. Looking into his eyes that had welled with fluid, Margaret read all the answers she'd sought.

CHAPTER 17

ALTHOUGH THEY'D SPOKEN ON THE phone daily during the past week, they were now at a loss for words. "There is so much I want to say to you, Margaret dear, but it will have to wait for later." Slowly pulling away from her he added, "Unfortunately, I have to attend a business lunch. And, you have only a short time before you begin your rounds of the hotels. I've arranged for Anna to accompany you to ease any language problems you might have. Will that be okay?" When Margaret nodded her approval of the plan and thanked him for his foresight, Tomas appeared satisfied. Margaret added, "Anna seems like a neat kid, and I'm so relieved not to have to go it alone." Tomas smiled with pleasure, but interjected somewhat awkwardly, "Anna is a good friend of my daughter." "Oh," Margaret intoned while laughing and sending him a wink, "I guess I'll have to behave."

Tomas' posture relaxed. He kissed her gently on the forehead appreciating her prudence. Then, he altered his stance and stiffened as he said, "Now Margaret dear, we need to get down to business." Quickly stepping behind his desk, he proceeded to call in Anna so that the three of them could sit and, together, review Margaret's notes. Tomas intended to add any ideas he might have while Anna could become familiar with the topics and questions

Margaret would be posing to the hotel representatives. They spent about twenty minutes at this task until Tomas was convinced that they'd covered all bases. Tomas rose, patted each of them on the shoulder and proceeded to his luncheon meeting.

Margaret, meanwhile, was left to admire Anna's efficiency. The young woman had set up a meeting at the Hesperia Hotel, for Monday where they would have a representational lunch with a member of the staff. At the Suecia, where Margaret would be lodged, they would canvas the rooms tomorrow morning.

Anna asked, "Do you mind walking? Even though it's winter, it's sunny and quite warm. It's not very far, and I can help you with your bags."

"That's so kind of you. That would be great. Thanks." She was really enjoying the company of this young lady.

The weather was quite balmy, and Margaret delighted in walking after being confined to the train for three hours. It seemed that all of Madrid were out and about enjoying this pretty day, and she and Anna were just joining the crowd.

She was buoyed by a sense that Tomas' plan for her involvement in the conference might work out after all. Hence, there was a spring to her step.

Margaret wheeled her medium-sized suitcase along the sidewalks while Anna held Margaret's smaller bag of cosmetics and toiletries. As they circled near the Museo Thyssen, Anna slowed her pace, "You know, it would not be a bad idea to pull in here for a second. We don't have to walk through this museum, or even go all the way inside. I would just like you to see the grand foyer. Would you be all right with that?"

Margaret looked past the wrought-iron fence that surrounded a large garden. There were a few souls seated on benches just inside the fence. She readily agreed to Anna's plan.

The two women trod down the entry path within the garden to the large doorway. Inside, Anna explained to the young ladies at the entrance that she and Margaret were interested in possibly renting the Thyssen's foyer for an upcoming event. Might they do a walk through?

Seeing Margaret, the women switched to English. "You are more than welcome to view the great hall. Would you like to leave the luggage behind this desk while you browse?" Anna and Margaret immediately handed over the bags and walked inside. They were soon accompanied by Ms. Ruiz-Rivas, the young woman in charge of special events for the museum.

Margaret inhaled. Such a sight! The room felt cavernous. Not only was it large in length and width, but also the ceilings were extremely high. Antique wall hangings were on her left. To the far right, she glimpsed two massive portraits. The event planner for the Thyssen explained that they were of the Baron and his very beautiful wife. "They are a handsome couple, indeed."

Ms. Ruiz-Rivas summarized the Thyssen's brochure to say, "The first Baron Thyssen was a German industrialist whose iron and steel factory was amazingly successful. Some of his descendants, 'vehemently opposed to the Nazi regime', moved to Switzerland and took their art collection with them. While in Switzerland, they expanded this treasure of German paintings to where it is one of the largest, possibly THE largest, private collection in the world."

When Margaret asked as to how this vast foyer might be used by the International Olive Oil Council, Ms. Ruiz-Rivas informed them, "It depends on what you are planning. Of course your event will have to take place when the museum is closed which is after seven p.m. Are you anticipating a sit-down dinner or a cocktail party?"

Margaret and Anna responded practically in unison, "Oh, we don't know that as yet."

Anna continued, "I expect the IOOC will make the final call."

"Well, then let me give you the specifics, and your organization can decide. This room can hold five hundred people standing. It seats three hundred. You would have to provide the caterer, bartender, tables and chairs, and so on. Of course, no candles or any open flames are permitted."

"Would our guests be permitted above this floor?"

"Oh, yes. In fact, you can have an hour and a half private tour. That should give your members sufficient time to see everything, hear explanations, and have their questions answered."

"Have you been through this museum?"

Anna said she had. Margaret replied, "I was here ten years ago and have a faint recollection of the works. Maybe, I can browse through while I'm here this weekend. I'm hopeful if it all works out, I'll get to see the exhibit during the IOOC event."

Margaret was elated. She'd been in Madrid for only a few hours and already things were starting to fall into place for her assigned tasks. She knew they'd have to work through the details of time and date, but the IOOC staff would deal with that.

Margaret and Anna thanked Ms. Ruiz-Rivas for her time and patience. This young lady had been most helpful and professional in her response. Margaret said, "We're so grateful to you. Can't thank you enough. I do hope we can use this facility. We'll request that the IOOC contact you shortly."

Margaret and Anna continued on foot heading toward the Marques de Casa Riera where the Suecia was located. Margaret noted that it was a four-star hotel, next door to a theater, and very well positioned for guests to walk to any of the major museums.

The lobby, registration desk, and coffee shop formed a wide-open expanse. Bright red walls and Chinese-red Oriental area rugs gave extra pizzaz to the black and white theme. Throughout, the pops of red in vases, pillows, flowers, and knick-knacks caught the eye in a most attractive fashion. She had not expected such a lively, contemporary setting.

Anna piped up with enthusiasm, "the Hotel Suecia is where Hemingway stayed whenever he was in Madrid. I suspect he was holed up here for long periods of time."

"I suspect the hotel lobby and coffee shop were not furnished in this manner at the time of Hemingway."

"No, I believe they did this for the 21st Century," Anna said with a laugh.

Margaret was not prepared for the young man behind the registration desk. As if he, too, were a part of the red pops in the scenery, he sported a full head of red hair. She scrutinized him closely. Yes, clearly, it was real; no toupee.

Margaret queued up in front of the reception counter. Margaret guessed that the desk clerk would have a working knowledge of English and she was proven correct. After giving her name at the reception desk, she was quickly identified in the computer. Margaret Cleary was assigned a room number, offered a computer card, and directed to the elevator.

She and Anna asked about the conference accommodations. After listening to their queries, he assured them that the hotel did, indeed, offer meeting rooms for corporate events and a restaurant. Anna questioned, "Can you check, please, to confirm that we have an appointment with someone for tomorrow morning to see the facility?"

The gentleman behind the counter promised that he would see to it.

Anna drew Margaret aside. "Do you mind spending a portion of your Saturday looking at this hotel?"

Margaret, a little bewildered, said, "That's what I'm here to do."

Even if Tomas were free to spend time with her, he certainly couldn't mind her spending an hour in the morning to take care of his business. After all, it was he who had arranged her Saturday morning meeting. She quickly reassured Anna, "Don't worry about a thing. I'll be fine."

Quite relieved, Anna rattled off as if in one breath, "If it's OK with you, I'll see you tomorrow morning. Can we meet on Monday morning at Tomas' office? Maria called earlier to arrange for us to meet with the convention manager and to eat a lunch at the Hesperia Hotel. Oh, and I almost forgot, Tomas will take you to dinner at the Hesperia this evening where the two of you can appraise the menu. It's a five star hotel with equally impressive restaurants. The chefs are world renowned. Lucky you!"

The last utterance took Margaret by surprise. It finally hit her that perhaps Tomas had made these arrangements to look as if it were a business dinner in case the two should be seen together. She did manage to ask Anna if she knew the time for the dinner reservation. Anna had not been informed, but surmised that it would be sometime after nine or ten in the evening since that was the earliest people would sup in Madrid.

Checking her watch, Margaret noted that it was half past four in the afternoon. Anna suggested that Margaret might wish to check into her room, rest and/or see some of the city. Margaret was grateful for the recommendation.

"Anna, I can't thank you enough for all your help. I'm sincerely looking forward to working with you."

Anna seemed amazed that her efforts had made any difference, but Margaret assured her that she'd saved her time and had been most thorough in organizing.

She also suggested that if Anna had other prospects for Saturday, Margaret would be happy to take stock of the facilities at the Suecia by herself and report to them all Monday morning.

Anna, with a show of emotion, quickly kissed Margaret on both cheeks. "Well, truthfully, I do have plans with a bunch of friends. I hated to have to cancel. Are you sure you're fine with this?"

When Margaret persisted, the relief on Anna's face was most apparent.

The two women smiled at each other and simultaneously and sincerely thanked each other and, waving good-bye, said, "Have a great weekend. See you Monday."

CHAPTER 18

SHE EXPECTED TOMAS TO BOOK her into a European-style hotel, but arriving in her room she viewed a very modern decor. It was clean and smelled fresh. She went right to the window and drew back the drapes to view Madrid. The room overlooked the Banco De Espana. She knew she was in the heart of the city and not far from Tomas' office. As she stepped back into the room, she noticed a vase containing a beautiful Spring bouquet of multi-colored fresh flowers that had been placed on the desk along with a small basket filled with some fruit, processed cheeses, crackers, chocolates and mints. Alongside the basket was a bottle of Muga, one of the red wines from Duero. Tucked inside the basket was a sealed envelope. Margaret removed it and tore open the contents. It read:

Margaret, my dear,

I trust you will find everything to your liking. I shall arrive at your room as early as possible. Unfortunately, I expect it won't be before 5:30.

If I'm to be much later, I'll telephone and leave a message. Can't wait *to spend time with you. Reserved a room next door in my name.*

Margaret sputtered and grinned broadly. It seemed that Tomas had thought of everything. He must have taken the second room for propriety, but upon closer examination, Margaret saw that the two rooms were connected through a doorway. If he possessed a flat in Madrid, it didn't appear that he would be remaining there for the weekend.

She unpacked her few items and set them into drawers and closets. With delight, she placed toiletries in a cabinet under the sink. She really would have disliked having them on display along the vanity. One contained her birth control pills which she'd acquired during the past week from a local gynecologist in Nerja. Her decision had been made, and she wished to be prepared. Now, she decided to soak in a tub and allow all the nerve endings to open.

At ten to six, Margaret heard a quiet knock at the door. She'd been trying to read, but had great difficulty concentrating. It seemed whenever she prepared to greet Tomas her stomach would churn, her legs barely holding her up, and she was almost out of breath in anticipation. He was standing on the other side of her peep hole, and she quickly opened the door.

He grabbed her up. Her breath came in gasps. No words were uttered. They tore at each other like animals. Tomas must have stopped first in the adjacent room, because his suit jacket and tie were absent, his top button opened. She was so aroused by the sight of him. His mouth felt fresh and clean against hers as her tongue probed his mouth. He slid his hand beneath her robe as she attempted, with unsteady hands, to unbutton his shirt and loosen his belt buckle. They were on the bed in seconds, or so it seemed.

He proceeded to kiss, suck and gently bite every inch of her. . . front and back. . . slowly moving along her body. . . whispering how much he'd missed her. She could only hear herself murmur grunts and groans. She indicated that he needn't use his condom which caused him even greater arousal. When he finally plunged inside her, they both were moving at tremendous speed and rising from atop the linens. She heard her voice screaming as the motions built in intensity. The release drove her to ecstacy. When her body finally stopped shaking and relaxed, Tomas turned her over and held tightly to her buttocks as they both lay panting.

Two hours later, Margaret awoke and looked at the clock. She had this warm feeling within her and a wetness between her legs. She gazed down at a sleeping Tomas. He reached out for her. She rested her head back on the pillow and replayed their latest love making in her head. He satisfied her in oh so many ways. Margaret couldn't believe the intensity of her desire for this man, nor the heights of passion she experienced when with him. As she let her mind concentrate on this most recent interlude, she felt twinges and edged her body closer toward Tomas.

As if to read her mind, Tomas awoke and gently stroked her breast. She barely felt his fingers as they softly ran down her leg and up toward her groin. This time when he entered her it was a very slow and deeply penetrating rhythm. He did not rush, but undulated as if he were playing a delicate instrument. Her response was quiet, but deeply satisfying. Tomas, also gratified, seemed unable to pry himself from her.

When at last he spoke, there was a rush of words like streams of consciousness. The words poured forth in bursts and in whispered tone. Tomas reiterated that in the last few years he'd found himself too busy for relationships and had not sought any nor come upon anyone with whom he'd wished to spend time. He'd been wrapped up in his business, the gym, some tennis, and his boat. His male buddies served as his companions.

"You have given me such joy. You have such an exuberance for life. You have unparalleled energy and share so many of my interests. I love the way you respond to my love making. I can't believe my good fortune. I'm not a religious man, but I feel so blessed." Then, as if shocked that all this had blurted out of him, he lightened and chuckled, "You are making me fall in love with you, Ms. Margaret", and tweaked her under her chin.

Margaret emitted an embarrassed giggle, but was clearly moved by his words. Shyly, she smiled up at him and struggled to find a response. Instead, she dug her face into Tomas' neck and snuggled into his chest. She was sure he could feel her tears running down. She felt he'd said it all.

They stayed in this position for several minutes. Tomas' stomach grumbled from hunger. The sound broke their spell, and they both tittered awkwardly. "Shall I phone room service and have dinner delivered to the room?"

Margaret protested that she was here on business, and Anna had stipulated that Margaret and Tomas were to taste the foods at the hotels and pronounce upon their fitness for the upcoming meeting of the olive producers. "I've produced a business automaton," Tomas squeaked. "Okay, let's gather ourselves for dinner. I have a reservation for ten o'clock."

That gave them a little over an hour to shower and dress. Tomas wanted to take a quick shave with his electric razor and went next door. He opened the connecting doors between their room and marched out of Margaret's into the one that was reserved in his name. So much for private rooms Margaret's mused as her face lit into an impish grin.

When they arrived at the dining room, they were seated in a far corner behind a large palm. Margaret wondered if Tomas had arranged for that particular secluded table. As if to read her mind, Tomas commented, "I thought we'd be able to discuss business more easily away from any hustle and bustle from the kitchen or other diners.

"Anna was thoroughly smitten with you. She was so excited at how much she learned from watching you in action today. In fact, she didn't feel that her presence was necessary as a translator, but was thrilled to be included in the shaping of this event. Although her dad is in the diplomatic core, members of their family are still in the olive and olive oil producing business." Tomas reached out his hand to cover Margaret's. "My instincts have served me well both from a personal and professional basis where you're concerned." Margaret just beamed.

Tomas' stomach gave another growl. They both laughed and turned their attention to the bowl of olives placed in the center of the table. They approached the olive bowl as herons diving for fish. Margaret suddenly became aware that, oddly enough, they had never been issued menus. She wondered if this were customary for this hotel's restaurant. As she glanced around her, a sommelier appeared with two bottles of wine and one of champagne. Instead of requesting their selection, the sommelier placed all three on the table with the appropriate wine and champagne vessels. Tomas performed the obligatory sniffing and tasting of each.

The crystal stemware now covered most of the table. Alongside, sat three coolers to keep the bottles chilled. Margaret shot Tomas an inquisitive look. As she did so, the sommelier bowed slightly from the waist saying something in Spanish, "I do hope . . . ," and that was all Margaret understood. When the young man finally backed away from the table, Tomas said, "He hopes that these will satisfy our taste buds."

Margaret was aghast. Here's something she hadn't known about Tomas. "Do you expect that we'll finish off three bottles of alcohol at one sitting?," Margaret blurted out. Tomas, understanding the nature of the question, burst out laughing. "I'm sorry, sweetheart, I guess I should have explained the agenda for the evening. It truly is a business dinner, you see. I have spoken with the chef requesting a tasting of his favorite menu items. They've just offered us a sampling of their grape and bubbly. No, I do not expect that we'll finish it all . . . and still walk upright out the door.

We'll have a platter of teasers for appetizers. Then, they will probably suggest a medley of the kitchen's most popular fish, chicken and beef entrees. I believe you will find the food and service here much to your liking. It is one of my favorite dining experiences in Madrid."

"My word, Tomas, you have thought of everything!"

"Hardly. It was you, honey, who thought of everything." When Margaret looked at him perplexed, he added, "Remember when we were at lunch on Sunday and how you went flying through a list of items we needed to cover in readying this meeting for the olive oil industry? I realized then that I didn't have a clue as to how much was involved. You got my wheels churning, and I began to take some action. I realized you'd need some help. . . a translator, possibly, and another pair of hands. That's where Anna steps in. When I thought further, I understood that I have dined in most of the high-end spots in Madrid. I assumed you've not spent the time here as I have, so I decided to step in and do the little bit I could to smooth the way."

Margaret was sitting with her mouth open. She was amazed that he had listened to all of her thought process which had come out sounding more like a grocery list. Not only had Tomas heard what she'd said, but he'd remembered, and then attempted to assist her in putting things in order.

While Tomas excused himself to use el bano, Margaret had time to reflect. Here was an adult treating her like another adult. Here was someone who respected her thoughts and observations. Here was someone who acted on HER behalf. Here was someone who built her stature instead of trying to undermine it at every turn. From their first encounter on the airplane, where Tomas had held her through the rocky portion of the flight and commiserated with her fear, Margaret had felt this man's mettle and sensitivity. Was it any wonder that she'd fallen in love with him?

Furthermore, she was so happy in Tomas' company and so pleased to be able to play a role in his business. To be able to do something that might prove productive for his corporation made her feel useful and capable. She realized that both Father Eduardo and Tomas, by bothering to get to know her and unearthing some of her strengths, had played to those strengths and fostered Margaret's confidence at a time in her life when her self-assurance was at an all-time low. It had been shattered when she'd caught Andrew with another woman. No, quite honestly, the downward slide had begun earlier in her relationship with Andrew. His arrogance and his family's airs had undermined her fierce pride and belief in herself.

Tomas returned to the table observing Margaret deep in thought. He joked, "I think in America you say, 'Penny for your thoughts'?"

Margaret sensed that she ought not to reveal her true ruminations at that point in time. She decided that, for the moment, she'd stick to business. "I was attempting to come up with some activities for the spouses. I presume that, in this case, most of the 'significant others' will be mainly middle-aged to older women and few, if any, men. Would that presumption be correct?"

When Tomas nodded in agreement, Margaret continued, "Would it be possible to do a tea at the Palace, or a private tour in the Prado, and catch a fashion show at one of the major department stores or boutiques? Ideally, we could do one or another or a combination of the above. I know it's a little late to do this sort of planning, but could we pull if off? I sense you have the names of contacts you've not shared with me who probably owe you."

Hearing her thoughts, Tomas emitted a belly laugh. "You're always happily surprising me with the unexpected. Yes, I might be able to drum up some contacts who can help us out. I guess I could call in a few chips as you put it. I'll think it through and place some calls on Monday."

Still chuckling softly, he very tenderly placed a hand over Margaret's. In almost a conspiratorial whisper he said, "I sense that there is more that's on your mind. Am I right?" Shyly, she nodded as he continued. "Let's discuss your concerns in a more private setting." Margaret looked about her. Although the tables were widely separated, indeed, the people at the next table were sitting with ears erect, and waiters and busboys were hovering in the distance. Margaret acknowledged his plan with a smile. She felt so comfortable and safe in Tomas' presence. Yet, she was still unclear as to how she would approach her areas of discomfort in their relationship. How could she best word her feelings of apprehension? Taking quick counsel, Margaret flashed him an ingratiating smile, "I don't know about you, but I am so stuffed. Are you up for a nice long walk before we return to the hotel where we're staying?"

They took a taxi down to the Plaza Mayor. Tomas suggested they have an after dinner drink at one of the café tables, but Margaret was truly feeling full from all the food and wine. "May I take a rain check on that? It's just such a pleasant night and the music in the distance adds so much color to the scene." Tomas nodded, indicated that he would follow her lead. They covered the huge plaza twice around while Margaret contemplated the crowds; mused about all the people who lived in the small apartments above; listened to music playing off in the background; oohed and aahed at the beautiful clothes, hats, and jewelry displayed in the many shop windows inserted into the buildings surrounding the plaza; and breathed deeply the clear night air. They spoke little, but felt the comfortable presence of each other and the mutual enjoyment of the moment.

Tomas offered to hail a cab back to the hotel. However, Margaret wished to continue walking. It was such a glorious night, and, though tired, she hated for it to end. Tomas, pleased that she was obviously enjoying the evening and the city, enthusiastically pointed out landmarks and statues, as they ambled along the brightly lit streets.

A good half hour later while strolling toward their hotel, he asked if she wished to continue on Arcala for several blocks to reach the Plaza de la Cibeles. Margaret readily agreed. With the many lights playing on the great fountains spewing water in the center of this immense thoroughfare, Margaret found herself mesmerized. If Paris is the city of love, Margaret thought, Madrid could not be far behind. She settled her head on Tomas' shoulder and nuzzled close. He placed an arm across her waist. Neither spoke. They stood positioned in this manner for several minutes. "Paradise, this is just heavenly," Margaret sighed.

"I have witnessed this scene so many times; it always lifts my spirits. Tonight, you have made it VERY special for me."

CHAPTER 19

MARGARET AWOKE TO THE MUFFLED sound of beeping tones. Confused at first by not being in her own bed in Nerja, she looked about. As she did so, Tomas was attempting to quietly ease out of bed so as not to awaken her. When she groaned audibly and grimaced, he looked in her direction but said nothing and headed for the adjacent room. She could hear him trying to drown the sound of his BlackBerry as he closed the doors between them. She supposed she could try to fall back to sleep, but the suddenness of waking had left her brain going full speed ahead. Instead, she remained with her head on the pillow and viewed her surroundings in a relaxed, leisurely fashion not wishing to pull her body out of bed.

Tomas returned to the room about a half hour later. He was visibly annoyed. "An oil press is not working properly and the foreman took sick during the night. I expected that I might have to run to my office for a short time this morning to tie up some loose ends. I had not contemplated spending the day in this fashion. I am NOT happy."

Drawing open the two sets of drapes blocking the hotel's window, Margaret looked out on a gloomy, gray, overcast sky. Rain was coming down in sheets. She sang the first line of *The Rain in Spain* from *My Fair Lady*. This would be a good day for remaining indoors; she would explore Madrid under roof.

"I'll be perfectly fine," Margaret assured Tomas. "I'm eagerly anticipating taking a tour of the Prado and, if possible, of the Thyssen museum nearby. If I have the time and energy, I hope to hit El Corte Ingles, and do some damage. Besides, you arranged for me to see the facilities here this morning. I believe you want them for additional meetings, breakout sessions, whatever." Tomas nodded.

He seemed relieved and a bit surprised that Margaret had adjusted so easily to his change in plans. Her confidence in tackling Madrid independently gave him cause to look at her with new admiration. Unbeknownst to Margaret, she was constantly rising in stature in his estimation. Her willingness to go it on her own merely intensified his terrible disappointment at having to relinquish her for the day.

She, on the other hand, was not entirely displeased. Although she'd been eagerly anticipating spending time with Tomas, she relished the thought of viewing works of art at her own pace. Her recollections of Andrew rushing her through the Prado, years back, prompted her wish to explore at will.

The hotel's room service delivered their breakfasts as Margaret and Tomas each donned casual attire for the day ahead. Tomas said, "I'm aiming to be back here between five and six. You have my cell number so we can keep in contact throughout the day. Let's alert each other if there's a change in plans."

Although the hotel's convention manager was off duty for the weekend, Tomas had arranged with the reception desk for one of the staff to allow Margaret access to the meeting rooms and restaurant in the Suecia Hotel. Thus, Margaret found herself beside a young lady who graciously escorted Margaret from room to room. As Margaret inspected the physical layouts to see if any would suit the needs of the olive producers, she made several notes on her yellow pad before feeling satisfied that she'd covered all her bases.

Promptly at ten, Margaret set off for the Paseo del Prado carrying a large umbrella and trying to keep her feet dry. The latter was no mean feat. The rain was coming down in buckets and splashing back up along the sidewalk. The scene appeared as upside-down waterfalls. She stepped gingerly to avoid the larger puddles. She wished she'd bothered to pack her short hiking boots. They would have given her some protection from this pouring rain. Better still, she thought, I wish I had those little red, rubber boots my mother insisted I wear as a child. She recalled hating them and believing her classmates thought them babyish. Today, however, they would have been most welcomed.

Fortunately, she was an experienced enough traveler to know that one always took some form of rain gear such as a poncho, slicker, jacket or coat. Margaret had toted her Gortex jacket which was doing a fair job of keeping her clothes dry beneath.

The Prado stood just a few short blocks from the Hotel Suecia. As she approached the Museo del Prado, a horde of tourists was alighting from the buses parked beside the building. Margaret quickened her step to reach the ticket booth before the crowds converged. She was determined to spend her time enjoying the art, not waiting in line. She paid the small fee and entered the first room.

Once inside, she tried to recall the individual works of art that she would like to linger before. Unable to hark back to any particular pieces, she decided to go through the museum one piece at a time stopping to view a work as long it captured her attention. She did remember that she had seen some marvelous creations by the Spanish artists Goya, El Greco, and Velazquez, along with other European masters Titian, Tintoretto, Raphael and Botticelli. She wove her way through the assorted rooms and chambers quickly glancing at some and stopping to thoroughly examine others.

The lighting had been updated since she'd visited last. The depth of color and clarity of the pieces was far more noticeable. The immensity of the number of acquisitions starting from the 15th and 16th centuries still amazed her. Most had religious themes. She drank in the reds of Titian; was intrigued by the regal finery, ornate jewels and furs, elongated lace collars, elegant full skirts and draped arms depicted in the works of Alonso Sanchez Coello; and marveled at El Greco's use of deeply somber backgrounds to bring light and color to the foreground. A young man standing nearby assisted her with many of the translations. He, also, informed her that El Greco had used mentally ill models for their "far away" look.

She lingered at great length before Titian's *Santa Margarita*. The symbolism sent shivers through her. It was eerie to see this virgin martyr with a distressed visage, on the run, fleeing a storm, bearing her cross. Titian had painted his subject wearing a green dress and brown shawl.

Margaret saw herself in HER green dress wrapped in her own brown shawl. She, too, was on the run, fleeing a storm. . . a torrent of emotional abuse, lies and heartache.

It was almost too much for Margaret to incorporate. She stood motionless, transfixed for quite some time trying to digest it all. Was this a sign? Was there a lesson in this for her? It left her confused, rattled, depressed.

Finally, she climbed several steps to reach the Goya exhibits. After viewing Goya's black period, she entered the main room to observe eleven new acquisitions of Goya. These portrayed the everyday life of the 18th and early 19th centuries. Margaret was charmed by the depictions of dancers, lovers, card players, and kite flying. She only wished she could step inside the canvasses and join the participants. Her mood lifted significantly.

When she had completed her tour of the two floors, she stopped to look at her watch. Unbelievably, three and a half hours had passed. Margaret was beginning to feel faint from hunger.

Outside the museum, she purchased the equivalent of a Dove bar and strode toward Parque del Retiro. The rain had ceased, but the arcing steps overlooking the large pond of water remained too wet for the usual crowds to converge in order to rest, chat, munch and enjoy the beauty of the numerous statues and fountains in this lovely environ. Margaret stopped long enough to admire them and the park and buildings sited around the vast Plaza de la Cibeles. Although unlit by the sun, the edifices still retained their old-world charm and magnificent architectural design. Their immense proportions, Greek columns and ornate carvings never failed to captivate.

She stood apart from the scene trying to preserve it in her memory. Standing in front of the Prado, and facing the waters rising from the Cibeles fountain, Margaret looked out upon a sea of cream-colored buildings that softened the view. She was able to identify the Palace of Communications with its striking, classical lines. The enormous structure comprised an entire city block.

On the opposite corner, she noted another ornate building that typified the exquisite carvings; this one with a rounded front. She thought it was the Palace Hotel, but never had time to really see. The heavens opened up, and Margaret made a dash for the Suecia. She walked the several blocks as quickly as possible, trying not to get too soaked beneath the thinsulate jacket and her umbrella.

She went directly to the hotel's coffee shop. Feeling chilled from the rain, Margaret ordered a bowl of hot soup and sifted through some of the coffee-table books she'd bought at the Prado gift shop. She debated about getting the Crepes Rellenos de Verdura on Salsa de Setas. The English translation said the crepes were stuffed with vegetables with a mushroom sauce. It sounded delicious. Nonetheless, she'd wait. She was sure Tomas would want to eat something when he returned early this evening.

Now, feeling rested, warm and dry, she rode the elevator to her room. It was past two o'clock and there were no messages from Tomas. She tried his office, and no one answered. Then, she tried his cell phone number and sent a text message. After a fifteen minute wait, Tomas returned her call.

Instead of the usual warmth and enthusiasm his voice held when speaking with her on the phone, Tomas' tone was clipped, dejected and muffled. The problems at the olive groves demanded his attention, and he'd driven the two hours to oversee the repairs. He had no idea when he'd be able to return to Madrid. Margaret was crushed. She suddenly felt her whole body deflate. Not only was Tomas unavailable to her, but also, his tone was brusque, cryptic, hushed. What was she to make of this?

While she put her iPhone into 'sleep mode', she thought about what he'd said and the tone of his voice. Was he trying to hide his relationship with Margaret? Was he with his wife? Was he just exhausted and as disappointed as she? Was Tomas blowing her off, or was Margaret blowing this all out of proportion?

She rested on the bed for a short time, and then decided there was no point in lying there stewing. She went down to the hotel lobby and asked directions. The rain had halted and the sun was peeking through the clouds when Margaret walked to the nearest metro stop. The air, after a downfall of rain, is often sweet-smelling and fresh. Margaret inhaled deeply and felt rejuvenated.

Walking in her beige Clark sandals, chino slacks and ivory-colored cotton sweater set, she felt well-groomed and comfortable for her day ahead. Europeans, in general, appeared more staid in their manners and dress than their counterparts in the States. Madrid, in particular, was a city of beautifully groomed individuals. Men wore suits, ties and jackets. Women still wore heels, suits or elegant dresses. Even in jeans, they looked well put together. Their hair coiffed as if they went to the hairdresser on a daily basis. . . perhaps they did.

Margaret did not wish to look like an American tourist. After all, she was living in Spain and paying rent. Margaret almost felt smug. She walked at a brisk pace, head held high. With one arm swinging and the strap of her small brown purse lightly resting on her shoulder, Margaret felt confident and secure. Suddenly she realized, although no one was gawking, people were obviously eyeing her. Vanity and pride goeth before a fall? Margaret, amused, saw her folly. With her stature and flaming red hair, she couldn't possibly meld into a crowd!

She boarded the subway and alighted at Goya station. Looking about her, Margaret located the sign proclaiming El Corte Ingles. Nothing like a little clothes shopping to lift the spirits. . . retail therapy!

Margaret made her way through the large department store, stepping off the escalator at each floor to examine the diverse and attractive merchandise. The leather goods were particularly appealing.

Margaret purchased leather belts for each of her sons. Then, she returned to the upper floors where she'd seen an exceptionally beautiful black leather jacket for herself. She paraded in front of the mirror looking at herself from every angle. She liked what she saw. The jacket was a good length, the material soft as a baby's tush and the style flattering. The weight of the garment would allow for early spring and late fall. It was roomy enough to accommodate a heavy turtleneck sweater during milder winter days, as well. At three hundred dollars, she knew it was an excellent buy. Could her budget allow for it? No, she'd have to scrimp on something else.

She did not deliberate long. Feeling down in the dumps since speaking with Tomas, this was as good a pick-me-up as she could imagine at the moment. Surprising herself with this sudden and impulsive act, she propelled herself and her purchase to the cashier's table and proceeded to finalize the sale.

Too many times before, she had hesitated, thought she didn't need an item, or felt she could do just as well or better on the price if she found it at home. Inevitably, she'd regretted her decision. The hot pink, hand-knitted, bulky sweater being sold on the street in Mexico City: the one-of-a-kind, sculptured earrings fashioned in Carmel, California; the work of a street-artist in the south of France. All left behind.

As the escalator carried her to the main floor, she reflected. Perhaps, had she not been so willing to forego acquiring belongings that she'd selected and she and Andrew could afford, she would not have been perceived as a doormat. Had she made her desires known and raised her expectations, perhaps Andrew would have treated her with greater respect.

As she reached her destination, Margaret stepped off the escalator into a sea of exquisitely-crafted leather handbags. She gazed at them briefly. Better not. Save it for another day. Margaret reined in her appetite. In addition to the euros fast outstripping the U.S. dollars, her body was feeling depleted along with her bank account. She was showing the effects of being on her feet for the better part of the day.

She retraced her metro experience and returned to her hotel room. It was now almost six and no sign or word of Tomas. She threw her purchases on the bed. After using the bathroom, she picked at some of the fruit and cheese and crackers from the basket Tomas had left for her the day before. The delicious tastes reminded her of his kindness. While wondering how things could have changed so abruptly, she collapsed into an easy chair and put her feet up on the adjacent ottoman. She heaved a sigh and closed her eyes. Numbing sleep arrived within seconds.

She did not know how long she'd been in this position. When she opened her eyes, she could see only darkness.

Night had fallen. The clock read 8:37. As her eyes adjusted, the clock cast some light into the room. Margaret noted the outline of a shadow on the bed. Stealthily moving forward, her eyes rested on the body. Tomas sensed her presence and awoke with a grunt.

In slow motion, he switched on the low-level light above the bed's headboard. They both flinched at the slight illumination. He patted the bed as a gesture for her to sit. "I'm totally exhausted. This was one of the worst days of my life. I cannot even begin to elaborate; I am so spent." Then, looking up at Margaret, Tomas reached out his hand to lay it upon hers. As if he suddenly realized that she, too, needed his focus, he asked if she were hungry. Up until that point, Margaret hadn't noticed. Now, she replied, "Well, I only had a Dove bar and a bowl of soup for lunch." "In that order?" he laughingly inquired.

"Yeah."

"Well, I guess we do need to feed you then. I'm so tired, though, I'm not sure I could chew."

He did seem wiped out both physically and emotionally. His voice was almost a whisper. Yet, he spoke tenderly to her and still had her interests in mind. Margaret's heart went out to him. She only wished to comfort him.

She stroked his brow and kissed him gently on the forehead. Tomas' hand reached to pat her cheek. "Would you mind very much if we ordered from room service? I really don't feel up to getting dressed and going out."

Margaret, too, was experiencing fatigue. And, sleeping in the chair left her feeling like a pretzel.

Margaret retrieved a menu from the desk drawer, and they each chose an entree. The decided that if they were still hungry, they could embellish the meal with some of the goodies remaining in the large basket that Tomas had supplied.

So tired, they barely spoke while eating. Supper seemed to revive them, however, and Tomas began making plans for the next day. He suggested they drive out of Madrid to Escorial and Avila. Margaret, having never visited there, readily agreed. Tomas started to elaborate on the itinerary for the next day. Since they were both enervated, they could retire early and awaken early tomorrow morning and get on the road first thing. "No," Margaret protested, "it will be Sunday and we need to get to Church." Tomas protested, but then relented. "What if we go to Avila first and make one of the Masses there. It's a beautiful Cathedral; I know you will love it."

Thereupon, they got their belongings out for the next day, changed into nightwear, and crawled into bed. No sooner had Tomas used the remote to put on the TV and lower the volume, when Margaret curled into a ball and fell into a contented sleep.

CHAPTER 20

GRABBING SOME COFFEE AND PASTRIES, they stepped into the Alfa Romeo and wended their way toward Avila before most of Madrid had awakened. The city's streets were fairly deserted. A clean, washed look greeted them en route. That, along with the rising sun, heightened the sense of expectancy one feels at the start of a new day.

Tomas deftly steered the car through the many residential neighborhoods of the city and out into the mountainous regions where the foliage had not yet come into its full promise. The car climbed northward and west toward the plateau. There, festooned with gray boulders, sat the town of Avila.

As they approached, Margaret could discern the medieval walls surrounding Avila which catapulted her into the Middle Ages. Within the walls stood the massive Cathedral whose beautiful apse was built in the late 12th century. In her Fodor's, Margaret read how the structure had not been completed until the 18th century.

Tomas explained that the town gained prominence as the birthplace of Saint Teresa, patroness of Spain. Saint Teresa, a Jewish child from a family of nobility, became the subject of many European artists who depicted Teresa's vision of an angel piercing her heart. Margaret, again read from Fodor's, that Teresa's legacy included several convents and *"yemas* (egg-yolk sweets), originally distributed free to the poor." Margaret wasn't certain that she wished to indulge in either legacy, but thought the nuns must certainly have faced fewer dilemmas than she had to contend with.

As they entered the church and were almost nearing the font, Margaret hung back. Tomas, sensing her hesitation, looked at her quizzically. Margaret drew him aside and placed her mouth at his ear. In a quivering voice, she murmured, "I don't know if I can go through with this . . . certainly not taking Communion . . . with our situation and all that." A slight cry escaped from Tomas' throat.

"I have not taken Communion for years," he uttered in a whispered tone. "I'm sorry you're having such a hard time with this. I don't know what to do. Do you want to leave?"

Margaret caught her breath, "No, I'll stay. It's just that I . . . I can't possibly take Communion. Haven't been to confession . . . I didn't know where to start . . . or where I could confess." Now, trying to get a hold on her emotions, almost sobbing, Margaret continued, "Let's just sit through the Mass. I'll pray that God will help me find the right path."

Tomas felt this heavy weight bearing down upon his chest. Margaret was struggling so deeply. What was the right thing for HIM to do? He didn't know. For years he had been agonizing, torn betwixt and between. Today, it was different; he was not the only one who was caught in the tussle.

Throughout the service, he sat with his arm protectively around Margaret's shoulder. They knelt in silent prayer and avoided each other's eyes. Margaret swayed toward him during the processional of those who were receiving Communion, but she made no motion to follow. She and Tomas were grave and drawn into their own thoughts . . . hardly hearing the sounds about them.

She had anguished all week, and particularly yesterday, over her conflicted feelings. She was so torn. Her strong feelings for Tomas set against the mystery surrounding him gave her cause for concern. She wanted so much to quiz him concerning his whereabouts yesterday. During their drive this morning, she had tried to broach the subject of his long absence and obvious fatigue on Saturday. Instead of relaying his whereabouts and problems, he'd launched into a history of the oil-producing industry and some of the pitfalls one encountered. Nothing was said of a personal nature. She hesitated to pursue the inquiry.

Margaret, once again, felt Tomas' strength and warmth beside her. His presence continued to give her great comfort. It was such an enigma. She suspected it would take some time to puzzle it out.

When they started down the steps of the Cathedral, Tomas reached for Margaret's hand and held it to his side. She welcomed this reassuring gesture and thanked him with a gentle smile as their eyes connected.

He steered them to a restaurant in one of Avila's Paradors. "In this town, the Paradors were renovated medieval castles. The State had acquired many of these former castles, as well as monasteries and convents throughout Spain. They've been converted into very accommodating inns and hotels. The Paradors are owned and operated by the State and, generally, well run." Tomas continued to explain, "Some of the Paradors in Avila have views of the river while others were built atop the town wall."

Many of the Paradors in Spain had lovely gardens. Tomas steered Margaret to the rear of this Parador where a beautiful park-like setting was laid before them. Margaret allowed herself to be enveloped by the light scent of early springtime aromas and an array of colors that forecast a bountiful season ahead.

Neither of them spoke. They walked among the pathways, enjoying the rich display. Here, more than in the Cathedral, Margaret felt the touch of God's hand, of Nature's gifts.

They entered the Parador through a rear door. As they traversed the building toward the lobby and restaurant, Margaret glimpsed some of the bedrooms where housekeeping was preparing for the day's arrivals. The rooms were stark in their simplicity, yet inviting. White walls, polished wood floors with wood moldings, and cleanly-carved wooden doors gave an uncluttered appearance. In each of the bedrooms, twin beds were covered with simple striped spreads in green and yellow hues with touches of red. Matching drapes stood flanking each window.

The views from some of these bedrooms and from the restaurant looked out upon the garden. By the time they were seated at the dining table, Margaret was feeling calmer.

Since they hadn't had much breakfast, they were famished. Sunday dinner seemed most appropriate. They each ordered a salad to start. Tomas told her, "I would highly recommend trying the fish here. Most probably, it was caught this morning in the nearby river." Margaret welcomed his suggestion; she loved the idea of fish that didn't smell or taste fishy. After Tomas conveyed their orders to the wait staff, they continued to gaze out the window at the garden rather than engage in conversation.

Almost immediately, their glasses of wine and salads were brought to the table, and they fairly dove into the crisp greens and freshly-baked breads. As they ate, Margaret debated as to how she might raise the subject of her apprehensions. She knew she didn't want to put Tomas' reassuring and uplifting presence out of her life. Nonetheless, how could she reconcile herself to this relationship given that she was still a married woman in the eyes of the law and in the eyes of the Church. In addition, if she were honest with herself, she knew so little about Tomas.

As she was silently contemplating all of this, Tomas came up for air, looked at his clean plate, and quietly cleared his throat. With great hesitation in his voice, he began,

"I'm aware that we have known each other a relatively short time and really know little about one another. Still, it would be so painful for me to give you up."

His words startled Margaret and her body flew forward while she blurted out, "No, I don't want to lose you either." Quietly, she added, "You are the best thing to come into my life in a long while . . . other than my sons."

Tomas smiled mischievously, "Well, that's a relief. I thought I might have to lose my best press agent and party planner."

Margaret grinned and looked at him with great affection, appreciating the lighter touch of humor, but quickly lapsed into a crest-fallen demeanor. "I'm really losing lots of sleep over this one."

Tomas took her hands in his, "You need to talk to someone; I can see this is eating at you. Do you want to talk with me about it? Have you an understanding girlfriend? Would you feel more comfortable talking to a priest? No, I guess the latter is not such a great idea . . . given our situation." His words were tumbling out now, his usual composure gone.

"I do feel rather awkward talking with you about my feelings. Everything seems so premature." Tomas nodded encouragingly, wishing to keep her talking. Margaret continued, "My closest friend from early childhood is back home in Boston. Telephone conversations get stilted or garbled, and the time difference makes it so hard to connect. It's difficult for me to pour out my feelings in an e-mail, particularly with no immediate feedback. Something like this requires more of a conversational mode with a face-to-face audience."

Tomas nodded again acknowledging her needs. Margaret resumed her train of thought, "I've been pondering going to Father Eduardo. He's become a good friend and I trust him implicitly." Margaret's voice was now almost a whine, and her words started to drift off.

At the mention of the priest's name, Tomas started. "How well do you know Father Eduardo,?" Tomas questioned.

"Oh, he has been wonderful to me. I told you how he'd arranged for me to teach English at his church. He also helped me purchase my car. And, he's been wonderful about introducing me to different features about Nerja, particularly the Caves. . . and some of the restaurants. We even spent an evening together watching *The Phantom of the Opera*."

Without coming up for so much as a pause, Margaret rattled on, "I know Father Eduardo worries about me. When I hadn't shown up for Mass that Sunday that you and I were playing tennis, Father was phoning the house to see why I wasn't at church. Apparently, he kept phoning throughout that Sunday until he reached me Monday morning. He was truly concerned. He's a really sweet guy. When he learned that I'd been playing tennis, I thought I'd hear a lecture. Instead, he volunteered to get out his racquet and hit with me. Imagine?"

Had Margaret been less engrossed in what she was saying and more focused on Tomas' expression, she would have noticed his eyes growing ever wider with each of her pronouncements. All Tomas could get out of his mouth was an astonished, "Really!"

At that moment the staff delivered their entrees. Tomas seemed relieved to tackle his dinner without the need for further conversation. He wasn't certain he liked where it was leading.

The presentation of the main course afforded an opportunity to change the subject. They found the food simply prepared and most kind to their taste buds; the freshness of the fish and vegetables was evident. Margaret and Tomas, as if it were a balm, turned their attention to the excellent wine, food and surroundings.

After the entree was completed, however, Tomas' curiosity was getting the better of him. He wished to steer the conversation to a resumption of matters regarding Father Eduardo.

Before he could so much as move in that direction, Margaret jumped in and peppered him with questions pertaining to the upcoming conference. She then informed him, "As you wished, I saw the conference rooms and restaurant at the Hotel Suecia yesterday before heading off to the museum. The meeting rooms seem very adequate as a gathering place for the attendees staying at this hotel. Also, the restaurant is very inviting. Tables are covered with white cloths with thin black lines drawn in large squares. Each chair is overlaid from top to bottom with white linen. It's most attractive."

Immediately, thereafter, she proceeded to launch into another round of questions and suggestions. "Do you think our plans for the spouses of participants will come to fruition? I really would like to arrange for an afternoon function at the Palace for a lunch or tea or an evening reception in the large foyer of the Thyssen museum and, hopefully, plan a fashion show at El Corte Ingles department store. I'm hoping you'll be able to use your contacts."

Smilingly, "I know, I know. I promise you I'll make those phone calls first thing tomorrow morning. We'll just give the guys time to get into their offices and loosen their ties, okay?"

With that, Margaret laughed and wickedly stuck out her tongue which caused Tomas to laugh heartily.

Margaret, getting back to business, launched into another round of ideas that were swirling in her head. "Additionally, I've been thinking of social activities for the entire group. A friend of mine in the States is now posted with her husband in Washington, D.C. It seems they are often being entertained at the different embassies there. If those embassies open their doors in the States, perhaps we can get the American Embassy in Madrid to allow us to use their facility for an evening's cocktail party and buffet dinner. I know they would only provide the space; we would have to line up the bartenders and a caterer. Is that doable? Shall I phone the Embassy in the morning?"

In order to give intelligent, honest, and realistic opinions, Tomas had to focus on Margaret's questions and recommendations and be ready to respond to them when she finally came up for air. As he did so, he realized that her ability to think at such a clip was beginning to amaze him. He had always enjoyed people who thought rapidly on their feet and, even more so, would grab hold of a task and pursue it with almost child-like enthusiasm. He felt his interest in her and his admiration and approval were escalating with each succeeding exchange of ideas.

By this point, Tomas' attention had been completely diverted, and he dropped all hopes of reviving the subject of Eduardo. Moreover, Margaret's head was now forging in another direction. "How long will it take us to get to Escorial? Have we time enough to see it today?"

Tomas glanced at his watch. "Well, we could linger over coffee and dessert, or we can get the check and head for Escorial. The choice is yours. If we leave now, we can get to see Escorial in daylight and spend some time at the museum before it closes for the day."

Margaret debated. She liked the thought of lollygagging around with Tomas, and perhaps getting to stroll through the streets of Avila. Tomas seemed most content to just sit. She suspected that he was still worn out physically and emotionally from his experience the day before. Nevertheless, she didn't know if she were to be in this region again. "I guess I'll have to vote for Escorial since I don't know if, or when, I'll have another opportunity."

Tomas looked taken aback and then disappointment showed on his face. The revelation seemed to rest on both their shoulders; their time together was limited. Margaret would have to be returning to the States at some time. And, that time was looming. With that, Tomas' hand reached out to press Margaret's as he signaled to the waiter to bring the check.

CHAPTER 21

URING THE SHORT TRIP TO Escorial, Tomas elaborated on the financial cost and years of building that had transpired in order to complete the gigantic monument which Franco had designed to memorialize his reign and those war heroes who died fighting for Spain. Margaret was eager to see the structures and grounds which Tomas was describing. More than that, she was most curious as to how Franco, the last dictator of Spain, impacted on Tomas, his family and the nation. She was hesitant to ask, but Tomas took it upon himself to refresh her memory of that era.

Tomas explained, "Franco, as an army officer and aligned with the moderate conservatives, had participated in a revolt against the leftists who'd won the election in the mid-1930's. Bloody civil war ensued. The outcome was Franco's rise to power as dictator.

"Although pretending neutrality during World War II, Franco had actually sided with the Axis of Germany and Italy for their earlier assistance to his fledgling regime. He had sent 'volunteers'. In fact, my Dad's youngest brother was severely wounded in combat. Franco's allegiance did not sit well with the United States and its Allies, and, consequently, Spain suffered economically.

"However, Franco was vehemently opposed to Communism, and, as a result, after World War ll, won economic and military assistance for his country while allowing the U.S. to build air and naval bases on Spanish soil. Internally, Franco ruled with an iron hand over the unions, the press and police. Not a happy time for our people."

As they approached Escorial, the Alfa Romeo climbed the steep hills through the narrow tree-lined highway. Standing in the immense parking lot, Margaret felt herself surrounded by the mountains of fir trees that blanketed the vista. Although the orange trees were not yet in bloom, early spring buds were appearing on some of the numerous deciduous trees in the densely packed woods. Everything about the terrain felt larger than life. The gray boulders along the ground gave way to the gray mountains rising in the beyond. If the purpose was to feel the power of the man and the reach of his arms, this landscape was a reflective message of Franco's career.

His strength was echoed in the cement, granite, stone, and marble that formed the man-made paths, steps and buildings that comprise the Valley of the Fallen.

Behind the main edifice was a cross the likes of which Margaret had never seen before. It was the tallest and most imposing figure and soared over the whole. Standing beside Tomas, Margaret needed time to absorb it all. She wanted to imprint it on her memory.

Once inside the building, they entered the church. There lay the remains of the fallen leader in a massive stone coffin bedecked with colorful floral wreaths. The inscription on the casket said simply: FRANCISCO FRANCO. A large, narrow cross was etched above.

Margaret seated herself in one of the pews and bowed her head, her hands covering her eyes. The quiet in this church, devoid of parishioners, allowed her to sit with her thoughts and to meditate more easily. Unmindful of the few tourists and of Tomas, Margaret sat, composed herself, and silently asked God for guidance. When she rose, Tomas headed toward one of the figures of a saint and the two of them lit candles in supplication. Although Margaret had performed this simple act innumerable times in her lifetime, sharing it with Tomas seemed to further their closeness on a more spiritual level. They said nothing as they took in their surroundings one more time and left the Valley. Margaret curled up into her seat as the car retraced its route down the mountain. Along the way, Tomas spotted a farmer's stand and purchased some fruit and baked goods to tide them along. At this juncture, they were more tired than hungry.

Today was their first real outing together, and it had left Margaret feeling emotionally drained. Tomas, although exhausted from the events of yesterday, had proceeded to drive through Avila and Escorial because he had originated the plan and cared enough to fulfill his promise. Margaret felt that she needed to address that.

"This was such a lovely day; I thoroughly enjoyed the experience. I had been to Granada and Toledo, to Cordoba and Sevilla when I was here last. Today, was a special treat seeing Avila and Escorial with you. . . and getting the real poop." They laughed.

She continued, "I want to see as much of Spain as I can. . . and seeing it through your eyes . . . makes it doubly special. I really loved seeing more of your country, but I know you are still worn out from all the aggravation and driving you experienced yesterday. "

"Well, I had a good night's sleep last night, but, yeah, I was feeling kind of worn out. It doesn't matter. I wanted to spend the time with you, to have the day . . . alone with you."

Margaret suspected that it was becoming apparent to BOTH of them that they sought out each other's company and enjoyed similar activities and each other. They seemed to be ensconced in a truly deepening relationship, yet knowing that it might be of a very tenuous nature. Margaret would have to return to the United States at some time . . . and probably in the near future. With this thought, involuntarily, her bodied shuddered.

As soon as they reached the hotel and the elevator door closed, Margaret pressed against Tomas as hard as she could, wrapped her arms about him and placed her mouth firmly on his. She seemed to be trying to convey to him, without words, all the tenderness she was feeling. His lips parted and they kissed deeply for several seconds before reaching their floor. Margaret's emotions were tightly strung. She cared so strongly for this man who gave so much of himself to her. The realization was painfully present that she might have to leave Spain and, in the process, leave Tomas behind.

As they lay on her bed, the depth of her ardor poured forth in her kisses, her embraces, and her longing to be close to him. Although his body was exhausted from the day before and from all of the driving and walking today, he responded to Margaret's initiative. Her massages, kisses and fondling awakened his lust. Their passionate lovemaking reflected a growing love for one another.

When they finally culminated in exhausted climaxes, they clung to one another . . . never wishing to let go.

When Margaret awoke, she heard the shower running and then stop. She surmised that Tomas awakened, shaved and would now be toweling off and getting dressed. As she reached for her robe, there was a knock at the door. Through the peep hole she could see a hotel staff person with a rolling cart. The smell of bacon and eggs and coffee greeted her upon opening the door. Margaret signed for breakfast and added a tip to the bill. Tomas had thought of everything.

Tomas emerged, dressed and ready for the day. They pulled up two straight-backed chairs from the desk and sat across from one another at the small round table. Neither said anything until they had digested a few bites and swallowed some juice and coffee.

At last, Tomas looked up at Margaret, "You are terrific! It's been years since I have felt so happy with my life." Margaret felt a rush of blood fly toward her cheeks, so embarrassed by her advances the night before. She said nothing, just looked demure. Her face reddened further and she looked down at her food with a grimaced smile.

Tomas guffawed, but took the hint and quickly changed the subject. He began to list the phone calls he would make today on behalf of the conference. "May I suggest, also, that after the four of us review the various features offered by each of the hotels and restaurants, if necessary, feel free to look for additional options."

He took off for the office leaving Margaret to dress leisurely. She arrived an hour later. Anna and Maria were already hard at work. They greeted Margaret warmly and inquired as to her weekend activities. Neither seemed to suspect that there was any personal connection between her and Tomas, Margaret noted, happily relieved.

After a few moments, Tomas emerged and wished to review their tasks for the day. He let Margaret itemize what she had seen at the Hesperia Hotel, and drew from her the social activities she had suggested to him privately. He listened with rapt attention as if he were hearing it for the first time. Finally, he said in Spanish, "I guess we'll have to get on the phone and see if we can get some of these people from the Embassy, palace, department store, and so on to get on board." Turning to Margaret, he switched to English, "Why don't you try the American Embassy, while Anna tries to reach some of the others. I'll hang around here for awhile to speak with some of them personally."

Margaret was given a desk and phone in an office in the rear. She invited Anna to join her. Anna initiated the call to the Embassy and asked to speak with an American there who had decision-making power. As soon as an American voice came on the line, Anna handed the telephone to Margaret. Margaret inquired as to whether or not the use of the Embassy was proper. When told, "yes", they resorted to their calendars to try to find a mutually agreeable time and date. Margaret was given two possibilities which she promptly held. She told the woman on the phone that she'd be back to her with confirmation within the next two days.

Later in the morning, Tomas stuck his head through the door. He was feeling quite frustrated. It seemed that either people were not yet at their desks or were in conference or constantly on the telephone. He shook his head, "It's a Monday morning . . . *deja vu* all over the world". They chuckled and broke for a cup of coffee. Afterwards, Maria offered to keep trying until she reached the parties who could open the doors to the Palace and El Corte Ingles.

They left Tomas to his own devices, and Margaret and Anna grabbed a taxi to head north along Paseo de la Castellana to the Hotel Hesperia. In the daylight, Margaret could see that the hotel was located in a very upscale residential area along with high-rise office buildings. She noted the large sign atop one that screamed Price Waterhouse Coopers.

The women entered the beautifully modern, sage-colored lobby and approached the desk. Almost immediately, a Senor Garcia greeted them and led them into a small conference room a level below. There, a lovely table had been set with beautiful china, silver service and crystal stemware. The director of event planning excused himself to allow Margaret and Anna to sample a variety of menu options. Many of their selections were those that Margaret and Tomas had previously enjoyed at dinner.

Attentive, white-gloved waiters carried in a succession of fish, poultry, beef, lamb and pork in addition to salads and desserts. Margaret and Anna reached for the foods and slowly and deliberately tasted each of the items. They designated an array of menu choices that could be served at lunch and dinner to the assembled IOOC members, spouses and guests.

In consideration for members who represented countries with Muslim and Jewish populations, pork was eliminated from the menu. In addition, Margaret included several substantial vegetable choices for those not wishing poultry, beef or lamb.

Senor Garcia returned to the table to discuss their selections and answer Margaret's questions regarding continental breakfasts, coffee breaks, seating arrangements, table placement, total capacity of rooms, sound systems, available computers for power-point presentation and videos, check in and bathroom locations, availability of pencils and pads, number of hotel staff allocated to the event, and any time constraints. Margaret insisted on getting a breakdown of costs of the food and any incidentals.

To satisfy Margaret's concerns that all their requirements would be met, they toured the available meeting rooms. Senor Garcia led the way and Anna translated as needed. Margaret eyed each one and noted its size, configuration, accessibility to a podium, buffet table, bathrooms, and so forth.

Then, Margaret questioned him regarding additional facilities: bar, beauty services, health club, spa, swimming pool and other possible amenities. When Margaret had exhausted all the questions on her list, and then some, she and Anna profusely thanked the gentleman for a lovely lunch and for his patience.

Margaret assured him, "Someone from our office or from the IOOC will contact you by Tuesday with a decision. I'd greatly appreciate it if you can hold these rooms for twenty-four hours. If there is any further information or questions, I can be reached at the Hotel Suecia. I'll be staying there for the remainder of my time in Madrid."

As their feet found the pavement, Anna glanced down. "You're wearing suitable shoes. Would you mind walking several blocks to the IOOC? I'd like to show you their building and where some of the functions will take place. I think you'll get a better picture of the events if you can visualize the facility."

MARGARET: FROM NEWTON TO NERJA

"That's fine. It's a gorgeous day for a walk, and we've been sitting a long time. Don't mind if I walk off those pounds. I have never been this far north of the museums and other tourist attractions. It's quite modern and pleasant."

The two women strode briskly making small talk as they went. Margaret was amazed when they finally reached their destination. The International Olive Oil Council was housed in an ultra-modern, five-story building that encompassed the entire block on Principe de Vergara. Flags of many nations flew across its exterior. Anna proudly showed Margaret the small olive trees planted in front. The entry was surrounded by floor-to-ceiling windows allowing light to enter.

When they returned to his office, Tomas had managed to reach the Palace. Since the King and Queen actually used it as a residence, it was never open for special events. However, guided tours were available to the public.

Maria had managed to reach the public relations person at El Corte Ingles. A Roberto Verino trunk show would be occurring during the time of the IOOC conference. Spouses and guests of the IOOC would be most welcome.

Margaret was elated; she felt 'in the loop'. "I just saw his clothes in a special area of the department store when I was there on Saturday. They are beautiful. Such gorgeous fabrics, and the designs are cutting edge."

"Yes!" Anna chimed in. "His son and he have opened boutiques in various parts of Spain. I do think we are lucky to showcase such fine Spanish talent to our international membership. The women should love it. And, maybe some guy will buy an outfit or scarf for his lady love."

Margaret felt much relieved as she and Tomas climbed aboard the plane he'd chartered to return to the Costa del Sol. They would arrive in time for Margaret to wash up and head to the church to teach her class. In addition, she felt the satisfaction of completing the task she and Tomas had set for themselves. They had lined up the hotels, conference center, restaurants, and most of the social activities that would be a necessary part of the olive producers' meeting. The little details were inconclusive, but they could be arranged in the next few weeks prior to the event. It was now, pretty much, left in the capable hands of Maria and the staff at the IOOC.

Presently, seated in the rear of the plane, they had time for conversation. Tomas, for his part, was still agitated by Margaret's description of her relationship with the priest. All weekend long he'd had disquieting thoughts niggling away at him. What was Eduardo's interest in Margaret? Was he a philandering priest? Somehow, he thought not. Yet, Tomas could not quiet his feelings of jealousy and irritation. He wondered how he might raise the issue without Margaret hearing any rancor or suspicion in his voice.

They were seated in the small private plane just behind the heads of the pilot and co-pilot. The sound of the motor, however, drowned out conversation. Tomas felt he could speak without being overheard. He asked Margaret if she usually saw Father Eduardo on the nights that she taught. When she said that she rarely did, Tomas relaxed. Then Margaret added, "But, if I have something that comes up in class or Father needs to hear about one of the parishioner's progress, we meet for lunch or dinner to talk." Tomas bolted upright in his seat. "Why would he need to do that?"

Margaret, surprised by his inquisitiveness, asked if Tomas ever frequented the little church. "Never!" was Tomas reply.

Tomas' interest in the priest was confusing to her, and she pressed him further. "Then, how DO you know Father Eduardo?"

She could see Tomas' body tense and then a look of resignation creep across his face. Tomas was not liking this line of interrogation, but since he, himself, had begun the probe, he was now caught in his own trap. He sensed that there was an almost unspoken agreement between the two of them to get some of these particulars out into the open.

Looking down, he began, "I've known Eduardo all of his life. His family is also in the olive and olive oil business. Our families have been the closest of friends . . . for generations, actually."

With a look of astonishment advancing across her face, Margaret uttered a surprised, "Oh." The full impact of Tomas' pronouncement took time to seep into her brain. Slowly, it penetrated. If Tomas knew the priest and his family all that time, Father Eduardo must know stuff about Tomas. How much time have the two of them spent together, she wondered. How well do they really know one another? She leaned her body toward Tomas and again said, "Oh," but with a look that said, "Continue."

Tomas, as if to do her bidding, "I never really got to know Eduardo until we were both in the States. He is quite a bit younger than I, but we were both living in New York State at about the same time. Before I began my MBA program, I took a job on Wall Street and worked there a year. I had a small place, a rental apartment in the Village.

"Eduardo, at the time, was a freshman at Siena College in upstate New York about two and a half hours from the City. He'd had no thoughts of entering the priesthood and showed no inclination for the vocation. He was a bit of a wild kid and a real ladies' man. He used to love to accompany me to the Village Vanguard to hear jazz and, also, to some of the crazier parties in my neighborhood. From time to time, I'd get tickets to the Broadway theaters from some of my clients. Occasionally, Eduardo would come as my guest. Sometimes, we'd double date; he escorted a succession of very attractive young ladies."

Margaret sat quietly, all absorbed. Her silence caused Tomas to continue his recitation. "He's an athletic guy, and we'd sometimes find a vacant court and get up a tennis game. Often, Eduardo . . . Eddie, as he was known then, would just bring a couple of guys down from Siena and crash at my pad while they pursued the joys of Manhattan."

Margaret observed with delight Tomas' enthusiasm and pleasure in relating these distant memories. Tomas acknowledged as much when he suddenly reverted to a solemn, almost wistful tone, "The freedom we felt in those days. It was a heady experience."

Margaret felt herself cherishing this revelation. She closed her eyes for a second in order to focus her thoughts on those younger men. She tried to draw a picture of them as they might have appeared.

Margaret did not wish to let go of this moment; she wanted so much to learn more. "What prompted Father Eduardo to go into the priesthood do you suppose?"

Laughing, Tomas replied, "I suspect he could tell you more about me than I can about him. My only perception is that perhaps all his carousing the first two years at college seemed pointless. I'm not certain."

Now in a morose voice, Tomas continued, "Unfortunately, I had to return to Spain after Eddie's third year at Siena."

Then quickly, as if not to dwell on himself, Tomas continued, "Eddie was a terrific golfer, and the Franciscans loved to get out on the golf course with him. I've heard that Eddie spent a lot of time with his teachers in this pursuit and really became close with several of them. I suspect he began to appreciate their lifestyle.

"Being the youngest in his family, he had been a rather indulged child as I recall. I know he became active in some of the Franciscan pet projects . . . even spending a year after college tending to the needs of residents in a run-down section of The Bronx. I would have thought he would have found that depressing and difficult and run in the opposite direction." Tomas shrugged, "Perhaps, Eduardo saw a way of life of giving to his community and found it rewarding." Margaret, almost abstractly, acknowledged that the priest, certainly, seemed to bask in the glow of helping others.

However, her thoughts were racing beyond their present conversation. Last week, she'd been dreading the prospect of having lunch with Father Eduardo. Although still feeling tentative, she was now hopeful that he might fill in many of the blanks surrounding Tomas. By saying that Eddie could tell her more about Tomas than Tomas knew about the priest, Margaret took that as permission to inquire.

CHAPTER 22

ARGARET WALKED INTO HER SMALL classroom in the church just twenty minutes before her students' arrival. She had hoped to run into Father Eduardo this evening to set up a time for them to get together. His office door was closed, and she could hear muffled voices within. He must be involved in a meeting, Margaret thought. She would try his office again after teaching her class.

She sat quietly in almost total darkness while attempting to clear her mind of all the happenings and conversations relating to Tomas and the past few days. She focused her mind now on the curriculum for the evening.

As her students entered, usually one by one, she would engage them in brief conversations. "How was your weekend? Did you do something special? That's such a lovely blouse . . . shirt; where did you get it?"

After they all filed in and she'd taken attendance, she would try to engage them in a group discussion of their weekend activities. Occasionally, the students would turn the tables and ask Margaret what she had done during the weekend. Today was no exception, and Margaret found herself launching into a description of her trip to Madrid.

She briefly told of her visit to the Prado, El Corte Ingles, and of some of the hotels and beautiful sights along the way. She tried, also, to explain her trip to Avila and Escorial. Using pictures from coffee-table books and pamphlets she'd gathered while traveling, she was able to surmount some of the language barriers.

She stressed the necessity of English fluency. "The people who helped me through my trip managed to speak English well enough for me to be understood and for me to understand them: office workers, train attendants, desk clerks, waiters in restaurants, salespersons in the shops and many personnel in the museum, many of the visitors, too, I might add. I can see even more now how important it is for all of you to speak and understand English well. I promise I will try very hard to continue to help you."

Many of her students smiled in response. Some shook their heads to concur. Margaret then continued replaying more of her weekend activities.

After she spoke of her ride on the train and her return on a private plane and explained the idea of a charter or private vehicle, Margaret could see Luis' face scowling at the depiction. It left her with a sudden queasy feeling in her stomach. She quickly shook it off and asked if anyone else in the room would share an experience or personal view of Madrid. A few of the students attempted to do so and Margaret encouraged them in expressing their thoughts in English.

Next, she grouped them for conversations using terms such as, "How may I help you? What are you doing? May I have the . . . ? Where may I find the . . . ?" Each group practiced their assigned phrase and responses; then shared their conversations as a whole.

Margaret then launched into a "Simon Says". These adults would commence to jump, hop, walk, run, stop, come, turn, laugh, and frown as Simon directed. She allowed others to take turns being Simon. The activity allowed lots of motion, silly child-like responses, and a shedding of inhibitions. Everyone loved it.

With some easy texts which Margaret had managed to secure from the used-book store in town, each of her pupils had a turn to read aloud. Margaret would question the group about the material or ask that they write a simple paragraph that related to the topic. Corrections were made with an upbeat turn and a light hand. She was lavish with her praise. Many in her class were making excellent progress. It made Margaret extremely proud of them and, in turn, proud of herself.

The atmosphere was relaxed and each individual treated with dignity. Any laughter was good natured and not derisive. Margaret wanted her students to come away feeling good about themselves and about Americans. In addition, she wanted them to enjoy learning the language. They were coming to her because they wanted to be there, and she wished to make it as pleasant for them as possible.

The time moved quickly. Often when the class was over, Margaret would encourage students to linger and chat. It allowed her to become better acquainted and, with several of them, she enjoyed the camaraderie.

Today, however, she was tired from her trip and anxious to find Father Eduardo. She gathered her belongings and proceeded to walk out of the classroom almost immediately after dismissal. Nonetheless, she was too late for the priest. He was nowhere to be found. Hurriedly, she scribbled a note and slid it under his door with the hope that he would find it in the morning.

She could barely keep her eyes open for the few miles it took to drive home. As soon as she arrived on her own threshold, she deposited her belongings in the entry, used the lavatory, barely washed her face and brushed her teeth, and crashed on her bed. She was asleep as soon as her head hit the pillow.

Before she was fully awake, she could feel the morning sun playing across her unopened eyes. The light was streaming through the windows where she'd left the drapes agape the night before. The brightness of the sun dancing directly in her eyes caused her to awaken quickly and reach for the clock. It was just past nine, and the day was well on its way. She'd missed the opportunity to reach her sons in the States. By now, classes had ended and they were probably at extra-curricular activities. She'd try later.

While preparing her coffee, she switched on the telephone's answering machine. There were messages from Missy in Massachusetts saying "hi" and one from Father Eduardo. She listened intently to what he had to say. He had come upon her note this morning and was able to meet for lunch today. Unfortunately, he had no further openings this week. Where Margaret had been dreading her encounter with the priest, she was now eager to connect. She immediately phoned the priest's office, and they agreed upon a time and place.

Her hastily unpacked traveling outfits and gear lay strewn across her bedroom and bath. While in the shower, she started to compose her ideas as she planned to present them to the priest. Her imaginary dialogue emerged with little effort. Basically, she'd been preparing her speech for hours.

She decided to dress demurely so as not to give Father any hint of her fallen status. Margaret chose a high-necked, navy blue blouse topped by a navy blue sweater and a plaid, Catholic school-style, skirt. To round off the outfit, she wore low navy blue pumps with a matching purse. Glancing at herself in the mirror, she saw an aged parochial school clone. Satisfied, she began to tackle the onerous job of sorting and putting away her belongings. She knew it would depress her to come home to an unmade bed and cluttered rooms. Besides, her pulse was beating so rapidly in anticipation of what the priest might reveal about Tomas, she needed to distract her thoughts.

With plenty of time to spare, she hopped into her car to drive down toward the northern end of Nerja where she was to meet the priest for lunch at the Garden Restaurant at the Hotel Carabeo. From the small outdoor dining area, she looked out upon the large expanse of the Mediterranean waters that dropped precipitously beneath her gaze. Margaret cogitated . . . the movement of water or a fire in a fireplace always has a calming effect. Right now, she needed some calm. Margaret allowed the sight of the sea to offer its powers of tranquility before Father Eduardo entered the restaurant. Five minutes later, he came toward Margaret with a grin that reflected his happiness at seeing her.

After they exchanged the usual pleasantries about the weather, how her classes were proceeding, and what selections they would make from the menu, the priest began to shower questions upon Margaret. "What have you been up to these days, Margaret? You seem to be all over the place from the tennis courts, teaching, and now

Madrid." With a kind smile and a bit of a laugh, "What gives?"

Margaret, returned his smile, drew a long breath and launched into her prepared response. With her voice rising and falling, "On my flight from Boston to Madrid, there was a businessman from Spain seated next to me. He was with another man, and they were heavily engaged in rapid conversation in Spanish and French, so I understood nothing. However, my seat mate and I got to talking briefly while we ate. He told me that he had lived in the States for a time and flew back and forth quite frequently. We shared reminiscences of Boston and our love of Italian food and lobsters." To this, the priest let out a hearty guffaw.

"Immediately after the meals had been served, the pilot came on to warn of inclement weather." Father Eduardo joined her laughter as in unison they said, "Isn't that always the case?"

Margaret continued, "This man was so solicitous during the rocky portions of the flight. In addition, when we landed in Madrid, he offered his business card if I were to need assistance during my stay. I was so grateful to him."

"I had no reason to reach him, but ran into him when I was out with Luis one day." The priest's eyebrows raised in sudden surprise. Margaret quickly rushed ahead with her story. She explained, "Luis was using me as his model while he sketched me in front of the yachts docked at the marina in Puerto Banus."

"Ah," the priest responded, nodding.

"Anyway, we spoke briefly and this gentleman took my phone number. I wasn't expecting to hear from him."

At this, Father Eduardo laughed a knowing laugh. "Margaret, you're an attractive, bright, and witty woman.

Why wouldn't a man want to seek out your company?" Margaret, though startled by the priest's remark, took pleasure from it.

Blushing, she added, "Well, we did meet for dinner and got to talking about our interests and his business. It turned out that we both like tennis. He also is involved in getting together a major business conference, and, before I knew it, I was itemizing all the features that needed to be addressed. Ergo, that's how I landed in Madrid."

Their lunch was delivered, and Margaret felt as if she'd been given a reprieve. She'd managed to summarize a rather long, involved story, delivered it truthfully, but revealed no details that would embarrass her or Tomas.

As they ate, Margaret mulled over how she might broach the subject of Tomas. She really hoped the priest could, and would, fill in a lot of the gaps. She felt her head spinning. She thought she'd planned her strategy, but now she wasn't sure.

As if by some miracle, Father Eduardo handed her an opening as his words came gushing forth, "This man . . . that you met on the plane . . . what business is he in? What kind of a conference is he running? For whom?"

Margaret couldn't stop herself. A huge twinkle formed in her eyes as she responded succinctly and in a most pseudo-casual voice, "Oh, the olive and olive oil business."

She had to contain her laughter as the priest's jaw dropped simultaneously with his eyes bulging. "Really," he wheezed.

Margaret nodded. She was prepared now for his follow-up question.

"Who is this man?"

Margaret knew she'd only have to speak one word, "Tomas."

"Tomas," the priest repeated heavily accenting the second syllable and exhibiting a look of incredulity.

To which, Margaret burst out laughing. " You two do have quite a history."

"And, just what has Tomas imparted, pray tell"?

Margaret realized that the priest was not going to reveal anything which would compromise his friendship with Tomas or the confidentiality he upheld as an ecclesiastic. "Well, I know you both go back a long way," Margaret commenced, "and you must have had one hell of a time together in the States." Margaret's hand flew up to her mouth, "Oh, excuse me, Father."

Father Eduardo, again, burst out laughing. "It's okay, Margaret. You obviously have been made aware that I've had a former life and have heard it all before." Then, his thoughts seemed to lose themselves in that history. His voice drifted off and appeared to be coming from another place. "Yes, Tomas and I, our families go back a long way." With an enormous boyish grin he added sotto voce, "and we did have one hell of a good time in the States! Ah me, it seems light years away and on another planet. And, just what did Tomas impart with regard to those bygone days? Whatever he told you, we weren't really all that bad," the priest chortled.

"I know that," Margaret responded lightly. "Tomas said that your families were both olive growers and had been friends for generations. When you began college at Siena, I guess Tomas took you under his wing. It sounded as if you both not only enjoyed many similar interests, but you, also, enjoyed one another's company."

"Yes, very much," the priest concurred. "Tomas helped me greatly through a kid's initial homesickness. And, remember, being from Spain, we were very far from our families. It was so reassuring to have someone in my life who had experienced those doubts and longings upon leaving home. No one in either of our families had ever done this. My financial support came from my family in Spain, but my emotional support came from Tomas. I was very lucky to have him in such close proximity."

"I know you saw a lot of each other while Tomas was living in New York City."

"We also saw a lot of each other when Tomas entered the MBA program at Harvard. Driving between Loudonville, NY to New York City or to Boston is very doable."

The dessert menu was offered. Each of them sensed there was more ground to cover. Dessert and coffee would prolong this interlude. As they made their selections, Margaret reflected. All this interchange had added no new knowledge or cast any new light with regard to Tomas. Father had merely confirmed all she knew. How was she to probe without pushing the boundaries? How far could the priest step out of his role?

Perhaps it was the lay clothing the priest was wearing today, or the fact that she'd ignited memories for him that pre-dated his entering the priesthood, Margaret saw him for the first time as Eddie. In all those years of parochial school and worship at the Church, Margaret had always held the clergy as an entity separate from other worldly species. Suddenly, Margaret let down her guard. Somehow, the courage rose within her, "May I talk to you, not as a priest, but as a friend, Tomas' friend and mine?" With this mention of Tomas name, the love she felt for him came oozing through. As she sought the answers in Eduardo's face, she knew the sound of her voice had not gone unnoticed.

"How well do you know Tomas," the priest ventured.

"Well," was all Margaret replied, yet it was the equivalent of a thousand words.

She sat silently letting Father Eduardo collect his thoughts and construct his own depiction of the relationship.

She continued, "While we were in Madrid, Tomas was summoned to the olive groves due to some faulty equipment and the fact that the foreman had called in sick. Tomas seemed quite agitated when he left. I'd managed to check with him during the day, and he seemed very annoyed and elusive, very unlike his usual self. When he returned, he was totally spent. I understood that he was exhausted from the drive and from the task of retooling the equipment. However, he had no desire to talk about his day. It seemed as if he had been suffering unbearable pain."

After what seemed an interminable silence, the priest finally began.

"I guess I've known Tomas all my life. His family and mine were such close friends . . . really like family. With Tomas being older than I, I looked upon him as one of my older brothers. Tomas had no brothers, so when I got to the States, I guess he treated me as a younger member of his clan.

"And, as you've heard from both of us, we did have terrific times together. However, although I had several different female acquaintances throughout those years, Tomas was heavily involved with only one." Now, the priest's face turned pensive, "They were truly in love."

Now drawn into an almost dream-like state, Father Eduardo continued, "Cassie was a tall statuesque blond, long-legged, chiseled features, porcelain skin, with bright blue eyes and an intellect to match. She was an expert horsewoman, played a good game of tennis, was a competitive golfer, and swam with elegant strokes. In addition to possessing all the 'country club' attributes, Cassie loved to hike and bike as well."

Margaret sensed an almost reverent tone each time he pronounced Cassie's name. "What happened to Cassie?" Margaret almost demanded to know.

The priest paused to catch his breath. Margaret guessed that he was wondering if he were going too far in exposing his friend's life.

After another pregnant pause, Father continued, "Tomas had met Cassie when they were both at Berkeley. When they'd graduated and Tomas moved east, he asked Cassie to join him. They were sharing an apartment in New York City when I met up with them. Later, she took a job in Boston to accommodate Tomas who was pursuing his MBA at Harvard. They truly made an ideal couple.

"I sincerely believe that if it were just the two of them, they'd be happily married today with a house full of gorgeous, bright offspring," the priest mused with the hint of a remorseful smile.

At this point, Margaret was bursting with curiosity and dread, "What happened?"

"Well," Father Eduardo continued, "They each had families."

At this juncture in the story, the waitress set the bill on the table and interrupted the flow of conversation. Margaret and the priest rummaged through purse and wallet, respectively, to extract a credit card. They then began the ritual, oft-practiced after the meal dance performed to determine who would foot the bill. "You paid last time." "No, you paid last." Margaret, anxious to return to the priest's tale, laughed and said, "Why don't we just split it down the middle." That agreed upon, Margaret urged the priest to continue.

"Where was I? Oh yes, they each had a family." At this thought, the priest shook his head. "Tomas had met Cassie's family on many occasions when they were students at Berkeley. Her folks owned a home in the California hills, and Tomas often joined them there or at their country club. Tomas reportedly felt that he was treated with respect and enjoyed his times with Cassie and her folks. Still, Tomas knew they had their reservations. After all, Tomas was from Spain, Catholic, and not of their country club set.

Cassie, for her part, reasoned that Tomas was not a practicing Catholic; he had the finest education; and, although her folks viewed his family as farmers, they were actually running a, quite comfortably-fixed, business corporation. Besides, she loved Tomas and wanted to spend the rest of her life with him. In general, Cassie had always trusted her instincts. They'd served her well, and she'd been happy with her choices thus far.

One Christmas, after he'd completed the MBA program, Tomas had brought Cassie home to Spain. All went smoothly. However, there was a sharp contrast between Cassie and his sisters and with the family's secluded lifestyle. Cassie appeared restless after a few days among the orchards, and she and Tomas left to tour the Spanish countryside and neighboring Portugal.

Although Tomas' family did not openly disapprove of Tomas' choice, they noted the fact that Cassie was not Catholic nor seemingly inclined to live out her life in Spain. Tomas, being the only male heir, was expected to take charge of the family's growing olive conglomerate. He'd been allowed to go to the United States for his business education with the expressed intent of returning home to take up the reins."

Then, with a rueful laugh, the priest added, ". . . 'to take up the reins' seems like an apt phrase. I do believe Tomas must have viewed himself as a young stallion having been put out to pasture, allowed to kick up his heels, to gallop freely, but then forced to return to the barn to live out his days as a workhorse and stud.

"No sooner than he and Cassie had returned to Boston, Tomas' mom passed away. Tomas was called home; never to return to Cassie."

Margaret gasped and leaned toward the priest. She was itching to hear more of the story. With the waitress hanging over their table, Father Eduardo suggested that they head for the caves and he'd continue there.

Margaret didn't know how she could keep her automobile firmly on the roads. She was so anxious to get to the caves and hear the rest of this saga. Her heart was breaking for Tomas. What a dirty deal he'd been handed. But, what had actually been his deal? She'd just have to wait through all the traffic lights to have her curiosity satisfied. Why is it when you are in the greatest hurry, every traffic light is red?

She rushed to his car as she saw the priest approaching the caves and walked with him down into the deep, dark passages. Margaret did not say a word, but Father Eduardo knew she was waiting for him. Teasingly, he questioned, "I can't imagine that there's more I can tell you or that you'd want to know?" At this Margaret's mouth fell open and no sound came forth. The priest laughed and then became solemn, "As soon as the mourning period was over for Tomas' mom, life at the orchards began to settle into a daily routine of checking market prices, supervising workmen, fixing equipment, phoning potential clients, and dining around the large kitchen table with his dad, his two sisters and their husbands.

"Tomas had written to me at this time; I still have the letter. It was similar to a letter he'd sent to Cassie. In it, he poured out his insurmountable grief and despair.

"He had loved his mother deeply, and missed her presence in their home. More than that, he missed his life with Cassie. Yet, he was drawn home as the dutiful son and necessary heir to the family's means of support. His father was, by nature, a superior business man, but he was growing elderly and in failing health. His dad could not maintain the pace the business demanded if it were to remain a success. Tomas observed his brothers-in-law and realized that, while they were fine men, they were not equipped to run the organization. All their incomes would suffer.

"Tomas felt assured that he could return to the United States, marry Cassie, and find employment or start a business that would feed their little family very well. He knew that he and Cassie could surmount all obstacles and lead a very happy life together.

"However, taking that option would feel disloyal and would leave his family in Spain in the lurch. The orchards were a defining part of his heritage and of himself. He could not turn his back on them.

"He begged Cassie to join him. She wavered in her decision. But, in the end, she could not bring herself to move across an ocean, far from her family and friends to a life that bode more tranquility than a young, cosmopolitan woman would crave."

Margaret interjected, in a somewhat impatient tone, "I still don't understand why Tomas was so curt with me on the phone and so miserable after returning from the orchards." The priest put out his hand to lightly touch Margaret's arm in a gesture of stemming her impatience while leading her into one of the narrow, deserted, and dimly lit corners of the caves. "I am getting to that," he assured her.

"Tomas worked long-hard hours at the business. At night, he sat around watching his brothers-in-law playing cards, his father watching television, and his sisters doing needlepoint. Life must have seemed very routinized and agonizingly dull for a young man accustomed to exciting campus life, thriving metropolises, and a vibrant, young woman at his side.

At about that point, I lost touch with Tomas. In preparation for taking my final vows as a Franciscan, I entered the monastic life." Margaret sighed audibly. She could not conceal her growing anxiety that she would never get to the source of Tomas' angst. She could hear the continuous dripping of water seeping within the cave that enfolded them; it added to her melancholy.

The priest continued, "It wasn't until I returned to Spain, as a young priest in my first assignment, that I again had an opportunity to meet face to face with Tomas.

Tomas was one of the first people I telephoned. As I recall, his voice sounded strained. We made arrangements to meet for dinner. Since we hadn't seen each other for a few years, we were eagerly looking forward to the evening.

"When I first spied Tomas walking toward me, I noticed how much he'd aged. He no longer walked with his old bouncy gait.

"After the usual formalities, Tomas asked if he could speak frankly. I, of course, reassured him that he could. We had a history. Neither of us had ever divulged any of our past conversations or talked with anyone about our escapades in America. That night, Tomas spoke freely.

"Tomas' father was now quite frail and had pretty much relinquished the chain of command to Tomas. With Tomas as the head of the business and the household, you would have thought Tomas would have had the final say as to his personal future. That was not to be the case, however.

"Apparently, shortly after Tomas had returned to Spain, his father kept inviting another of his olive-growing buddies to come 'round the house for dinners, Sundays after church, or in the evenings for a beer. As was the case with my own family, these families had known one another for generations and socialized quite regularly. Anyway, when this man came to visit, he'd often bring his daughter along, ostensibly as company for Tomas' sisters. Although Liliana is about five years older than Tomas, we all knew her from the time she was a young girl. She was always presentable, sweet, active in the church, a decent sort of person. Now, Tomas' dad wanted him to marry Liliana."

Margaret couldn't stand it another second and interjected, "What happened to Cassie?"

The priest responded with a quick laugh, "That's just what I'd asked Tomas that night. He had seen Cassie a couple of times when he made business trips to the States, but their time together was not as of old. It seems neither of them would back down. Cassie wanted him in America; he felt he had a duty to remain in Spain. An across-the-Atlantic relationship did not appear feasible. It just felt like a hopeless situation for both of them." And as an aside, the priest added, "You must remember that this was before the time of faxes, modems, e-mail, conference calls, cheaper phone rates, cell phones, text messages and Skype, and before people were flying so frequently for business."

Margaret nodded. She could comprehend the situation Tomas faced. However, in retrospect, she didn't believe she'd ever experienced such filial devotion.

"Liliana's a kind, decent and presentable woman. She loves to cook, is a good mother, and maintains an immaculate household. I rarely have contact with her and haven't seen nor heard from Tomas in several years.

"I've been able to piece together some of Tomas' more recent goings on from snitches and snatches of conversations. Since it is mostly rumor, innuendo and gossip, I won't repeat what I've heard."

The priest didn't see Margaret's crestfallen expression. He had glanced at his watch and almost choked, "Margaret, do you know what time it is? We've been talking the entire afternoon. I have a board of directors meeting at my office in half an hour. I must leave immediately. I'll barely make it." As he hastened to leave, Margaret thanked him for his time and for sharing so much with her.

The caves were closing to the public, but Margaret walked slowly through the labyrinth trying to collect her thoughts in the calm of the underground. The priest had told her a lot, but there were still so many unanswered questions. Why hadn't Tomas ever mentioned his wife? Why were there no pictures of Liliana in his condo on the Costa del Sol? How did he manage to spend weekends with Margaret? With all the information Father Eduardo had imparted, Margaret was still at square one. Were Tomas and his wife separated? Divorced? Still married, but living apart? Was it an arrangement they both agreed upon or was it decided unilaterally?

Margaret now knew that Tomas' wife existed. And, Margaret surmised she must live at the orchards. Perhaps, that was the reason Tomas was so upset when he was there on Saturday. Had they argued? Had she found out about Margaret? Was Margaret one of a long list of Tomas' flings? No, she couldn't believe that. Was Margaret being delusional?

Maybe she'd learn more when she spent the coming weekend on Tomas' yacht? Poor Tomas. Instead of marrying the one woman he'd really loved, he was maneuvered into an arranged marriage. She felt such love and pity for him. No, Tomas would not want pity. He did what he felt he had to do, and probably with no remorse.

She started up the engine of her car and smoothly slid from first to second and into third gear as she drove from the caves through the now-familiar streets of Nerja to her welcoming abode.

CHAPTER 23

THROUGHOUT THE WEEK, MARGARET SEARCHED for the remaining clues. As determined as she was to find the priest and complete their talk, she could not locate him. When she did, he was surrounded by a group of school children. It seemed as if Father Eduardo did not wish to continue their conversation regarding Tomas. Margaret was on an emotional see-saw.

She was looking forward to spending the weekend on Tomas' yacht. She adored being in his presence. His kindly, gentle manner, his sense of humor, his delight in her and in their shared interests, and their satisfying lovemaking all gave her delicious pleasure. She knew she had fallen in love with this man and ached to be in his company.

Yet, all of her being was telling her to step away. "Once burned, twice shy," her mother used to say. Margaret was instinctively trying to protect herself. She knew she could not bear further rejection; she'd suffered enough from the Cleary clan.

These thoughts gyrated through her head; the proverbial emotional roller coaster. Overtly, she went about her daily tasks, but her brain was continually in a spin. Her heart was heavy one moment and light-hearted the next.

When Tomas phoned each evening, she did not mention her luncheon conversation with Eduardo nor verbalize her misgivings. However, Tomas seemed to grasp her feelings. His voice, always calm and reassuring, elaborated on their weekend plans. He drew a mental picture for her of the yacht, which waters they would ply, where they could swim, what they would eat, what clothing would be needed. He named a marina where they would tie up on Saturday evening to enjoy an elegant, superb dinner.

Occasionally, some of his guy friends or his son or daughter accompanied him on board; but, Tomas intimated that, other than his daughter, Margaret was the first woman to join him. His enthusiasm for the upcoming weekend and his intense desire to be with her buoyed Margaret's spirits. By Friday, she was as much looking forward to the weekend as he.

She drove into a visitor's parking spot at the condo shortly after three in the afternoon and transferred her belongings into Tomas' Alfa Romeo whereupon they headed directly to the marina. Tomas had stocked up on all the necessary provisions. He had purchased salad ingredients, juice, wine, beer, coffee, fresh breads. Margaret had prepared a spinach lasagna and the makings of an egg souffle; both of which she'd frozen and would simply require reheating.

Tomas quickly located *The Respite*. Margaret caught the significance of the name. The happiest days for Tomas, apparently, had been as a youth in an English- speaking country. In America, he had found peace and contentment. This modest yacht now offered healing and release from the cares of his work and personal circumstances.

He proudly conducted Margaret through a tour of the deck, galley, two heads containing tight-fitting showers, and sleeping quarters for six. It was a compact affair, but comfortable. A little city . . . self- contained. The teak trim was beautiful and the furnishings sleek and modern.

Margaret sensed that *The Respite* was a truer reflection of Tomas than the more impersonal style of his condo. Here, there were pictures of his children Antonio and Maritza, of his fishing buddies, his parents, and of himself. Margaret commented on some lovely acrylic paintings. There were renderings of the yacht and of vividly colored flowers and gardens. Tomas held up the picture of his daughter, Maritza, and said, "Doesn't she do beautiful work? I believe she inherited her mother's ability with her hands. I am trying to encourage her talent."

This was Margaret's signal. She rapidly settled herself on a small settee located beneath the deck and patted the seat beside her while motioning Tomas to sit. She had found her opening, and so in a soft voice, asked him, " And, just where is Maritza's mother now? I feel I need to know."

When she saw Tomas' dejected expression, she covered his hand lightly with hers, "I don't want to press you. If you cannot talk about it now, I'll be patient."

"No, I guess this is as good a time as any. With our feelings escalating, I realize we have to be honest with each other regarding our circumstances . . . no matter how disquieting the conversation."

To save him from having to go through all the painstaking memories, Margaret quickly glossed over the information she'd gathered from Father Eduardo regarding Cassie and Liliana. Tomas continually nodded his head throughout Margaret's recitation. "Eddie certainly enlightened you. He did me a favor by sparing me from having to tell you myself. He really wasn't evading you, because he doesn't know my present circumstances."

At this juncture, Tomas reached out for Margaret's hand and escorted her to the upper reaches of the yacht. While climbing to the deck, he continued, "It will be more pleasant continuing my story up here." Indeed, the sea's undulating waters lulled the senses and the water slapping against the sides of the yacht emitted a comforting sound.

"Father Eduardo got it right. My marriage was one that was arranged and not to my choosing. I was deeply in love with Cassie and heartsick at not consummating that relationship. After Liliana and I were married, I desperately tried to make it work. In her way, I believe Liliana did, too. We were just too disparate human beings. We shared nothing except the love of our families and of the land.

"When my children were little, I spent a lot of time with them. They were my outlet. On weekends, I would take them skiing, horseback riding, or traveling to another town or city. Finally, I purchased this boat for short excursions. Their mother had no interest in leaving the house nor the grounds save going to church.

"As the kids became teenagers, I convinced Liliana that their education would benefit from the schools in Madrid. To this day, I don't know if this was accurate or merely my rationalization for setting up housekeeping in Madrid. Anyway, I took a large apartment in the city for the children and me, while Lilana continued to reside in the country.

"Often, Maritza and her brother went back to the orchards for the weekend while I spent the time in New York or back at the little condo near the marina. As I told you once before, I spent my time working, or out on this boat with my friends, or off at the tennis courts or health club.

"Only when business demands it, do I return to oversee the olive trees. Mainly, I leave the running of the day-to-day operations to my brothers-in-law and to the hired foreman.

"Last weekend when I was called back to the property, I hated and resented having to leave you. I had been looking forward to spending every minute with you. Managing the business suddenly seemed horribly onerous. And, Liliana is peeved that I am rarely there to manage the estate, or the business, or to keep up appearances that we are still a married couple. Always, I had loved being in the home where I grew up and wandering the property and working the land. Now, I dread going home to my birthplace. When I leave it, I feel drained."

Although Margaret nodded her understanding, they remained in silence for several minutes. Tomas' pain hung heavily in the air.

Saying softly, "I guess that's why I heard a sharpness in your voice when you were talking to me from the orchards. I thought that you were annoyed with me."

"No," he said emphatically. "I was not upset with you. Margaret, you have brought me such hope and happiness for the first time in, oh, so many years. When I am with you, it is the pure joy that I experienced with Cassie and still enjoy with my offspring. My only fear is that at some point you will return to the States. By God . . . ," his voice now hushed, "I don't want to lose you. I already have absorbed so much pain."

His shoulders drooped as his voice dropped. The sincerity of his words was not lost on her. Margaret choked back a sob and drew him to her. Margaret gently stroked the back of his head, his neck, his back. Tomas rested his head on Margaret's shoulder. Nothing more was said.

They sat quietly for some time, each in his own thoughts. Slowly, Tomas led them toward the helm and deftly started the motor. The yacht put out to sea.

They sailed along in continued silence, enjoying the smell of the salt air and the moist spray licking their faces. When dusk blanketed them, Tomas pulled into an uninhabited cove and dropped anchor.

The stars rose one by one. Pulling her toward him, Tomas identified Orion's belt, the Dipper, and Cassiopeia's Chair, the five brightest stars in the heavens. As the darkened sky filled with stars, Margaret thought she'd never seen so many thousands lighting up the view. It was an awe-inspiring sight.

Beyond prying eyes and with only the stars to guide them, they moved together as if in a choreographed ballet. Tomas drew her toward him. They locked together in a deep embrace. Slowly, very slowly, Tomas unbuttoned each button in turn, kissing her lips, her neck, her shoulders while he continued down the front of her blouse. They progressively disrobed as if in a magical trance. Now, moving toward the deck floor, Tomas slowly and carefully rolled Margaret onto her belly. He dug deeply into her as he drew her buttocks toward him. When he was finished, he was startled to hear Margaret quietly, but uncontrollably, sobbing.

"What's the matter?" He turned her body toward his and, lovingly, cupped his hands around her face. When Margaret continued to cry, Tomas asked, "Are you crying for joy, or did I do something awful?"

Margaret continued to sob while shaking her head. Now, Tomas was utterly perplexed. What had happened? What had he done?

It was quite some time before Margaret was composed enough to blurt out, in between sobs, "I'm sorry. I don't know why I reacted this way. The only thing I can think of is that many years ago when my sons were very young and had the flu, I had been left alone all day with the children. Never once did my husband phone to find out how the boys were feeling or how I was managing. By nighttime, I had come down with the virus and felt like I wanted to die. I was running a high fever and tossing my cookies and running to the bathroom and all the time trying to get the boys comfortable and settled down for the night."

"Why didn't YOU call your husband, or find a friend or ask your sister for help?"

Margaret, at first, couldn't respond. Her voice quivered with soft wails. In staccato bursts she whispered, "I don't know. I guess I was used to relying on myself. I know I was praying for someone to take care of us, but I was too busy taking care of the boys and me to find the time. Also, I was so worn out, I don't think I would have had the strength to pick up the phone and explain. Once the boys were asleep, I just dosed myself with the medication the doctor had prescribed and finally collapsed.

"Late into the night, Andrew came home. He'd had too much to drink and pounced into bed trying to turn my body to suit him. I guess he couldn't flip me over. I was dead to the world . . . he . . . he . . . he . . . mounted me . . . like a dog."

Margaret began to cry uncontrollably. Her entire body shook.

Now it was Tomas' turn to say, "I'm sorry."

"It's, it's, its not your fault. How would you have known", Margaret asked, now trying to reassure Tomas.

"When this happened, I was burning with fever and proceeded to heave into the pot beside my bed. I'm afraid my memories are not very pretty."

"What was your husband's reaction? By then, he must have realized how sick you were."

"Oh, he did," she replied while still sobbing gently. "He left to spend the night in our guest room. He didn't want to catch what I had. I guess it was the first time I allowed myself to see how selfish, self-centered, and inconsiderate Andrew was. My feelings for him altered from then on."

Margaret and Tomas sat in stunned silence until her racking sobs subsided. It was almost too much to absorb. After all these weeks, they'd finally spilled their guts.

Her disclosure must have resonated with Tomas as well. He held her tightly, stroking her head, purring into her ear. Gently, always gently. He held her close to him and lightly massaged Margaret's back until he sensed her body relax.

Margaret felt safe with this man. She suspected that he would not hurt her, at least, not intentionally. He held her close until she was lulled into a peaceful, dreamless sleep.

There, on the deck, Margaret had fallen into an exhausted sleep in Tomas' arms.

Sometime during the night, Tomas must have helped Margaret into bed. She had no recollection of the event, but awoke in the yacht's cabin. She heard Tomas' rhythmic breathing and sighed a sigh of contentment.

It was still dark. Lying there, she thought, once again, of her confession of pain which she'd poured out to Tomas last night. Margaret, while feeling emotionally depleted, also, felt a wave of relief wash over her. It was as if a sore or wound, that had been festering for years, was suddenly healing.

While Tomas still slept, she rose to a bright sunrise awaiting her on the deck. Since her arrival in Nerja, Margaret could not recall many days without clear, blue skies. The Costa del Sol (Sun Coast) was aptly named.

Gazing out on the waters, Margaret saw a sparkling array of colors . . . shadings of blues, yellows, greens, aquamarine, pinks, and white. The sea was as a magnificent diamond surrounding her with its brilliance, capturing her with not only its beauty, but also with the sense of freedom it evoked. Margaret luxuriated in the surge of pleasure and inner peace.

So much had happened within the past year. Had it been such a short time ago when Margaret was in the depths of despair? Her marriage eroded, her status in limbo?

Since that fateful day in Andrew's office, Margaret's life had been totally dismembered. Upon reflection, she recalled being unable to function. Her once immaculate home became riddled with dirty dishes and an unmade bed, what little food she ate was taken while standing at the sink or in front of the refrigerator, phone calls remained unanswered, e-mail unopened. Days were spent alone in fits of crying jags.

She had never been closer to feeling suicidal. How had she survived? How had she ever moved forward? What inner strength had helped her? What propelled her to this place?

Her dear friend, Missy, and her sister, Eileen, had been her rocks. Through their persistent encouragement, she was able to will herself to gather her resources, to repair and reposition. Margaret had often preached to her sons that tomorrow always held promise. Now, as she looked out upon these waters and upon Tomas who was coming up the steps to greet her, she knew she had found her tomorrow.

But, what would they say to each other? She was hit with a wave of embarrassment. They had been so forthcoming last night. Only people who are traveling can open up like that to perfect strangers; they know they'll never cross paths again.

How were she and Tomas to face one another?

Rely on Tomas! As he reached the boat's deck, he contorted his body into a huge stretch and exclaimed, "What a glorious day. Hey, you're looking much more relaxed and chipper than last night. That's good. I was worried about you. Come, I brought these. Have a look."

Tomas handed her a pair of binoculars. The Coast was clearly visible.

"I can almost make out Nerja from here," she told him. "What am I seeing to my left?"

"Oh, let me look. Probably San Roque. We're seeing most of the Coast from here."

He handed the binoculars back to Margaret. She continued to marvel at the sparkling waters beneath them that were pushing toward the beautiful carpet of white-sand beaches along the shoreline, beyond which rose the modern high-rises and ancient white Andalusian homes built into, and surrounded by, the rugged mountains. Wafting from somewhere came the mixed aromas of jasmine and honeysuckle.

"This is Heaven," Margaret sighed, and stood enraptured for several minutes.

"Last one in is a rotten egg."

She followed Tomas' lead and plunged into the waters of the cove. The cold water left her gasping, but invigorated. As she swam, Margaret felt cleansed and refreshed. She suddenly understood the symbolic rituals of the Catholic baptism and the Jewish mikva. Water permitted the purification of body and soul. She was in a state of ecstacy, tensions gone.

CHAPTER 24

THEY EACH GRABBED FOR TOWELS as they emerged from the chilly water. With barely a wisp of movement, Tomas brushed his lips lightly against her forehead. Margaret shivered. "Is that what I do to you?" He laughed to see Margaret's grin.

While giving her a playful pat on the rear he said, "Why don't you go and get a hot shower. Just don't use up all the hot water; I'm feeling a bit nippy, too."

Margaret proceeded down to the head. She could hear Tomas off in the kitchen.

When she was sufficiently warm and cleansed, she toweled off and donned her bikini and coverup.

"Your turn to shower," she yelled to him. "Hope there's still some hot water remaining, or I'll be in hot water." He laughed as he quickly stepped into the small stall.

So often now, he felt himself laughing aloud. He realized that he was truly happy. He needed a woman like Margaret in his life. Someone who really enjoyed living, tasting all that life offered. She heartily gave of herself. A beautiful person inside and out.

After Margaret's response last night, Tomas felt his intuition validated. Margaret was so receptive to love and appreciative of kindness. They had been grievously lacking in her marriage of that he was sure.

Margaret followed the coffee aroma as it beat a path to the galley. She was pleasantly surprised to see that eggs and bits of cheese were sitting in a bowl, thoroughly beaten; bacon was simmering in a fry pan on the small stove; and bread was arranged in the toaster slots waiting to be crisped. Two trays were set with unbreakable plates, utensils, napkins and plastic juice glasses.

As soon as she heard the water cut off in Tomas' shower, she quickly removed the bacon and patted down the grease with a paper towel; poured most of the grease from the fry pan into an empty coffee tin which sat on the counter; and proceeded to scramble the eggs. With one eye on the eggs, she poured some orange juice into the waiting containers. As she gave a last stir to the eggs, Tomas arrived to pour the coffee.

They worked in silence. Margaret believed that, after last night's gut-wrenching, emotionally-draining confessional, they had a tacit agreement to keep today's conversations light and impersonal.

Seated at the table on deck, they ate with rarely a word passing between them. It was not an awkward stillness, however, but almost a relief.

Since neither had eaten much last night, they hungrily attacked the meal. When they finally came up for air after the last of the coffee, Margaret spoke in an off-hand tone, "You know I hadn't mentioned this, but I was flabbergasted at how clean Madrid seemed as opposed to five years ago. Even the buildings all looked as if they'd been washed, waxed, and polished until they gleamed. And, all this building! There are new structures rising everywhere the eye can see, here on the Coast . . . and in Madrid. What gives? Is Spain that prosperous?"

"Well, Spain was doing well until this current recession. Many in the European Community had been benefitting from the new arrangements. But as far as all the new construction and clean up . . . yes, you are right."

He said nothing further, but seemed to be searching for the right words. Averting his eyes, he continued, "When the euro was instituted as currency, there were individuals holding pesetas unknown to the government. To avoid paying taxes, people sought investments where the money would not be traced. Hence, the building and cleanup." He finished his sentence with an awkward grin of amusement, as if to say, "Isn't that typical anywhere in the world?" Margaret returned a knowing smile, but said nothing.

They let the words hang in the air. Was Tomas one of those individuals whose money needed laundering? Margaret decided not to go there. There had been enough soul searching last night; let sleeping dogs lie.

They reached for the soiled tableware and proceeded below deck. Compatibly, they washed and dried the breakfast dishes. Tomas remarked, "I had hoped that we could sail today, but, thus far, there's no wind in sight."

"Maybe it will pick up later, but I'm perfectly happy to stretch out on deck."

Indeed, the sun was rising higher in the horizon, and Margaret settled into a comfortable, spacious lounge chair and opened a book she was reading. "The Secret Lives of Bees" had once been on the best-seller list, and she was immensely enjoying re-reading it . She read rapidly while admiring the beautiful writing of its author.

Her body gave a spasmodic jerk as she awakened from sleep. The sun's heat must have lulled her into slumber.

She looked about and saw Tomas at a nearby table. His body engulfed in piles of papers covered with numerical columns. Could all that apply to the olive groves and their production?

"My, my you never stop working! I never knew that all those little olives could produce so many columns of figures. There appears to be one column for every tree."

Tomas chuckled, and threw her an appreciative glance, but gave no sign of going into details regarding his business enterprise.

Margaret did not continue her questioning, but felt as if there were so many intricacies surrounding Tomas. Did he think of her in that light? She thought she'd been rather forthright with him, particularly considering last night. But then, he'd unburdened a lot himself. Slowly, slowly they were unfolding. It's so different, she mused. They each had a long history. It's not as if we're still in our teens or early twenties where a few sentences just about sewed up your bio.

As the heat bore down, Tomas stopped, carefully returned his paperwork to his attache case, and suggested a swim. Margaret welcomed the suggestion, and they dove off the side of the boat into the cooling waters.

They swam steadily for almost half an hour until each was breathless. Tomas caught Margaret and held her to him. He kissed her soundly as they bobbed above the waters. The heat of the sun mixed with the lapping of the waters heightened sensations in all their nerve endings. They quickly swam to shore, and Tomas had both their suits stripped by the time they'd hit the deck.

Holding Margaret in one arm, Tomas worked the mechanism on the rear of the large lounge chair until it reclined fully. Margaret settled on her side leaving room for Tomas. She expected Tomas, who was obviously aroused, to jump right in. Gently, ever gently he kissed and fondled. Finally, unable to restrain himself any longer, Tomas asked, "May I?"

Margaret, wanting nothing less, couldn't choke out the words, but nodded emphatically. Tomas straddled her and slowly proceeded. With a pressured grip on his buttock, Margaret urged him toward her, and they escalated the pace until each was gratified.

"I can't believe I'm acting like this."

"What do you mean?"

Embarrassed now, she hung her head and in a muffled voice continued, "I can't believe I'm so hungry for you . . . for sex. It's so unlike me."

Tomas smiled deeply. "That's how it's supposed to be, Margaret. And, you are delicious. I could have eaten you up out there in the bay."

"Then how come you were taking your time? You seemed so, well . . . hesitant?"

"After last night's description of your husband," his voice rising, "I felt I owed you that."

"Thank you. But," laughingly kissing the tip of his nose, "I think I like it better when you're hungry."

Tomas joined her laughter and enfolded her in a long squeeze. He held her close, exhaled, closing his eyes. He felt satisfied in many ways.

CHAPTER 25

INSTEAD OF TYING UP AT a marina and spending the evening having dinner at a lovely restaurant, they decided to finish off the spinach lasagna Margaret had prepared and dig into the souffle. Perhaps, not a well-balanced diet, but it suited them, nonetheless.

They watched a video of an old classic movie wrapped in each other's arms, and fell asleep to the boat's rhythmic motion.

Margaret awoke to find herself sprawled on the couch and covered with a worn afghan. She inhaled deeply of the aroma of coffee. She brightened hearing Tomas, "Hey, sleepyhead. I thought you'd never waken. There's a wind, and by God, we're going to sail today."

He left the room and returned with a pot of coffee and a tray of cups, a variety of Spanish cheeses and crackers and Boston creme-filled donuts . . . Margaret's favorites. "This is the best I could do for breakfast in bed, considering we fell asleep on the sofa."

"Did you sleep here all night, too?", Margaret queried.

"I woke about two a.m. in such a cramped position, I moseyed off to bed. You were so deeply asleep, I thought it best not to disturb you."

Margaret softly thanked him for his consideration.

They ate quickly, donned shorts, tee shirts, and hats and lathered each other with SP30. He checked the yacht's ship-to-shore radio listening to the Coast Guard and weather reports. His ensuing war whoop reminded her of a kid who'd just discovered a longed-for bike under the Christmas tree. Margaret laughed. He was ready for a day of sailing, or, at the very least, for as long as the wind held.

Tomas scurried on board deck headed toward the mainsail and jib. Straightaway, he set to work unfurling the sails and readying them for action. Margaret's role was very secondary as first mate . . . only giving a hand when Tomas requested. With both sails securely in place, he deftly found the wind and began tacking back and forth.

When she thought it safe, she proceeded to the bow to watch as the boat sailed along chopping the water in its path. Later, Margaret settled back in the lounge chair at one side of the ship and only moved to duck her head when Tomas yelled, "Comin' about!"

It was a glorious day and a beautiful sight to see the sails catching the wind and the boat moving steadily over the sea. Margaret could not remember a happier moment. Tomas, too, seemed exultant; he was in his element.

Margaret gaze was fixated on the boat's movement through the waters. She felt herself relax, contented, almost mesmerized by the choppy Mediterranean.

They were en route for almost an hour when, suddenly, Margaret's body was lurched forward as the wind abruptly picked up its pace. Now, the yacht seemed to be moving of its own accord. She could hear Tomas yelling at her, but her feet could barely hold as she tried to rise.

He was desperately trying to latch onto the rigging in order to release the mainsail and fold it, securely attached, to the main sheet beneath. Margaret could see Tomas in the distance as a driving rain hit their faces. She thought, for sure, Tomas would be knocked out by one of the booms, or one would hit her in the head as she inched her way to the fore of the boat.

As if the torrential downpour were not enough, the rough seas were causing Margaret both fear and a roiling in her stomach. She had all in the world to do to suppress the urge to heave.

Finally within earshot of Tomas, she could hear his voice shouting above the storm, "Douse the sail; release the jib." Clearly, this was not a task for which she was prepared. Even through the curtain of rainwater, Tomas must have read the expression on her face and realized their plight. He quickly tried to wrap the foot of the sail around the boom. He secured the mainsail as best he could and began on the jib. When he thought she might be able to handle it, he put her hands on the mechanisms to finish the job.

"You do this. I'm going to start the motor," he roared above the noise of the weather and water. After several minutes, Margaret listened. Her spirits sagged as she heard nothing and felt no movement that would indicate an engine in use.

Now, the boat was surging from side to side and water was splaying and splashing across the deck. Tomas caught her as she almost slipped across the bow. It was obvious, even to a novice such as Margaret, that they had to get below. Tomas placed both hands under her arms and tried to ease them forward. They were rocketed to and fro barely able to keep upright. As if sensing her fear, Tomas yelled above the squall, "Don't worry, Margaret, we're going to make it. Just keep holding on and moving toward the hatch. I'll put in calls to the Coast Guard from the ship-to-shore radio and from my BlackBerry. They'll be looking for stranded ships." She could barely hear his voice, but caught enough to focus on the mission at hand. After much effort, they finally reached their destination. Together, they lifted the hatch as water continued to pour over the deck. Their soaked feet slipped and slid precariously down the steps while they clung to the banister.

Still being thrown from side to side, now careening back and forth against the walls, Margaret fled to the nearest head where her innards poured into the bowl. Tomas, right behind her, held her head in his hands and softly stroked her brow. As sick as she felt and as deathly afraid, she was able to process that moment when her Dad had held her similarly when she was a very young child. Tomas' actions gave her some comfort and relief.

When her stomach emptied and dry heaves were the norm, Tomas escorted her to a bed. She gratefully fell upon it although the wrenching movement of the boat was increasingly terrifying.

Tomas left her and returned shortly, his face ashen. Since he was ranting in Spanish, Margaret could only assume he was letting out 'expletive deletives'. With desperation in his voice and a sharp tone, "I can't seem to reach the Coast Guard. All their lines are busy or full of static. The yacht's radio is no better; it's all static.

My choices are to ride out the storm with a double anchor, or attempt to bring this sloop into a safe harbor where we can moor for the night. I'll need the motor for that IF the motor is still operable. I'm going topside to try again to start the motor and check the navigational gear.

The compass should point me to shore. Whatever happens, YOU remain below, is that clear?"

Margaret couldn't imagine moving anywhere. The constant surging of the yacht was causing her to feel as if she wanted to die. Neither opening her eyes nor speaking, she merely shook her head in recognition of his request. She wasn't budging.

As he was about to leave the cabin, she roused herself, "Will you be OK on deck? I'm so frightened. Please Tomas, be very careful."

"I'm not planning to get myself killed; I've been in situations like this before." Now, his voice gentle, "Don't worry, Margaret, I'll be all right. I love you."

With that, she could hear his footsteps recede. Her head fell back on the bed, her eyes closed, her body and soul drained. She felt sick and useless, but very loved.

CHAPTER 26

MARGARET AWOKE FROM A FITFUL slumber thinking she must have dreamed of pirates. The voices drifting from above sounded gruff and intense. Were there really pirates on board? It was hard to discern which was reality and which a nightmare?

To her relief, the yacht appeared to be moving more gently. She could no longer hear the howling of the winds. Her watch indicated that she'd slept for maybe twenty minutes. Margaret rose, went to the bathroom to wash, and then to make her way to the deck. She continued to hear several men's voices, but their Spanish was so rapid that she comprehended little.

Slowly, she released the hatch to peek. The rain was more like a drizzle, and she could observe three men standing on the deck facing away from her. They were talking, gesticulating wildly as they hovered around the motor. She eased the hatch higher, and Tomas spotted her. With fatigue and great relief in his voice, "Come here. We are being rescued by the Coast Guard. The Coast Guard had us in their sight. Maybe my SOS had gone through although I didn't hear a response. Anyway, they headed in our direction."

Margaret felt all her fear release in a sudden swish as she crossed to the little cabin housing the motor. She stood beside Tomas and put her hand within his. Gathering her strength, she smiled at the assembled crew and, in Spanish said, "I am so grateful that you are here. I was VERY scared. Thank you, thank you so much." The men looked up in surprise at hearing the accented Spanish and seeing a thatch of red hair on the American woman. They nodded in her direction with hurried smiles and immediately returned to the task of roping the Coast Guard cutter to the large yacht.

Margaret realized that they were going to be towed to shore. She eyed Tomas who had a set, determined look upon his face, but she could not read his thoughts.

There was little conversation between them throughout the remainder of their time on board the yacht or during the ensuing car ride to Tomas' condo. They had merely agreed that neither of them was equipped to drive a distance. Hence, Margaret would spend her first night at Tomas' place.

She was too exhausted to quibble about proprieties and welcomed the bed and Tomas' arms. Neither of them had been hungry for dinner. All their bodies wanted was a rejuvenating sleep.

After an unusually sound sleep, Margaret had to orient herself when her eyes opened. For the first second or two, she was not sure where she was. Then, all of yesterday came rushing back. Margaret felt her body shiver at the memory.

When she looked at the clock on the night table, she could not believe the time. It was 10:15. She hoped it was, at least, morning. Pulling back the drapes, she saw the de rigeur blue skies of Costa del Sol.

Tomas' voice rose from somewhere in the apartment. His rapid Spanish was indistinguishable. He must be on the telephone.

Tomas had taken her small carry-on off the boat last night and laid it on the bedroom dresser. From this, Margaret got out her toiletries and the outfit she'd worn onto the boat. She quickly slid into the bathroom, showered and dressed.

Tomas had defrosted some English muffins, and they sat down to eat. When Margaret heard Tomas' voice, she did not realize he was addressing her. They had barely said a word to each other since the Coast Guard boarded *The Respite*.

Tomas began, "About yesterday," Margaret could feel her stomach tighten into a knot. She could hardly look at him or register what he was saying. She knew he was going to hit her with both barrels. She had to force herself to process what Tomas was continuing to say.

Noting the great agitation and remorse in his voice, she forced herself to focus on his words. Tomas proceeded, "I can't believe I couldn't get that motor started. I had my man check it out this morning. He just phoned to say that there were some wires that were loose and should have been tightened. I guess some water got into them as well. I can't believe my carelessness and irresponsibility. I should have had *The Respite* checked before taking it out this weekend. I apologize to you, Margaret; I put us both in danger. There is no excuse for that."

Margaret appeared confused and quizzical. Before putting head in gear, she quickly blurted out, "You're not blaming me? You're not going to say that I was the cause, that I prevented you from getting the motor serviced, that I didn't give you sufficient help?"

"Why would I do that? How could I blame you? You're not responsible for *The Respite*."

Margaret shrugged, and in a small voice continued, "Because. during the past few years of our marriage, I felt Andrew always blamed ME . . . for whatever went wrong." Margaret's voice trailed off . . . not allowing herself any further thoughts.

Suddenly, Tomas lashed out in a voice full of rage, "Why are you incessantly comparing me to that man you married? Are you always weighing the people you meet, one against the other? Why can't you accept me for who I am and not make comparisons? Everyone has faults and good points. Your ex must have had some good points, or you would not have married him in the first place. I'm beginning to feel as if I'm under a microscope." And, with that, he stormed out of the room.

Margaret sat there stunned. She was so taken aback. She had not expected an explosion toward, what she considered, a compliment to him. She rose, picked up her overnight bag and walked out of the apartment without saying, "Good-bye" or looking back.

Fighting tears, she willed herself not to cry. Margaret struggled to her car which was parked across from Tomas' apartment in a visitor's spot. She sat for a few minutes to steady herself before adjusting her seatbelt and starting the motor. She had her foot on the clutch and was putting the car in reverse when she felt something pounding on the left rear of the convertible.

She could see nothing out the rear view mirror, but immediately saw Tomas approaching the driver's side. She did not roll down her window, nor take her foot off the brake. Her fingers tightened around the stick shift.

Tomas was motioning her to come out. She remained affixed. He, then, motioned for her to lower her window.

She lowered it by an inch and heard herself saying, "I really think I need to get home. We obviously are on different wave lengths, and you aren't happy with me."

"I am very happy with you, Margaret. I wasn't lying to you when I said that you were bringing me back to life, that I love you. I haven't been this content in years. We're both wrought up from yesterday's experience and our nerves are frazzled. Please come back in and let's talk."

"Are you sure there's anything left to be said? I thought you'd said it all."

"I do NOT like you comparing me to your husband. I think of him and me as two very different entities. In addition, I'd hoped that you'd totally forget about him with me in your life. Do you understand how I feel, what I'm saying?"

"Yes . . . I guess I do."

With that, Margaret put the car in park and slowly released the handle. She lowered the car window. "You know I really feel exhausted. Perhaps I should go home. You need to go to work don't you?"

He hesitated, "Yes, I guess I do. But I hate to leave us at this juncture."

Brightening, Margaret paused and said, "How about if I fix us some dinner at my place. Is that OK?"

She could see Tomas' body relax and he beamed. "Yes, that's a great offer. Say about eight o'clock? Would that do?"

When she nodded in approval, he added, "I'll bring the wine." As she was about to drive off, he leaned into the window and placed a butterfly kiss on her forehead. He held her with his eyes in a hypnotic gaze . . . daring her to blink or look away. Margaret felt her tummy turn to mush. She stared back, then finally looked down.

He leaned in again. This time, his lips brushed hers. "Have a good day," he said. "I'll see you tonight. Drive carefully." And, almost in a whisper he added, "I love you."

CHAPTER 27

As HE RETURNED TO HIS apartment, Tomas realized that he'd been on the phone earlier this morning canceling all his appointments in Madrid. Now, what was he to do for the remainder of the day?

He had surmised that he and Margaret would spend the day together after yesterday's horror show on the Mediterranean. They were both so unhinged by the experience. He now realized they were more traumatized than either imagined.

Yesterday's storm had arisen so quickly. He suspected that Margaret realized they were in great danger, but was not fully aware enough to panic and become hysterical. He had tried to keep his fear at bay so as not to incite hers. He would not have had time to deal with that circumstance along with safeguarding the yacht.

Although he was not much of a believer, it was surely a God-send that the Coast Guard arrived when they did. *The Respite* would not have made it back to shore very easily, if at all. There were times he had doubted they'd make it back; there was so much water crashing over the deck. Reliving the memory, he felt as if he could use a drink even if it were only noon.

Instead, he jumped in the shower where he could clear his head. Thoughts came in a rush. Despite his self-warnings, he knew he'd fallen for Margaret. As much as he enjoyed and loved her, he knew the relationship had many challenges, perhaps insurmountable. Was he up to dealing with them? Did he want to?

Margaret was virtually alone, vulnerable, emotionally sensitive and needy. But hadn't he been in that shape years back when he was forced to break his relationship with Cassie to marry Liliana, whom he respected but did not love? Didn't he run from the situation by immersing himself in work, and finally setting up shop in Madrid and New York . . . finding more and more ways to keep him from home?

Margaret was courageous to have left her husband, to have come to Spain. It flew in the face of her upbringing. Furthermore, he knew she was not financially secure.

He had far greater means to deal with his problems. Women in his circles, and he suspected in Margaret's as well, purchased freely . . . loved to shop. He'd noticed that Margaret was frugal in her spending habits, and he assumed, out of necessity. He needed to give Margaret some slack.

If he had to rely on the farm to feed the entire family, they'd be in a sorry state. Tomas had spent years building a corporate base. Now, he had property and businesses here in Malaga and Marbella, in Madrid, the family farm and in New York.

He knew many olive tree growers who subsisted on the outcome of their crops and were at risk of bad weather, poor yields, fluctuating prices, weak markets, and any and all of the dangers that accompany farming. As a result, few of them were men of means. There was a great dichotomy among the olive oil producers which was evident at their annual meetings. At which hotels the representatives stayed, how they dressed, which restaurants they frequented, and, often, their interests, education and worldliness were dependent upon whether or not they were financially successful or teetering on a borderline existence.

As he climbed out of the shower, he realized he could put on some casual clothes. He did not have to go to the office or meet business associates. What WAS he going to do today; a full day without a schedule?

He would check on *The Respite*. Could he have prevented the motor from conking out? He must learn the facts to prevent another occurrence.

And, thank goodness for computers, fax, e-mail and apps. He would track a lot of his stocks, real estate properties, and contact the estate to gather current progress on the olive trees.

Furthermore, he would take time to select a very fine wine for this evening. He might even purchase some excellent olive oils to bring to his hostess.

By the time he was ready to drive to Margaret's, Tomas was well-rested and in a fine fettle. His mind was free of business concerns and free to roam. While driving, it occurred to him, hadn't he contrived means by which he kept his children near him? Having them in school in Madrid, then in New York? Taking his kids skiing, boating, on trips through Europe? Perhaps Margaret was correct in comparing him to Andrew.

Had he dealt squarely with his wife? Perhaps, in some ways, he was as guilty as Andrew. Until Margaret, though, he had never betrayed Liliana's trust. What had made him succumb to Margaret?

So for the ninety-ninth time, he found himself recounting Margaret's attributes. He had found her immediately attractive when she was seated beside him on the airplane. She had that natural, unaffected beauty. Her good health, active lifestyle, and sculptured Irish features shown through. Those high cheek bones, tilted nose were always a plus in his book.

In addition, Margaret had spirit, was smart, looked great in clothes (and without, he thought wickedly). Her warm personality came through, too. Not only he, but also his staff, Eddie, and those she encountered in public were easily drawn to her.

It was scary to him how much he looked forward to being in her company. Furthermore, she certainly mustered a lot of courage and independence to break free. She had left the security of her home with no personal means of support having sacrificed a career to being a homemaker. From bits and pieces, he gleaned that Margaret was a great mom and her sons adored her. In so many ways, he admired her and felt she was perfect for him.

Decisions and actions might have to be made. The obstacles were many. From experience, Tomas knew for every problem, a solution could and would be found. He would see to that.

Tonight, however, he would just enjoy the moment. It was a happy, relaxed Tomas who arrived at Margaret's doorstep.

CHAPTER 28

MARGARET HAD JUST REMOVED SOME canapes from the oven when the doorbell rang. She'd known that he'd be prompt.

As she opened the door, both of them appeared tentative. Tomas gently kissed her on the cheek, and she returned it with a shy smile. Some water had passed over their bridge, both literally and figuratively, and each of them was treading cautiously.

The night had a slight chill in the air, and Tomas proceeded to light a fire in the fireplace. Slowly, he uncorked the wine. Tomas had purchased a blended Rioja and pronounced, "This is a Spanish wine which is considered the world's masterpiece for blended wines."

"I've never heard of such a thing as blended wine. Is it really good?"

"Just you wait and try it, especially with the dinner you've prepared. I believe you'll like it."

She checked the standing rib roast in the oven. Having him in the kitchen beside her, each doing mundane routines, felt familiar and added to their comfort level. By the time they'd seated themselves on the little rug in front of the fireplace, glass in hand, with the canapes and napkins on the small cocktail table beside them, they were beginning to feel more at ease with one another.

"How did your day go? We started the day so late; were you able to get all your meetings and tasks out of the way?"

Tomas looked surprised. He smiled down at her. "Oh, I guess your Spanish or your hearing isn't quite good enough. I phoned everyone this morning and canceled my work day . . . probably a first. I figured that it was a late morning, and we'd had such a scare. I thought we'd both need to come up for air."

"I did hear you rattling off this morning. And, no, my Spanish doesn't process at ninety miles an hour," she said, laughingly, as she leaned in toward him.

The oven timer gave out a sharp, incessant buzz signaling the readiness of the roast. Margaret reluctantly rose and removed the meat from the oven.

"Would you like me to carve the roast?"

She laughed. "What a chauvinist thing to say! Yeah, I'd be delighted to have you carve. Let's just give it several minutes to let the juices set." She returned to sit beside him in front of the fire.

Margaret proceeded to open the gifts he'd brought. While she removed the store wrapping, Tomas interjected, "I should preface this by saying that each year the Spanish Ministry of Agriculture offers a prize for the best olive oil. Over the course of time, different growers in Spain have been awarded that honor. You can imagine it's quite prestigious. Anyway, these olive oils were current winners and are two of my particular favorites."

He began to explain the nuances of the two olive oils he'd selected. One from Cordoba was awarded for its medium green ripeness; the other, for its ripe fruitiness, was from Sevilla.

When he finished his recitation, Tomas placed his hand on hers. "You know we've been sort of beating around the bush, making small talk, ever since I arrived. I need to tell you something."

Seeming to grope for words, he continued "When I didn't find you in my apartment this morning and realized you'd taken off, a stab went through me like a knife. I really thought I'd lost you. It was the most awful, empty feeling. I know I can't let my happiness slip away again. I wasn't old enough to fight for Cassie, and have had many a regret. But one can't dwell in the past. I must look at NOW and, hopefully, forward and what I want for my future. I don't know how we'll do it, Margaret, but I sure want to try,"

Margaret said nothing but motioned him toward the kitchen. She took the individual salads from the refrigerator and placed them to the left of the forks on the table. Tomas, following her lead, carried their wine glasses to the table and arranged them to the right and just above each knife and spoon. In the kitchen, he sliced the juicy, medium-rare roast, and they placed slices on individual platters which held baked potato and fresh green beans.

They each carried a plate to the table where Margaret had earlier set a white cloth and napkins, two candles in the center, a small basket with bread wrapped in a matching cloth napkin, pats of butter and a small bowl of sour cream containing fresh diced chives.

They proceeded to eat with relish making little conversation. Tomas complimented the chef several times. Indeed, it was a delicious dinner far better than many a restaurant. Margaret was proud of herself; it had been a long time since she'd attempted a roast. And, the Rioja blended wine did complement it well.

"I don't believe I ate lunch today," Margaret said with amazement in her voice.

"I grabbed something from the fridge, though there's not much in it. I guess I was too upset to think about food. I had so much else on my mind."

When they'd consumed most of the dinner, Margaret swallowed a bite of food and blurted out in a soft voice, "You weren't wrong to blow up at me this morning for comparing you with Andrew. At times, I guess I do. It's hard not to."

Tomas placed his knife and fork on his plate, "I know. I found myself doing the same after you'd left. I continued to think about that on my way here tonight. I used to feel so claustrophobic staying within the confines of the orchard. I welcomed the expansion of my business, maybe subconsciously fostered it, as a means of escape."

Tomas paused and continued eating. After a few more bites, he resumed. "Yet, I wasn't like Andrew, at least my picture of Andrew as you've drawn him. I DID try to involve Liliana right from the beginning. I'd suggested we honeymoon on the Costa del Sol. Her response was that she'd been there once with a bunch of girlfriends so she'd already seen the Mediterranean.

I finally convinced her to go to Madrid. We toured the museums, the palace, saw a show, went to fine restaurants, bought her some outfits at department stores and boutiques. Liliana couldn't wait to return home. Some might call her an armchair traveler. She reads books and the daily newspaper and is fairly knowledgeable and up to date about a great many places and events. She just feels more secure within familiar parameters. I guess some people are this way. It doesn't pay to try to expand their world if it makes them miserable.

The outfits we'd bought for her on our honeymoon and the occasional purchases I'd made on trips have hung in her closet and sat in the drawer all these years. She's never once had them on her back. She claims she has no place to wear them. And, in truth, she really doesn't.

Her life consists of reading, her quilting group, church-related friends and activities, her sisters, my sisters, their husbands, and sitting around watching TV while she knits, sews, does needlepoint." At this, Margaret grunted.

Tomas rose to his wife's defense, his voice getting gruff, "It's what gives her pleasure, and I can't change that, nor drag her to do what suits me. She never cared to ski, hike, bike, go out on the boat. She's just not into athletic pursuits. The children and I always invited her to join us on one or another of our outings, but Liliana found a million excuses not to come. Planning ahead, readying items to take, packing, traipsing about by car, train or plane just never appealed to her and still doesn't. And, it can be a hassle . . . no doubt about it."

At this Margaret concurred. "Don't I know. Your highways in Spain are lovely. Nonetheless, crawling along the coast from Malaga to Nerja can be a nightmare. At home, more and more, the Boston area is being choked with traffic. Also, there are always accidents. I sometimes get to the point that I wonder if I really need to run a particular errand. I find that I arrange appointments and errands so that I'm traveling at times of the day where traffic is lightest."

Tomas added, "What about traveling by plane," his voice hinting at annoyance.

"Oh," Margaret concurred, "going through security, having flights canceled, over bookings, lousy food and cramped seating; it certainly isn't a picnic."

Margaret rose from the table and began putting away the food and placing the dirty dishes into the sink. She talked as she walked, "Speaking of cramped seating, how did you happen to be flying coach and seated next to me on that flight from Boston to Madrid?"

"How did you know I always fly business class?" he laughed.

"Come on, now. I know you well enough for that," she giggled in embarrassment.

"As it happens, I was flying with the Director of the IOOC. His son, too, is a college student in the States so we were both mixing business with pleasure. He's a very gifted and pleasant fellow, by the way, who owns a large olive orchard in Morocco. We had business to conduct and viewed the lengthy trip as a chance to talk undisturbed by phones, clients, admin. staff, whatever. We arrived early at the airport, but they couldn't find seats together for us in business or first class. We were not, as you say in America, 'happy campers'. If you remember, the flight was very full. So there we were seated next to you in the way back. Do you believe in fate?"

Margaret set their coffee and a variety of Pepperidge Farm cookies on the little table Tomas had earlier deposited in front of the fireplace. He joined her on the rug.

"I do believe that though we are supposed to be masters of our own fate, fate does sometimes step in and take a hand. I do believe I was lucky to be sitting next to you on that flight." She inched closer to him placing her left hand across his back as she steadied her coffee in the right.

"Margaret, we really do need to plan ahead. The IOOC Conference is just weeks away, and your boys will be arriving from the States shortly thereafter. We'll not have much time together for a while. I think we need to clarify where we are and where we want our relationship to lead. And, what's feasible, or how we can make it feasible."

Margaret could hear a slight tone of pleading in his voice. She was stunned at hearing his thoughts articulated. She said nothing for quite some time. The silence was audible.

Finally, she replied in, what she hoped would be, a calming voice, "As much as I'd like to plan a future for us ... it seems far too premature for us to make a commitment now. Don't you think? We're both still married to our spouses, and I've not even come to grips with my present situation. For me, up until now, looking into the future has been terrifying. I have so many questions reverberating in my head. This is all so new for me.

"I must have been aware, on some level anyway, that my marriage wasn't nirvana. But, people get so mired in daily routines that we don't always allow ourselves to stop and think, to feel, to make note of whatever feelings we ARE experiencing. Too, I guess I didn't want to think about it. It's too unnerving, particularly if you can't readily change things. As I'm discovering, I'm now in a worst-case scenario."

"You are?" Tomas wheezed completely taken aback.

"NO, I'm not referring to you. Perhaps, other than my sons, that's the best thing that has happened to me. But, I have little income and no visible means of support that will allow me to stay in my home and keep afloat. I'm presently separated from my sons, my home, my friends and neighbors, my sister and whatever felt comfortable to me. Hell, since I've been living here in Spain, I can't even understand ninety per cent of what's being said around me. Except for you, Eddie and his assistant, Helen, with whom I've had an occasional cup of coffee or a quick lunch, I'm pretty damned isolated." Margaret paused to come up for air, surprised at her own vehemence. "Yet, you know, I don't remember when I've been so happy." She smiled in astonishment at what she'd just said.

"And, pray, how might that be?" Tomas quizzed her with a grin from ear-to-ear.

"Let's see." Measuring her words, Margaret began, "Well, for starters, I'm basically responsible for only myself. I do what pleases me. I can worry about my kids and where life will take me, but my sons are too far away for me to know what they're doing minute by minute, and the future can only be in the abstract, pure conjecture. On a daily basis, I'm finding satisfaction teaching English to my students at the church, I'm managing to get around on my own despite the language barriers, and I've found people in my life whom I respect and enjoy and who enjoy me . . . basically you and Father Eduardo and Helen."

That, too, elicited a broad grin and nod from Tomas.

"More than that, the daily tensions that used to eat away at me are gone. It's nice not to feel harassed. When Andrew came home expecting to be served dinner the minute he crossed the threshold, I'd always get knots in my stomach; or he didn't come home until the wee hours and I'd no idea where he was. Was he working late? Did he have a car accident? Was he out carousing? Should I phone the police?

"In addition, he'd leave orders for me to do this or tend to that when it wasn't always feasible given other demands on my time. It's certainly liberating to, pretty much, set your own agenda.

"My God, Tomas, how did our lives get into such a heap? You were coerced into a marriage not of your choosing, and Andrew and I were so ill-suited."

Tomas seemed to be weighing her words carefully. After an ensuing pause of some length, he replied, "You know, we really cannot fault our decisions however much we may regret them. Although we were not children when we married, I was still very much under the influence of my parents, and you had barely experienced life. It is my belief that, after having many years to reflect, young people cannot make life-long decisions about selecting a partner or even a career until they really know who they are. Who are you as a person? What pleases you? What feels good to you? What do you enjoy? What puts you at ease? What challenges you? What values do you hold? And, no one can give you those answers. You have to learn them for yourself, usually by trial and error.

"Well, you and I, dear Margaret, have made our errors. Now, what I'm asking you is whether or not we can take the next step?"

"The next step?" Margaret questioned.

"What I guess I'm asking is, where do you and I go from here? I, sincerely, would like for us to spend more time together, to move in together to allow us to see how well we fit." He was carefully observing Margaret's reaction which was rather stunned and perplexed. "Have I overstepped my bounds?"

"No." Looking down at her toes in a bashful gesture, Margaret continued, "If I'm truthful with you, I have to confess I have painted scenarios of us together on a more permanent basis. And, I must admit, I've found the picture very appealing. But then, reality hits!"

"I know, we are both still legally married, and not even legally separated from our spouses. In addition, I live in Spain and you live in the States. We each have two children whose lives would be greatly affected by any and all decisions that we make.

"It is a heavy burden. Is it insurmountable, that's the question I've been asking myself."

"And, what answer have you come up with?"

"I think if we proceed very cautiously, one step at a time, carefully considering all the circumstances and people involved, we just might be able to pull it off. That is, if you and I decide that we're the perfect team . . . well, almost a perfect team. And, I think we just might be."

"I think we do make a good pair in many ways. And, I'd love to believe that we can make this happen. It just feels overwhelming. I don't even know where to begin except having you in my life feels good, and I fervently want you to remain."

"Well, what I'm suggesting," Tomas continued, "is that I remain in your life, that we move in together. At least it's a start."

"My gosh, Tomas. I wasn't prepared for this . . . even in my wildest dreams. I don't know what to say."

"How about, 'yes'."

"Wouldn't that put you in jeopardy? It's more likely that someone would recognize you and become aware of the circumstances. What if Liliana or your children heard about us, or Eddie? What if Andrew had a private eye following me; I'd never put anything past him."

"I, too, have had those thoughts, sweetheart. We would be putting ourselves at some risk, true. I wouldn't worry about Father Eduardo. Eddie is a dear friend first and foremost. He'll have our best interests at heart. If we are certain that it is right for us . . . to be together . . . we can file for legal separations. Then, our risks would be greatly decreased."

"How will you leave Liliana and the orchard that's been in your family for generations?"

"Sadly, my emotional bonds with the orchard and all it holds for me were broken long ago."

"Yes, I can see that. And I guess I can understand it, too."

Margaret's voice became wistful, "I never thought I would wish to sever my ties with my beautiful English Tudor in Newton. Would I be able to keep my house? Do I want to keep that huge place just to rattle around by myself? It felt so lonely, empty, and useless after the boys went off to boarding school. Worse, now, it's a symbol of my failed marriage."

Abruptly, Margaret's mood turned brusque, "How will I be able to get a legal settlement, a financial settlement from Andrew? He's sure to be furious if I initiate divorce proceedings, and it's not unlike him to exact revenge."

Tomas startled Margaret with his laughter. "You've certainly painted him as some kind of monster. Even if he does try to bring the house down around you, your boys are old enough to decide how they'll spend time with their parents. From a financial point, you surely will be awarded something by the courts. Even if you had to go it alone,

Margaret, you are a bright, attractive, talented, very capable woman. You'd find something that would allow you to support yourself."

Tomas persisted, "I do believe your lawyer should make the best settlement that he can on your behalf. And, I would wish to treat Liliana with respect.

"Even without the income from the farm and family holdings, I receive substantial income from real estate I own in Spain and in the States, along with stocks, bonds, and all. Despite this recent world-wide recession, I believe I can manage to feed us, so don't go worrying on that account. As it happens, my financial adviser and I, were uncomfortable with the soaring housing market, unstable mortgage contracts, exorbitant executive salaries, and flagrant public spending leaving many in debt. So, we'd sold many of my stocks before the boom went bust.

"I was looking to sell one or two of my apartments in Manhattan, but with the plunge in real estate, I'm holding on. In a way, it's been fortuitous, my son is residing in one apartment while taking courses at Columbia, and there's another coming up for lease at the end of the school year. It could have our names on it in the foreseeable future."

Then in a sweet, whimsical tone, Tomas said, "I brought my toothbrush, Margaret in the hopes you'd agree to let me stay."

"Well, aren't we presumptuous!" Margaret tried to sound haughty and keep a straight face, but her joy and amazement came through.

Then, her practical nature took hold. "Here? How would you ever get to work? We're forty-five minutes from your office, from the nearest airport. How would you manage?"

"I honestly don't have an answer for that. One, I should think it would only be temporary until we figured out what we want to do on a more permanent basis. Two, you'd be less uprooted. Three, I can make the accommodation in traveling for that limited a time."

When he saw that Margaret was trying to sort it all out, he pursued his plan. "As it happens, we'll both be in Madrid for the Olive Oil Conference in two weeks time. Then, your boys will be visiting."

"And, all traces of YOU would have to be erased before they came."

Now, with a crooked grin, "You think they'd hate me or find me wanting?

"I'm glad you agree with me that we have to be absolutely certain of our feelings for each other and our plans before we involve our kids."

"Absolutely! Also, I don't want my sons to think you were the cause of my divorce from their father."

"Wise thinking. Now, may I help with the dishes . . . and move in?"

Margaret threw back her head in laughter and threw her arms around him.

"I love you so much. I'm the luckiest woman in the world."

CHAPTER 29

ARGARET FAIRLY FLOATED DOWN THE aisles of the local supermarket, still euphoric from their conversation/decision the night before. She was scurrying to stock her small fridge and cabinets with whatever she and Tomas might require for the next couple of weeks. He had definitely moved in.

Before heading off this morning for business meetings in Madrid, Tomas announced he would be gone for an overnight and would return Wednesday evening for dinner. This was Tuesday. Suddenly, Wednesday seemed so far away.

However, Margaret knew she could occupy the day with things that pleased her and would make the time go faster. She had lined up an early walk and cup of coffee with Helen. Afterwards, she focused on her plans for tonight's class.

She was creating individual menus in English, and the group would pretend they were going out for a meal in America. Her students were eagerly anticipating this event. After some individual research, students had even suggested foods they would like to see on the menus. Margaret had made a list of their choices along with additional items. She'd asked that they be able to describe the contents of various dishes.

As soon as she got back to her house, she stored the groceries and went to work creating the menus. She hadn't much time remaining. She'd encouraged Luis to meet her for lunch at the café facing the church at one o'clock. Afterwards, they would head to the classroom, and Luis would decorate the five menu covers. She had started typing in the information on Friday before they'd left for *The Respite*. Her plan was to complete the task yesterday, but her flare-up with Tomas had upset her powers of concentration.

Just past noon, Margaret saved her information and turned off the laptop. She'd just have to take it with her. She freshened up, grabbed what she'd need for the remainder of the day, and was out the door feeling perky and chipper.

She parked her car in the lot and crossed the square. Luis was already seated at one of the outdoor tables.

"It is a beautiful day, no? I think we can sit here."

"Of course, Luis. This will be fine," grateful that she'd remembered to bring a jacket with her. There was still a bite in the air.

At lunch, Luis eagerly told her, "I sell two paintings. I get good money for them. I paint lots more."

She decided she wouldn't dampen his enthusiasm by correcting his grammar.

"Luis, that's fabulous, wonderful. I am so happy for you. What were your paintings about?"

At his confused look, she reiterated, "You know, what were they . . . people, water, trees, the sky . . . ? What did you paint that you sold?"

"Oh, I see. The paintings of you. I sell, sold? (Margaret nodded approval) the charcoal drawings I made of you, so I made paintings of you."

"Oh my!" Margaret blurted out with a fearful look on her face.

"That no good?"

"Oh, it's good. I'm just surprised. I'm so happy for you, Luis. That is good news, wonderful news."

While they studied the menus placed before them, Margaret contemplated more than the food. Luis had remained aloof in the classroom ever since she'd asked him to leave her home so she could prepare for her evening. She'd never told Luis she had a date that night, but he must have sensed that she was preparing for something bigger and better than spending her time with him. In some way, his feelings were hurt.

She'd been very leery about requesting his help with the menu covers. However, he'd readily accepted her offer and with much enthusiasm despite the fact that it meant losing precious time from his job and loss of income.

Perhaps, the sale of his paintings had taken away the immediacy of needing every penny earned as a day laborer. Furthermore, she WAS the subject of the work he managed to sell and she WAS the one who'd given him a capacity to communicate with the English-speaking tourists. Margaret surmised that those factors might account for the amelioration of Luis' harsh feelings toward her; he appeared truly grateful.

After they'd ordered some nachos as starters and wraps for lunch, Margaret said, "I hope you'll sell some of your beautiful landscapes."

"Landscapes?" he pronounced with difficulty.

"Yes, you know, the water, trees, the sky." Margaret pointed to the objects as they were mentioned.

Now, Luis' head was bobbing in recognition. "Yes, I will sold those."

Margaret looked quizzical and a gentle laugh escaped. She decided the time was right for some explanation. She gently placed her hand on Luis' to soften what she was about to do. "Luis, 'sell' is now or future, 'sold' is past. Today, I will sell my painting. Yesterday I sold one. Do you understand?"

"Si, si. I get it now. Thank you," he smiled thoughtfully.

They set about eating their lunch as Margaret wondered who had purchased her likeness. She was trying to think how she might ask in English simple enough to get a clear response.

Her thoughts were distracted as Luis asked, "What you want me paint on menus?"

"I made a list of restaurant names. You can write those with pretty letters. You can make pictures of food, flowers, anything you like that would be nice. OK?"

Luis felt as if she'd given him full reign so he smiled happily. He also studied the menu cover in front of him. It was not terribly creative or appealing he noted with some disgust. He could do better.

"You won't have too much time. Whatever you can do in the time we have will be lovely, I'm sure. Do you understand?"

Luis nodded. Yet, Margaret knew that nods from her students did not always signify understanding, but just an earnest gesture of trying to please the teacher.

Oh well. She'd know soon enough how much Luis understood. Besides, she'd be right by his side if questions arose.

After they finished eating, they walked across the narrow lane to enter the back of the building. Her classroom was a very multi-purpose affair. Fortunately, Margaret was able to reserve the room for the afternoon in addition to her scheduled evening class.

While Luis drew the menu covers, Margaret finished typing the menus and used the copier in the church office. She was accustomed to praying in church, but now she prayed that she didn't run into Eddie while she was standing at the copier. His office was practically adjacent to her classroom, as well. If he were in the building, it would be hard to escape his presence. She knew he'd ask about her and Tomas and, well, he was still Father Eduardo. She wasn't ready to lay the details of her life at his feet.

She and Luis worked diligently for the next few hours. Using crayons and colored pencils that Margaret had provided, he worked with little input from her. When the menus were placed in their sheaths, they both looked with admiration at the finished products; Luis had done an amazing job on the covers.

So much so that Margaret addressed him, "Luis, I could see you painting covers for menus and posters for businesses. You work so quickly, and these covers look FABULOUS!"

"Quickly?" he queried.

"Rapido."

"Ah, yes. I guess I did work fast . . . quickly. His smile showed his bolstered confidence and delight."

Luis helped her arrange the chairs in small groups to accommodate the 'diners'. They moved the two large, oblong tables to the sides of the room and arranged four chairs in five groups. At each group, one 'diner' would take a turn at being the waiter.

Luis now produced the names of his fellow classmates. He'd used a calligraphy pen to write their names on the name tags Margaret had given him at an earlier session. They were beautifully written, and Margaret exclaimed, "Luis, you have such talent. These letters are magnificent. It must have taken so much of your time. Thank you. I'm sure the others will be impressed . . . love it . . . "

Luis smiled proudly. Then sheepishly asked, "Where you want I should put?"

"If you'd like, please put one on each chair as I've assigned them in this chart."

Margaret aimed to get a balanced fluency in English. When her students arrived and were seated at their assigned chairs, she noted, too, that she'd balanced the diversity of her students as well. Her class represented varied age groups, occupations, and lifestyles. She was teaching everyone from blue collar to the wealthier snow birds who wintered along the Costa del Sol.

Satisfied with the results, Margaret now noticed how enthusiastically individuals were greeting this project. People oohed and aahed at their names and at the menu covers which were now being distributed to each of the groups. She had Luis stand for a round of applause. It quickly dawned on her that several of her students were in a position to purchase his work or encourage their friends to do so. Perhaps, she might foster this idea.

Margaret mingled among the 'tables' to answer questions, make suggestions, overhear the description of the foods that were listed, and to generally gauge how the assignment was progressing. She had asked that, after placing their food orders, they be prepared to make light conversation.

She'd written on the board some suggestions for topics:
1. What did you do today?

2. What is the weather forecast for tomorrow?

3. Where will you go on your next trip?

4. Describe some family member or love interest.

The last topic elicited much giggling. She noted that some of the more senior members had no trouble holding forth about grandchildren, but younger individuals were somewhat stymied as to what they cared to disclose. Yet, Margaret marveled at how well the disparate groups coalesced. She was pleased and proud that she'd had a hand in making it happen.

Margaret was elated to see how well the project was going. Everyone seemed to be participating and with a lot of gusto. Occasionally, she'd overhear a bit of Spanish and had to scurry over to cluck with a laugh, "English only, people. Thank you."

The session came to a close much too quickly. Her students were actively engaged in animated conversations in English. They seemed reluctant to leave. Although, several commented that the food descriptions had made them hungry, and, after thanking Margaret even more profusely than usual, they left for their respective dinners.

Margaret had made a point of publicly thanking Luis again before class dismissed. She was surprised and perplexed when Luis lingered after the others had left. She said, "You did a wonderful job today. I think all the class loved your work. You know, why don't you bring some of your landscapes to class in a few weeks. I can do a lesson about them. Also, there are people in our class who might enjoy your work. Who knows, maybe they might buy something or have a place of business to display the art."

"Display?"

"To show your work."

Luis looked delighted at the idea. He said, "You and me go for dinner?"

"Why yes, Luis, I'm going home now, and I'll get something to eat." Probably leftovers Margaret surmised as she remembered the remains of last night's rib roast. She'd planned to make a sandwich.

In a frustrated tone, Luis continued, "No, Ms. Margaret, you and ME go to dinner. I pay."

This last remark caught Margaret off guard, but she managed to think quickly. "That's so sweet of you Luis, but I am sooo tired. I was at the grocery this morning, working together with you this afternoon, and teaching this evening. I need to get home, grab a sandwich, and get to sleep. I am exhausted."

And, Margaret thought, spent from trying to speak English in simple sentences within the grasp of your vocabulary and that of your classmates. An entire day of it was truly draining. She couldn't imagine continuing this speaking pattern throughout dinner.

"I'm sure you're tired, too, Luis. Another day, perhaps."

Luis understood enough to know that she was not taking him up on his offer.

He nodded in compliance, but looked like a cat curled quietly in the corner ready to pounce on his prey.

How creepy! A sense of dread shot through Margaret. However, she regained her composure and added, "I'll see you in class on Thursday. Why don't you bring some of your work for us to display?"

"Ah." Luis left with a bounce to his walk.

Margaret sincerely hoped she hadn't offended him and that his feelings were assuaged. Language barriers aside, he was a complex fellow.

CHAPTER 30

AN UNEASY MARGARET STEPPED INTO her car. What was she to make of Luis?

Her sleep was punctuated by disquieting dreams, nightmares really. She slept fitfully, waking often. How she wished Tomas were here.

As it usually does, things looked brighter in the morning. Margaret had checked her e-mails, ignored since she and Tomas had gone sailing. The boys were eagerly planning to come to Spain for an extended Spring Break. They had received permission from both their dad and the school. Margaret wondered what motive Andrew might have for allowing her a lengthier visit with her sons.

To no one in particular she said aloud, "What a cynic I've become! I shouldn't even 'go there'. I'm just going to enjoy Brandon and Richard every minute they're around!" Her spirits soared. Margaret turned on the radio and danced a bit around the house before busying herself in the kitchen in preparation of the evening meal.

Although she'd brought no cookbooks from America, she grabbed two from the shelf. These had been presented to her when she'd visited the International Olive Oil Council building in Madrid several weeks ago. As she perused the titles, Margaret realized they'd been published by the IOOC. She opened *Cooking with Olives* where recipes were divided by the contributing countries . . . Algeria, Cyprus, Egypt,

Spain, France, Greece, Israel, Italy, Morocco, Portugal, Tunisia, Turkey. Chapters began with a picture of the identifying country. The opposite page was explanatory, describing the country's culinary history which was often related to the region and to its religious traditions. Beneath, in the left hand corner, an inset of olive trees or an olive-related carving was depicted.

On the following pages, each recipe was exhibited with a gorgeous photograph of scrumptious food displayed on an elegant platter atop a magnificent tablecloth or mat. The expensive paper made the pages slick to the touch. The recipes were all in very legible English beneath the photo. The measurements, however, were in the metric system . . . a dilemma for Margaret. She'd have to 'wing it'.

The same was true of the second book, *Mediterranean Cooking With Olive Oil*. It, too, had crisp, richly-colored photos along with each recipe. In addition, the recipes were also from the member countries of the IOOC. However, the introductory pages of this cookbook focused more on olive oil and how it related to the maintenance of good health. Margaret vowed to read the beginning chapters when she had more time.

Since this latter cookbook was divided into classifications of foods: appetizers, salads, pastas, veggies, fish, poultry, meats, sauces and desserts, it proved easier for Margaret to find a recipe for the scallops she'd purchased yesterday.

Turning to the section on fish and shellfish, Margaret found a recipe from Greece for a prawn casserole. She would substitute the scallops for the shrimp. The remaining ingredients she knew she had on hand including the remainder of last night's splendid white wine. She now set about finely chopping a medium onion and tomatoes, crushing two garlic cloves, and crumbling feta cheese. How many tomatoes, how much feta???? She'd just have to guesstimate. The same with the white wine and olive oil. She'd use what she had on hand and hoped it would suffice. Carefully, she added four shallots and the garlic to the frying onion. After two minutes, she added the tomatoes, wine, a tablespoon of chopped parsley and the teaspoon of oregano called for in the recipe. She added salt and pepper to taste; Margaret used little salt in her cooking.

She covered the pan and allowed it to cook over low heat for thirty minutes until it was thick. She laughed aloud when the recipe said to pre-heat the oven for two hundred twenty degrees Celsius. She must have been absent or 'phoned in' the day that topic was covered in math. She didn't have a clue, but surmised that a three hundred fifty degree oven would equate. Fortunately, when in Spain, one has an oven that is equipped with a Celsius gauge.

As called for in the recipe, Margaret placed half the thickened sauce in the bottom of a small casserole dish, added the scallops, and covered them with the remainder of the sauce, covered it all with aluminum foil, and placed it in the fridge. When Tomas returned this evening, she would sprinkle the cheese on top and bake it in the preheated oven for ten to twelve minutes, or however long it took to heat through and brown. She'd have to watch closely so that nothing would burn. When they were ready to eat, she'd add the remaining tablespoon of parsley for garnish.

Tomas had suggested they go out for dinner tonight. However, Margaret decided that the time would pass more rapidly if she prepared something at home. Besides, Tomas would probably be weary after trekking back and forth to

Madrid. Now, he had the extra burden of driving from the Malaga airport to Nerja, a good forty-five minute trip.

Indeed, when Tomas arrived at the door that evening, Margaret could see he'd had a very busy day. In addition to his business agenda and flight from Madrid, he'd taken the time to stop at his condo to collect personal belongings. His arrival with a large suitcase and many items on hangers floored Margaret. "I see you're serious about moving in," in a voice that carried some surprise. Still, she recovered her sense of humor and added, "Did the landlord kick you out?"

"I thought that's what we'd agreed upon," Tomas replied in an injured tone of voice. "What did you expect?"

"I suppose I thought we'd be venturing into this day by day . . . kind of on a need-to-know basis. No, I guess it would not have been practical to keep running back and forth for your belongings."

"Just practical? I thought the idea was that we'd be together from here on in."

"I believe I was just preparing dinner for tonight, not contemplating the rest of my life." Then, in a more serious tone, "I do want so much for this to work, Tomas. Simply the fact that I can speak my mind so openly to you is very reassuring."

"Well, now that we've spoken our minds, where may I store these; these hangers are getting mighty heavy? Have you some room in a closet? Oh, and I'll need a few drawers or shelves."

"Well, don't YOU make yourself right at home!" she laughed delightedly. "I can't believe you are doing this, but it's feeling better every minute."

Margaret steered him to the closet and bureau in the second bedroom. "Am I to sleep in here, as well?"

"Only if you don't behave."

Now that his hands were free, he gathered her to him in a deep embrace. Suddenly, it all felt so right. Margaret wanted to hold on to the moment.

"Something smells divine. Did you go and cook dinner? I thought I'd suggested dinner out. Okay, I'm not sorry you opted for this route."

'The way to a man's heart is through his stomach', trite but true thought a glowing Margaret. Tomas washed up, and together they prepared the salad dressing. Tomas wanted to use one of the new olive oils he'd purchased for Margaret and show it off to its best advantage. Margaret deemed it, "wonderful."

Over the very delectable dinner, Tomas described the painstaking progress being made at the International Olive Oil Council for the upcoming conference. "But," he assured her, "I have faith that the planning is in good hands. I think it will all come together in the end."

"Don't worry. Events like this usually do pan out well. There is so much preparation and angst beforehand by staff and volunteers, there are usually few glitches. Moreover, the invited guests are rarely aware of any mishaps if the function, over all, is a success."

Margaret told him of her sons' extended visit to Spain. At that Tomas exclaimed, "Why not let the boys fly into Madrid. I had hoped you would have some time to tour that city with them. I took the liberty of arranging for Maritza to visit her brother in New York right before Easter Sunday; she wishes to interview for some graduate programs in the States. She'll vacate the Madrid apartment and stay at the orchard for a week before she leaves. The apartment will be free if you wish to use it.

"As a matter of fact, I was hoping you'd agree to remain in Madrid after the IOOC Conference, and we could spend a week together prior to your sons' arrival. I can acquaint you with the apartment, neighborhood, shops, et cetera. Do you think you can arrange to do that? I'll have finished my immediate obligations to the International Olive folks, and I think I can arrange some time away from my businesses, so we can just enjoy." He laughed, "Can you play with me?"

Margaret giggled, "I don't know. You are certainly the persuasive one; it sounds like a wonderful idea." Then she hesitated, "I would have to clear the time with Father Eduardo. It means my taking an extended leave of absence from teaching, and I do feel an obligation to my students. They are doing so well." She excitedly described the class from the previous night.

Tomas beamed at her. Margaret became so alive and vivacious in the re-telling. He could see she was pleased not only with her students' progress, but also with the job she'd accomplished.

"You should be feeling very gratified. You're really seeing results. I'm proud of you, Margaret. And, Father Eddie will be delighted, too. Did he manage to see your 'restaurant adventure' last night?"

"No, he wasn't there. Frankly, I was relieved. I'm not quite sure how to broach the subject of 'us'. He's your friend, but he's still a Catholic priest. He may be happy for us on a personal level, but I'm not ready to hear his professional thoughts."

"Mmmm. Not ready for the 'sweat-box'. Confession can wait."

"Actually, what concerns me more are my sons. I really don't want the boys to know about you just yet."

Tomas weighed her words before replying, "I fully understand." In what he hoped would be his most reassuring voice, he continued, "Don't worry, I won't be in Madrid when the boys are there, and we'll erase any traces of me from the apartment. We'll say you're renting the place if the doorman or a neighbor might ask."

Margaret's body relaxed, and she slid her hand atop Tomas'. "I'll. fully consider your offer; it's very kind. I will have to have my English class at the church covered for the time I'll be in Madrid. The students certainly deserve that much, and I cannot disappoint them nor Eddie. You can be sure I'll work on it. The thought of spending a whole week with you in Madrid by ourselves, undisturbed, sounds too good to be true."

As he cleared some plates from the table, he leaned into her neck and planted a huge kiss. Margaret jumped in surprise and pleasure. "Hey, you break those and my landlord will throw us both out of here."

After they'd finished dinner, Margaret suggested he relax while she rinsed the dishes and put them in the dishwasher. "There's not much here, and you've had a long day. I'll only be a few minutes."

Tomas shuffled off to sit on the sofa. Seemingly uncomfortable, he wandered from room to room getting better acquainted with his new quarters. On the few occasions he'd spent the night, he hadn't the time nor permitted himself to wander the premises. This time, taking it all in, he carefully noted his surroundings while judging how he'd fit on a permanent basis.

Returning to the couch, he was joined shortly by Margaret who snuggled into the crook of his arm, knees folded under her. "You know I was just thinking, I see pictures of Brandon and Richard, of your sister and her little family and of your friend. I see no photos of Andrew."

"Why would you be looking for photographs of Andrew? Do you want to know how you compare?"

At this, Tomas let out a hearty roar. "No, for heaven's sake. I just want to know what this guy looks like if I run into him. What if he showed up at this door? I'd probably take a punch at him . . . or run like hell."

"Why on earth would Andrew 'show up at this door' to use your terminology?"

"Margaret, sweetheart, Andrew has a beautiful, bright, fun-loving, affectionate wife, a doting mother to his sons. Don't you think at some point he'll come to his senses and try getting you back? He'd be a fool not to. You certainly must be an asset as a social and business partner to him if nothing else."

When Margaret grasped what he was saying, she could barely breathe. Gasping she said, "What a notion! I can hardly believe or imagine such a thing. When all this happened, I kept focusing on all the things I might have done wrong to cause Andrew to stray. I played out every scenario in my mind, again and again. I was sure it was all my fault. Yet, I was so deeply aggrieved. All I wanted was some semblance of an apology from Andrew, some sign from him that he regretted his actions, that he still loved me. I would have welcomed him back with open arms. I would have tried anything to stay in my marriage even going to the priest or a marriage counselor. It was that important for me that my marriage remain intact, my children have a stable home. Also, it was so scary for me to be on my own; it had been so many years since I'd been financially self-supporting."

"Well, has he made any overtures in that direction? What do you hear from him?"

"Initially, when he phoned, he never mentioned the situation in which I'd found him. Andrew's conversations were related to returning home as if nothing had happened, or concerned with his need to retrieve his personal belongings. Once he was out of the house, we really didn't speak for months except if a decision had to be made regarding the boys. Unlike other women I knew who had to track down their husbands or exes for alimony and child support, Andrew paid his share of the bills. My friend Missy termed it hush money. Anyway, I don't have a clue as to where he is living or with whom. For all I know he took up residence with the bimbo."

"Hasn't he tried to reach you since you moved here?"

"I hear nothing because I don't answer his e-mails; I block them. I have an unlisted phone number and made my kids, sister and Missy swear on pain of death they'd never let him know. I really wanted to take these six months and get some distance. Find out what I, Margaret Cleary, wanted for MY life. What would be best for me and for my sons."

"And, now that you've had some time to think?"

"I think that I am married to a man who is egocentric . . . meaning self-centered, self-absorbed . . . at times cruel, incapable of feelings, insensitive, contemptible, demanding, pompous."

Never before had Tomas heard such vehemence or bitterness in Margaret's tone of voice. To allow himself time to reflect on her words, he busied himself in the kitchen removing the clean dishes from the dishwasher and putting them in the cupboards. He recalled reading a book by Elizabeth Kubler-Ross regarding death and dying.

A failed marriage, too, presented a great bereavement, not unlike a death. Perhaps, Margaret had passed through many of those same stages: denial; asking what did I do wrong and how could I have made a difference; grieving the loss of the family structure. Now, she'd reached the stage of anger.

To deflect, he said in a humorous voice, "I can see you really like this guy!"

"Tomas, since coming here, I thought for sure, I'd be so lonely, so homesick that I'd be flying home at the first opportunity. And, I have had bouts of loneliness and being homesick. I do miss my sons, my sister, my friends. But, I don't miss Andrew. In fact, this has been a most liberating experience. I feel reborn, as if I've come into my own. I like my independence, and I now like who I am. I no longer feel that I was solely to blame for the break up of my marriage."

"This all must have been quite enlightening and a relief."

"Yes. And, the best part has been meeting someone who truly loves and respects me, who makes me laugh, who allows me to be me, and enjoys me and our times together."

"You talking about me, lady?" Tomas smiled teasingly. "Why don't you show me how great I am; I promise I won't let it go to my head."

At this, Margaret gave him a playful poke.

All the fatigue left him. Tomas pulled her toward him and showed her just how much he loved her with every stroke, caress and kiss. Feeling her respond, he knew they were exceedingly compatible.

CHAPTER 31

TRUE TO HER WORD, MARGARET was determined to provide teaching material and an instructor before acquiescing to Tomas' plan for them to remain in Madrid between the Conference and Margaret's sons arrival in that city.

Margaret was sure that Helen would be up to the task, and might welcome the few extra dollars with the Easter holiday approaching. As it happened, Helen readily agreed to substitute for Margaret if Margaret would prepare the lesson plans or, better still, worksheets for the class. Margaret dutifully complied.

She explained to her students that she would not be in class the two weeks before Palm Sunday. After the requisite groans, she assured them she had prepared a lot of work for them, and the substitute instructor was well-equipped to assist and answer questions.

Picking and choosing her words carefully for her students' full comprehension, Margaret continued, "I expect that most of you know Ms. Wetherly from the church office. She will be here to help you if you have questions.

I shall prepare some work sheets for you to do while I am away. They are not tests, and you will not be graded. I would like to see where I need to teach more of something and where you need the most help. This will help me and you to know where we need to take more time for learning new things. Then, we can review some things that we already talked about, but, as yet, some of you may not completely understand."

After Margaret felt satisfied that her students understood what would happen while she was not present and they would attend the classes with Helen as substitute, she proceeded with a new lesson for the class. She wished to clarify what they sometimes heard in English, and what was traditionally considered correct.

"I know that the English-speaking world is far more relaxed than in years past, and many people are not interested in speaking English perfectly. However, the rules of grammar really do make sense. I feel that as your teacher, I have been trying to speak correctly, and need to give you the proper forms of speech. I learned proper grammar and, as a result, it's easier on my ears. In addition, if you are in the business world or in an educated setting, proper grammar may be a big help to you." Smiling broadly now, Margaret continued, "However, it's up to you as to how you wish to speak English. As the teacher of English, it's up to me to teach the correct form."

Margaret had decided to do this by giving very simple examples. "Lots of people, when asked, 'Who is it?' will reply, 'It's me'. I know you've heard this many times. Except that if you reverse it, you'd be saying, 'Me is it'."

Margaret had prepared several sheets of material to offer her students, and the first was passed around the class, one per student. It read as follows:

WE NEED TO SAY:	BECAUSE:
It is I.	I am it.
It is he/she.	He/she is it.
It is they.	They are it.

**WHEN WE TALK ABOUT TWO PEOPLE,
WE NEED TO THINK OF EACH ONE.**
For example: I am talking to Jane and
John. I am talking to her and to him.

WE NEED TO SAY	BECAUSE:
I am talking to Jane and me.	I am talking to Jane and to me. We would not say, "I am talking to I."
I gave the book to John and them. He answers him and us.	I gave to the book to John and to them. He answers him. He answers us.

**WHEN MAKING COMPARISONS, FINISH
THE THOUGHT IN YOUR HEAD ( ).**
He is taller than I (am). She is faster than
he (is). They work better than we (do).
Makes no sense to say, "He is taller than me
(is)." or "They work better than us (does)."

Margaret spent the better part of the evening's lesson explaining the sheets and answering questions from the class. She tried to make the ideas come to life by involving the students. First, she had individuals lining up to compare heights, then giving notebooks to two people, and finally, knocking on a door and asking, "Who is it?" Several in the class initiated further questions and responses.

For further re-enforcement, Margaret separated students into groups of four and asked that they converse using the material in hand. She then wandered from group to group listening to conversations and urging self correction when needed.

By the end of class, Margaret felt reasonably sure that her students grasped the concepts. At home, she composed a dozen worksheets which Helen would distribute to the class. They comprised much of the information Margaret had been teaching throughout the course and served as a review and test of what she hoped they'd learned. Over lunch, Helen and Margaret agreed that Helen would review the answers to the worksheets during each session if time permitted.

The next two weeks flew. Besides fulfilling her responsibilities to her night class, Margaret needed to pack for the two-plus weeks in Madrid. In addition, she and her sons were planning, via the telephone and Internet, what the three of them would be seeing and doing after the boys' arrival in Spain during Brandon and Richard's extended Spring Break.

Margaret savored the evening hours and weekends when Tomas managed to travel to Nerja. He had expressed his desire to see more of Margaret, and clearly, he was trying his best to do so.

Before she knew it, they were headed to Madrid for the annual gathering of the International Olive Oil Council.

CHAPTER 32

THE EFFORTS OF THE IOOC staff proved fruitful. With Tomas' administrative aide, Maria, in the forefront accompanied by the input of Tomas, Anna and Margaret, the conference ran quite smoothly. There were some unexpected arrivals, as well as the name tags that sat idle, unclaimed, indicating no-shows. Mainly, any glitches went unnoticed. Few of the participants griped about their lodgings or food, and there was a general vivacity and comradeship among the attendees.

Margaret marveled at the transformation of the huge lobby at the IOOC building the night of the welcoming cocktail party. The lights were all aglow, most men in sharp business attire with stylishly-clad women milling about, drinks flowing and hors d'oeuvres offered by crisply-suited wait staff. Voices rose and fell in a cacophonic rhythm. As Margaret circled among the guests, she heard a vast array of tongues . . . French, Hebrew, German, Italian, Arabic, English and, of course, Spanish. There were some languages she could not even identify. Newer members from Brazil, Uruguay, Albania, Argentina, Turkey, Japan and South Korea were given special recognition.

When the conference did convene in the adjacent room the next morning, English was the favored tongue. However, translations were available for those who needed it.

Due to the size of the crowd and the limited space, Margaret was unable to be the proverbial 'fly on the wall'. It was left to Maria and other staff members of the IOOC to provide the written material, writing instruments, mike checks and beverages.

Everyone was justly proud of the very professional, efficient and immaculate olive oil laboratories that were scattered throughout the building. Staff and elected officials accompanied many of the IOOC members on tours of these areas giving extensive information and trying to answer the many questions that were posed.

Since the idea originated with her, Margaret felt responsible for the event at El Corte Ingles. To Margaret's delight, the showing of Roberto Verino's Spring line of clothing met with great enthusiasm. The beautiful silks, uneven hems, graceful blends of colors and patterns worked well for the younger women as well as for the more matronly. In addition, some of the soft lines of skirts were beautifully paired with stylishly long cashmere turtleneck sweaters for cooler weather and a more conservative, daytime look. The women's rapt attention and vocal enthusiasm gave Margaret positive feedback. She felt happily rewarded for this achievement.

Moreover, Margaret overheard some unique publicity gimmicks that were bandied about. Goya was planning to place an attractive advertising label that slipped over the neck of the bottles of its cold pressed Extra Virgin Olive Oil announcing a chance to **Win a delectable adventure to Spain**. The contest would be sponsored by: *Olive Oil from Spain*. Someone who has the skills to plan a simple, tasty dish using olive oil with a good selection of ingredients could be the recipient of a "six-day culinary adventure for two." Travel would include Barcelona, Cordoba, "tours of olive groves, cooking classes and delicious meals prepared by Spain's great chefs."

Upon seeing it, Margaret had exclaimed to Anna, "How neat is that!"

Margaret and Anna had urged the IOOC to do an evening at the Thyssen Museum. Since the two were not familiar with the caterers in Madrid, they relied on the recommendation of Ms. Ruiz-Rivas who provided the name of a well-established, reasonably priced firm.

Heavy hors d'oeuvres and drinks were served in the immense foyer ringed by café tables where guests could light for a spell or mill about at leisure. The magnificence of the area created quite a stir, and guests were encouraged to ascend to the upper level to view the many paintings. The evening was a definite stand out, and Margaret and Anna privately congratulated themselves on their choice.

The days flew by, and Margaret barely registered her fatigue and tension; it was a heady experience. The over-all picture was very good. Folks certainly appeared to be enjoying the Conference, and the feedback was very positive.

The evening at the Hotel Hesperia proved a success, as well. Ordinarily, food, when served in vast quantity, does not quite measure up to the tasting. Margaret was greatly relieved and pleased with the results.

From experience, Margaret knew it was always difficult to serve large groups in quite the same manner as smaller gatherings. Foods sit longer in the kitchen, are not as hot at presentation, and orders are occasionally confused. Yet, the Hesperia had done an amazing job in replicating the choices from the menu that she and Tomas had experienced on the night they'd visited.

Since this was the last evening of the Conference, members of the IOOC Board and Tomas, in particular, were recognized for their contributions to the IOOC and, especially, for the success of the Conference. Tomas was called to the microphone as spokesman where, in Spanish and in English, he thanked all those in attendance and for their year-long support of IOOC endeavors. "We, as a group, are, also, beholden to the international community for their burgeoning use and growing sophistication in the purchase of olive oil. I, personally, must add my thanks to the staff members of IOOC, to my colleagues on the Board, and to my personal assistant Maria, and to Anna and Margaret for taking sole responsibility for the planning and execution of this Conference. I am grateful to each of you."

The inclusion of her name and the standing round of applause thrilled Margaret who beamed with pride and happiness. Goose bumps along her arms expressed the joy of her involvement.

Privately, Tomas handed each of the women an envelope. When Margaret returned to the hotel and opened hers, there was a thank you note citing her professionalism and capability, plus a one thousand dollar check in her name for Event Planner signed by the Treasurer of the IOOC. Margaret was ecstatic.

CHAPTER 33

AT THE CONCLUSION OF THE Conference, Tomas and Margaret retreated to his apartment in Madrid. Margaret had never seen an apartment as spacious. The elevator arrived at the apartment door which led to a long, wide foyer containing two small settees and chairs, a large side table, a smaller table, a chest of drawers and built-in shelves above it. On each flat surface, there was an array of beautiful objets d'art collected from various cultures. In addition, Tomas had arranged a lovely bouquet of fresh flowers that he'd placed on the larger table. The floor was almost totally covered with a magnificent Oriental rug. "What a gorgeous entry," Margaret almost shrieked in delight.

Tomas continued, "The previous owner was looking to sell quickly. I just came along at a fortuitous moment."

"I'm glad that you and your kids have had the chance to enjoy this for so many years."

Off the foyer and adjacent hallways were four bedrooms, three full bathrooms, a powder room, a very large kitchen and an equally large laundry room, a den, and a mammoth living room surrounded by huge windows that overlooked the Italian Consulate's park with its multiple gardens. There was a dining table and chairs at the far end, better to catch the view. Most of the furniture consisted of period pieces set on Oriental carpets. Lovely paintings and gilded mirrors added to the elegance of the whole. Margaret felt herself gasp as she attempted to take in the sight. "My God, this is BEAUTIFUL!"

Tomas, acting with some embarrassment replied, "Yes, it is, but I cannot take the slightest credit for this place. When I purchased it many years ago, it was already furnished just as you see it. My kids and I have added some of our own personal contributions in the way of posters in the kids' bedrooms, photographs and the like. Other than the occasional re-upholstering, painting walls or fixing, we've done little else."

Tomas continued, "It has been very convenient to my office as you know, and well located for both Maritza and Antonio's schooling. Liliana was here only once if you are wondering. City life was way too overwhelming, and she hurried back to the olive groves. So, there are no ghosts of my wife lurking in the shadows."

"Well, that's comforting. There doesn't seem to be any place where I've been with you that I would be disturbed by a 'wifely presence'."

"No, I guess you would be right about that. Liliana has never been to the condo in Marbella. . . and has been out on the boat only once. Another indication of why she and I are so poorly matched, and why I've chosen to spend so little time together."

As if he felt he'd said enough and wanted to move on, Tomas suddenly changed his stance. Straightening, he queried, "Would you like to put your things in the bedroom and get settled into the place?"

Margaret followed him into the large bedroom and started arranging her clothes into the drawers and closets where he'd made space for her belongings. Somehow, he'd anticipated her needs, because everything fit quite well into the spaces provided.

"What will I do when my boys arrive? They will surely see that you live here along with your kids."

"Nothing to concern yourself. There's a locked closet in the apartment where I can put my clothing and the photographs. Much of Maritza and Antonio's things are off with them. Will it really upset Brandon and Richard that someone else lives here and has rented out, or allowed you to use the place for a few days?"

"No, I guess not. It's just that I wouldn't want my sons to learn about us. At least, not yet. If I were officially divorced, or even legally separated, I would feel more comfortable. Also, I wouldn't want anything to slip out where Andrew is concerned."

"Okay. It's interesting, though, how Europeans have a much more relaxed view of marriage and extra-marital affairs." Noticing Margaret's stiffening demeanor, Tomas immediately interjected, "Am I upsetting you, dear? I'm sorry. I didn't mean to sound crass or make you uncomfortable. We'll work this out somehow." Then in a quiet, hesitant voice, he added, "I promise."

Margaret lurched toward him while putting her arms around his neck and laying her head on his shoulder. Nestling in, she felt as if she could not draw herself close enough to this man . . . both physically and emotionally. He seemed to hold just the right keys for her. She trusted him.

Tomas lifted her head and kissed her soundly on the lips. Margaret opened her mouth as if to welcome him. Long, protracted, lovingly-deep kisses ensued. It had been a full week of the IOOC Conference where they'd been avoiding any eye contact or physical contact. Now, the hunger swelled inside each of them as they moved toward the bed.

Now, driving to the airport, reflecting on the Conference and the subsequent week holed up in Tomas' flat in Madrid, the whole experience seemed surreal . . . like a dream . . . a wonderful, 'this couldn't be happening to me, Margaret', kind of a dream.

CHAPTER 34

MARGARET WAS HAVING A DIFFICULT time constraining her body. She wanted to fling herself, leaping skyward, shouting with glee for the whole world to hear. As excited as any teenager who was awaiting the arrival of some favorite pop stars; she was a 'groupie'. Only, her idols were the two tall, handsome teenagers who were to alight from the airplane she was now so eagerly awaiting at Madrid's airport . . . her sons, Brandon and Richard.

Margaret was one of those moms who truly delighted in her kids. When they were little, she would arrange play dates for the boys and always welcomed their friends into her home. She offered snacks and beverages, materials necessary to engage in projects, a large selection of creative games and toys, and a loving tone if one of the boys was hurt or had his feelings bruised.

Margaret, Brandon and Richard would often go to the library, the playground, a petting zoo, a children's theater production. Margaret particularly liked taking them into Boston to the Fine Arts Museum. It housed a world-class permanent collection as well as periodic special showings. Brandon and Richard were drawn to many of the paintings. At a rather young age, they were able to identify several of the painters and showed a preference for the works of particular artists. After the boys no longer required naps, Margaret would time her visits to the museum to include afternoon tea. Being served tea in these elegant surroundings accompanied by classical music was one of the few bastions of civilization remaining, and she wanted her sons exposed to it. They, too, enjoyed their afternoon tea time, perhaps not for the elegance, but most certainly for the delicious desserts.

Margaret was a car-pooling mom. She frequently laughed to herself while recalling a friend's needlepoint. "If I'm a housewife, how come I spend most of the time in my car?" However, Margaret would love to sit in her station wagon as a fly on the wall hearing the boys' silly banter. She knew she should force herself not to laugh and not to inject her thoughts; easier said than done. Occasionally, she'd pick up some important information regarding a child's infraction of school rules, who started the food fight in the cafeteria, who threw a spit ball at the math teacher, which girl pulled the hair of another, which classmates were in a fight. She was kept abreast of neighborhood doings . . . an impending divorce, a mom's pregnancy, a planned trip. It not only gave her clues to the school and surrounding community, but also a peek at what might later prove to be a dilemma for her kids. She hoped she'd be able to draw questions from her sons and be prepared to answer to their satisfaction.

As the boys grew older, she drove them to lessons, practices, games and meets. She sat on the sidelines and found that her foot automatically flew out in front of her as if to kick the ball that was rapidly spinning toward one of her sons during their soccer match. She happily cut oranges for half-time snacks as did most of the families.

Margaret acted as one of the timers during swim meets. Brandon and Richard participated mainly in soccer, ice hockey, tennis and swimming. They were welcomed on the team as able participants, team players and good sports.

They enjoyed many unstructured sporting activities in addition. Andrew had erected a basketball hoop at one end of the driveway which led into the three car garage. When the boys were very young, they set the net a little lower. Margaret drew circles on the driveway for 'Around the World' and a game called 'Horse'. The entire family participated in dribbling and shooting. Even when the guys were in middle school and shooting hoops with their friends, they still enjoyed their time with her and Andrew.

Along the way, Margaret had purchased a volleyball set, strung it from atop the basketball pole, across the driveway, and latched it to the garage. They had some fierce matches which left Margaret winded and a poor candidate for a manicure.

A well-kept grassy lawn at the back of the house was the setting for games of croquet, an elaborate swing set, relay races, potato sack races, three legged races, and occasional pony rides. The Clearys would often invite friends with their children to join them in testing their skills in the various sports. Their laughter and shouts could be heard throughout the neighborhood. Everyone would lose themselves in the merriment of the games. How, she pondered, could Andrew forsake all of that?

Margaret tried to enrich her sons' lives by immersing them in joyful activities and widening their horizons. She loved the city in which she was raised and felt it had so much to offer. The Boston area is filled with history and historical sights. She and the boys followed the Revolutionary War's events going from Village Green to Village Green, from Lexington to Concord, visiting the Old North Church and Bunker Hill. They took in Plymouth on their way to the Cape, the plays and art museum at Williams College, the maritime museums, and the homes that inspired poets and writers such as Lowell, Hawthorne, and Wadsworth whose works she shared with her boys.

From the get-go, she approached their growth in a creative fashion, always providing fun. They would bake cookies and cut them in various shapes; build monstrous-sized edifices and towns with the boys' blocks, Legos, and varied-sized pieces of cardboard; make potato heads, sock puppets, and masks with scrap materials of twine, yarn, ribbons, buttons, paint and paste; drape blankets over chairs to devise forts, tents, and bears' dens. They sang, danced and marched to tunes she played on the piano or on their stereo. The family owned an extensive CD and tape collection and Margaret would select folk music, show tunes, jazz, marches and classical pieces.

She read to them, heard them read, and encouraged her sons to create stories of their own. Their video games and television watching were monitored. As they got older, Margaret had often viewed shows with them to answer questions or just for the sheer enjoyment of their company.

She'd been aching for their company ever since her arrival in Nerja. The almost daily e-mails, texts, Skype and phone conversations kept her in touch. However, it did not allow for lengthy and deep conversations nor the ability to read expressions of pain or joy in their eyes. She was longing to spend unfettered time, to hold them, to gaze at them and shower them with love.

CHAPTER 35

ARGARET HAD QUITE A LENGTHY wait since she'd allowed so much extra time for Madrid's commuter traffic tie-ups, finding parking, driving very carefully behind the wheel of Tomas' vehicle, and the possibility that the plane might arrive early. Finally, people began to slowly stream through the gate tugging overnighters, laptops, infants, toddlers, tennis racquets and purses.

Margaret was holding her breath until she, at long last, saw her sons emerge. Mixed emotions suddenly hit her. She was thrilled to see how many inches they'd grown in the few months, but was overwhelmed with the sadness that she'd not been there to witness it.

Now she had to wait further while they cleared customs and had their passports stamped. As soon as her sons spotted her, she heard, "Mom, Mom." They hurried toward one another, all arms and cheeks readied for embrace. Margaret held them to her as if she'd never let go. Laughingly, Brandon cried out, "Ma, you're smothering us; come up for air." She, too, laughed, and with that they marched off to the baggage gate to await the boys' luggage.

Although Margaret had been apprehensive about the possibility of awkward communication between her and her sons, the frequent phone conversations and Internet connections must have bridged the gap. The boys were quick to fill her in on their experiences during the flight, what they were hoping to see and do in Spain, the fact that they'd been working hard to master some Spanish, and how happy they were to have this extended Spring Break.

They all talked incessantly while waiting for the luggage and during the twenty minute drive from the airport to the "Gucci Gulch" section of Madrid. Margaret pointed out all of the designer-boutique shops as they slowly wove through the traffic toward the building where they'd be staying for the start of their vacation.

The boys' mouths were totally agape while Margaret showed them through the apartment. "Wow, Mom, how did you ever snare this place? You must have some great connections. This place is awesome!"

Margaret merely replied, "I try!"

She and Tomas had done a clean sweep of the place before he'd left. There were no clues remaining as to its owner. Now, all Margaret had to do was exorcize the memories of herself and Tomas' delightful week in these same rooms; not so easy to do. She'd have to force herself to compartmentalize if she were going to truly enjoy her time with her kids.

Each of the boys selected a bedroom and unpacked. Afterwards, Margaret escorted them through the immediate neighborhood. They eyed the very attractively- arranged windows of the designers' shops and, occasionally, strolled within to view first-hand some of the beautiful, and very expensive, items.

At the end, Margaret led the boys into the El Corte Ingles department store where they could appreciate the vast array of merchandise, and finally led them to the basement where the entire floor held a huge supply of food items. The boys marveled at the immense variety of Spanish olives. Margaret suggested that they select a sampling which they did. They were a bit grossed out at the prawns completely intact including their heads, and Margaret rejected her impulse to offer them a sampling of those, as well. The boys had a field day selecting a variety of cheeses, cold meats, fish, bread and fresh produce to amply stock their larder for lunch and dinners. Margaret derived much joy from their enthusiasm.

Since they did not appear to be worn ragged from their flight or their morning walk, Margaret suggested a trip to the Reina Sofia Museum. If they had little time and stamina enough to glimpse the rest of the art work here, she knew they would wish to concentrate on the immense, artistically and politically powerful *Guernica* of Picasso's. Indeed, both Brandon and Richard were blown away by the vastness, eloquence and sheer force of the piece. They were transfixed by the work for well over half an hour. There was so much to absorb and discuss.

Margaret was pleased that they were as enraptured with it as she, and were familiar enough with the history of the Nazi and Fascist movements to understand what Picasso was expressing. The *Guernica* is a bold statement of the losses and destruction that war brings, and Margaret was glad that her boys had the opportunity to learn from it.

Back at the apartment, Margaret fixed a light supper. Instead of sitting in the immense dining room with its very large table and grand chairs, they opted to sit at the smaller, more intimate round table in the corner of the living room surrounded by windows that overlooked the scene below. Shortly thereafter, the boys fell onto their beds and were out for the night. Margaret did not see them again until late morning.

They walked to a boulevard where cafés abounded. At one of the cafés, they ordered a sumptuous brunch of Spanish delights. Her sons gamely tried ordering from the Spanish menu. Fortunately, she and Andrew had introduced their sons to a myriad of food tastes from early childhood. Thus, the boys were willing to try just about anything.

They enjoyed the egg dishes which included potatoes in one omelet and ham, tomato, onion and peppers in another. A variety of sausages and cheeses was set before them. Margaret pointed out the delectable, and very popular, Manchego and some cheese from sheep called Roncal from Navarre. It's a fairly firm cheese, moist, smooth and pale ivory in color. A light nutty and herb flavor lingers on the taste buds. In particular, the blood sausages were pleasing to the boys' palates; something they'd not had at home.

After being fortified with this hearty brunch, the three meandered along another couple of miles westward. Margaret pointed out an older, historic section which quite recently had been extensively renovated into lovely boutiques, restaurants and art galleries.

"This area had been extremely run down before some artists and business people decided to turn it around. Isn't it lovely?"

The boys' heads bobbed in agreement. Margaret refrained from sharing the fact that the neighborhood had been the former site of rampant prostitution, drug deals and other unsavory activity.

Eventually, they reached the Royal Palace. They traversed the imposing structure and admired the lovely gardens and views of Madrid while they waited for an English-speaking tour.

Once inside the very magnificent building, they listened to their guide describe the French influences, the elaborate Rococo designs, the ornate chandeliers, marble floors and artistic walls. Brandon cupped his mouth over his mother's ear and whispered, "Gee, Mom, I thought we grew up in a beautiful, expensive home; this makes ours look like a slum."

Margaret stifled a giggle. She felt warm all over. Her boys were with her, and they were obviously enjoying the time together as much as she was.

The following day, they hopped on a bus to Toledo. The ride took less than an hour to this walled city which reached its zenith as the center of arts and economic and political power before the 15th century. After the expulsion of the Jews in 1492 and the persecution of the Moors, Toledo was on the decline.

Today, it looked very beautiful with its immense Cathedral and hilly, winding and convoluted streets within the ancient city walls. A teacher going home for her lunch break and later an elderly woman out walking her dog, when asked to point Margaret and her sons to a particular site or restaurant, stopped what they were doing and walked them to the location. Richard quipped, "They're just like at the Safeway. You need something, and they take you to it."

"Nice, eh?" Margaret queried. Again, two heads bobbed in agreement.

They'd agreed, also, to have a typical Spanish meal for lunch. Margaret explained, "In much of Spain, lunch is dinner . . . the big meal of the day."

"Oh, Mom. We knew that already."

Margaret, said nothing, but just grinned at their desire to show sophistication.

The waiter placed three small glasses of sherry on their table. They sipped leisurely while they read the menus.

Interestingly, both Brandon and Richard chose the same dishes. Margaret knew they were familiar choices as she'd served her version of them at home. She did interject, "I know you've tasted these before, but I'd guess that this preparation is different from mine. This should be much more authentic." And, Margaret decided to go along with the choices as they were typical Spanish fare.

The first course was a refreshing gazpacho soup. The cold soup was accompanied by small dishes of chopped tomato, chopped cucumber, chopped onion, and chopped green and red peppers and one with croutons, any or all of which the diner might add to suit his palate.

Margaret explained that those ingredients, except for the croutons, were already blended into the soup which, also, probably had garlic, shallots, red vinegar, and extra virgin olive oil and presumably contained flavors of cilantro, lime, chilli flakes, salt and pepper and Worstershire sauce.

They'd ordered one family-sized Paella. The boys were wide-eyed. "Wow! Look at the size of this thing," Brandon exclaimed.

Richard added, "Mom, I don't think your Paella at home ever had this many things in it. I'm seeing sausage, chicken, shrimp, squid, clams, mussels."

Brandon chimed in, "Look at the chorizo. Mom, what makes the dish so yellow? And what are those little thingies on top?"

Margaret chuckled, "I'd guess it's saffron that gives the dish a yellow coloring. Also, there's probably some chicken stock, garlic, onions, and those doohickies on top are parsley, rosemary and thyme."

"Just like the song," the boys chorused. "What happened to the sage, Mom?"

Laughing together, they attacked the bowl, spooning portions on to their individual plates. "Okay, guys. Eat up!" Silence ensued as they happily dug in to enjoy the tasty dish.

Fully satisfied, they decided to head back to Madrid. It took several stabs to try and puzzle their way out of the maze within the walled city in order to return to the bus stop. Once on the bus, all three dozed off.

Refreshed, the boys were, once again, ready to roll. Margaret suggested that they might wish to try one of the neighborhood night spots that the local teenagers frequented. Although she didn't say it aloud, Tomas had mentioned that his kids enjoyed dancing there when they were younger. "Gee Mom, that sounds like a great idea," Richard responded already feeling very grown-up and looking forward to a night on the town.

Immediately, Margaret had second thoughts. "OK, but please don't turn into pumpkins. I'll be worrying until you return."

"We'll be home by midnight. Okay, Mom?"

"Okay. Here, let me get you some money."

"If they take credit cards, Dad gave Brandon one for the trip. In fact, he said we should pick up the tab for some of our meals, any tours and transportation. Did you forget you had a VISA card, Brandon?"

"Guess I did. Sorry Mom. We'll use it from now on so you don't have to keep shelling out."

Margaret, amazed, said, "Really! Oh my. What do you know. Well, have fun guys."

As soon as they were out the door, Margaret collapsed onto a couch. She was totally confused. Could Andrew be turning over a new leaf? Had she judged him too harshly?

Again, she found herself wondering if she were to blame for the collapse of their marriage. Was this something they could work through with marriage counseling? Would Andrew be willing to undergo it? Would he take the time? Was he ready to give up the other woman or women? Was Andrew ready to be a full-time husband and dad?

Hey, wait a minute, Margaret. Do YOU want to return to Andrew? You've finally found your own voice. You're finding success and validation leading your own life. You've really felt good about yourself. You've had a great thing going with Tomas. I like Tomas' company, and he truly seems happy to be with me. We work out our differences with respect for one another. It's been feeling so good.

Then other thoughts weighed in. Was Tomas' interest in her appealing only as a reaction to Andrew's rejection? Was she just flattered by being wanted and admired? Was this like a summer romance, an infatuation? Would the real world descend on her and Tomas? She'd been so content in this new relationship. Could it last?

It was almost eleven in the evening. Would she awaken Tomas? Perhaps, he wanted to hear her voice as much as she his. She punched in his number in the Costa del Sol.

"Hi, I was hoping you'd call. How are things going?"

"Oh, I'm so relieved I didn't waken you. It's been great. The boys and I are having a super time. In fact, they're out at the teen club you'd suggested. That's how I have time to talk."

She then related the adventures of the last few days.

"You're having such a good time, and without me; I'm feeling jealous."

Margaret caught his humor and the underlying longing for her. "Well, it is wonderful being with my kids, and they are terrific company. But, if I weren't missing you, too, I wouldn't have phoned first chance I could."

"That's nice to hear, sweetheart. By the way, I need to remind you, I'm heading to New York City in a couple of weeks. You can reach me on my mobile. I'll be there for a week or two, depending on how long business will keep me and how much time my son will be able to spare for his dear old Dad."

Margaret laughed aloud, and inwardly smiled. She appreciated how much she and Tomas truly enjoyed their own offspring.

"Tomas, I had a sudden idea. If I were to invite Helen and Eddie and you for dinner before Richard and Brandon returned to the States, do you think we could pull it off without it being awkward or giving us away? I would love for you to meet them, and I think they'd enjoy meeting the folks that were influential in smoothing my path in Nerja."

"Well, if we could manage to keep our hands off one another . . . a dead giveaway."

Giggling like a foolish school girl, but in a slightly scolding voice, Margaret injected, "Stop that. Really, you and I can certainly behave as adults."

"Well now, I guess if you can show restraint, so can I," replied Tomas with an obvious smile in his tone. Bright, interesting table of people should make for a splendid evening."

"I gave the boys a midnight curfew, but I have no idea what time they'll be returning. I hate to end this conversation, but I better go. Goodnight dear fellow."

Margaret fell into a lovely reverie as she sank deeper into the couch. She must have dozed a bit as she didn't hear the key in the lock when the boys returned.

Startled, but awake, she glanced at the clock on the mantle. One minute to twelve; some things never changed. They always slipped in just before curfew.

"Mom, you wouldn't believe the time we had." Richard and Brandon couldn't get the words out fast enough, each speaking so rapidly their words crossed linguistic paths as they went. "These Spanish girls were all over us. I don't know how they knew we were from the States. Everyone wanted to dance with us. Some wanted to teach us to Salsa, and other stuff. And, both the girls and the guys all wanted to try out their English. They were asking us a million questions."

"Wow, sounds as if you had a busy, fun night. Maybe, I shouldn't have given you guys a curfew."

"We did have fun, but we were glad of the curfew."

Margaret raised her brows in surprise and questioning.

"Some of them spoke English well, but the ones who really wanted to practice didn't, and, honestly, they were giving us a headache."

Margaret guffawed, "I guess I must do that to most of the people I meet between Nerja and Madrid. My Spanish needs a lot of work."

In a tired, but concerned voice, Brandon spoke up, "Do you still struggle to speak Spanish with everyone you meet?"

"Oh, not everyone I meet is from Spain and as you've noticed, many Spanish-speaking individuals have a command of English. In fact, I wondered if you'd like to have dinner with a few of the people I've befriended while I've been here. I think I've mentioned Father Eduardo and his office assistant, Helen, and the gentleman I met on the airplane who involved me with the Olive Oil Conference here in Madrid. We could invite them for dinner at the house I'm renting."

The boys gave her the thumbs up, but Brandon added, "It sounds great, Mom, but if you don't mind, we're exhausted. Let's not plan the menu tonight."

Margaret laughed. She kissed and hugged them soundly as they each headed off to bed.

CHAPTER 36

FOR THEIR LAST MORNING IN Madrid, Margaret suggested that they head to Museo del Prado. Although Margaret would have loved several days at the Prado for her sons to fully appreciate the immensity and quality of the museum's collection of more than three thousand works of art including more than four hundred sculptures, she was pleased to be able to give them a quick taste of some of the Rubens, Bosch, Brueghel, Titian and the Spanish painters: Goya, El Greco and Velazquez. They scanned the museum's large map to determine where to find the artists and paintings of greatest interest to them. In the religious-oriented paintings, the boys recognized the biblical stories, many from the New Testament. They were obviously embarrassed and disconcerted, however, viewing Goya's *The Naked Maja* and El Greco's portrait of a man's hand upon a woman's breast while in the company of their mother.

As they were approaching the lunch hour, Margaret could feel her stomach rumbling and figured the boys were getting hungry, too. Their brains were quite satiated; time to call it quits. Margaret rejected lunching in the Prado's new cafeteria.

"The weather is gorgeous. Let's head to the park."

Outdoors, they found some food trucks from which they purchased slices of pizza. Ice cream was too tempting.

"Okay, guys. Let's all start our lunch with dessert. We can munch on the ice cream while we walk."

"Great plan, Mom," Richard chimed in while Brandon quickly nodded his head in agreement.

Before setting out for their picnic, they stopped to admire the various fountains in the vicinity of the Prado. Across the street was Neptune rising from a giant sea shell spewing water and being pulled by two gigantic horses. Down the street was the very popular Plaza de la Cibeles where the over-sized marble statue is pulled by two equally-sized lions. The ornately-carved Apollo fountain spews water that is illuminated at night. Margaret explained this to Richard and Brandon, but chose not to disclose how she'd stood there one evening breathing it all in with Tomas.

Fortunately, her sons were captivated by the colossal-sized mythical figures and were attempting to recall the stories related to them as Margaret steered them east toward the Parque del Retiro. The boys halted along the edge of the enormous pond with views of a castle, fountains, swans, and an enormous structure. "Mom, that looks like a cross between the Lincoln Memorial in Washington, D.C. and an ancient outdoor amphitheater."

Margaret laughed, "Why don't you dig out that little guide book from your back pocket, Brandon, and see if you can find the details. What does it say?"

"Let me see. Okay . . . got it. This park is one hundred fourty-three hectares. How many acres is that?"

"I believe I read somewhere that this park has an expanse of around three hundred acres," Margaret answered.

"Man, that's huge!" Brandon continued to read from his guide book. "The castle is called the Crystal Palace, and the other building, um, it just says that atop of that structure is Alfonso X11 on his horse. Guess that was a king. Whatever . . . I'm hungry. Let's find a place to sit and eat our lunches."

"I second that," added Richard. They plopped where they were, and rapidly ate their pizza slices. After which, they strolled to the magnificent gardens. The air was perfumed and the sight breathtaking to behold. Although they would only see a portion of the horticulture, Margaret thought . . . a perfect way to end their stay in Madrid. Always go out on a high note.

After a very long walk back to the apartment, they were all exhausted. However, Margaret was intent on returning to Nerja to begin their sojourn on the Costa del Sol. They could rest on the train.

En route to their bedrooms to begin packing their belongings, Margaret mentioned to her sons that the weather would probably be warmer as they headed south. "Do you have suitable clothing?"

Richard piped up in an unsteady voice, "Well, that's been a bit of a problem, Mom. You see, now that there are renters, we can't get into the house to get our spring and summer clothes. Actually, we may have outgrown last year's stuff, but I usually get Brandon's hand-me-downs and do keep those I like." His voice trailed off while he looked for support from Brandon.

Margaret was struck by his words as if he'd thrown a dagger at her or poured cold water over her body. She shivered slightly, but quickly sought equilibrium. Trying to summon some enthusiasm and encouragement for the boys, she managed a false bravado, "Oh, I'll get hold of the renters. I'm sure they'll find some time to accommodate your entering the house. They indicated that they were not planning to use your bedrooms, so everything should be just as you left them." Then she added in a soothing tone of voice, "Why don't we phone them before you leave Spain and set a time for you to go round. If we find that you need something while we're in Nerja, I'm sure we can find it there."

Later, on the high-speed train to the Costa del Sol, Margaret was overcome with remorse as she struggled with her thoughts. How could she have done this to her boys. She'd not only thrown their father out of their home, but her sons had their home pulled out from under them, too. The impact and realization of what she'd done was just beginning to surface.

She had not wanted to indulge in self pity before Brandon and Richard, nor had she wished to paint their father in the very black light he deserved. How was she to present a balanced view that would allow these teenagers, on the cusp of manhood, to understand what led to her present circumstance and, ultimately, to theirs.

While she was attempting to compose a response, Brandon and Richard were exclaiming over the cleanliness of the train, the speed it was traveling, the beautiful scenes they were viewing as they passed, and the lovely dinner that had been set before them. Their comments, to her relief, jerked her from her agonizing rumination.

CHAPTER 37

ARRIVING AT THEIR DESTINATION, MARGARET was relieved that Tomas had managed to deliver her car and leave it at the railroad station. The boys both whistled in unison as they spotted the Ford Escort convertible. "Wow, Mom. You didn't tell us!"

"No, I thought I'd leave this as a surprise. I take it, you like my choice?"

"Boy, and how!"

The boys started to bicker as to who was sitting in front. "Good grief, some things never change!" and Margaret quickly pulled out a tissue and tore it into two unequal parts. Turning away from her sons, she placed each in a palm of her hand and curled her fingers around the tissue. "Okay, pick a hand."

The boys deliberated, but each chose a different hand. Margaret let out her breath and opened her hands. They measured the pieces, and Brandon was clearly the winner. Richard, of course, protested, but Margaret assured him that he'd drive in front on another, even longer expedition. With each of them appeased, she had them hurl their baggage and hers into the trunk of the car.

Dusk was setting in, and Margaret wanted to catch as much daylight as was still available. The boys uttered a few comments regarding the scenery as they drove along the highway, but mostly remained in their own thoughts.

When they pulled into her driveway, the boys became very animated as they saw the exterior gardens and pool. Margaret turned on the pool's heating unit so they would all be able to swim whenever the weather permitted.

Indoors, Margaret put on lights and the place felt very welcoming. Margaret was home. Her sons, undoubtedly, were caught up in her sense of familiarity and relaxation. She ushered them through, and finally settled them in the bedroom the two would share. The following morning, they had a leisurely breakfast before setting off for a walking tour of the beautiful hill town of Fragiliana just above Nerja. The sun shone and the scene shone with it as they climbed the mountain ridge and looked down toward the sea and the little white houses tucked beneath them and out to the mountains in the distance. Margaret could hear the boys' intake of breath as they came upon this awe-inspiring, sensational view.

Eventually, they gradually descended to the cobble-stoned streets. As it was a Saturday, artisans were displaying their wares. While stopping now and again to admire the lovely handcrafts, Margaret encouraged the boys to select a small piece of the local pottery that would fit in each of their luggage, and to purchase T shirts as souvenirs.

They then drove to the Safeway to pick up food for the remaining time the boys had in Spain. She allowed their sons to use Andrew's charge card for the groceries.

After a late lunch, the pool beckoned. The boys were content to relax, swim, read and listen to music. That evening, they worked together in the kitchen creating dinner. Margaret knew that this was what she'd been missing ever since Andrew had relegated the boys to boarding school. She wondered if they felt it, too, but dared not ask.

The boys accompanied her to church on Sunday. As always, it was a packed affair. Richard and Brandon admired the edifice and were relieved that much of the service was in English. After Mass, Margaret showed the boys the classroom where she taught English as a Second Language and then stepped into the adjoining offices where she introduced the boys to Father Eduardo and to Helen. Margaret extended an invitation for them to join her and her sons for dinner at her home on Tuesday evening.

"That's perfect for me. I'll be having to prepare for Holy Thursday, Good Friday and all the Easter rituals, so that's about the last evening I'll have open this week. And, you are saving me from having to prepare a full dinner. But, I'd like to contribute something to the meal."

"And, so would I," Helen added.

"Gosh, the boys and I haven't even thought of what we're serving."

"Well, may I whip up a dessert? I really do like doing that, and I'll try to think of a recipe that will go with anything."

Margaret looked at the boys who looked back at Margaret in sheer bewilderment.

Margaret laughed. "That was not what I'd intended. This is not a pot luck." Yet, seeing the glum expression on Helen's face, Margaret acquiesced, "Okay, Helen, you'll make dessert." At which point, Helen's face brightened. Poor Helen, Margaret thought, she really doesn't have many interests in life after working all day at the church.

Margaret turned to the priest, "It's such a busy week for you, please don't feel as if you must bring something; I'd prefer it."

"I do have a bottle or two of wine at the ready, and I'll happily share it. What time will be good for you?" And, then rapidly added, "Would seven be OK? There will be a lot for me to tackle this week, but I know I'll be ready to quit by then."

Margaret turned to her sons wanting to get their input. The two teenagers just shook their heads in dumb-like, awkward approval. So, all was settled.

The boys perked up as Margaret took them to an outdoor café for lunch and afterwards stood on the Balcon De Europa gazing into the distance and observing the rugged, rocky shoreline and the mountains beyond. They rambled leisurely in and out of Nerja's narrow streets.

"Gee, Mom, you really know your way around here. It's like you've been here forever," Richard said with amazement in his voice.

"I guess I do feel as if it's all very familiar," and then she added, "and comfortable. Although I don't speak the language very well and know very few people, I feel needed by teaching English, and, as you can see, I've made a few friends whom I really cherish. One doesn't need a huge number of people, if those that you know are truly good, good friends and the few I've met have proved to be just that. They've been extremely helpful, supportive, and we do enjoy each others' company. I really do feel relaxed here, but I miss you boys terribly." And, her voice choked on the last few words. Her sons moved in toward her in comfort, but said nothing in reply.

CHAPTER 38

THEY STARTED OUT EARLY THE next morning for Granada. Margaret knew it could take from two to three hours to reach their destination, but the boys should not visit Spain without seeing Alhambra. While Margaret worried about finding a suitable parking spot, that is, one that would not be prohibitive in cost nor susceptible to break-ins, her sons read from their guide book.

Before they'd arrived at their destination, they were aware that the monumental project originated in 1240 with work continuing into the 1300's, had been destroyed or disintegrated over time, and was reconstructed beginning in the 1860's after Washington Irving's publication of *Tales of the Alhambra* in 1832.

They expected to see a complex comprising several buildings including the Royal Palace with its staterooms, a harem, pathways and courtyards which covered more territory than a football field squared. They read of the major influences from the Koran, the Moorish culture, and giggled over the Harem's Eunuchs.

Reading about it, however, did not prepare them for the marvels of Alhambra. The craftsmanship; the intricacy, gorgeous array of bold color and variety of the mosaic-tiled patterns; and the delicate, lacy-like structure of others.

The boys kept repeating, "Mom, this is totally awesome! Each area we enter is different, but equally spectacular."

"Indeed it is! I'm so pleased that you are enjoying the magnificence of this place. It truly is amazing . . . the workmanship . . . beauty . . . magnitude. It's barely comprehensible. It's been many years since your father and I were here, and I'm struck again by how fabulous it is."

They continued to admire the many superbly carved arches and doors; domes, cupolas, towers and turrets; the fountains and ponds; the flora; the twelve sculptured lions, and on and on. "I think I've entered Paradise," Richard exclaimed. "I believe if there is a Heaven, it should look like this."

They continued to wander from sight to sight and back again, drinking in all of it, in order to commit the scenes to memory. Eventually, they realized they'd not even attempted to identify the many different structures; they'd been so engrossed in the overall splendor. Margaret was delighted at her sons' response; it was far more than she'd anticipated.

Time flew and hours passed; no one was ready to leave. Yet, despite the snacks Margaret had provided for the car ride, stomachs were ready to be re-filled. Very reluctantly, they moved on.

While searching out a suitable establishment for lunch, they walked across to the large fort that overlooked the Moorish neighborhood below. It, too, held a compelling scene.

After lunch, they roamed the streets of the old city before driving back to Nerja. A tired, but very satisfied threesome returned to Margaret's condo. They took a quick swim in the pool before preparing dinner.

"Boy," exclaimed Richard at the dinner table, "is this the life, or what! You're giving us a fabulous vacation, Mom. Thanks."

"Well, it's fabulous for me, too. In addition to seeing these sights through your eyes, just having you boys with me is everything. I've really missed you guys, not only here in Spain, but even at home."

As soon as the words were out of her mouth, Margaret regretted them. After all, the boys were at boarding school through no fault of their own, and they were enjoying the experience. Instinctively, as if to take back her words, Margaret put her hand over her mouth. "I'm sorry, I shouldn't have said that. You guys are receiving a first-class education and enjoying your classmates and the activities the school offers. I shouldn't be running a guilt trip on you."

"Mom, we're not as innocent as you might think. We're not totally unaware of your reasons for landing here in Spain."

"Yeah," Richard interrupted Brandon in a defiant voice. "Brandon has sworn me to secrecy, but I think we should tell Mom, Brandon."

"Tell me what?"

Brandon said nothing, and Richard took it as a sign of acquiescence.

"Mom, Brandon went back to Newton for a weekend to stay with his buddy George. You remember George?"

"Of course I do. He lives just a few blocks away and has been Brandon's good buddy for years."

Richard continued. "Well, George and Brandon went into Boston to spend the afternoon and evening. They were in the North End and looking to eat Italian food." Now, almost choking on his words and obviously in discomfort, Richard resumed, "From a distance, Brandon spotted Dad and what appeared to be a younger woman. You might say they were quite chummy."

Margaret sighed heavily and looked down toward the floor. "I'm sorry you had to witness that, Brandon. It's the last thing I wanted for myself and certainly for you two."

"We know that, Mom." Brandon had decided to take up the story from there.

"Richard and I discussed this a lot. We knew there had to be a very good reason for you to ask Dad to leave, and then for you to take off for Spain six months later. Seeing Dad that day on the street, just confirmed what we'd suspected all along.

"For years, Dad had been there to shoot hoops, golf, ride bikes, swim and play tennis with us. Suddenly, he was always going into the office. It did start to add up when Richard and I talked about it."

"I'm so sorry guys. I'd hoped that since your routines didn't vary, you weren't at home anyway, I was hoping it would have less impact on you. I guess I was wishing it so, but not seeing the reality of how much you would comprehend and how much it had to affect you, also."

Brandon said, "While we were flying here, Richard and I had lots of time to talk about things. Although as you well know, we don't always think alike, we're actually feeling the same way on this score. We both are doing well at school, but we'd do just as well at the high school in Newton." And, in rapid succession as if to get it out in one breath, he added, "It has a great reputation, kids get into good colleges, and we'd much rather be at home."

Seeing Margaret ready to protest their decision, Brandon interrupted her, "Mom, we'd really rather be at home. We've made good friends at school, but our very best friends are still the guys that we've known forever. And, although we're OK with the boarding school, we'd really prefer to be at home with you." At which point, Richard burst into tears with Brandon just about ready to follow suit.

Margaret thought she'd have a nervous breakdown. What had happened to her picture-perfect family.

She gathered her boys to her and held them tightly. "I guess we should have had this conversation earlier, before I took off for Nerja. I should have leveled with you, but I hated to ruin your Dad's image in your eyes, and I really didn't know where all this was going. Frankly, I'd hoped your Dad and I could sort it all out. Was this a one time thing? Could we go into marriage counseling? I just didn't have the answers."

Margaret heaved another huge sigh. As a Mama Bear, she'd wished she could protect her cubs. She was finding, unfortunately, that's not always doable. Such trauma for her and her sons; she really abhorred Andrew. Why had he chosen to cause them all such pain?

She held her sons to her for quite some time, no one wishing to speak. Finally, Margaret whispered, "I'll give your wishes strong consideration, but I'd like you to think hard. In the long run, is this what you REALLY want? Do you really want to leave where you are? Will you be giving up some independence, the whole campus life that you presently have, the chance of, perhaps, getting into a better university? You're both engaged in sports and extra-curricular activities in which you've obtained success and enjoyment. You're both doing well academically and have found the courses informative and interesting. I believe you need to allow yourselves some time to weigh this decision very carefully. "

They cleaned up the kitchen in silence, each in his own thoughts. When the job was complete, Margaret said, "I don't know about you guys, but I'm beat. Do you mind if I head off for bed? We can talk further in the morning."

They embraced Margaret with an understanding that Margaret deemed beyond their years; she felt as if some of their childhood had been stolen.

CHAPTER 39

THEY MUST HAVE ALL SLEPT soundly as each of them looked quite refreshed. Perhaps, thought Margaret, last night's conversation was much needed. It was the elephant in the room and needed to be faced.

But, today was not for wallowing in self pity. She knew just the cure. Off they went to Gibraltar.

Just as she'd hoped, as soon as her sons caught a glimpse of the darling, tailless Barbary Apes, they became young teens again. Richard yelled, "Mom, can we keep one of these little guys? They're so cute!. They remind me of 'Curious George' . . . that book you used to read to us when we were little."

"Sure, just put one in your knapsack, and you can carry him home on the plane."

And, rapidly shouted, "Oh, oh, watch your cameras! Those apes will grab them in a blink of an eye." They clutched their cameras, but remained in place while doubling over in laughter at the many antics of the several monkeys gadding about and hopping on and off folks' shoulders. As Margaret had predicted, those monkeys lift spirits.

Since The Rock is only about four miles in length and a half mile across, they agreed to hoof it rather than take a tourist bus. However, Margaret did suggest that they take the cable car to the top. From there, they looked across the Mediterranean waters on one side and the Bay of Gibraltar on the other. Margaret pointed at Morocco in the distance.

From their perch on high, Brandon commented, "Now, I can see why so many countries fought for this piece of real estate. It allows a perfect view of any naval contingents beneath."

Richard lifted his head from the guide book, " 'This property was held by the Moors for seven hundred fifty years, then ceded to Britain in the Treaty of Utrecht in 1713, and Admiral Nelson used it as a base while fighting the Battle of Trafalgar during the Napoleonic Wars'. Hey, we learned all of this in history. I'll bet I might remember it all, now that I've been here." Margaret observed how he looked very pleased with himself, and she smiled within and without.

Brandon added, "Don't forget Richard that the Allies used Gibraltar for naval and air bases during both World Wars. But, today, it looks like a spot for tourists."

"Indeed it does," Margaret chuckled. "Yet, when I was in high school, I had a dear friend who subsequently joined the Navy and his ship was stationed just beneath the Rock. He'd written beautifully descriptive letters to me from Gibraltar. At the time, I'd never thought I'd have the opportunity to be standing here. How lucky we are!"

Two heads nodded in unison as they proceeded to descend. They hurried along to the main street and arrived just in time to catch the Changing of the Guard in front of the Governor's Residence. Afterwards, they grabbed a quick lunch before strolling along the various streets. They came upon one impressive older building which the guide book identified as the Nefusot Yehudada Synagogue built in the 18th century.

Richard asked, "I wonder why so many people are streaming out of here?"

"Oh, I believe this is part of the Passover observance. It usually falls very close to Easter. You recall that the Passover Seder and the Last Supper are one and the same." Her sons nodded in acknowledgment.

Brandon added, "I remember going to my friend Ben's house for a Seder. Do you remember that, Mom? They were so nice to invite our whole family. That was a long dinner, but the food was delicious and it was a fun evening."

"I remember it, too, I was there," Richard piped up as they all stepped into the car to head back toward Nerja.

Margaret would have liked to mosey along the shorelines of opulent Marbella and Puerto Banus showing the boys the beautiful seascape, fabulous yachts, and, perhaps, dine in one of the restaurants facing the sea. But, tonight was the night for her sons to meet her dear friends, and so they went straight-away toward Nerja.

"What do you think we should serve for our dinner tonight, guys?"

"Your leg of lamb, Mom."

"Yeah, that's always a winner."

"Or, maybe your Chicken Cacciatore."

"Uh-huh, that's delish. Or, how about we grill some steaks?"

"Bet you have something in mind, Mom. Right?"

"Actually, I do. There's not much room on the table as it only seats six, and we'll be six people. I thought it would be easier if each person has his own serving. I was thinking of doing Cornish Game Hens. I phoned the butcher this morning, and he is saving several of them for us. Are you up to doing some stuffing with wild rice?" Richard noted, "Always ahead of us, eh Mom?" This declaration tickled their funny bones.

"Okay, Mom, what else is on your menu for tonight?"

"I was thinking of some light appetizers: cheese and crackers, shrimp with cocktail sauce, and, maybe a veggie platter or some other item that catches our eye."

Margaret pulled into the Safeway parking lot. They cruised the store looking for a suitable cheese. Margaret spotted 'San Lazaro'. "I had that once when I first came to this region; it's a delicious cheese. Let's get that. I'm sure you'll like it."

They found some pre-cooked, frozen, ready-to-eat jumbo shrimp and bottled cocktail sauce. Over at produce, Margaret grabbed a firm lemon, "This will add flavor to the cocktail sauce, and we can use it as a garnish to decorate plates."

Brandon exclaimed, "Look at these beautiful asparagus. The deep green will 'pop' against the hens and wild rice and make a contrasting shape on the plate.

"This bunch is healthy. Right, mom? All the tips are in good shape and tightly closed." Margaret, amused, thought he'd been watching too many cooking shows on TV.

"Good job, Brandon! Those do look great, and what a good eye for aesthetics. Maybe we'd better get two bunches for six people. Can you find another bunch looking just as fine?"

The boys wanted to get another selection of olives as they had earlier in the week. Shrimp, olives, cheese and crackers would suffice for hors d'oeuvres.

Margaret added ingredients for salad to the cart. She went through the rice aisle and added one box each of Wild

Rice and a Pilaf Mix with Wild Mushrooms. "I have pine nuts at the condo that I can add to this mixture."

At the bakery department, Margaret asked for two freshly-sliced sour dough breads. She requested that they be placed in only paper bags. The boys knew their mom believed plastic bags tended to soften the crust.

As promised, the butcher had the hens waiting for them. At the check out, Brandon said, with a slight smirk, "I think we should have Dad pay for this dinner," and he whipped out the charge card.

"Good idea, Bro."

"Is that ethical?" Then, with some remorse in her voice, "I guess your Dad hasn't acted very ethically has he. Okay, I'm in."

They, hastily, put away their bundles. Margaret quickly washed and seasoned the hens while the boys prepared the wild rice and pilaf from the boxes and added the pine nuts. They all worked together to stuff the rice pilaf inside the hens.

Margaret placed the largest saute pan on the stove. She added some good quality, buttery-flavored olive oil, and when it was hot, tossed in the asparagus. She added some pepper to taste and a medley of fresh herbs.

In the meantime, the boys set the table with a cloth, napkins, utensils, dinner plates, and wine and water glasses. Margaret sent them outside to gather some bougainvillaea that was just coming into bloom. They distributed the flowers into two small vases and placed each toward the head and foot of the table.

Once the table was set, and the food and a pitcher of water in the fridge, there was time enough for relaxing at the pool. They'd been on their feet all day and even her sons collapsed into the lounge chairs and dozed. Margaret woke first and quietly slid into the pool to do a few laps.

While swimming, she contemplated the evening ahead. Margaret always relished giving dinner parties, but tonight would be special. All the people who'd be in attendance were very dear to her . . . her little fan club of personal boosters . . . and, additionally, very enjoyable.

She was looking forward to Tomas' presence with great anticipation, but wary of what vibrations her sons might glean. Her guys were very perceptive. She and Tomas would have to be careful.

She looked at her watch . . . 5:30. Just enough time for her to shower, dress and make up. The boys could sleep awhile longer.

When she stepped out of the shower and peeked outside, her sons were horse playing in the water. It was good to see them just being kids. She knew they could shave and shower and dress quickly. Shave! It still took her by surprise that her sons were old enough to shave. . . although Richard's beard was ever so slight.

As Margaret was putting on mascara, she heard the boys entering the house to get ready for the evening. Such a joy not to have to go calling them in from play; they really were getting to be responsible young adults.

Entering the kitchen, Margaret melted butter and mixed in some red wine that remained from a bottle Tomas had supplied. She poured the concoction into a Pyrex baking dish to baste the hens as they cooked.

Margaret arranged the shrimp and cocktail sauce on a dip platter. The olives were spooned into a beautiful bowl that the condo owner had left on display. Cheese and crackers went on a wooden cheese board with an accompanying slicer.

When the boys emerged freshly attired in chinos and button-down shirts, they whistled at their mother who was clad in a three quarter sleeved, cotton-jersey shirt with a low V neck that tucked securely under the bust line. The material was patterned in bright bold purples and oranges set on a white ground. Her white cotton/spandex Capri pants clung to her shape, and were accentuated by white, high-heeled, open-toed mules on her feet.

"You like?"

"Very fetching, Mom."

"It's such a lovely evening. Shall we have the cocktail hour out on the patio around the pool? If we're lucky, we might even catch a beautiful sunset."

"Let's! We'll help carry out stuff for you."

Margaret set the oven temperature. The boys transported the hors d'oeuvres while Margaret grabbed cocktail napkins, plastic cups and small paper plates.

On the dot of seven, Helen appeared in a white blouse with modern-looking dangling chains, and a long, full skirt in multiple hues. She'd made a marvelous looking strawberry-rhubarb pie and a fruit salad for her dessert contribution.

"Oh my, you really overdid it! So much labor. Thank you soooo much. It looks fabulous. Bet it's delicious. Wait until my boys see this! Wait until the men see this!" Laughingly, Margaret added, "I don't think anyone will want to eat dinner . . . just go directly to dessert."

Helen blushed, a bit embarrassed with the accolades, but smiled brightly in appreciation of the comments. She replied demurely, "They may look better than they taste."

To reassure her friend, Margaret patted Helen's arm, "I'm sure they'll be great. However, we'll have the taste test later . . . and do expect compliments." Both women were smiling as Margaret popped the Pyrex dishes containing the hens into the oven.

Thoughtfully, Tomas did not use his key, but rang the doorbell. He offered a dozen mixed roses into Margaret's waiting hands and kissed her on the cheek along with a Puritanical hug. Suspecting that Tomas would bring flowers, Margaret had already set out the vase. She quickly filled it with water, arranged the roses and set them prominently on the counter separating the kitchen and dining area . . . a nice touch of color and additional warmth to the room.

Tomas greeted the boys as they escorted him and Helen onto the patio. "What have you been doing since you arrived? How did you like Madrid? What has your Mom shown you in Nerja?"

The boys duly answered Tomas' questions in turn while growing more and more forthcoming as he listened intently and without comments other than to say, "Oh nice . . . great . . . fun."

Margaret listened to their conversation with one ear while the other ear listened for the doorbell. As soon as the priest arrived, everyone dug into the food. Margaret took the opportunity to check on the hens and do some basting before re-joining the group.

She noticed that Tomas and Eddie greeted each other with fervent bear hugs and fell into rapid conversation in Spanish. She knew they'd not seen each other in many years and were delighted to reunite. Their affection for one another was readily apparent, and everyone allowed them the time together. Margaret made a mental note to get these two old friends together more frequently.

Finally, Margaret said with amusement, "Okay you two, enough with the Spanish; join the party. What will everyone drink? Father Eduardo brought some wonderful reds and white wines. I have beer, and of course, water and sodas."

They each registered their requests, and her sons returned with her to the kitchen to start filling the drink orders. Once again, Margaret checked the hens and basted. Eventually, Tomas joined them in the kitchen and out to the patio to help proffer the drinks.

Margaret observed that much of the conversation was geared to the boys with everyone asking about their stay in Spain, their courses at school and their favorite sports. Even Helen, who had no children, was getting into the act.

Margaret was concerned that Brandon and Richard might find the attention a bit much. However, both Tomas and Eddie were so natural in their questioning that her sons appeared at ease and happily engaged.

She left the group in order to lay the salad bowls atop the dinner plates at each place setting and to remove the hens from the oven to cool slightly prior to serving. The bread basket went onto the table along with two small pitchers of olive oil convenient to all. Before calling them in for dinner, she lit the fragrant candles scattered around the living room and dining area.

Everyone carried in a drink glass and an hors d'oeuvre platter which the boys returned to the refrigerator. Margaret chose to sit nearest the kitchen and asked the others to find a spot. Perhaps, she thought, she might have made up place cards, but that did seem a bit formal and pretentious in this setting.

When everyone was comfortably seated, the priest offered a short blessing over the food. Despite having consumed much of the appetizers, the group commenced to eat heartily of the mixed salad topped with sliced radishes and scallions . . . and silence reigned.

The boys helped Margaret clear the dishes. While conversation resumed, she and the boys laid a stuffed Cornish Game Hen on each clean dinner plate along with asparagus spears served at room temperature and garnished with lemon slices and cherry tomatoes.

"Sweetheart, what a beautiful presentation!" Catching himself, Tomas blanched.

The priest, sensing the situation, immediately added, "Margaret, dear, you really have outdone yourself. And, it appears your sons have had a hand in all of this, too. Am I correct?"

"Indeed they have, and thank you for the compliments." She shot the priest a thankful glance . . . hoping they'd dodged that bullet.

Father Eduardo continued, "Has your mother brought you to see our marvelous caves? They are inspiring."

Richard, matching the priest's enthusiastic and sincere tone, "No, she hasn't, but we know that's on her list to explore with us."

"Well good. If I weren't so caught up this week in Easter rituals, I'd take you there myself. It's quite amazing."

"Well, I'm not caught up in Easter rituals, at least not until Friday when I fly to New York to join my son and daughter. Do you guys like the water? Do you know anything about sailing? How would you boys like to head out on my boat?"

Margaret snapped to attention. She was not expecting this at all and threw Tomas a look. Just as she was about to say something, Brandon clamored, "That sounds like a wonderful excursion. Huh, Mom? We'd love that. That is so kind of you to invite us." Richard, too, was practically jumping out of his seat with enthusiasm.

"Hey, you and your Mom just served us a great dinner. I can try to repay in kind.

"Why don't you meet me tomorrow morning, say about elevenish at *The Respite*, that's the name of the sail boat."

"Do you know how to find your way, Mom? Would you please give us very explicit directions; Mom isn't too good at finding her way around."

Tomas turned to Richard, "I don't know about that. She's been managing fine in a foreign country, but I'll certainly give you clear directions." He restrained himself from winking at Margaret.

These youngsters did ingratiate themselves. There was nothing uppity, false or contrived about them. He found he was enjoying them more and more every moment.

Then, remembering his manners, Tomas sought to include Helen and Eddie, as well. The priest answered for both of them. "We would love the outing, but duty calls."

Margaret started clearing the table and taking beverage orders to accompany dessert. Before she knew it, Tomas and Eddie had rolled up their sleeves and were rinsing the dishes and stacking them into the dishwasher. She was about to stop them when she realized the two were engrossed in conversation, and this was their outlet for some private time. She recalled their fond remembrances of days spent together in the States those many years ago. Perhaps, here was an attendant sense of *deja vu* . . . of a time when these men were young and unencumbered. She decided to give them space.

To Helen she said, "You know, why don't we use the coffee table to finish dinner. Would you care to slice your pie into these little dessert plates? Here are some small forks. I'll just put your lovely bowl of fruit in the center and folks can help themselves."

She set the boys to wiping off the table as she prepared tea for everyone . . . the drink of choice. Eddie had suggested that since Helen had prepared the desserts, British tea should rule.

Now seated on the living room couches and chairs surrounding the coffee table, they chatted amiably. No one rose. Perhaps too much food and spirits had slowed their metabolism, but everyone seemed reluctant to leave, lingering far longer than expected.

Finally, Father Eduardo pulled himself up from the sofa. "This has been one of the most pleasant evenings I've spent in ages. You've connected me with a very dear old friend, family really. Your sons are terrific, just like you, Margaret. And, the cuisine and conversation have been divinely inspiring."

They all laughed and, with that, everyone gathered the dishes and mugs to place in the kitchen sink and headed for the door. Margaret and the boys were hugged, kissed on the cheeks and thanked profusely again and again for the superb evening.

As they put the remaining few items into the dishwasher, Brandon remarked, "You know, Mom, we thought we'd be bored out of our gourds tonight. You really made some neat friends here. They're really cool. No one was stuffy and pretentious."

"Yeah," chimed in Richard, "and they even seem to like you."

Margaret was so startled, she almost inhaled the candle she was extinguishing. "Excuse me??? They seem to like me? Are you so surprised at that?"

"Oh Mom, Richard doesn't know what he's saying. Why wouldn't they like Mom?"

"I don't know why not, but they sure do. And, we're getting out on Tomas' boat tomorrow. You certainly made great connections. How did you meet this guy?"

Margaret beamed, "I'm so glad and relieved that you boys had such a good time. I could tell that you found Father Eduardo and Tomas interesting, and Helen is such a sweet lady. However, why don't we talk more and I can answer your questions while we're driving tomorrow morning. It will take about forty-five minutes, so we'll have plenty of time. I don't know about you, but I'm exhausted. It's been a fantastic day, but very long."

"Love you, guys. You were a great help today. Thanks," and she kissed them soundly.

Richard said cheerfully, "No problemo, Mom. Night."

CHAPTER 40

A S THEY WERE GETTING READY to leave, Margaret called out to them, "Don't forget to put sweatsuits, hats, bathing suits and deck shoes or flip-flops in your backpacks. I have sunscreen in mine. You might, also, want to take a change of clothing in case we go out for a bite to eat."

"Yeah, Mom, whatever."

"Well, aren't we getting persnickety. Mind your manners, fellow, or your chauffeur will declare a day off."

Brandon giggled and went with the program.

As they were snapping their seatbelts, Richard commented, "I hope that this sail- boat has a crew aboard."

"I am certain it doesn't."

"Yuck! That means we'll have to help with the sails, the mast, the jib, whatever they're called. And, do you remember when Dad rented that big sailboat and we all were aboard, and we were all expected to help him? My hands were rubbed raw from those ropes."

"I believe we all remember that, honey! Yet, you survived. And, yes, I'm certain Tomas will expect you to help, and why not. You're two strapping young fellows, and your skin did grow back. Right?"

"By the way, have you boys been on any outings with your Dad recently? I know you told me you'd gone to a Red Sox game with him. Where else have you been?"

"Absolutely nowhere," was the reply in a desolate voice from Brandon. "We went to Newton a couple of times for long weekends, like President's weekend. Grandma and Grandpa had invited us to stay with them. Grandma keeps mumbling how you ran off and left us, implying you're an awful Mother and care nothing for us."

At this news, Margaret whimpered audibly.

Brandon continued, "I got so fed up, especially having seen Dad in Boston, I finally told her that you had good reason for going, and there weren't two sides to this story. That kind of took her aback. Anyway, Dad joined us for dinner. He was so antsy and uncomfortable the whole time. It was if he were on a time table and couldn't wait to get away."

"Yeah," Richard spouted, visibly subdued.

Oh Lord, thought Margaret. Now they're in a pissy mood, and poor Tomas will have to put up with all of us. Thanks a lot, Mr. Andrew. Not only are you ruining my life, but our sons', as well. Think fast Margaret, think fast. Let's get rid of the melancholy.

"You guys are going to be blown away when you see these yachts at the marina. Some are absolutely huge and outfitted in mahogany or teak wood. They are just exquisite and horribly expensive. Those probably have crews on board, but I'd bet that Tomas' is not ostentatious in the least. Read those instructions to me, will you please." And shortly thereafter, they pulled into the parking area and looked for Tomas' boat.

They arrived at 11:10, and Tomas was awaiting them. With a huge smile on his face, he waved energetically in their direction, and the three clamored aboard.

"Welcome to *The Respite*. I'm hoping you'll enjoy the day." This time, while the boys' attention was elsewhere, he did wink at Margaret.

Tomas provided a quick tour of the boat to orient them. The boys were drawn to photos of Tomas' children. He explained that Antonio was a graduate student at Columbia University in New York City and Maritza was an undergrad at the University in Madrid. He added that he'd be seeing them both when he flew to New York tomorrow to celebrate the holiday as Maritza was visiting with her brother.

"Do they have a mother," Richard blurted out. "Oh sorry, I guess that's not a good question, huh."

"No, it's not," his mother said in quick reproach.

"That's okay." Tomas knelt to the bottom of a chest of drawers and from the back withdrew a framed picture. "Here is Liliana when the children were small."

Margaret saw a youthful brunette with hair in a ponytail, wearing a house dress and sandals while holding a baby and clutching the hand of a very young Antonio. Liliana was smiling broadly, a proud and happy mother.

The picture disquieted. A wave of pity for Liliana swept over her. Margaret knew there were photos of her smiling happily with her young sons. How life could turn on a dime; in her case in an instant.

Almost to break the spell, Tomas interrupted their thoughts, "It's a wonderful day for sailing. The weather is so pleasant and we should have enough wind to catch the sails, but not enough to heave. How do you say it? Last one in is a rotten egg; in this case, it's 'up'." Everyone raced up the steps and willingly plunged into the tasks of getting the boat underway.

It was a picture-perfect day for sailing. Richard did not seem to mind the related tasks. Both boys were glowing.

Tomas pulled into an area where he knew they all could swim safely. They plunged into the brisk water. When Margaret and Tomas emerged, the boys asked if they could swim a bit longer. "If you can stand the cold temperatures, fine. Just don't wait until you turn blue."

"Margaret, it really feels as if this will work. I feel so comfortable with your kids, and they seem fine with me."

"Can you offer them a boat ride in the Mediterranean on a daily basis," Margaret asked playfully. "Unfortunately, from their comments to me, it doesn't sound as if Andrew has spent very much time with them since he and I split. Maybe, he thinks he's punishing me by disassociating himself from his sons. It's a loss, loss situation that I deeply regret."

"His mid-life-crisis behavior sounds very immature to me. It, also, could mean that Andrew is freer to 'sow his wild oats', and he's doing just that. Ergo, leaving him no time for his sons.

"You can't beat yourself up about this Margaret. You didn't bring this on yourself or your boys. There are things in life we simply cannot control. One of them is trying to alter another human being.

"However, I'd like to alter your behavior. Do you think you could take your eyes off the swimmers for about three minutes and duck behind this door?"

"Oh, you naughty boy." Margaret gave a quick look at her sons who were lying on their backs, floating along on the gentle waves.

They ducked behind the door for a quick, but meaningful embrace. Their arms around each other locked in a deep kiss. As much as they would have liked to continue, they emerged on the other side of the door within the three minutes.

Margaret sighed with relief to see the two heads bobbing on the water. Tomas gave her hand a quick squeeze, and she smiled up at him with sheer joy on her face. If she could just freeze-frame this moment in time.

When the boys finally climbed back on board, Tomas went beneath to surface a few minutes later with all the fixings for sandwiches. They ate hungrily having worked up a great appetite.

"Mom tells us that you have fields of olive trees and produce olive oil."

"That's true, Brandon, although I'm not personally involved with the everyday hands on anymore. Is there something special you'd like to know about the industry? Maybe, I'd have some answers."

"Well, we're only acquainted with the olive oils we see on the grocery shelves. We know to look for the Extra Virgin, cold-pressed and first-pressed varieties. And, Mom did show us some new brands that she has at the condo."

"There are jillions of brands of olive oils." Tomas was surprised and pleased to see the boys' faces registering interest in the subject so he continued. "Basically, there are four categories of olive oil: regular, organic, for seasoning as in a salad, or for cooking. The olive oils can have buttery flavors or fruity or peppery or in combinations. Some may be of lower acidity than others."

The boys nodded in understanding, and with looks that suggested they wished to hear more. "Are there price variations as there are with wines?"

"Absolutely. You can go from the less expensive oils that you see on grocery shelves to . . . "

"Oh, I know," Richard interrupted. "Mom's bought olive oil for special occasions that can be as much as sixteen dollars a bottle."

"Well, there are some that can go as high as seventy dollars."

"Really," whistled Brandon. "Wow! Is it made with gold?"

They all laughed. "Not quite, but there are olive oils infused with say wild mushrooms, or truffles which sends the prices soaring. Also, there are olive oils that are sold in containers made of expensive glass or ceramic which drives up the price."

"Is your olive orchard nearby? Maybe we could visit it today?" Richard was carried away with curiosity and eagerness.

Margaret and Tomas shot each other a furtive glance which read . . . as long as Liliana is at the orchard, there will be no visitation by Margaret and her sons.

Tomas injected, "It's way too far," and deftly changed the subject. "Do you boys know how to fish? I believe there might be some old fishing rods below. We can get them out and give them a try. What say?"

Margaret offered to dispose of the lunch remains while the boys and Tomas descended to look for the rods and reels. Emerging, they baited the hooks and attempted to follow Tomas' movements in releasing the lines. The equipment was negatively impacted by weather and time, but the boys pursued until the lines arced toward the water. Whatever they managed to hook brought delight to her sons' faces, and they were content to 'catch and release' for some time. Margaret was grateful to Tomas for introducing her sons to a new skill, and both she and Tomas were beaming.

As the winds subsided, Tomas suggested they pull in the sails and rely on the motor. To the delight of Brandon and Richard, they moved full speed ahead toward the marina. Once they were tied securely to the dock and all items removed, they walked to their respective cars.

The boys and Margaret thanked Tomas profusely. They'd all had a fabulous day and were sincerely grateful.

Knowing they'd not see each other for some time, Margaret and Tomas were reluctant to part company, but Tomas needed to get back to the condo to pack for his extended time in New York. They parted with a bear hug.

Once settled on the airplane headed to his destination, Tomas found he could not concentrate on his reading. He longed to have Margaret beside him. He was realizing more and more how much she filled his life. And, he had so enjoyed her sons. What an easy camaraderie they'd formed. He found himself smiling at the recollection.

However, in truth, it was Liliana whom he had tried to persuade to accompany him. Weeks ago, he'd driven out to check the orchards. While en route, he'd been struck by guilt. He and their kids would not be with Liliana for the holiday, and he knew that would upset her.

Therefore, he did try his best to convince her, in a reassuring voice, to join them in Manhattan for Easter. Her response was not unexpected; she'd sung the same songs before. "From the very beginning, you were taking those children here, there and everywhere. You've given them your wanderlust. You even introduced them to all those foreign foods. God only knows what those kids are putting inside their bodies."

"Liliana, you knew that I'd lived in the States and traveled extensively through Europe for many years before we'd married. What did you expect? That I'd give up an interest in seeing new places and meeting new people, enjoying restaurants, museums, theater?"

"I thought you'd have it all out of your system and would be content to settle down and enjoy the peace and quiet of this beautiful piece of the world. Now, you want me to go to New York City with its filthy streets, crime, and hordes of people pushing and shoving? As much as I want to be with Maritza and Antonio, I will not abide that. Moreover, you want me to get on an airplane? You've heard me say it a million times, if people were meant to fly, God would have given us wings."

In spite of himself, Tomas couldn't stifle his laughter. "Calm down, Liliana. Airplanes are a safe means of travel. And, New York City is a lot cleaner with far fewer crimes than in the past, and the people can be rather nice. Besides, you'll be staying in a very lovely neighborhood, the kids and I will be right with you, and I'd try to get us into St. Patrick's Cathedral for Easter Sunday. That should be a very special treat. And, we could all be together for the holiday."

Despite his show of enthusiasm, as he'd anticipated, Liliana would hear none of it. She refused to move out of her cocoon, and there was no convincing her. She was a genuinely good woman, a devoted mom, but, sadly, he and Liliana were a poor match.

She was correct, however, their children had tasted his love of adventure and were not turning back. At some point, Liliana would have to know that at this moment, with encouragement from her brother and dad, Maritza was investigating graduate schools in Manhattan.

Was he like Andrew? No, he and Liliana had grown apart before they were ever together. He hadn't left Liliana for another woman or women, nor had he tried to separate his children from their mother. He'd merely introduced them to his world, and they preferred it. His children had simply outgrown their mother's life view and her fears. Was that wrong? He genuinely thought not.

The problem, as far as he could see it, was how to bring Margaret into his life on a permanent basis without hurting either of their offspring or Liliana? Having now spent time with Brandon and Richard, Tomas felt strongly that they would get along well with Antonio and Maritza. His chief dilemma was how to affect this without causing additional pain for Liliana. He did owe her that.

CHAPTER 41

OR THE NEXT FEW DAYS, Margaret flung herself into a myriad of activities with her sons. While it dulled her pain of Tomas' upcoming departure from Spain, it gave her the opportunity to focus on the boys and enjoy their last few days of vacation.

Since they'd heard so much about the Nerja caves, the teenagers were very much looking forward to their visit. Margaret explained that only about a third of the caves was open to tourists. The caves dated from the Paleolithic era and could have been inhabited as much as twenty five thousand years earlier. Richard and Brandon were fascinated with the fact that the caves were not discovered until 1959 and, then, by children playing on the surrounding hills.

When the three climbed down the stairway into the caves, her sons commented on the eerie feeling from the dark, dampness, sounds of dripping water and the many spires, turrets and stalactites. Richard pointed to the one suspended two hundred feet in length. The guidebook claimed that it was thought to be the largest in the world. They dallied in the caves for some time; Margaret never tired of this experience and was glad her boys were intrigued, as well.

Afterwards, they shopped for groceries in preparation for Easter dinner. At their request, Margaret promised to make her traditional leg of lamb and the accompanying assortment of vegetables. A bakery nearby offered a small cake in the shape of a lamb. They hoped it would be as delicious as it looked. "If nothing else, it will make a lovely centerpiece for our holiday table," Margaret exclaimed as she made the purchase.

That night she lay in bed thinking of the many Easter Sundays where she and Andrew and their sons had enjoyed Sunrise Services and the numerous dinners celebrated with her family or Andrew's. Given the circumstances, perhaps it was better that she and the boys would be observing the day far from home and from the usual traditions.

Might it be less painful? Is it something she should discuss with Brandon and Richard? They had initiated the topic of the marital split at different instances while they were here. I guess I'll just wait for their cues.

To her surprise, the boys had awakened earlier and were reading in the living room. "Well you're up bright and early,"

"No, Mom, you slept in late," Brandon chuckled. "We're just waiting for you for breakfast. The eggs are all ready to go. Richard and I decided to cook for you this morning."

"How nice. Thanks guys."

As they sat around the table finishing their breakfasts, Richard remarked, "That was such fun yesterday on the boat. When I grow up, I'm definitely going to buy myself one of those babies."

"Those babies don't come cheap, Richard," Brandon warned him. "You better study hard and plan to earn lots of money, and marry a woman who doesn't get seasick." At that, the three burst out laughing.

When they'd all regained their composure, Brandon said, "We know you met Father Eduardo and Helen through the church and how he'd asked you to teach English, but you never did tell us how you met Tomas. Is it some deep dark secret?"

"Hardly," Margaret grinned. Having realized that this topic would eventually be broached, Margaret launched into a very abbreviated, cleaned-up version she'd run through her head many times before. She wished to tell her boys the truth, yet not put them into a state of shock.

"We met on the airplane from Boston to Madrid. Tomas was seated with a business colleague and busily engaged in conversation . . . but not in English. I absolutely hadn't a clue as to what they were saying.

Then, when the food was served and we were all eating, Tomas made some casual remark to me in English that held only a trace of a Spanish accent. I was really taken by surprise, and especially when he identified my Boston/Irish brogue.

He'd been a student at Harvard's grad school many years before and enjoyed reminiscing about the Boston area. When he heard that I'd be living in the Costa del Sol region for six months, he offered his business card if I needed any assistance.

Well, I did not get in touch with him as I was doing quite well on my own. As I told you, Father Eduardo, 'Eddie', really came to my rescue in helping me find the car, visiting the caves and offering me a part-time position. And, I was enjoying learning Spanish, the seclusion here, and being on my own to think about our lives.

Lo and behold, one evening when I was having dinner with one of my young students, Tomas appeared at my elbow. He was dining there, too."

Margaret paused, coming up for air. "Go on, Mom. Tell us the rest," they said in unison.

"Okay. Well, after that, Tomas phoned and we met for dinner. That's when he was bemoaning the fact that he was asked to help run this Conference for the Olive Oil Council, and I offered some suggestions. I guess my suggestions were good, because I managed to land an additional job.

Tomas provided his secretary for an occasional assist. In addition, a daughter of a friend of his, who happens, also to be a friend of his daughter, acted as my translator during a long weekend in Madrid. They are all EXTREMELY gracious and generous human beings, so it was a delight to work with them. In addition, I learned a lot about the olive oil industry and the extra money allowed me to squire my two boys this week. A win-win situation, don't you think?"

Satisfied, the boys rose from the table. As they cleared breakfast Margaret said, "Since it's raining, why don't we prepare the lamb roast and the veggies today. Then, we'll only need to re-heat the food when we return from services tomorrow."

Richard added, "Besides, everything will be tastier after the food sits for a day in the fridge."

"Right you are. Let's get to it."

Brandon seasoned the leg of lamb with salt, pepper, paprika and lemon juice while Richard and Margaret sliced three onions and washed a couple of stalks of celery.

Neither of her boys wished to mess with the garlic, so Margaret diced two cloves and rubbed them into the lamb and placed them into little pockets. While she was thus engaged, the boys placed a half cup of water and three tablespoons of butter into a baking pan with the onions and celery. They opened two cans of whole potatoes and placed those along the sides. Margaret added the roast.

They'd set the baking thermometer to what they hoped was four hundred degrees. Once the roast seared, Margaret lowered the temperature to three hundred fifty degrees. She removed the baking pan from the oven and covered the roast and potatoes with a mixture of two tablespoons of Worcestershire sauce and a half cup of lime marmalade. While she did so, Richard intoned in a deep, vampire-voiced baritone, "Grandma's secret ingredients from *Have Cookbook Will Marry*."

Indeed, Margaret still had the dog-eared, tiny cookbook at home which her mother had received as a wedding shower present decades ago. As they were all doubled over in laughter, Margaret decided this was a good ritual after all.

Margaret explained, "We'll need to baste this, but I'll cook the roast only partially and finish it after church. In this way, it will marinate during the night and be hot and tasty when we're ready to eat."

The following morning, Margaret was pleased to see her teenagers dressed in the outfits they'd worn on the airplane, but having added a necktie. "You boys look handsome, indeed," Margaret told them with a broad grin.

The three had chosen to attend an Easter service conducted by Father Eduardo. Margaret positioned herself in the pew so as to read her sons' expressions. She wondered if they were missing their usual church service, plus their Dad and friends at home in Newton. The boys, however, appeared relaxed and absorbed.

Although she did not feel she deserved to do so and had struggled with her decision, Margaret joined her sons to receive Communion. She was sure Eddie must have 'read' her relationship with Tomas, yet had not spoken of it to either of them.

Afterwards, the priest stood in the doorway greeting each of the parishioners. Margaret hung back and let the majority of the worshipers pass through. She suspected the priest would wish to spend more time with her and her sons.

Indeed he did. He greeted each of them by name along with a big bear hug. "Thanks again for a fabulous evening. Did you boys enjoy the boat ride? Did you see the caves? Is it tomorrow that you leave us?"

After hearing a positive response to each of the questions and some hasty back and forth, he wished the boys a safe trip home. "Enjoy your Easter dinner; I'm joining my family later today."

As soon as they returned to the condo, the boys removed their ties and rolled up their sleeves. They helped Margaret put the roast in the oven. While that was cooking, Margaret fixed a large salad and the boys set the table. "I'm going to make this easy," Margaret declared as she pulled some frozen vegetables. "These will cook in a matter of minutes," and she popped the peas and baby onions into the microwave.

Shortly after, they were enjoying their repast. Margaret wondered if they were missing the camaraderie of their dad, grandparents and many cousins. Almost with mental telepathy, Richard questioned, "Do you think that our family is eating dinner right now?"

Gently, Margaret explained, "Well, there is that time difference of several hours, honey, so I doubt they're at the table. Are you missing everyone?"

"I guess, yes and no. I have to say, I'm not missing the formality of sitting at the table all buttoned to the collar with a tie and scratchy woolen pants."

Brandon added, "I think it's kind of nice that we can sit here without neckties and with our shirts askew. It's certainly a lot more comfortable and far less noisy."

"Oh, it's too quiet in here," Richard proclaimed. "I'm missing the fun of lots of people around and especially the cousins."

Brandon interjected, "It's just . . . that is what we've always done. Will it ever be the same again, Mom?"

"I honestly don't know, sweetheart, but I suspect it might not be the same again. I'm sorry. I certainly did not expect this nor wish it.

"It does feel less of a holiday. If my friends here weren't going to their respective families, we could have included them. Except even that would not have felt the same, would it?"

"Right, Mom. However, you didn't ask for this anymore than Richard and I did. It's just going to be a big adjustment for our family."

Margaret sat stunned. It seemed as if her boys were already looking at their family's situation as a *fait accompli*. She wasn't there yet, but, at the same time, she did not wish to give her sons a false sense of hope.

Now they spoke openly of contemporaries whose parents had separated or divorced, especially guys they knew at their boarding school. Margaret experienced a knot in the pit of her stomach and a sense of apprehension shot through her. Never had she expected that her family would be classified in this category. What was she to do?

"I have no idea what my next step has to be. However, we'll get through this. It won't be easy, but somehow we'll get through. As the saying goes, we'll just have to 'hang tough'."

With that, Margaret rose from the table carrying in some of the empty dinner plates and serving platters. The boys rose to help her which caused the conversation to segue to happier thoughts. Margaret was intent on not spoiling their holiday.

"What are you betting on our dessert? Will it cut it?"

Richard piped up, "Mom, we'll not know that until you cut the cake and we taste."

Their mood lightened. "I'm so full, Mom. Perhaps, Richard and I can get our belongings together and start packing. Afterwards, we'll have more room for sampling the lamb cake."

"Sounds like a plan," Margaret replied happily.

The remainder of the day and into the evening, the three chatted, but stayed away from the plight of Margaret and Andrew's dissolving marriage.

The teenagers had an early flight and Margaret saw them off with a heavy heart.

She held onto them as long as humanly possible, wishing she'd never have to let them go. But, go they must, and the three bravely smiled their good-byes.

Margaret knew she'd have to get very busy to numb the pain and loneliness. Since it was Easter Monday, she headed to the church. As soon as she could find Helen, Margaret proceeded to collect the worksheets her students had completed in her absence. After thanking Helen for overseeing her classes, she and Helen made a lunch date for later in the week,

Throughout the day and into the next, Margaret pored over her students' responses. In most cases, Helen had marked incorrect answers. Margaret would want to thank Helen again for her professionalism and industry.

Margaret categorized and tallied the errors. After itemizing the results, she ascertained which topics needed to be reviewed and in which order of importance. She set about writing her lesson plans for the remainder of the next several weeks.

Once again, and for the next ten days, Margaret was power walking, swimming when the weather permitted, shopping groceries, occasionally visiting the caves, preparing for and teaching her classes and having a lunch with Helen and one with Father Eduardo. It was enough to keep her busy and prevented her from missing Tomas or her sons too much. She felt her life was back to a comforting, steady rhythm. Then, suddenly, her world came crashing down around her. Turmoil ensued.

CHAPTER 42

MARGARET COWERED AS SHE CROUCHED in a corner of the cave. Seeking protection and cover, she felt herself backing as far as possible into the recesses of the rock.

She had come to the caves of Nerja, as she did routinely, whenever she wished for quiet and a place to gather her thoughts. Now, a refuge was being threatened.

On Saturday, she had been sipping coffee with Helen at an outdoor café when she became aware of someone watching her. At the time, she rejected a surging sense of fear and continued to enjoy the early spring warmth as she lifted her face to the sun. Nonetheless, the hair on the nape of her neck began to prickle. Someone was observing her. Margaret turned her head just slightly. A man, or what she presumed to be a man from the look of his fingers, ducked his head beneath the open newspaper. When she dared turn again, the figure was gone. Helen had noticed him, too, but hadn't been able to describe the person as his face had been hidden by the newspaper.

Margaret dismissed a feeling of alarm and continued her usual routines of teaching English to her Spanish-speaking classes at the church, taking her long walks, and swimming in the pool behind the home she'd rented. Nerja had afforded Margaret a sense of freedom and abandon, security and privacy. Swimming topless in her private, heated pool, she again sensed someone watching her. Grabbing for her towel, she climbed out of the pool and looked far up into the hills. Without a doubt, there was a person looming at the top of the crest. Even from this distance, Margaret could tell that it was a masculine figure staring down at her through a set of binoculars. As soon as Margaret's actions were noticed, the figure fled. He was gone too rapidly for her to examine him carefully. She could not distinguish his features, nor decide on his height or complexion.

This sighting left her feeling very apprehensive and exposed. This man had seen her. . . and fully well at that. Was it just a random tourist who, while eyeing the scenery, glanced upon a semi-clad female form? These hills did seduce those who had a penchant for traveling off the beaten path. She would just have to shake this feeling of being stalked.

Margaret resolved to continue as if nothing had happened. After all, nothing had really happened. Perhaps, she was just overreacting.

On Sunday, Margaret went to Mass. This Sunday, the church was crowded with more worshipers than usual. Perhaps, because it was shortly after Easter, greater numbers of people were caught up in a religious mode. Father Eduardo's assistant, Helen, waved to the entering Margaret. Margaret, gratefully, eased her way into the center of one of the pews where Helen had saved, what looked to be, the one unoccupied seat.

After profusely thanking Helen, Margaret became totally absorbed by the beautiful young voices singing some of her favorite hymns. Was there any music more beautiful than the *Panis Angelicas* or the *Ave Maria*?

As Father Eduardo rose to give the homily, someone in the rear gave a short cough. Margaret turned toward the sound. A man quickly turned his back and exited rapidly.

Had Margaret been imagining all of this? Was she becoming paranoid? She had been so surprised by the presence of this man that it took her a few seconds to focus and comprehend. With several Masses recited on Sunday, why was he present now? Was this the same individual who'd had his binoculars trained on her earlier in the week?

This was the longest and closest view she'd had of this person. There was no denying that it was a he. In addition, she could see that he was quite tall and moderate in build. He had moved so swiftly, Margaret noted nothing more. Now, her fear was tangible. The incident left her with a tingling spine and dry mouth. She was barely able to make it back to her house. As she entered, she searched each room, looked out the windows up into the hills, and made certain all outer doors were locked. She remained indoors throughout Sunday afternoon and evening. She regretted terribly being too frightened to swim or lounge by the pool. She found that she jumped at any noise, at the ringing of the telephone.

There was no one in whom she could confide. Tomas was in New York on business, and today, he would be dining with his son and daughter. Father Eduardo was busy all week with visiting church dignitaries. She didn't wish to intrude on the priest's time nor distress Helen. She would just have to be wary.

There were no further sightings of the man and, by Wednesday, Margaret began to relax. As she frequently found great comfort there, she decided to head to the caves.

She wandered along, captivated as always by the magnitude and beauty of this underground wonder. Suddenly, she became aware of a figure lurking in the shadows along the edges of the caves' walls. At first, she backed into a large group of tourists and continued to move among them. She was able to blend for some time because of the numbers. However, when the guides called out individual buses, smaller groups of passengers began to assemble. Margaret could not make herself invisible while the leaders were counting heads, nor could she ascend with them from the caves. Her car was parked at the farthest side of the lot while the bus drivers stationed themselves at the ticket booth. She would have to traverse the entire parking lot alone and in the darkness.

Acting quickly, she jumped, balancing unsteadily over some rocks and water as she sought to melt into a niche in the rocks of the cave. She curled her body into the tightest ball, her head tucked under. Margaret prayed she would pass unseen.

Margaret listened intently. All the tourists had left and she heard no voices. She could hear her rapid breaths and the thumping of her heartbeat. She felt as if her chest would burst.

The cold was seeping through her veins. Her body shuddered and she could hear her teeth chattering. Could someone else be hearing them, too? As quietly as she could, she unfurled her torso, reached for her backpack, and withdrew her ever-present Gortex jacket and slipped into it. She knew she had a power bar in the pack, too. If she became hungry, could she risk the sound of crunching?

The silence of the caves was broken only by the occasional sound of dripping water. The mood was ominous, and Margaret cringed.

Who could be pursuing her? She was certain someone was. Who was this tall man? She contemplated all those whom she knew? Could it be Luis, Father Eduardo, or even Tomas? Why would one of them be trying to spy on her? Stalking her? Could it be Andrew, or even one of her sons? Was it one of her students? Was it a total stranger? What would be his motive?

Luis, of course. Hadn't he shown terrible mood swings? Wasn't he often angry with her when she refused to spend additional time in his company?

Could it be Eddie? Had he completed his conferences with the church leadership and sought relaxation at the caves? Had he spotted her there? Why wouldn't he have called to her and joined her there? Was he suspecting that she and Tomas were living together and thought her a poor role model to be on staff? Had the elderly priest, who was Father Eduardo's superior, heard of her indiscretions and wanted her dismissed?

Had she somehow slipped up while her sons were visiting? Had she aroused their suspicions? Had one of her sons returned to keep tabs on her?

Would Andrew leave his busy law practice and girlfriend or, maybe, girlfriends to follow Margaret to Spain? Would he care enough to want to drag her back to Newton? Besides, he didn't know where she was. Or did he? No. As they were heading toward the airport's gate, Margaret recollected calling to her sons, "Remember guys, don't divulge my whereabouts."

"Don't worry, Mom. Mum's the word." And, she trusted her sons to keep their word.

These were preposterous thoughts. Totally unimaginable. Nothing that would have credibility. Certainly, she would recognize any of these men even from afar and at a cursory glance. She felt as if she were being driven insane.

Footsteps! A shiver shot through Margaret. Suddenly, a light shone in Margaret's eyes. Instinctively, she covered her face with her hands, drew into herself and screamed. The man who'd rushed toward her, and spoke in a mix of rapid Spanish and broken English, tried to convey reassurance. "It is OK, senora. You are OK. What you do here?"

At this, Margaret looked up with one eye peeking from behind her hand. Her quivering body disassembled into a heap . . . a heap of relief. Fortunately, she was looking into the face of one of the many uniformed security guards who lined the pathways of the caves and guided the tourists along their way.

Having heard her screams, several of the guards rushed back into the caves. One, a younger man who usually was at the information center, spoke English more fluently than most of the guards. Margaret had chatted with him on numerous occasions in the past. Now, she turned toward him. Trying to keep her voice slow and steady in order to be understood, she explained. "Some man has been following me all week. I saw him in the outdoor café, and in church, and he was in the caves today. I was too frightened to try to get to my car because it is parked on the far side of the lot."

"We know. We saw the parked car as we were leaving."
Now, he translated her English into Spanish for the benefit
of the guards. They nodded their understanding. "Come,
we'll get you to your car. No one is left on the premises.
You will be safe. Have you told the police?"

Margaret suddenly felt so foolish. Why hadn't she called
the police? Why hadn't she told someone?

Margaret suddenly recognized that the concept of being
stalked was beyond believing. She didn't want to believe it
and expected few others to fathom her plight.

She realized, too, that she was very lucky that some of
the staff recognized her, or she'd be in great trouble for
loitering past the hours of operation. The Nerja caves had
posted times that were strictly adhered to by the great
multitude of visitors.

Margaret became aware that her body was visibly
trembling and tears had started to quietly flow.
Embarrassed, she wiped her sleeve across her eyes. The
younger man placed his arm around her while the security
men unlocked the information office and shepherded her
into a chair in the main room. Once she was seated, one
of the guards offered her a Styrofoam cup of hot coffee. A
grateful Margaret sipped its contents. The warmth of the
liquid seemed to flow through every seam in her system,
gradually restoring her to a modicum of calm.

The guards spoke in Spanish among themselves. They
appeared to feel that Margaret was now in control of
herself. Anxious to complete their workday and return to
their homes, they now rose to leave.

"Will you be okay?"

Margaret, not wishing to detain them further, replied, "Yes, I'm feeling better." Nonetheless, her voice, betrayed her.

Thanking them profusely both in English and Spanish, Margaret allowed them to escort her to her vehicle and follow her car onto the main highway. In a robotic trance, Margaret let the car guide her toward home.

How was she to go home? What if this man were lurking in the shadows? What if he'd managed to break into her house and was awaiting her there? Should she phone the police? What could she tell them? Would they think she was some crazy American woman? Paranoid, that's what she was! Yet, she couldn't quiet the jitters in her stomach.

Impulsively, Margaret reached for her iPhone that she'd left in the car. She reached her next-door neighbors whom she'd finally met and they'd exchanged some brief conversations. Just last week, Margaret had helped them carry in groceries and lent them some extra pillows for their visiting grandchildren. She hoped they'd be home and receptive to her needs.

Now, in broken Spanish mixed with English, Margaret explained to Olga that she'd spotted some man following her repeatedly throughout the week. Margaret continued, "I'm heading home. Would you and your husband be kind enough to walk through the house with me? I'm so scared. I just want to make sure no one is hiding there."

Would they think her nuts? Would they want to go along with her plan? In addition, as she spoke, Margaret realized she could be putting this elderly couple in jeopardy.

Olga, in a reassuring voice, said they'd certainly watch for her car and meet her in the driveway. Margaret choked up with relief and gratitude. "Gracias, senora, mucho, mucho gracias!"

Together, the three approached Margaret's rented home. They stood aside as Margaret inserted the key in the door and pushed it open with one hand while turning on the entry light with the other. Margaret, accompanied by her neighbors, put on every light in the house as they thoroughly searched room by room, in each closet, under beds, and across the patios and pool area.

Finding nothing and no one there, Margaret felt abashed and foolish. But, her neighbors reiterated that she should call on them anytime she needed.

Margaret offered the couple a glass of wine and some cheeses. They sat compatibly, and Margaret felt her equilibrium slowly returning. When her neighbors suggested she join them for dinner, Margaret, suddenly feeling totally exhausted, declined their kind invitation. She escorted them to the door offering profuse and heartfelt thanks. She reassured them that she'd be okay.

When she was alone, Margaret mechanically set about getting something to eat. She pulled a can of Campbell's vegetarian soup from a cabinet, emptied it into a bowl which she placed in the microwave along with a platter of leftovers from the fridge. Without much appetite, she set the food on the table and proceeded to slowly eat. The BBC echoed in the background reporting the news from Britain and around the world. She heard nothing as her mind ran in all directions.

Who could this man be? Now, the sanctuary of her home in Nerja, her life in Nerja felt threatened. Was it time to return to the States? To her marriage?

She'd submerged so many moral and religious convictions since meeting Tomas, she was getting better at squelching any misgivings. Yet, the concept of divorce was still a bitter pill to swallow. It had never been in her vocabulary regarding her marriage.

She believed she would have to return to Newton, her boys, and her former lifestyle . . . probably to Andrew as well. Despite the reality of half of all marriages ending in divorce, in her mind, the Church would never condone her leaving her husband. Nor could she handle her in-laws' remonstrations, nor her feelings of self-scorn if she were to disrupt the life of her sons. Her time in Spain and with Tomas would have to remain a sweet memory.

With a heavy sigh, Margaret rose from the table and placed her dishes in the sink. She ran some water through them, but could not summon the strength to place them in the dishwasher. They'd be there tomorrow.

Without removing her clothes, she collapsed atop her bed, her thoughts racing helter-skelter. She could almost see and touch the beautiful azalea bushes, yews, liriope, skimmia, astilbe, hosta, and variegated acuba that surrounded the English Tudor house in Newton which she had lovingly tended.

Now, crunched under the covers in her bed in faraway Nerja, Margaret's shuttered eyes visualized the circular driveway and expansive lawn which rose to meet the large imposing brick Tudor. Mentally, she opened the oversized-double doors to reveal the double-story foyer from which hung a cut-crystal chandelier that threw a soft light along the graceful, winding stairway.

She and Andrew, with the help of his mother's decorator, had chosen mahogany French provincial furnishings from

Baker and Henredon with materials and wallpapers culled from Stroheim and Romann and Schumacher. Expensive. Elegant. The taste of her mother-in-law?

The living room and dining room reflected her earlier, happier years of marriage. However, after eighteen years, they, too, were beginning to show wear.

And, a very weary Margaret finally fell into a fitful sleep.

CHAPTER 43

As she sat curled in a corner of the sofa, Margaret heard the phone ringing in the States. A woman's voice answered with a groggy, "Hello."

"Missy? Did I wake you?"

A whispered voice answered, "Huh . . . I'm barely up. Hold on a minute."

Margaret held the phone to her ear. Finally, Missy returned to the line, "Sorry, I needed to leave the bedroom; Johnny is still asleep. What's the matter? Your voice sounds awful . . . as if you've been crying."

"I have been hysterically crying for hours." In an unsteady voice, Margaret began to blurt out the events of the days before.

"Remember when I spoke with you a few days ago, I'd told you that I thought I'd seen a man staring at me through binoculars while I was swimming topless in my pool. And, you and I had laughed it off saying that I was just imagining that this almost, middle-aged bod would attract some guy's eyes."

Margaret's voice choked as she described the very brief sightings of this man at the café outside the church, during Mass, and then at the caves. Upon hearing all of this, Missy's voice took on a tone of alarm.

"Margaret, did you phone or go to the police station? Is someone with you now? Where are you?"

Between sobs, Margaret said no, she hadn't gone to the police and then continued her story. "The morning after I was spooked at the caves," and she gulped, "I drove the car to a family grocery just below the highway and parked there. I continued on foot toward the main drag of Nerja, down the hill to the Balcon de Europa near the church. From there, I started walking along the shoreline. I wanted to clear my head and get some perspective."

Margaret's voice faltered. Missy, wishing to encourage her friend to keep talking responded, "And?"

"Well, the shoreline along there to the beach is very narrow and rocky, so I was walking more slowly than usual. I heard someone calling my name and the voice sounded familiar. I turned to see who it was . . . Missy, it was Andrew!"

"Oh my God," gasped Missy.

" I know. I took off like a shot!. I navigated the remaining shoreline, raced across the beach trying to avoid stepping on the older ladies." With some humor returning, Margaret added, "It was like a sea of sagging breasts."

"Yes," laughed Missy. "Our time for that is coming, too."

Concerned for her friend, Missy wanted Margaret to continue her story, and so she urged Margaret to do so.

"Well, I raced up around a hundred steps to the top. By this time, I was so winded, I had to stop. I ran across the street and plopped down on the first chair at this outdoor café where I've eaten lunch several times with Father Eduardo. Andrew, barely able to breathe, followed shortly after and sat opposite me. Frankly, now that I think about it, I wished he'd had a heart attack in the process."

When he finally caught his breath, Andrew, in this admiring voice said, "You are really in amazing shape, Margaret. I couldn't keep up with your pace at all."

"I don't recall my exact words, but it came out something like 'So, it's YOU who's been STALKING me. You couldn't let me know you were planning a trip here, but had to sneak around? I guess that's just like you . . . in every way . . . true to form'.

"I had the upper hand here, Missy, since Andrew was still trying to get his breath. I must have continued to rant and rage.

"Then he said to me, 'I wouldn't call it that. After all, you are my wife, and I just needed to see for myself what you've been up to. Also, you need to return home'.

"At that remark, I thought something had happened to one of the boys. Andrew did reassure me that was not the case, but persisted in ordering me home.

"I can't quote myself, but the conversation went something like this; 'And, pray tell, why should I cancel my six month lease and return to Newton? I've just spent time with my sons, and I have no plans for returning, at least before my six month lease expires, if then. I'm making a good life for myself here, and I'm happy'."

"May I remind you that you have two sons, a home, and a reputation at stake."

"So, you're threatening me?"

"Perhaps, but let me tell you the neighbors and our friends are asking questions. I find myself making excuses to my colleagues when you are not in attendance at social events, and my mother is irate that she has to explain your behavior to her contemporaries."

"And, what's it like for you, Andrew? Are YOU missing me, your home, what? Have you decided to give up the bimbo or however many women you are seeing? His face turning from red to purple, and in a choleric, raised voice, he blurted out, 'Cheryl is NOT a bimbo!'

"With those words, I almost croaked; my whole world was totally upending. Cheryl was the young lawyer in his office for whom he's, supposedly, acted as mentor during the past couple of years. I'd met her at office parties, picnics, and the occasional dinner at someone's home.

"As if to weigh this essential piece of information, we sat in silence for some time. I'm sure Andrew had not intentionally revealed his little secret and sorely regretted his unexpected outburst.

"The café owner approached our table for our drink orders while handing us menus. He looked at me a bit quizzically as if he recognized me and seemed to sense my angst. Since we were the only ones camped there in that interlude before lunch, surely, he couldn't help but notice that Andrew and I were in a very heated discussion. Furthermore, I suspect, he recalled seeing me at his establishment before with Father Eduardo and felt a bit protective.

"As the owner was about to re-enter the kitchen, I hurriedly grabbed my backpack and told Andrew I needed the restroom. Following the owner/chef whose name I suddenly recalled, I whispered in English and Spanish and said something like, 'Carlo, you have to help me. Can you please quickly drive me to my car parked at the small supermarket at the top of the hill, I need to get far away from this man right away'.

"I guess I kept repeating 'rapido, rapido' because Carlo immediately said something in Spanish to his helper as he grabbed his keys off the hook near the back door of the kitchen and whisked me outside. We were in his car probably in a matter of seconds, although it felt like forever. Missy, I've never been so terrified in all my life."

Missy's voice could barely be heard. She sounded shaken as she asked, "Are you OK? Are you in a safe place? Is Andrew anywhere around?"

"I believe I'm safe. Truly, Carlo drove as fast as he could, even going through a couple of red lights. Although I was feeling paralyzed, I kept turning to see if anyone were following us.

"As soon as we reached the small, family-owned market, Carlo made sure I was secure in my car and watched me head toward the highway."

"You drove onto the highway in that condition? Are you completely nuts?"

"Oh Missy, I knew I just needed to get as far from the rented bungalow as possible. I realized that it was Andrew who'd been staring at me through binoculars, so he knew where I was living."

"But why would you take off on a super highway feeling so jittery?"

"This I get from the person who has spent a lifetime taking risks? Honestly, Missy. I did count to ten several times and took some deep breaths to try and calm myself. I wasn't completely berserk, only partially.

"I was able to clear my head enough to make some judgement calls. Since I hadn't been with Tomas all week, I believed that Andrew would not know about him or where he lives. So, I headed toward Tomas' place in Marbella.

"I tried calling Tomas from my iPhone, but could not reach him on his. I left a message for him and sent a text which I was praying he'd pick up quickly. I knew he'd hear the tremor and fear in my voice, but I didn't want to upset him further by going into details. I just prayed he'd get my message in time. I wasn't sure how I was going to talk my way through his community's gate.

"However, at that point, there was a more urgent need. I had a sudden bout of sheer panic. I realized that Andrew had kept showing up wherever I was all week long. I worried and wondered whether or not Andrew had hidden a device on my car to keep tabs on me.

"As soon as I was able, I pulled off the highway and checked all around the car inside and out, over and under. There was nothing visible although, I must admit, I was not totally relieved. I ain't the most high tech person on the planet."

Missy added, "Well, neither am I, but you were certainly brave, Margaret. Actually, even though I encouraged you, I thought you were mighty brave heading off to Nerja on your own; and, you've done surprisingly well. Anyway, continue."

"Well, I had left the message for Tomas. I didn't give any details because I knew Tomas would be worried, and he was too far away to do anything about it. However, I did ask him to let the guard know I was arriving and I'd explain everything when Tomas returned from New York.

"Luck was with me. Since I had a fourty-five minute window of opportunity, Tomas was able to alert security at the gate in time for me to drive onto the premises. I mentioned to the guard not to let in anyone for that condo other than the owner, Tomas Nunez.

"I was not aware of anyone following me. Nonetheless, I took the precaution of parking away from Tomas' apartment and walking a circuitous route. After locking myself into the place, I just burst into tears.

"While I'd been driving, I kept thinking of how much time Andrew had spent with Cheryl on the pretext of working late hours or occasionally on a Sunday evening. All that time away from our sons and from me.

"My rage was boiling as I suspected it was one of the reasons he insisted on the boys going to boarding school. If they weren't at home, he wouldn't have to feel guilty about not being at home with them, or have to make excuses for his hours away.

"It was humiliating for me and absolutely despicable of him. How could I have been so easily deceived!

"I was not comforted by the memories of other women in my same shoes. Men who'd married into wealthier families to see them through law school, and then left the marriage once their practices were on firm ground. Or guys who fell for the young woman lawyer and led a double life for tons of years before approaching their aging spouse for a divorce. I knew it happens, but hadn't dreamed it would happen to me."

"Oh, Margaret. I am so, so sorry for you and hating Andrew more and more every minute. I guess you no longer have a choice, do you?"

"No. I must find a good lawyer in the Boston area, preferably in Newton, and go through with a divorce. I have no recourse.

"Oh, Missy, what am I to do? What if I lose the house? Will I have money to live? Where will I get the money to pay a lawyer? I don't have a job; I haven't worked for years. Will I get custody of the boys? Will I need to share custody with Andrew? I am beside myself with hurt, anger and fear for the future. I have sat here by myself just bawling."

"Well, I'm glad you phoned me. At least, it helps to have someone in your corner. It's important, Margaret, to get things in perspective.

"You are not totally helpless. You do have a university degree, a few years of teaching under your belt, and innumerable volunteer experiences in a leadership capacity, plus a jillion folks who admire you and may be helpful in finding a position for you even in this present job market.

"Just think how you've managed to keep afloat in Nerja. True, you've had monetary assistance from Andrew, but the courts will certainly award you some alimony and child care benefits. That's usually customary. And, you've been able to find a part-time job at the church and assisting with that olive oil conference in Madrid.

"I'm sure Father Eduardo and Tomas would give you stunning references, and those are recent work experiences. Margaret, don't sell yourself short."

Choking back tears, and in a tentative voice, Margaret responded, "I'll try to think positively, but it won't be easy. Thanks for the pep talk, Missy; I'll try to keep your words in mind. You are a dear friend, and I am feeling somewhat better."

"Good. Keep me posted. I do need to go. Johnny and I have an appointment this morning, and I hear him up and about. Need to get on with my day. When are you expecting Tomas?"

"He reached me here awhile after I'd come in. I'm sure he heard the terror in my voice, but I really didn't want to give him details until I saw him. Bless him, he said he'd fly home from the States immediately. I expect him in a few hours. It's certainly a change in my life; it's nice to feel loved. It does take the edge off my pain.

"Thanks again, Missy. And, give my love to Johnny. Bye."

CHAPTER 44

THE RINGING PHONE MUST HAVE awakened Margaret who'd been fitfully dozing on Tomas' living room sofa. "Hi, I caught the last plane out of JFK. I'm at the Malaga Airport. I'll grab a cab, and should be arriving shortly."

"Do you want me to drive over and get you?"

"No, I don't want you to move from the condo. Stay where you are. I'm hoping you won't leave the place until I learn that Andrew Cleary's name is on a flight manifest leaving Nerja from the Malaga airport or from Madrid's."

Margaret felt her shoulders relax. Suddenly, she was in capable, caring hands. She washed her face and tidied herself before standing in front of a window to watch for Tomas. It was shortly after midnight when the taxi arrived.

Tomas looked very exhausted and harried as he walked through the door. Margaret fell into Tomas' arms with relief and gratitude. "Thank God, you're all right. I have been out of my mind with worry. I couldn't sleep a wink on the plane."

"I'm so grateful to you for rushing back here. You must have had to cancel meetings, and it must have cost you a bloody fortune to fly last minute."

"Yes to all of that, but now tell me what happened."

Margaret, weary and knowing how tired Tomas appeared, gave a much-abbreviated description of the last week. While he quickly unpacked, and they each readied themselves for sleep, Tomas asked in a somewhat irritated tone, "How did you let this happen, and why didn't you telephone me and the police?"

"At first, I thought it was all a coincidence and that I was being a bit paranoid. I seemed to be taking all the necessary precautions and really had nothing tangible to offer." Feeling defensive, Margaret's voice rose, "It never entered my mind to phone the police. My Spanish is halting, and I just felt uncomfortable relating what might have been just my imagination playing tricks. And, I didn't think there was anything YOU could do from New York except worry."

"Well, that was certainly not your imagination. I wish you had let me know; I would have reached someone on duty at the police station and explained. In addition, I'd probably have hired a body guard for you. You really need to trust your instincts, Margaret."

"I know. You are probably right." Sensing a confrontation of two tired individuals, Margaret quickly interjected, "Why don't we talk about this tomorrow when our heads are clearer; we're both worn to a frazzle and need to sleep."

With that, Margaret cuddled into Tomas' chest where he enfolded her with his arms. For the first time in a week, Margaret felt safe and secure. Within minutes, they were both sleeping soundly.

In the morning, Margaret rose first. She washed and brushed, and seeing Tomas still in bed, lay down beside him. It was so comforting to have him here. She realized just how much she loved him. And, last night, he clearly showed how much that love was reciprocated.

When he finally woke, Tomas stumbled out of bed and proceeded to the bathroom. Upon returning, he noticed Margaret in bed with her arms stretched out to greet him.

She covered his face with kisses of joy and relief. He proceeded to appreciate every part of her as she groaned with a heightened sense of pleasure. When they finally united, it was as If they'd been walking through a desert and deprived too long of life-sustaining fluids.

They didn't move for awhile enjoying the closeness. However, since their stomachs were grumbling from hunger, they reluctantly went to the kitchen to fix some breakfast. Pickings were lean as Tomas had not been there for a couple of weeks. They found some frozen bagels and butter and some coffee. Enough to satisfy until they could visit the market and re-supply.

Over breakfast, such as it was, Tomas queried Margaret. "I thought you told me that you'd sworn your sister, your friend and the boys to secrecy as to your being in Nerja. Do you think the boys let it slip?"

"No, I truly do not. I can't imagine how Andrew knew.

"Oh no," Margaret screamed. "I do know! Crafty bastard! Here I was giving him points for his generosity."

"What do you mean?"

"Dammit! The Safeway!"

"Safeway? What does the Safeway have to do with this?"

"After the boys were visiting for a couple of days, Richard reminded Brandon that their Dad had given him a charge card to help pay for groceries, tourist attractions, and miscellaneous items. I was bowled over thinking that

Andrew had finally come to his senses. Boy, was I ever hood-winked.

"We used the card a couple of times in Madrid, at Alhambra, and once, no twice, we paid for groceries at Safeway. Oooh! How naive and foolishly trusting!

"The credit company charges us at the beginning of each month. I know because I always paid the bills. Once Andrew received HIS bill, it must have shown that our purchases were made at the Safeway in Nerja. Grrrr!"

"What's your plan, Margaret?"

"What options do I have? Divorce is the only one. I am not going to stay with Andrew for the sake of appearances. I do not care what he or his parents require to save face. My face has egg all over it, and especially if I were to remain married to him. Particularly now that my sons know the truth of the situation, I'd lose their respect and be a pretty poor role model if I didn't."

"I believe you're right. Although divorce is wrenching for kids, I can see where you might be faced with no other choice given the circumstances."

"It seems forever since we've been able to talk face to face. I need to tell you the boys are adamant that they want to return to our house in Newton and attend the local high school. I think they see the boarding school as their father's way of getting them out of the picture so he could enjoy his philandering. They're probably correct.

"I asked them to consider their loss of a prestigious prep school, their relative independence, etc. It wasn't much of an argument as Newton has two of the top high schools in the States, they miss their childhood friends, and, I believe, they miss their home and having their mother.

Particularly now, I probably represent some constancy in their lives."

"You do have a uniquely excellent relationship with them. I observed how they assisted in the kitchen, in serving the meal, and how they look at you. They truly adore you and enjoy your company. You can see the love in their eyes when they look at you, a real treat to witness. They are really nice kids Margaret, and, I'm sure, it's in no small part due to you. I believe you've missed them terribly.

"I should be resentful and jealous of them because they'll be taking you away from me. But, I honestly believe they need you at this time and you them. Moreover, before you know it, they'll be off to a university."

"I've thought that, too. Although the thought of moving back into that house will be extremely difficult to bear, I hope that I can provide a stable environment for them in that relatively short amount of time."

"You will. But, we must also consider 'us'. While I was flying back here yesterday, I was giving it a lot of thought."

"And, you came up with?"

"I guess this sounds silly, but you are still of childbearing age? Do you want to rear another child, my child?"

"Are you proposing that I do?"

Tomas laughed, "No, not really. Yet, your decision would influence mine."

"How so?"

"If you are comfortable 'living in sin', it would present far fewer problems for me, and would, most definitely, allow us a much higher annual income. If we had children together, not marrying would be out of the question."

"Living in sin, eh?" Margaret intoned in a pseudo angry voice, "What would my mother say to that? Do you realize the lady is rolling in her grave as we speak?

"But, tell me more of your thinking, I ain't my mom! And, it does have a kind of sexy connotation," as she slightly wiggled her fanny.

While chortling, Tomas silently prepared his thoughts. This was difficult waters he'd be entering. He wanted to make things very clear to Margaret, yet, not undermine their growing love for each other.

"In my heart of hearts, I would love to divorce Liliana and relinquish the business that connects her to me. It would make my psychological being far more carefree. I'm sure a divorce would be easily forthcoming as she and I have lived apart for more than the three years Spain requires if one of the partners simply does not wish to remain in the marriage.

"Nonetheless, the reality is that if Liliana and I divorce, I would have to eject her from the orchards . . . the only home she's known, and, as I've told you, she doesn't stray from it. That would be a terribly cruel thing to do to her, and she really has done nothing to deserve that.

"Moreover, it grieves me to think this, yet I must admit a more pragmatic and selfish view. If I allow her to remain there as part of a divorce settlement, then she would be owning my family inheritance and a business that provides a major part of my annual income. Do you see from where I'm coming?"

"Yes, I do. So, what are you proposing we should do?"

"Initially, I just thought the two of us could move into one of the two condos I own in New York City and divide our time between New York, Madrid and the Costa del Sol.

"As it stands now, it appears that you will be tethered to Newton for a few years anyway. As I have to be kind to Liliana, you need to put your boys' needs first . . . and yours. You need to be with them as much as they need to be with you."

"Then, is this good-bye for us," Margaret asked in a voice barely above a whisper.

"Oh, Lord. I was afraid this wouldn't come out right. Heavens, no! I only want to figure out a way that we can be together . . . at least for most of the time. We'll need to think this through very carefully to come up with a plan of action."

The phone rang and Tomas picked it up in his study. When he returned, he was smiling broadly. "That was my contact in Madrid that I'd phoned last night and asked a favor. Since I'm a frequent flier and they know me by name, they agreed to my unusual, and probably illegal, request. About an hour ago, your husband registered at the United Airlines Lounge for those boarding Business and First Class."

Margaret emitted a burst of air. She jumped up and gave Tomas a quick hug.

"Andrew sure got out of Dodge quickly. What a relief! Although, I've just had a horrible thought. Do you think he might have hired someone here to keep tabs on me?"

"I don't know, honey, which is why I wish you'd gone to the police. They might have been able to arrest him for stalking and harassment. Furthermore, that might have given you a leg up in your pursuit of a divorce."

Margaret, unhappily, considered his words. Then, she brightened a bit. "I did have witnesses though. Remember Helen noticed a man looking at us from behind the newspaper; and the minute I lifted my head, he fled.

Since there was a tour group at the caves, but few individuals on the premises, the guards had observed Andrew entering and leaving. In addition, they filed a report of my remaining after closing time."

"And, you did tell me about the incident at the café. You said Eddie had met you there for lunch a few times. Perhaps, Eddie could extract a statement from Carlo testifying to Andrew's badgering you. You'll need to tell him what occurred. Are you comfortable doing that?"

"That shouldn't be a problem especially now that he's met Brandon and Richard. Also, I'm sure Helen would write of our experience on my behalf. Do you think you could get something in writing from the guards at the caves? I believe they'd be more comfortable speaking with you, or would you prefer that I do it?"

"I can accompany you there. They'd probably need to see you as a reminder of the incident, but I certainly can act as translator."

"And, my support system. This whole thing is making me crazy, fearful and at my wits' end. Andrew has, once again, thrown a monkey wrench into my life. Now, I'm dragging you into this mess."

"Margaret, it was clear to me from the start that you came with baggage. I continued this relationship nonetheless." Then with a short grimace and chuckle, "Of course, I wasn't aware of how MUCH baggage."

CHAPTER 45

THE VERY NEXT MORNING, TOMAS took Margaret's car into his mechanic to check for any apparatus that might be affixed to the Ford Escort convertible. The mechanic found nothing. Surprisingly, Andrew had been able to stalk Margaret by merely hanging around the church that she had attended when they visited Nerja those many years ago. As for the caves, they surmised that either Andrew lucked out in finding her there, or had somehow managed to tail her automobile.

Not wishing to take any chances, Tomas hired a private detective to inspect every inch of Margaret's residence in the event that Andrew, or someone working for him, might have bugged the place. Once the 'all clear' was given, Margaret and Tomas returned to Nerja.

"What do you think?," Margaret asked Tomas.

"I suspect that Andrew was so certain that he could coerce you to return to Newton, he did not arrange to bug your car or house. When you lit out on him, perhaps he thought you might go directly to the police to file a report and get a restraining order. Too, he was out of his comfort zone, not knowing how the Spanish legal system works in these cases and not even knowing a lawyer to defend him. In any event, he probably did not want to call attention to the episode. It may well be that neither his office, your sons, his parents nor even his girlfriend knew of his whereabouts.

"Your bolting on him showed a lot of bravery and determination; it sent a very clear message. At that point, his subterfuge had been exposed and he no longer felt in control. Ergo, Margaret, my love, it's up to you to take the reins."

And, she certainly did. During the weeks that followed, despite returning to their daily routines, they put their plan into action as Tomas had suggested.

Margaret managed to have lunch with Father Eduardo at the café overlooking the beach. She informed the priest of all of her encounters with Andrew while he was stalking her in Nerja. Carlo immediately recognized Margaret and showed relief at seeing her in safe hands. When Eddie explained what they needed, Carlo wrote down what he'd heard and seen between the embattled spouses, and how he had helped Margaret escape to her car.

Eddie, also, insisted on accompanying Margaret to the caves. Privately, Tomas and Margaret agreed that it might be a wiser decision. On the appointed day, Margaret was surprised to see the priest in full regalia, but realized the "uniform" carried weight. Clearly, the guards were attentive and quickly acquiesced to their request for written statements.

"I guess now all a judge in Newton will require is a Spanish translator," Margaret laughed then sobered. "Do you think those notes will actually support my case? At least, they might make Andrew squirm. Despite the fact that I'm focused on tying up loose ends in Nerja, I have great trepidation at the thought of returning to the States."

Tomas' eyebrows raised in question. "I'm having a hard time picturing myself in my former surroundings. Will I have to explain my circumstances to friends and acquaintances? How will a judge rule? Would Andrew agree to a mediator? Will I get sufficient alimony, child support, custody of my sons? If the boys choose to stay in Newton, must they travel back and forth to Boston if Andrew is residing there . . . and with the girlfriend? Will Andrew wish to be a nurturing parent and assist his teenage sons financially, as well? Will Andrew be expected to pay for the boys' universities, or do we have to split the cost? How much will I be missing you, Tomas?"

"I'd presume we'll be missing each other a lot, at least initially. I imagine for your sake we cannot afford to be seen together."

"I know. It probably will be better to keep our relationship quiet until a divorce is finalized. If Andrew found out about us, I'd lose a lot of leverage. Furthermore, I wouldn't want my sons to think that I was the one having an affair that led to the demise of our marriage; it would not be true."

"I think your boys know that. However, you need to speak with a divorce lawyer in Newton. He or she might be able to answer the questions you asked me. The responses might not put you at ease, but at least you'll be dealing with reality."

The next evening when Tomas returned to Margaret's bungalow, Margaret greeted him with elevated spirits. "Bless Missy. I phoned a lawyer she recommended. His voice was warm and caring. He listened to my abbreviated version of my finding Andrew in his office and, eventually, Andrew finding me in Spain, stalking and threatening that

I must return to Newton and blurting out the woman's name.

"At present, I'm thinking that although I haven't incriminating photos and such, I'm hoping I have enough evidence to make Andrew willing to go through mediation instead of a court procedure. It would spare our sons, our pocketbooks, and, perhaps unwanted publicity."

"That sounds reasonable. How reasonably will Andrew behave? How generous will he be toward you and the boys . . . not only with economic considerations, but also emotionally. Is he so enraptured with this Cheryl that he excludes you and them in his life's equation? Harsh, I know, but something to consider."

"Yes, the lawyer mentioned that, too."

Rather abruptly, Margaret's face registered dismay and her voice sounded weary, "As I am not in a good financial position here either, the divorce lawyer indicated that I would be better off remaining separated rather than to seek a divorce. Andrew has been allowing me to stay in the house and providing funding. Currently, in Massachusetts, it's usual for the spouse to receive only one third of her husband's income for alimony and child support. It's rare to be awarded up to fourty percent, and Newton is an expensive area for living. Too, with my not being employed, that may well be counted against me even though my entertaining at home and involvement in leadership roles in the community and at the Club certainly helped Andrew's practice to expand. It was the role Andrew and I had agreed upon."

"Doesn't seem fair, does it?"

"No, not at all. What's even worse, according to this attorney, if I date, Andrew will probably feel less guilty regarding HIS infidelity. Moreover, it might make him angry and, subsequently, less generous. I walk a very fine line here.

Andrew may have been cheating on me for years for all I know. Yet, if I screw, I get screwed! Grrrr!"

At this, Tomas, unsuccessfully, tried to stifle a laugh.

Then in a more serious tone, "It will work out Margaret, of that I'm certain. In a few years, the boys will be in college. By then, you and Andrew, as Liliana and I, will have established a pattern of separation."

"Yes, that's true. Andrew may well wish to get on with his life and not be concerned about what others may think. At that point, or perhaps sooner, he'll agree to a mediated settlement whereby we split the proceeds on our home, retirement income, and any assets we accrued while living together. According to the lawyer, this is probably the best-case scenario. At present, that is what I'm seeking."

Tomas could sense the dejection and lack of conviction in Margaret's mind. To buoy her, and probably himself, Tomas proffered, "The International Olive Oil Council was formed by the United Nations. Perhaps, now that you've had some exposure to the IOOC, they might create a position for you in New York. Another possibility is to form a lobby to represent olive interests in the States."

Margaret looked at him quizzically, and almost as if he'd lost his mind.

"Since I'd lived in California while going to Berkeley, I became aware of the olive growers there, and subsequently, have followed their predicaments over the years. It's not a particularly pretty picture."

"Why is that?"

"California is battling an olive fruit fly which is not prevalent in Europe, the Middle East or in Africa.

Unfortunately, there are many in the U.S. Congress who do not see the need to financially assist research endeavors. In fact, while running for the Vice Presidency, Sarah Palin insisted that this money represented pork-barrel spending.

"Since the United States is one of the leaders in olive oil consumption, it would be economically prudent for California to be one of the leading producers. They truly need a strong representation on Capitol Hill. Come to think of it, perhaps, that might be a new role for me, too. We'll just have to maintain the status quo while exploring new options. It certainly won't hurt to try."

Although ameliorated to some degree, but not thoroughly convinced, Margaret tried to put the issues behind her as the remaining days in Nerja whittled down. Time spent with Tomas, her friends and students helped to cheer.

When Margaret entered her classroom on the last night she was to teach at the church, she walked into a sea of streamers and balloons flying high. A beautifully decorated cake sat atop her desk surrounded by handmade thank you notes. Each of her students had prepared a statement to address Margaret in English.

Then, one of the women who was quite fluent held a wrapped gift. "We are all most grateful to you for everything you taught us. You worked so hard to prepare for our classes. You were so kind, even when we made mistakes. Thank you so much. We give you this and hope you will not forget us. We will not forget you."

Everyone applauded while Margaret felt her face flush. She was simultaneously thrilled and, yet, embarrassed at all the attention.

The students urged Margaret to open her gift. She unwrapped an exquisite piece of painted pottery. "Oh my!

This is gorgeous, and what a beautiful reminder of all of you. I shall put this in my home where everyone can see it; it will have a place of honor. Thank you sooo much. You have given me far more than I could ever give to you. You are all very special to me. Thank you. Muchos, MUCHOS gracias." And, she held the platter close to her heart. Margaret could barely hold back the tears of joy mixed with the sorrow of leaving.

She continued in this manner throughout her last couple of weeks. Tomas, Father Eduardo "Eddie" and Helen treated her to dinner at Carlo's outdoor café. Although it wasn't the fanciest place in Nerja, they all felt beholden to Carlo for his courage and commitment to Margaret. It was a convivial group that gathered to exchange toasts celebrating their continued friendship.

Eddie promised to return to Siena College for five year reunions; Tomas mentioned his business interests in New York; and Helen expressed her desire to fulfill a life-long dream to someday visit the States. Margaret assured them all with "Mi casa es su casa."

CHAPTER 46

ALTHOUGH THE EVENING CONTINUED IN this jovial mood, by the time Margaret and Tomas reached her home, she was feeling dejected. Her leave-taking was an emotional drain. She'd sunk deep roots within Nerja and its environs.

In addition, she had many misgivings separating from Tomas. She realized he'd become her anchor.

At breakfast the next morning, Margaret felt compelled to confess, "You've become so much a part of my life, Tomas."

"As you have in mine, dear, but we'll stay in touch and see each other if and when we can. Your relationship with Andrew will have to resolve itself. I might add, hopefully, sooner than later."

"What if Andrew gets wind of us; he could tap my phones, hack my computer, intercept my mail? If we can't see each other, I'd at least want to hear your voice and have a continuing flow of conversation."

"So would I and I've thought about that, too. Perhaps, down the road, we can maintain contact through the Internet if we keep Eddie and Helen in the loop and our exchanges brief and casual. However, we might have to resort to a P.O. Box with our own passwords and security codes."

"I am so pleased at how thorough you've been, Tomas. I believe you really do love me. You've almost convinced me that everything will fall into place for us."

"On all counts, you believe right, lady. And, I have some news that might interest you."

"Oh?"

"Shortly after we became, what shall I say, rather well acquainted?"

Margaret found herself blushing and looked toward her toes. "Mmm?"

"I contacted the Dean's office at Harvard's business school and spoke with someone in the department regarding my business endeavors since receiving my MBA. Well, little lady, I've just been rewarded with a chance to speak to their students some time in the Fall. I'll be given a stipend to cover travel, lodging and food expenses as well as an honorarium. Cambridge, here I come!"

With that bit of information, Margaret leapt to her feet, jumping up and down with joy. Feeling much emboldened, to her surprise she blurted out, "I've been exploring the possibilities of our seeing one another, also. Let me know if I'm out of line here, but when you're in New York City, would it be asking too much for you to hop on the train or fly to Hartford for a day?"

Without stopping to catch her breath, or for Tomas' reply, she raced on with great exuberance, "If I left immediately after the boys went off to school in the morning, I could drive down and return later that evening. I'm sure that Brandon and Richard will be involved in multiple after-school activities, and I could arrange for them to stay at a friend's until I return. It might, also, be on a night that they'd spend with their Dad. I guess I might as well take advantage of joint custody; not that I ever sought it."

Suddenly, Margaret looked crestfallen. No, she hadn't sought this situation. Now that it presented itself, she'd have to meet it head on and, hopefully, come out on top.

"You certainly have pondered this long and hard. It's a great idea, honey. Have you come up with any others?"

Now embarrassed and giggling, Margaret added, "I guess I have."

"And?"

"The boys and I, and sometimes Andrew joined us, have often traveled into Manhattan just before Christmas to enjoy the store windows at Macy's and Saks, see the tree at Rockefeller Center and take in a Broadway show. My wish to continue that tradition with our sons would not seem farfetched. Would you ever be there at that time?"

"I'm sure that could be arranged. Do you want the boys to know that I'm still in your life?"

"Actually, at some point, yes. Although I don't know too many divorcees, I've been aware that some sons often feel their moms got a raw deal and take it upon themselves to be responsible for their mothers' well-being and happiness. By my taking charge of my own life and with your presence, it might reassure my boys that I'm not so alone and needy, and they can get on with their lives."

"Never thought of it in that way; it does make sense. I'm impressed, Margaret, at how you continue to tackle this position in which you've found yourself."

With an impish grin, Margaret uttered, "I am trying . . . and hope to continue to impress you I might add.

"Speaking of my sons, I have some good news, too. Remember when I was so concerned that I'd have to pay half of the boys' college expenses?"

Without giving Tomas a chance to reply, Margaret rapidly continued, "I suddenly recalled that Andrew and I had started a college fund for Brandon and Richard some ten years ago. Funds are automatically deposited monthly from Andrew's salary into an account which cannot be touched or used for any other purpose. Since the money gets invested, it has grown exponentially. Last time I saw the amount, it was rather significant."

"I'm sure that's the case. However, we have had a downturn in the stock market, and investments have fallen. Yet, the boys won't need that money for a couple of years. By then, optimistically, we'll see a more robust economy. In any event, it sounds as if the basic principal will remain untouched, and there will be a substantial amount to help your boys through their university years."

"I guess I should be prepared for some expenses on my part. As you've suggested, I'll still have to explore many options for career opportunities. Albeit, it does bring peace of mind to have remembered that trust fund."

"I had something similar established when each of my kids was born. However, there never seems to be quite enough," Tomas responded chortling. "Lately, Antonio has surprised me greatly by showing an interest in the farm. Although I can't picture him remaining there with a hands-on approach, I think he'd do well from the business end. He's spoken of applying for the master's degree program in olive growing and merchandising that is available at the university in Perugia, Italy."

"I never heard of such a thing."

"It is relatively new." What with Antonio's MBA from Columbia and this master's degree from Perugia, he'd have great tools to continue the family's business.

"You said that Maritza is looking at schools in the States?"

"Do you recall my showing you some paintings of hers that I have displayed on the boat and in Madrid? I think she'll try to pursue that talent and apply to New York University, Stony Brook and Pratt. At any rate, you and I are entering a very expensive time in our lives."

By their second cup of coffee, Margaret felt herself constantly wavering during this conversation between utmost hope and utmost desolation. Were she and Tomas caught in a vortex of descent? The reality must have imposed itself on Tomas as well. He, too, looked deeply dejected.

Both of them were sitting silently when they were abruptly shaken out of their reverie by the sound of the postman delivering mail through the door slot. Tomas bent to retrieve the small pile and quickly eyed the contents.

"Here's one for you, Margaret. I'm hoping it's what I'm thinking it is."

"Now, what's that supposed to mean?"

The envelope had a mailing address from the IOOC. Curiosity getting the better of her, Margaret ripped it open to find a letter of recommendation with dual signatures. She recognized the name of the Director, the Frenchman whom she'd met on the airplane and again at the Conference. The second signatory was the Algerian gentleman who'd recently been appointed as the Assistant Director.

She immediately shared the contents with Tomas. They read of Margaret's very capable handling of specific events and the success of her endeavors for the annual conference of the IOOC despite time constraints.

"And, I'm sure I have YOU to thank for it."

Tomas smiled sheepishly. "There's something you can proudly show a potential employer."

"Thanks to you."

"No thanks to me; you worked for it, and you earned it. I merely reminded them."

"Oh my, speaking of reminders, I totally forgot. Father Eduardo handed me an envelope last night, and I was too tired to open it."

She marched off to the bedroom and retrieved the envelope from the top of the bureau and began to read silently. "Oh, wow! Were you responsible for this, also?"

"No, I can't claim any credit for Eddie's note. Do you wish to share it?"

Written on church stationery with the priest's name on its letterhead, Tomas read:

To Whom It May Concern:

I recruited Ms. Margaret Cleary to teach English to members of our church parish. She enthusiastically accepted and quickly sought creative ideas to enrich the curriculum. I have been very impressed by her organizational skills, her work ethic, and her professional demeanor.

Ms. Cleary has shown remarkable interpersonal skills dealing with people representing different ages, incomes, backgrounds and education. She has caused each student to feel responsible for the work and pride in his or her achievements.

Ms. Cleary is an intelligent, caring, capable and energetic individual. I would highly recommend her for whatever

```
position she seeks. You are welcome to
reach me at. . .
```

Margaret began to visibly quake. "I did not expect this. Everyone has been so kind, and I'm so grateful. Even if these letters do not get me through the front door, I'm certain they will serve to bolster my confidence."

As Margaret was replacing the letter into its envelope, something fell onto the floor. Tomas raised voiced declared, "Margaret, that looks like a check!"

On closer inspection, Margaret clucked, "Indeed it is. I suggested that Eddie should replace his old black clunker with the Ford Escort. I offered it to him for twenty percent less than I'd paid . . . accounting for depreciation and the time he'd spent helping me find it. At first, he wouldn't hear of it, assumed it wasn't sedate enough for a priest. Guess he changed his mind."

"I can't believe he did this."

In a playful voice, "Look at the bottom left corner, and your answer will appear."

Where the line said 'for', Father Eduardo had written 'sporty white convertible'. Whatever tensions Margaret and Tomas had been experiencing this morning faded into roars of laughter. . . a welcome relief.

They busied themselves cleaning up after breakfast and dressing for the day. Their separate occupations gave Tomas time to reflect. Whenever life threw a hurdle at Margaret, she immediately caved. Then, he'd observed, she'd quickly summon her determination, resilience and perseverance to seek a happier outcome. Not a bad trait, not at all.

Margaret entered his space, and in a monotone, "I guess it's time for me to organize my packing. Can't put it off any longer. Best to get started today."

"Afraid we can't put off the inevitable, as much as we'd like to try. Do you want me to stick around, or shall I head to my office?"

"No, I'll be fine. You go ahead."

CHAPTER 47

EFORE DISTURBING ANYTHING, MARGARET LOOKED around her apartment as if seeing it for the first and last time, fixing it in her mind's eye. She then proceeded to empty bureau drawers, closets, desk drawers. After separating items she'd need to wear for the next day or two, and clothes for the flight to Boston, she began to fill her suitcase. She gathered together the remains of her toiletries and cosmetics to transport in small, separate containers. Her tennis racquet and laptop sat propped against the door.

Next, she cleaned out her car of all its personal belongings and headed for a car wash. Since the check was already in the mail, and she'd received it, technically the automobile was no longer hers. The least she could do was have it looking its best before presenting it to the priest. He was one of her favorite people. He had befriended her from the start and seen to it that she was a participant in the life of the parish. She was most grateful to him.

Afterwards, she headed to the family-owned supermarket to purchase the fixings for a lovely, but simple dinner. Tomas could grill some salmon to which she'd add rice and a vegetable. To empty the fridge and pantry, she drizzled some olive oil, melted butter and lemon on the salmon. With the scrapings of about a tablespoon or two of Greek Yogurt that remained in the container and some chives and dill tossed into the mixture, she would lightly cover the cooked salmon. She'd defrosted some leftover rice, vegetables and some slices of pie. Voila! Dinner!

Tomas arrived at her home earlier than usual that evening. "I see you're pretty much packed and ready to go. Can't say that I'm overjoyed."

"Nor I. However, I do want to share an epiphany I had while driving to the market. I had some time when I returned here and looked up job offerings in Newton for substitute teachers."

"Really! That's thinking ahead. Jobs are so scarce. Did you find anything?"

"Actually, I did. Amazingly, there was a position for a permanent substitute for a four month stint while a teacher is on maternity leave. Another site, for the Chestnut Hill section where our house is located, fills positions for four different elementary schools. I applied at each of the sites."

"In what way will this help you?"

"Well, I do enjoy teaching. Subbing will allow me to earn a little money sporadically, while giving me the flexibility to look for other positions in or out of the field of education."

"Flexibility works for me, particularly if you can take off to meet me in Cambridge, Hartford or New York City. Honestly, I guess it does make a lot of sense. It doesn't commit you to anything long-term, you can be home for your sons after school and during vacations, it shows a judge that you're no slouch, it looks good on a resume when applying for other positions, and it might give you and the boys a little extra pocket money and some independence if needed."

"My thoughts exactly." Margaret's decision felt validated.

Their love-making that night and the next was prolonged and tender, neither of them wishing to let go. Each was dreading her departure.

Since Margaret was to leave the following morning, they delivered her convertible to the priest. He couldn't wait to get behind the wheel. After a quick review of its features, Eddie enveloped Margaret in a huge hug. In a most solicitous voice, the priest inquired, "Will you be all right, Margaret?"

"After Andrew's very sudden and unexpected arrival in Nerja, I felt vulnerable, violated, threatened. However, since then, I've realized that I'm able to draw upon my own strengths and inner resources which I will need for myself and as a role model for my sons."

"You are very right, Margaret." And with that, right there at the curbside, he offered a prayer for safe passage, good health and serenity in her life. "We'll all miss you, Margaret. May God grant us many future happy times together and may He be with you and guide you in all you undertake." A somewhat tearful good-bye ensued after which Tomas led Margaret into his Alfa Romeo.

They decided to spend some leisurely time visiting the hills, the caves and the seashore. All too soon, the next morning arrived, and they were on their way to the airport in Malaga. Margaret would make a connecting flight in Madrid.

Now on the airplane, Margaret's head was in a tailspin. Would this be just a 'summer romance'? Could their hopes materialize? Up to the very end, even with eyes filled with tears, Tomas projected certainty in their future together.

She drew on the strength of his convictions, and settled back in her seat.

Mentally, she ran a quick check list. She'd contacted her renters, and they'd happily allowed her sons to retrieve their summer-weight clothing a few weeks ago. The couple planned to leave basic essentials in the fridge and freezer to ease her transition. They reassured her they'd started her car periodically, and it worked well. Despite the fact that they'd already closed on a house, the couple agreed to remain rent-free in Margaret's until her arrival; Margaret was not taking any chances of Andrew having access.

Her to-do list was longer. Prepare her home for her sons' return; follow-up on the substitute teaching inquiries; meet with the lawyer; enroll the boys at the neighborhood high school, take Missy to lunch one day and her sister, Eileen, another; invite her renters for dinner one evening as they'd been so cooperative and congenial.

Feeling better organized, she could relax. Most of the pictures she'd taken in Spain were stored in her digital camera. Now, she reviewed the trips she'd made with her sons, photos of her students, and group photos of Tomas: with his colleagues at the IOOC, with Helen, Eddie, and Margaret, and with her sons on *The Respite*. She had deemed it prudent not to have a picture of Tomas alone or of the two of them together. Captured, too, were memories of the little house with its swimming pool, the church, the caves and of Nerja and its surrounding views. She'd put them all into an album to reminisce at home. Six months out of a lifetime, but what an impact!

Would she be able to execute her plans to construct a fulfilling life for herself? Would she be able to profitably sell her home in a couple of years and retain some of their shared assets in order to maintain a decent lifestyle? Would she be able to land an interesting, challenging and well-paying position? Would she go from Newton, to Nerja, to Newton, and finally, to New York?

Only time would tell. Margaret mused . . . one cannot predict one's destiny, but a person could certainly try to create the destiny of his or her choice. She was determined to be the master of hers.

ABOUT THE AUTHOR

Joyce Grand was born and raised in New York City. She attended Skidmore College and earned a Bachelor of Science cum laude from New York University and a Master of Arts from Georgetown University in American Government (Public Policy). The author pursued her interest in writing with instructional programs at the New York State Writing Institute and at Georgetown University.

Her professional career has included: teaching; writing; leadership and development of a local federation and a community center; the executive director of a nonprofit related to youth issues; involvement in political campaigns; and the producer/moderator of a weekly local television show.

Joyce and her husband, who reside in Virginia, are fortunate to have their children and grandchildren living nearby.

ACKNOWLEDGMENTS

I owe a debt of gratitude to my family for respecting my closed office door and to my two book groups who generally served as my first readers and explored, in depth, the characters and content and pushed me to publish.

To my delighted surprise, a few readers were diligent editors. For that enormous effort, thank you so much Lois Scherbenske, Beverlee McCarthy, Sue Morse and Jane L. Winant.

To all who initially read *Margaret: from Newton to Nerja*, your positive feedback and suggestions were most helpful. Thank you: Lisa Mesirow, Paige Alexander, Gail Shaw, Jackie Browne, Gail Parsons, Beverly Welther, Shelly Miller, Fay Froh, my brother-in-law David Grand, Elaine Alexander, Miles Alexander, Robin Fetsch, Debbie Massey, Martha Romans, Joyce Hanson and AnnMarie Hicks.

Many thanks to those who so willingly shared their expertise on subjects new to me: MaryAnn Phelps; my sailing advisor, the late Dr. Kirk Burns of Falls Church, VA; the Spanish Embassy in Washington, D.C.; the International Olive Oil Council in Madrid whose members squired me through the building and plied me with books, journals, cookbooks and tons of information; and to Attorney Howard Goldstein of Newton, Mass. for patiently making sure that I 'got it right'.

I am beholden to Matthew Benjamin (VA) and to Glendon Haddix at Streetlight Graphics (IN) for their immense support, patience, and technical skills.

For their excellent suggestions regarding marketing strategies, a grateful 'shout out' to: The Honorable Leslie Byrne (former Congresswoman, VA), Peter Behr (former Business Editor of *The Washington Post*), and Seth Goldman (co-founder and CEO of Honest Tea and author of *A Mission In a Bottle*).

Lastly, a thank you to Chantal Burns former Social Secretary (Chief of Protocol) American Embassy, Paris and to Lloyd Fleck former Agricultural Counselor, American Embassy, Madrid. As their guests, my husband and I greatly appreciated their warm hospitality, knowledge and friendship during our second visit to Spain.

Photo: Lisa Mesirow
Hair: Nuri Yurt of TOKA Salons

Made in the USA
Charleston, SC
02 January 2014